Berkley Sensation titles by Victoria Morgan

FOR THE LOVE OF A SOLDIER
THE HEART OF A DUKE
THE DAUGHTER OF AN EARL

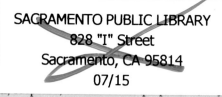

"Tender passi... ...along at a fine pace. Morgan's talents lie in creating realistic characters—a feisty heroine, honorable hero, and despicable villain—and then placing them into a smartly written plot. There's a bright future ahead for this newcomer."

—*RT Book Reviews* (★★★★)

"A historical romance with plenty of suspense and intrigue. The characters in this book were very well written . . . It was a great fast-paced read and a wonderful love story."

—Cocktails and Books

For the Love of a Soldier

"This book is an absolute gem. Morgan's story has combined complex characters, a satisfying love story, and a fascinating examination of the Battle of Balaclava . . . Bravo to Victoria Morgan for bringing this fascinating bit of history to life, and seamlessly weaving it into her storyline. Morgan's voice is perfect for this genre. She has just the right balance of history, romance, and intelligent prose. *For the Love of a Soldier* is a remarkable debut novel."

—PennyRomance.com

"Readers will enjoy Morgan's debut novel, with its charming characters and depth of emotion. Morgan deftly handles returning soldiers' trauma within the context of a love story and adds spice with a bit of mystery and unexpected secrets."

—*RT Book Reviews* (★★★★)

The Daughter of an Earl

Victoria Morgan

BERKLEY SENSATION, NEW YORK

**BERKLEY
SENSATION**

**An imprint of Penguin Random House LLC
375 Hudson Street, New York, New York 10014**

THE DAUGHTER OF AN EARL

A Berkley Book / published by arrangement with the author.

ISBN: 978-0-425-28077-5

PUBLISHING HISTORY
Berkley Sensation mass-market edition / July 2015

PRINTED IN THE UNITED STATES OF AMERICA

10 9 8 7 6 5 4 3 2 1

Cover art by Aleta Rafton.
Cover design by George Long.
Interior text design by Kristin del Rosario.

Penguin
Random
House

ACKNOWLEDGMENTS

Writing can be a lonely journey, so it helps when you have friends with whom you can share your ups and downs along the way. Friends who can push and pull you over the obstacles you encounter, cheer you on, and kick your butt when needed. Oh, and of course, celebrate your triumphs, usually over Thai food and a martini or two . . . Thanks to the wonderful and crazy Junior Mints—Samantha Wayland, Penny Watson, Stephanie Kay, and Bobbie Ruggiero—for being there for me! I would also like to thank my wonderful agent, Laura Bradford (bradfordlit.com), and my lovely editor, Leis Pederson, at the Berkley Publishing Group, for helping me to finally bring Brett and Emily's story to my readers!

Chapter One

❧≈≈

THERE were advantages in recovering from the brink of madness.

Or so Lady Emily Chandler believed. Nearly four years had passed since her fiancé's death, and she was better. She had learned how to keep the darkness at bay. How to sidestep the painful paths in her memory. To stay distracted and busy. Ultimately, she had learned how to not worry her family.

Most of the time.

Today was not one of those times. If cognizant of this morning's meeting, her family *would* worry, definitely disapprove, and in all probability, outright forbid her from following her present course. After all, a murder investigation was not an acceptable diversion for any young woman to pursue, let alone a safe pastime for the mentally fragile daughter of an earl.

But mad or not, her mind was set.

To advance her plan, she needed assistance. Lawrence Drummond had been her fiancé's closest friend and a trusted colleague. Both men had worked for the Honourable East

India Company, overseeing their trading accounts in Calcutta. More important, Drummond was with her fiancé during the time of his death. With such strong ties, she was confident that Drummond would share her determination to ferret out the truth.

A cool breeze brushed over her, and she wrapped her arms around her waist. She had arranged for the meeting to be held at her brother-in-law's former home, Lakeview Manor. She tipped her face toward the sky where the sun was waging a paltry battle against March's bitter bite. Her sapphire spencer jacket was more fashionable than warm. She rubbed her hands down her arms, her skirts brushing her walking boots as she paced a dirt path beside the lake.

Mr. Drummond was late. She scanned the grounds, skimming her gaze over the men toiling to rebuild the twice-burned-out house. She located Agnes, her abigail, perched on a stone wall, her legs swinging jauntily while she smiled up at a workman. The girl was a shameless flirt, but her distraction secured Emily the privacy she needed.

She turned her back on her maid, only to gasp and retreat a step. Conjured like a ghostly apparition, Lawrence Drummond stood but an arm's length away. "Mr. Drummond."

"Lady Emily, it has been too long." He dipped into a shallow bow. A smile warmed his features, and he lifted her hand to give it a gentle squeeze.

He wore a nutmeg coat, buff-colored breeches, and boots polished to a gleaming sheen. A flash of gold in his cravat and cuff links reminded her that he carried a bit of the dandy in him. With his auburn hair and golden eyes, he did turn his share of heads and was vain enough to appreciate it.

His gaze roved over her, his smile widening as he took her measure from the top of her bonnet to the tips of her boots. "You are more lovely than ever. A muse for a poet *and* a rival to nature's beauty."

She preferred not to be touched, so she gently disengaged herself and stepped away. "Thank you, you are too kind."

"That is candor, not kindness. Jason was a fortunate man."

"Yes, well, I was the fortunate one to have found Jason," she said. One of time's gifts was the strength to hear and speak her late fiancé's name without buckling.

He nodded. "I hear congratulations are in order. You are an aunt now, double blessed with a niece *and* a nephew. And your sister, Lady Julia, she is doing well? And Bedford, the proud papa?"

She responded and then inquired after his sister who had recently made her debut.

They eased into the age-old ritual of social etiquette, and she fought the tug of her impatience. One could not jump into embezzlement and murder right away. There were rules to be followed. Breaking them required a combination of guile and subterfuge. In order to do as she pleased without alarming her family, she had acquired an aptitude for both.

"I remember your debut," he said. "You left a trail of shattered hearts in your wake before you accepted Jason."

The husky tone in Drummond's voice troubled her. It reminded her that he liked to stretch the lines of propriety. It could prove problematic, but to achieve her goal, she would join forces with the devil himself.

She made light of his flattery, steering the conversation into safer boundaries and toward her purpose. "I doubt many men wasted their hearts on me, seeing as mine was firmly spoken for. Mr. Drummond, I wrote to you—"

"Yes, and I cannot tell you how much it meant to me to receive your letter. It encouraged my hopes that we can renew our friendship."

She ignored the warmth in his tone, because he had unwittingly given her the opening she sought, and she seized upon it. "Actually, it is due to your friendship with Jason that I requested this meeting. I hope that in the name of it, you might be willing to assist me on a matter of some delicacy. Before I broach the subject, I need your word that you will keep our conversation in the strictest of confidence. This is forward of me, approaching you in this manner, but I did not know to whom to turn."

A flicker of surprise lit his eyes, but after a moment, he

cocked his head to the side. "I am intrigued, and of course, at your service." He dipped into a bow.

He appeared more amused than intrigued. "You will keep my confidence? I have not shared this with anyone. My family would not understand. As Jason's friend, I hope that you do."

His smile wavered. "Definitely intrigued. I give you my word that you have my discretion."

She drew in a breath and ventured to win him to her cause. "About a year and a half ago, I reread Jason's letters and came across some disturbing information. I gave it little heed in my first reading, being very . . . young." *Shallow* and *besotted* were more appropriate, but *young* was far less damning. "I was dismissive of news not concerning me. I did not know what to make of the information at first, and then other events stole my time."

"For goodness' sake, what is this about? Whatever it is, I can see that it is upsetting to you. Please, tell me so that I may help you."

She lifted her chin. "Jason wrote of discrepancies he had found in the ledgers. The disbursements for payments were not adding up, funds were missing. It was his responsibility to determine—"

"My dear, say no more," Drummond said. His voice gentled, as if he were addressing an overwrought child. "This will not do."

His avuncular tone gave her pause. She had abandoned her pinafores when she pinned her hair up years ago. A child no longer, she did not care for men who made the mistake of treating a woman like one.

Oblivious to her annoyance, he continued. "Whatever it is that Jason wrote, it was years ago. Lost to the past. Why revisit it, delving into areas that are distressing to you?"

At his cavalier dismissal of her concerns, she drew even breaths and stifled the urge to curl her hands into fists. A woman had a right to question if her fiancé had been murdered. She would not be silenced—or worse, dismissed as a distraught female.

"Remember what happened to Pandora when she opened the box? Bad things were unleashed. Now I refuse to stand by and see a beautiful woman in distress. Not when I can alleviate it." He let his eyes drop to her lips.

What a patronizing, pompous arse.

She had made a mistake. He could not help her. More so, she refused to spend time with someone who condescended to her. They would not survive an hour together—as this ill-fated meeting had demonstrated.

She would have to find someone else to assist her. And she would.

"Emily, listen to me."

She bristled at his presumption, using her Christian name as if they were intimates. Fortunately, she had become well practiced in veiling her reactions. She schooled her features to look like an attentive china doll—serene, delicate, and mute–which in her experience was another expectation men of Drummond's ilk held of women.

"I am so glad you wrote to me, so that I could set your mind at ease," Drummond said. "Working with Jason as I did, I can promise you, had he uncovered anything questionable, he would have resolved the issue. Jason was very good at his job, so you need not fret needlessly over yesterday's troubles. If I cannot assist you with anything else, let me provide you with comfort in knowing that."

Her smile was brittle. "You are right. I am sure Jason did all he could to investigate the matter."

And paid for it with his life.

Drummond's features softened, and a gentle smile curved his lips. "I am glad that we agree. Now let us lay the ghosts of the past to rest. I think it is past time you found a more pleasant diversion on which to focus your attention. Like renewing old friendships. And perhaps, just perhaps, the hope of beginning something more . . ."

All her senses went on alert. She recognized his look. It was one a man gave to a prized stallion, a fashionable curricle, or a desirable woman. It was a look that said *I want, I covet.* She did not care for it. She was not a possession to be acquired, having long since taken herself off the marriage market.

He allowed his gaze to slowly drift over her figure, as if assessing her assets. She nearly shuddered when they paused on her breasts and then lifted to meet her eyes.

Oh dear. It was time she set the man straight. "Mr. Drummond, I hope we can maintain our friendship, but there can be nothing more between us. I loved Jason, and—" She inhaled sharply as Drummond grasped her arms and drew her to him.

"Jason is dead. I am not. It is past time you stepped into the present. I have waited a long time for you to wake up. Nearly four years. I think that is long enough." His eyes flared, then dipped to her lips as if anticipating a succulent treat.

She strained away from his heavy-lidded gaze. "Mr. Drummond, I apologize if my request to meet you gave you the wrong impression. Led you to believe—"

"Not to believe, to hope. Hope that Jason had stolen from me years ago."

Her patience snapped. "Mr. Drummond! Please, you are a gentleman! As such, I demand that you behave like one and let me go." She gasped as his grip tightened on her arms, and he leaned his face close to hers, his cloying breath hot against her cheek. She clenched her jaw and prepared to knee him where he deserved to be disabled.

"I cannot. I did that once and—"

A deep voice cut him off. "Allow me to assist you."

The frigid tone sliced through her anger and sent a different sort of shiver rippling down her body. Drummond was wrenched away and flung aside like a rag doll. A strong hand curled around her arm and saved her from an undignified sprawl on the ground. Landing on her arse would have made her humiliation complete. Not that it wasn't already, because she recognized that American accent. All too well.

It belonged to the one man who, for the first time since Jason's death, stirred emotions within her that she had no longer believed herself capable of feeling for another man.

Feelings she had thought were dead and buried with her fiancé.

Face burning, she looked up. Dressed in uncompromising black, he was austere and formidable. A cool breeze rustled through his thick golden hair. Sharp blue eyes impaled Drummond with a threatening glare, his mouth pressed into a disapproving line.

Brett Curtis.

Her heart jumped into a frantic beat. The man was as handsome as she remembered—even as she had fought so desperately to forget.

"Who the devil do you think you are?" Drummond brushed furiously at the debris dusting his trousers. When he straightened to his full height, he was inches shy of Brett's eye level. Drummond had to tip his head back in order to peer down his disgruntled nose.

"Who am *I*?" Brett thundered, his features contorted with rage. "I am the gentleman that you are not. For the moment, let us pretend you are capable of behaving as one, so you may apologize to the lady and promise to never lay a hand on her again. I suggest you then disappear into whatever hovel you crawled out of before I change my mind, regret my leniency, and take that ridiculous cravat—which your valet wasted God knows how many hours tying—and use it to string you up from the nearest tree."

Drummond's eyes bulged, his face going a molted shade of purple. "An *American*. I would expect no less than—"

Drummond's sneering aspersion to Brett's nationality snapped Emily's stunned senses back to the present. "That is enough!" She snatched free of Brett's grip and straightened the hemline of her jacket. "This was a misunderstanding between old friends. Nothing more. Mr. Drummond, I appreciate your taking the time to speak with me, but I believe our business is finished." She kept her gaze locked on Drummond's, while every muscle of her body vibrated with the awareness of Brett looming behind her. The air practically sizzled with his harnessed fury.

Drummond swallowed, and then brazened it out. "You

are kind to call this a misunderstanding, but the *gentle-man*"—he dubiously voiced the word—"is right, and I owe you an apology. I fear I forgot myself, and I beg your forgiveness for my boorish behavior. However, my intentions are honorable. If you would allow me—"

"Mr. Drummond, *please*." Horrified, she sought to derail him, while Brett's snort conveyed his opinion of Drummond's *honorable* intentions. She nearly snapped at Brett to shut his mouth, but knew her warning would be futile.

The man did as he pleased. Always had.

"I will address your father in order that I may state my case before word reaches him, and your reputation suffers—"

"Please, that is not necessary," she said evenly, desperate to stop Drummond from declaring himself, and Brett from strangling the blackguard, despite her wishing he would. "I appreciate the sentiment, truly I do. But like yourself, Mr. Curtis is a family friend. He is godfather to the twins and was in partnership with my brother-in-law before Daniel inherited the dukedom. As such, I am confident of his discretion. Thus, the only word to reach my father would be yours, so for the sake of our friendship, please do not compound this misunderstanding by carrying it further. Forgive me, but there can be nothing more between us. Let our friendship be enough."

Aware of Brett seeking to move around her, no doubt to expedite Drummond's departure, she shot her arm out, thwarting his advance. If he was the gentleman he claimed to be, he couldn't very well plow through her arm—or so she hoped.

A play of conflicted emotions crossed Drummond's features. Her heart thundered in fear of his pressing his advantage. After all, his earlier behavior had proven he had no compunction in doing so.

She cast a quick glance back at Brett. He had straightened to his full height and was opening and closing his hands at his sides. At the implicit threat, she prayed Drummond's vanity came to his rescue, because his wits appeared to have deserted him. If the dandy valued his face, she doubted he wanted to risk Brett inflicting his fist on it.

After a tense moment, Drummond nodded curtly. "I understand. Perhaps I read too much into your letter. Forgive me. While I wish it otherwise, I have to be appeased with what you deign to give me. Friendship it is." He gave her a rueful smile and dipped into a bow.

"Thank you," she said, relieved.

"I trust your Mr. Curtis, who, as you say, is a family . . . *friend,* along with your abigail, will escort you home. Lady Emily, until we meet again." He tipped his hat and then spun on his heel, leaving them alone.

She closed her eyes and exhaled. The silence was still and loud until Brett's scoffing disdain shattered it.

"What a tuft-up coxcomb. With his cravat tied so tight, I am surprised he doesn't choke over his words. Wherever did you find him? More important, what in the world possessed you to meet him here *alone*?"

The words cut like a knife through her tightly strung nerves. She wanted to rail at him, venting her frustration over the failure of her meeting, but she could not.

Contrary to what she had assured Drummond, she had no idea if Brett would keep her confidence. If he did not and spoke to her father, he could ruin everything. She had to stop him, and if that meant feigning sympathy for Drummond, she would do so. Tears made most men retreat, and she had no qualms in employing them now.

She drew herself up and whirled on Brett, letting her voice hitch as she spoke. "That is enough. He was . . . a . . . a dear friend of my late fiancé, and I have hurt him badly. I think that is punishment enough, so please refrain from airing your callous opinions of a poor man whom you know nothing about." She turned her back on him and walked away, curling an arm around her waist and lifting the other to her temple.

Let him retreat. Please retreat.

Silence met her. The distant sound of the workers carried to them, and still he did not speak. It never failed to amaze her that the bravest of men were flummoxed at the sight of a distraught woman. She bit her lip to curb her triumphant smile, but could not resist tipping her head to the side to surreptitiously study him from beneath her lashes.

She straightened like a poker upon discovering he had crept up beside her. Too damn close. Worse, his arms were folded across his chest and a smile tugged at his lips. The dratted man was laughing at her!

"Well done. You are almost as good as my sisters." He leaned so close that the teasing gleam in his eyes held her mesmerized. "But you forget, I am not as easily maneuvered as your family. I also am familiar with your talents with penning a clever note. I am sure your *friend* read exactly what you intended for him to read, which was your bait to lure him here."

She silently cursed him to perdition and back.

His humor vanished, and his eyes narrowed. "I repeat, what is so important that you risked your reputation and your safety to meet this man alone?"

His heated gaze burned through her carefully composed veneer and saw all she fought to hide.

It was just as she feared.

He was going to ruin everything.

Chapter Two

❦

BRETT kept his voice level, but rage vibrated through every muscle in his body, simmering since he'd stumbled across Lady Emily in another man's arms. Heard the distress in her voice.

What the devil was she doing with the bastard?

He flexed his fingers, which still itched to snatch the gilded pin that had pierced the fop's lace cravat and stab him with it. *Then* he would have strung the man up as he had threatened. His temper had eased somewhat at her decisive setdown of the whoreson. She had some sense left after all. And he could not fault the pathetic Mr. Drummond for his taste.

Lady Emily Chandler was a prize worth winning.

Tall, slim as a willow weed, fair of feature, and dressed in a sky blue gown that highlighted those long-lashed, luminous Chandler eyes. Eyes of such a deep, fathomless blue that Brett feared if a man stared too long, he would drown in them.

Another reason to keep his distance from Lady Emily Chandler.

Like the Sirens in Greek mythology, whose beauty and voice lured sailors to shipwreck their boats on the rocky shores of their island, Lady Emily was just as dangerous. Fortunately for him, having been splintered by another Siren, he had fortified his defenses and his heart—or the battered remnants of it.

Annoyed at his line of thought, he yanked his attention to the present. To Emily, who stood so still, but was clearly seething. She did not like his foiling her plans. But a man could not grow up with three sisters and not identify—and respect—feminine guile in all its forms.

She recovered her voice and drew herself up, her blue eyes snapping. "How dare you lecture me on deception. Was it not you who broke your *right* arm and cajoled me into drafting your business letters, choosing to omit the pertinent detail that you write with your *left*?"

She was never going to let him forget that. It had been a weak moment. After being tossed out of a speeding curricle, he had coveted a pretty face by his side to cheer his bruised spirits during his recovery.

"And I am paying the price for that. I am still clarifying your little addendums. Do you think it is easy explaining to clients that I do not suffer from gout, have no need of a loan of a cane, nor have I gained eight stones, thank you very much?" Drummond was not the only man that Emily's cleverly penned words had gotten into trouble.

She smiled. "Serves you right. Women do not like to be deceived."

He caught the gleam in her eyes, and arched a brow. "Spare me your apologies, and no, it did not threaten my relations with clients, but thank you for inquiring. I am touched by your concern, but you need not lose any more sleep over the matter."

She dismissed his sarcasm with an airy wave of her gloved hand. "Had I any doubts of your ability to smooth things over, I never would have written what I did. In drafting your business letters, I witnessed your ability to iron out complex problems without blinking an eye. It is why Curtis Shipping is a success. I am sure your explanations were charming and deftly handled, and the clients liked you all the better for adding a personal touch into your correspondence. No thanks are needed. Really, it was my pleasure."

"Oh, there is little doubt the pleasure was all yours," he said dryly, surprised and oddly moved at her compliment to his business acumen. "I do work very hard at—" He froze and shook his head, wagging his finger at her. "Very good. Distracting me with praise. Well done. However, let us return to the matter at hand. Why did you need to meet this man, Drummond, is it? And alone?"

She clamped her mouth shut, her expression mutinous.

"If you want me to keep my discretion and not speak to your father—"

"You wouldn't dare!"

"Oh, I dare many things, as do you. You wrote a letter to a man, inviting him to meet you alone in a private location." He amended his words when she opened her mouth to protest. "My mistake, you were not without a chaperone. You brought your absentminded abigail with you. You chose this location, scattered with workmen, knowing her penchant for—"

"You go too far!" she cried, then cast a glance behind him and tightened her jaw. "We will discuss this later. It appears my maid has disappeared. I must locate her before . . . ah . . . before those *penchants* lead her into deeper trouble." The last was muttered beneath her breath. She turned her back on him and without waiting to see if he followed, started up the bank.

Incredulous, he shook his head. Maid and mistress were a dangerous combination. It was time someone kept an eye on the two of them. For the moment, that appeared to fall to him. He stormed after her. "*I* go too far? *Your* actions show foresight, strategy, and determination, while exhibiting a total lack of regard for consequence. Do you have any idea what could have happened had I not come along as I did? Had he—"

"But you did and he did not!"

Her stride slowed and he heard the distress in her voice. Relenting, he gentled his tone. "Lady Emily, if you do not have a care for your own welfare, you must understand there are others that do. As they are ignorant of your activities, I insist on speaking on their behalf. What business could you possibly have that you clearly do not want your father knowing about, and that was worth risking your own safety for?"

She stopped a few yards from the construction site, a cornered look in her eyes.

A guttural cough shattered the stretch of taut silence, rescuing her, and she cleverly seized upon the distraction.

"Excuse me, but I am looking for my maid," she said to a burly workman, clutching her bonnet to her head as a gust of wind threatened to upend it.

"She went that way." The man pointed a beefy finger down the hill toward a dirt path. Its trail cut through a line of trees edging the banks of the lake.

"Thank you." Emily nodded curtly, and again leaving Brett behind, she started off in the direction indicated. Her strides were long, and her skirts flapped about her legs, accentuating her lithe figure.

He gritted his teeth and hastened to fall in step beside her. He wanted answers—not that she would willingly give them.

Over the past year, his encounters with Lady Emily had been akin to a fencing match, a delicate balance of parry and riposte, skirmishes but no blood drawn. It was inevitable. When two strong-minded individuals collided, one had to bend. If neither did—like a hammer connecting with an anvil—sparks flew. Yet he couldn't stay away from her, because beneath her calm façade, he had glimpsed something simmering just beneath her surface.

Buried secrets.

She was hiding something, but damned if he knew what. Now that it involved clandestine meetings with men in secluded areas, he vowed to find out. He frowned, because he carried scars from another encounter with a bold beauty. Needed no more. He would keep Emily safe, but that was all.

As if on cue, Emily broke her silence, saving him from memories more palatable with a stiff whiskey in hand.

"If you must know, I arranged to meet Mr. Drummond because I have questions in regard to my late fiancé's work. I did not confide in my father or Julia because I knew they would worry over my looking into matters that transpired years ago. They do not like to see me upset and can be overly protective."

He drew his brows together. Bedford had confided to him that Emily had taken her fiancé's death very hard. Despite over three years passing, he also knew that her family still worried over her. He was hesitant to tread onto sensitive ground, but as Emily had introduced the topic, he followed her lead. "What makes you think that Drummond could be of help to you?"

"Mr. Drummond and my fiancé were friends, and they were posted together in India. For those reasons, I sought his assistance, but as you witnessed, he had another agenda. I made a mistake, but rest assured, I will not make it again. That much, I can promise you."

"Drummond and your fiancé, Viscount Weston, worked for the East India Company?" Brett asked, furrowing his brow.

His own company, Curtis Shipping, dealt in importing goods to England, and his business interests and those of the Honourable Company had conflicted in the past. Years ago, when he had sought to expand into new territories beyond England, the East India's monopoly of the eastern trade routes thwarted his aspirations. More so, he could not compete against the company's flagrant bribery of government customs officials, who in turn renewed the firm's charter. They did so despite the malfeasance and the bankruptcies that had beset the firm for decades.

"Yes. They were posted in Calcutta together," Emily said.

"Ah, carrying out the Honourable Company's work of looting and scooting."

"Excuse me?" She stopped to stare at him.

He cursed his glib tongue. Her fiancé was dead, and

therefore unable to defend himself. It was bad form to force his bereaved fiancée to do so. "Forgive me. Being unfamiliar with the viscount's position, I spoke out of turn. If your questions are in regard to your fiancé's work, being in the trading business myself, I do have some contacts in the firm. Perhaps I can inquire—?"

"That is not necessary. Really." A flicker of panic crossed her features before she schooled them into a portrait of calm. "Considering your opinion of the firm, I do not think that wise." She hastened to clarify her response. "Not that I disagree with your views. The company's reputation is quite tarnished. It is for that reason that Jason was posted over there. He was part of a select group appointed with Parliament's backing to ferret out the corruption riddling the offices and clean it up."

"A Herculean task indeed," he said. The man would have had better prospects redeeming Lucifer himself. It was no surprise Emily had a difficult time recovering from his death. No other men, all mere mortals, could compete with a man of such mythical stature. It was a disturbing thought.

"Yes, Jason did like a challenge, which is why he undertook the project," she said. Shadows clouded those vibrant blue eyes. "Perhaps you are right, and it was a futile undertaking. Thus, there is little sense in either of us pursuing this matter further. However, I appreciate your offer of help. It is a far more honorable one than I received from Mr. Drummond," she ruefully added and then turned away.

He blinked, and nearly shook his head. Damn, she was good. As clever as a weighted die and just as deceptive.

Her explanations were smooth and plausible. A few questions needing to be answered. Her desire to not worry her family. The coup de grâce was lamenting the futility of her pursuit.

She had spoken the truth—just not the whole of it. Not once did she confide what answers she pursued. Answers she wanted so desperately that she had risked her reputation to get them—and so much more had he not arrived when he did. Whatever she sought, he would bet his whole company that she had no intention of abandoning her quest.

Only a fool risked everything for nothing.

Lady Emily Chandler was many things—bold, beautiful, and bright as the sun—but a fool she was not.

"Now then, I understand you have arrived for the christening of the twins," she continued brightly. "As the designated godparents, we will be busy with other responsibilities, and I do not wish to burden you further with this ill-fated affair. I appreciate your timely arrival and assistance, but let us start anew."

She stopped, and facing him, she sank into a curtsy. "Mr. Curtis, welcome back to Bedfordshire. It is good to see you again. Allow me to offer my deepest condolences over the loss of your uncle and your cousin last year. Despite your family's tragedy, I know how much it means to Bedford and my sister that you managed to attend the christening."

He stared at her and then he couldn't help it, he laughed. She had so cleverly set him up. He had no choice but to agree to her proposal or appear a boorish cad should he press the matter further. Fine. He would concede. *For now.*

She might have secured her secrets tighter than Drummond's ridiculously knotted cravat, but he would unravel them.

"Lady Emily." He bowed. "It is a pleasure to see you again. You are as beautiful and clever as I remember and still leading the gentlemen on a merry chase. I shall have to remember to tread carefully lest I be trampled in their pursuit." He flashed her a grin, pausing to admire the flush staining her cheeks. "As for your condolences, keep them. I have no need of them."

"I beg your pardon?" She frowned.

"My uncle was a despicable blackguard, and my cousin no better. Neither will be missed. My sympathy is for my younger cousins, but I do not mourn either man."

"Was he not the Duke of Prescott?" Emily asked, wide-eyed.

"He was. He was also my mother's brother, but neither affiliation could redeem him. As much as you English revere your lofty titles, and I concede their power to accomplish more than they should, they cannot eradicate a deficiency of character."

Emily smiled. "You may have a point. It is indeed a detriment to our peerage that distinguished rank is not always linked to persons held in the highest esteem. But not everyone's character is stellar; we all are comprised of different degrees of human frailty." She cast a furtive glance behind her, and then stepped in front of him. "That is, some of us are weaker than others and hence, fall to temptation."

A grunt and a suppressed giggle emerged from the vicinity of bushes farther down the path. Amused, he arched a brow. "Like Eve and the apple? And Agnes with her penchant for—"

"Trouble. Exactly. We all are tempted." Emily nodded solemnly, but her lips twitched. After a moment, she rolled her eyes, and lifted her voice to call over her shoulder. "Agnes, I am ready to leave. Please meet me at the end of the path." When Brett laughed, she urged him along. "That is enough entertainment for the afternoon. Let us at least give her a moment of privacy."

"I would think that is exactly what you do *not* want to give her." He couldn't resist teasing.

She stared at him, and then sighed. "Oh, for goodness' sake, Agnes is an accomplished flirt, not some London doxy. This is the country, not the city. Here a few stolen kisses are considered harmless. And for all her absentmindedness, I am confident she would have been at my side had I but called out and you had not intervened in so timely a manner."

"I agree. I never meant to imply otherwise." He eyed her full lips, intrigued to learn the prim and proper Lady Emily considered a few stolen kisses harmless. He smiled. "Now then, once Agnes joins us, in accordance with our new beginning, I insist on escorting you both home." He lifted his arm and amused, watched her eye it warily.

"I am sure that you do." Relenting, she curled her hand around his forearm. "You are the soul of kindness."

He ignored her sarcasm. "So my sisters tell me."

"I do not doubt it," she said dryly. "I am hoping that you are the soul of discretion as well. I prefer this meeting with Drummond be kept between us. It is over, and so I do not wish to worry my family over it."

"Of course. I can be discreet when warranted. As for Agnes, I never saw a thing. Harmless or otherwise." He patted her hand.

She arched a brow, looking dubious. She did not trust him. He could not fault her for that. He did not trust her either. It was not an auspicious start to a fresh beginning.

Chapter Three

❧❧

LADY Julia Bryant, the Duchess of Bedford, smiled at her baby daughter, Emma, cradled in her arms and who regarded her with wide-eyed wonder. "I think she will have Daniel's eyes. I have been told a baby's eyes can change color after a year, but I believe hers are destined to be moss green."

Emily sat beside her older sister in Bedford Hall's spacious drawing room. The sun streamed through the French windows, bathing the elegant gold and beige interior with light. "If you wish it so, I have no doubt that it will come to pass, because of late, all your wishes appear to be coming true." She spoke warmly.

Her sister's happiness had come to her late in life, and the journey had not been a smooth one, so Emily did not begrudge her any of her hard-earned joy. Even if it meant that Emily's new brother-in-law, Daniel Bryant, the Duke of Bedford, came with his former business partner and closest friend, Mr. Brett Curtis.

She pursed her lips and tapped her fingers against the sofa

arm, then froze at her rare display of impatience. It was difficult to remain unruffled with her plans in disarray and temporarily shelved, because she could not possibly proceed under the man's all-knowing, piercing gaze. When Brett locked those eyes on her, he studied her as if she were a riddle he had to decipher or a pesky knot he needed to unravel.

It was a problem. One she needed to remove.

The christening was a few days ago, so one would think his departure imminent. More important, he had a company to run, and she dearly wished he would disappear to do so.

She glanced across the room to where Brett stood conversing with her father and brother-in-law. Bedford, who held Emma's twin brother, Colin, lifted the boy and thrust him toward Brett. She half rose, prepared to rescue the baby, but instead, she found herself sinking back into her seat, her brow furrowed. Brett accepted the bundle and cradled Colin in the crook of his arm, smiling at the boy. At a comment from her father, Brett lifted his head and flashed that devilish grin of his.

She sighed. It was difficult to remain annoyed at the man when he did something so heartrendingly endearing. She *knew* he would be a problem.

"My father has a large family, and many of our cousins have children," Melody Curtis explained, having clearly noted Emily's surprise. "We are often having babies thrust into our arms, and Brett has a way with children. Always has."

He has a way with women, too. Emily cursed the unbidden thought, and summoned a wan smile for Brett's younger sister. While blond and blue-eyed like Brett, the resemblance ended there. Unlike her statuesque brother, Melody, at sixteen years, was a slip of a woman, barely reaching his shoulders, but her large, ebullient personality belied her size. Like her name, her voice carried a lyrical cadence, as if she was always on the brink of laughter.

"I can see that. He will make a wonderful father," Julia said.

"I used to think so." Miranda Curtis, another of Brett's sisters, joined the conversation. "But since Daniel's become a silent investor, leaving the daily operations of the company in Brett's hands, I worry about him. He used to be on the brink of marrying one woman after another. Now freight weights, cargo hauls, and trading routes hold his attention."

A year older than Melody, Miranda was a darker-haired version of her sister, but carried a more serious mien. Sometimes Emily caught Miranda quietly assessing her, and Emily had to glance away, fearing what the young woman might find. She hoped she was not as prescient as her brother. One meddling Curtis was enough.

Miranda's comment on Brett's multiple marriage prospects came as no surprise to Emily. The man could charm a statue to life, so it was inevitable that women were drawn to him. It was one of the reasons why Emily kept him at arm's length—despite the dormant feelings Brett Curtis awakened in her.

More important, she would not attach herself to any man ever again. To risk the passion, or worse, the pain of it a second time. The first time had nearly killed her.

The only surprise in Miranda's disclosure was that Brett had been too busy with work to pursue women. It was like a fox abstaining from hens. She doubted the man capable of such restraint. Perhaps he had changed. Mulling that over, Emily eyed Brett with curiosity.

"Yes, reproduction with freight weights or cargo hauls would prove a miraculous feat indeed, so his prospects for fatherhood do look bleak," Melody said.

"Melody!" Miranda gasped.

"Psshaw, Mandy. He was never serious about any of those women. Thank goodness." Melody's face scrunched up, revealing her opinion of Brett's taste. "And he has more time on his hands now that he has hired a new manager to oversee the company in America, as well as one to assist with the London and Bristol operations."

Miranda, bristling at her sister's cavalier dismissal of her concerns, opened her mouth to protest, but Julia intervened. "I have faith that he shall find someone special very soon. Being happily married myself, I wish for your brother to be equally as content. It is the least I can do for him after stealing

Daniel away. Since Emily tells me that of late all my wishes appear to be coming to pass, expect wedding bells to be in his near future." Julia winked at Miranda.

"Do not toss away a wish on a wife for Brett!" Melody said. "Once he sets his mind to the matter, he is quite capable of finding one himself. It is not like he has never asked—"

"What Melody means to say"—Miranda cut off her sister, a flash of warning lighting her eyes—"is that Brett has little trouble accomplishing what he wants once he sets his mind to it."

So Mr. Brett Curtis had asked for a woman's hand in marriage?

It was something else to mull over.

Had he loved the woman? Had she then rejected him? Or he her? Who was she?

A voracious reader, Emily loved a good story, particularly when it starred someone else's tragedy and helped her to escape her own. Guilt pricked her at the petty thought, and she chided herself for both it and her curiosity. After all, Mr. Curtis's ill-fated affair was not her concern.

"Emily?"

Emily stiffened at Julia's repetition of her name. The Curtis sisters watched her expectantly, and Julia was giving her a curious look. Heat climbed her cheeks. "I'm sorry, what did you say?"

"I was just commenting that the success of Curtis Shipping is a testament to Brett's talent at accomplishing what he sets his mind to. Daniel always quipped that Brett could charm, persuade, or talk a person to death in order to achieve his goals," Julia said.

"Do not forget begging and nagging," Melody added.

"He does have a talent for that," Miranda said, grinning.

"And chicanery and intimidation," Emily muttered, and then froze as Julia's lips parted. Had she spoken out loud? She cursed her forwardness.

"Yes, that, too." Melody rescued her, affably agreeing with a laugh. "Then let us leave Brett to fend for himself, because I have a better need for one of your wishes."

"Oh?" Julia looked amused. "Is there a handsome man who needs to be wished to your side?"

"I certainly hope so." Melody winked. "But do not send anyone my way just yet. First, I need one of your wishes or any assistance you can provide to address another matter. You see, I have a need to move a mountain."

Emily exchanged a bemused look with Julia, while Miranda clapped a hand to her mouth, eyes brimming with laughter.

"A mountain? Perhaps you should elaborate," Julia said.

"While we are here, we wish to travel to London. I want to go to the theater and to dance the night away at a ball. More important, we wish to shop for new gowns at Madame Duchard's infamous shop. Her designs are divine." Melody released a wistful sigh. "Then I shall be more fashionably attired to meet any suitors who come my way."

"Of course, you must visit London," Julia said. "A trip to England is not complete without a city excursion. I cannot believe your parents would oppose such a trip."

Miranda had told Emily that after the funeral, Brett's parents and younger sister Merritt had remained behind in Oxfordshire to care for the dowager duchess and her younger children.

"The ride from Bedfordshire to London in fair weather is but a two-day journey. While the road can be rustic in places, no mountains impede your travels," Emily said.

Melody's expression was glum as her gaze strayed to Brett. "I beg to differ. There is an insurmountable one about six feet tall, weighing just over twelve stone."

Miranda followed her sister's gaze and solemnly nodded. "Yes, with a deep-set scowl, and a canny ability of disappearing whenever the words *shopping* and *new gowns* enter the conversation."

Julia tossed back her head and laughed, and Emily smiled.

"We have been working on breaching his defenses. If as you say, your wishes are coming true lately, perhaps you can spare one for us," Melody said.

"He refuses to escort you into London?" Emily's smile faded. What kind of brother did that make Brett if he was so heartless that he could not find time to accompany his sisters to the city?

He may have spent the past year in London, overseeing his company's expansion, but his sisters had been home in America. Boston was far from provincial, but she doubted it could compete with John Nash's recently completed development of New Street. And Melody was right. Madame Duchard's gowns were exquisite.

Miranda glanced at Melody and appeared to choose her words with care. "It is not that he refuses per se, it is that another matter has arisen that requires his attention. He has promised to escort us as soon as it is taken care of."

"Yes, he did vow to do so," Melody agreed. "But he also said he preferred to take a long walk off a very short pier." Her tone, for once, was gloomy.

"He told me he would rather be drawn and quartered," Miranda said bleakly.

Emily ignored Julia's laughter. "I thought he had more time now that he has hired new managers?"

"It is not work stealing his time, but a family situation. He promised to assist my aunt with a matter of some urgency," Miranda said.

"Yes, he needs to locate her missing heir." Melody sighed. "The newly minted Duke of Prescott disappeared." She leaned forward and lowered her voice to a conspiratorial whisper. "I think he has run away. Brett said he hoped he had, infuriating my aunt—"

"Melody!" Miranda yelped.

"What? Andrew never expected to inherit the title anyway. He was the fourth in line and the black sheep in the family. So—"

"That is enough, Melody," Miranda chastised. "Aunt Beverly would not appreciate your publicly airing private family matters."

"Oh psshaw, Daniel is like family, practically lived with us for a decade in America. Now he is married to Your

Grace, so that makes *her* family. And Lady Emily is *her* sister and so by extension—"

"I understand." Miranda spoke with strained patience. "That still does not warrant a full account of—"

"It is not like they can keep his disappearance a secret." Melody's eyes sparkled with mischief, undaunted. "My aunt blames Brett for Drew's disappearance, so she has demanded Brett find and drag Drew home willing or not. If he fails, Aunt Beverly says"—Melody's voice dropped to a melodramatic contralto—"Brett will rue the day he was born. Brett said our aunt should have treaded the boards because she has a penchant for drama."

"Such talent runs in the family," Miranda said dryly, narrowing her eyes at Melody.

"Why does she blame Brett?" Emily said, edging forward on her seat.

"Oh, she blames Brett for *all* the trouble Drew gets into." Melody rolled her eyes. "After failing out of a few schools, my aunt despaired of Andrew getting any education. As a last resort, they shipped him off to join Brett and Bedford at Dunbar Academy. The three became inseparable. A *trio of trouble*, my uncle used to grouse. My aunt Beverly blames Brett for filling Drew with his American scorn for English ways, which, of course, in her opinion, comprises all that is good and proper in the world."

"Does Brett have any idea where your cousin has gone?" Julia said. "Or why he has disappeared?"

Miranda frowned. "I do not think so, but I have no doubt he will find him."

"If Drew is in London, I do not see why we cannot accompany Brett into the city," Melody said. "If Julia and Emily agree, I cannot see how his defenses can withstand a four-woman siege. The odds are against him." She beamed.

Emily straightened, inspiration seizing her. "Actually, your first idea is better. Removing the mountain from the equation altogether will make your journey a far smoother one. And I know how to do it."

"Really?" Melody's eyes widened.

Emily ignored Julia, who was looking at her as if she had sprouted a second head. Miranda's words had given her an epiphany.

What if Brett is not my problem, but my solution?

The man was good at resolving difficult situations, accomplishing what he set his mind to, and persuading people to do his bidding.

He was also slick as a cardsharp, and cardsharps always won.

She had vowed to consort with the devil to achieve her goal. Satan appeared in many guises. If he posed as a shrewd, handsome American businessman for this sojourn, so be it. She was a woman of her word.

She would get Brett Curtis to assist her.

In return, she would escort his sisters to London and to shop along Oxford Street, liberating Brett to search for his wayward cousin.

To set her plan in motion, she needed allies. Melody was right. Brett might be able to fend off two women, but four? Well, then it would be like trying to change the direction of salmon en route to spawn, or in this case, to shop.

"I would love to offer you my services as an escort in London. You can stay with us at Keaton House during your visit. Father has business in the city and has been badgering me to accompany him. What better reason to do so than to visit Madame Duchard's?"

Emily did not glance Julia's way after noting her parted lips and wide eyes. Julia must think Emily's two heads had sprouted horns, so stunned did her sister appear.

Melody clapped her hands in glee. "That is a marvelous plan."

Miranda's brow furrowed. "Lady Emily, perhaps you should confer with the earl before extending—"

"My father will be absolutely delighted to have you join us." She waved away Miranda's concerns. "He has been worried about my not getting out enough and encouraging me to enjoy the Season. I have a tendency to rusticate in the country more than I should, so a city excursion will alleviate my father's worries about my growing roots and sprouting leaves."

Once upon a time, she had relished the never-ending whirl of balls, garden parties, and elaborate dinners. Since Jason's death, Emily no longer felt as if she belonged there. Did not know if she ever would—or if she could summon the energy to try. But to obtain the answers she sought and for Jason's sake, she would force herself to return—and more difficult, pretend to belong.

"It is a grand offer. I do not know how to thank you. Brett will be indebted to you," Melody said. "After all, you are sparing him an evisceration at the gallows."

Emily hoped their brother shared their gratitude, but she had no idea how the man would respond. He was an American, and nor did he behave as one expected. He could be outspoken, irreverent, and unpredictable.

She hoped the positive attributes upon which she was counting overrode these problematic ones.

"This is a generous offer," Miranda said. "If you are quite certain your father would approve, we would be honored to accept." Her worried gaze drifted to Julia.

"As Emily says, I am certain Father will agree to the plan and the company." Julia hastened to assure them, recovering her power of speech and looking delighted. "But to alleviate any doubts, let him speak for himself." Julia clutched the baby close, swept to her feet, and with the Curtis sisters following, led their group over to the men.

Surprised at the speed in which the events were unfolding, Emily followed at a slower pace.

"Papa, Emily has had the most delightful idea!" Julia announced. "Miranda and Melody expressed an interest in visiting London, so Emily invited the girls and Brett to stay with you and her at Keaton House." Julia beamed at her father, as if she was bestowing on him a prized gift.

All the men's eyes turned to Emily. Usually a loquacious man, her father appeared to have been rendered mute, so stunned was he. Emily's cheeks warmed.

"Is that so?" Brett said in a slow drawl.

His deep voice rumbled through her body, and she blinked as she met his curious gaze. She had paused beside him, and he stood so close that she could smell the subtle fragrance of his cologne, see the gleam in his eyes. He wore his hair unfashionably long, so it brushed the collar of his shirt. She swallowed at the sudden dryness in her mouth.

In for a penny, in for a pound.

She lifted her chin and plastered a bright smile on her face. "Father has business in London, and your sisters tell me that you do as well, so I thought an invitation to Keaton House to be timely."

"It will save you that long walk off a short pier," Melody said, squeezing Emily's arm and shooting Brett a triumphant look. "You do recall saying that you would prefer to take—"

"Yes, Melody, my memory is just fine." Brett cut his sister off. "It is yours that I worry about. If you recall, I promised to escort you to the city as soon as I tied up my business matter. I refuse to impose on Lord Taunton or Lady Emily's generosity when—"

"Impose! Please, impose! In fact, I insist." Her father had recovered his voice, and it boomed out. He hastened to Emily's side, his eyes glowing. "I should have thought of it myself. Have to thank Emily for doing so."

"Really, we cannot—" Brett began.

"You can. You must! A visit to England is not complete without a trip to London," he said, echoing Julia's words. "As the Season is in its infancy, I am sure we can extract invitations to those events the ladies would enjoy. Isn't that right, Emily?"

Emily's smile wavered. A familiar quickening of nerves had her pulse racing and her heart pounding, momentarily paralyzing her. She had to tamp down the desperate urge to rescind her invitation and stay rooted in Bedfordshire. Safe. Protected. Away from the prying eyes, the censure, and those endless murmurs.

How is she? Better? She never was quite the same after the viscount's death. So very young. A tragedy.

She forced her breathing to level as she had practiced, calming herself. *For Jason's sake. For justice.*

"Of course. I am sure there is a pile of invitations awaiting us." She hoped they did not bury her. "I shall make a point of weeding through the most promising." And deadheading those from sycophants and tittle-tattlers. The former seeking favor from the earl, the latter looking for grist to feed the ever-churning gossip mill. "I am sure there are many that will suit our needs."

Daniel dropped a hand on Brett's shoulder, a teasing gleam in his eyes. "Actually, staying at Keaton House will suit yours as well, Brett. As you have given up your apartments and have been lodging in the room above your office. Keaton House is far more hospitable with Lady Emily and Taunton helping to make your sisters' visit to our fair isle an unforgettable one. Lady Emily will garner invitations to the very best events. While you may not appreciate the advantages that come with titled connections, you cannot deny your sisters the right to do so. To dance at the Duke of Hartwick's ball, to attend Lady Davis's garden party, and of course, to—"

"I understand," Brett said through gritted teeth. He shrugged his shoulder, dislodging Daniel's grip and addressing Emily and her father. "Lord Taunton and Lady Emily, to secure my two favorite sisters their happiness, I accept your generous invitation to—" He got no further. His words were drowned out by his sisters' squeals of excitement. Melody released Emily to tug Brett down by his shoulders and gave him a smacking kiss on his cheek.

His indulgent smile set off a flutter in Emily's breast.

When the silence settled, Miranda spoke up. "Two of your favorite sisters? What about Merritt?"

"Merritt who?" Brett winked.

Melody laughed and caught Miranda's arm to draw her away, their heads close together.

"Your sisters tasked me with moving a mountain," Julia said. "I thank you for enabling me to do so. I feel quite heroic."

"It is not me whom you should thank, but Lady Emily.

You do know they will not be fit to live with once they experience a London Season. But I admit, you have rescued me from a nagging, begging, and whining siege."

The Curtis sisters clearly shared their brother's tenacity in the pursuit of their goals. Emily would keep that in mind.

"I am indebted to you," Brett added, giving her a courtly bow.

And that was her plan—to have him in her debt.

She couldn't resist a smile of triumph, but when he straightened and those deep, fathomless blue eyes met hers, her smile wavered. Her heart skipped as if she had raced downstairs and missed a step. The man stirred up yearnings she did not want to feel. *Attraction. Desire. Lust.*

Worse, he dug up old memories. Tumultuous memories of joy and . . . pain. Everything she had fought to bury with Jason.

Chapter Four

❧❧

"W HAT business do you have in London? As your largest investor, I have a vested interest in matters concerning the company," Daniel said as he lifted a decanter of whiskey from the mahogany bar and collected two tumblers.

It was late evening, and Brett and Daniel had retired to Bedford Hall's billiard room. A blend of gray-green marble and red mahogany, the room was another legacy of Daniel's late brother and his lavish renovations upon his inheritance of the title. Brett had never felt at ease in the ostentatious room, but he gave neither his environs nor Daniel's words any heed. His mind was preoccupied with another matter—

Lady Emily Chandler's curious invitation.

For a woman bent on skirting his company over the past year, he could not fathom what had brought about this abrupt change of heart. She had been unwavering in her disinterest, her defenses entrenched and damn near impenetrable. Not that it mattered, because there could never be anything between them. A decade ago, another earl had told him exactly how they felt about their pampered daughters marrying untitled Americans who work in trade.

So it begged the question, after a year of doing the dance of avoidance, why had Lady Emily extended an invitation to stay with her and her father at Keaton House?

"That bad?" Daniel said.

Startled, Brett's eyes met Daniel's and he snatched the glass of whiskey from his friend's hand. "What the devil is her purpose in inviting me and the girls to Keaton House?"

Daniel paused in lifting his glass to his mouth, and a scowl blackened his features. "You best not rescind your acceptance. Julia will have my head, and I am not spending another night in the guest quarters."

"I am not . . ." Brett began and then paused, intrigued. "Another? Has the blush of wedded bliss faded so soon? Do you need advice? After all, I have a way with women and—"

"Yet you still remain a bachelor. I will keep my own counsel because my bed is almost never empty, which is more than I can say for yours." Daniel tipped his glass in a toast and drank.

Brett had no witty retort to refute the pitiful truth. His bed *was* empty. Had been for too damn long. His mood souring, he twirled his glass in his hand, brooding into the amber depths. When he met Daniel's amused gaze, he addressed his earlier comment. "Why, pray tell, is my head in jeopardy with your wife if I do not take Lady Emily up on her invitation?"

Daniel leaned back against the bar and sighed. "According to Julia, this is the first time since her fiancé's death that Emily has, of her own accord, extended an invitation to anyone, let alone expressed interest in rejoining society. So my lovely, overprotective wife is delighted with this turn of events, and you cannot cry off. It will upset Emily, which then upsets my wife, which will then upset me." He narrowed his eyes. "I will have to call you out. As you know, I am a lousy shot, so this will have a very bad ending for one of us. Do you understand?"

"I do." Brett's lips twitched.

"Good."

"What do you mean Lady Emily has not joined society? She has traveled to London numerous times. She was with us that autumn when I was tossed from the curricle."

"I did point that out to Julia, but she explained that while Emily visits the city, she declines most social invitations, preferring to avoid large gatherings of the ton."

"As do I. You said Lady Emily was a good judge of character." He shrugged. "This simply affirms your words."

Daniel laughed. "True. But your exile is due to your contempt for—to borrow your words—*the haughty pomposity of the vacuous half-wits who wear their aristocratic titles like haloed crowns. All the while, they are incapable of dressing themselves, adding a simple sum to keep their estates out of debt, toss down fortunes at the turn of a—*"

"I understand." Brett held up his hand. "However, I call them empty-headed peacocks, not half-wits. No need to mock poor simpletons for a mental deficiency that, unlike your ton, is no fault of their own. Otherwise, that is an accurate assessment of your aristocracy." Suddenly aware of his audience, he quickly added, "Of course, that is, with the exception of Your Grace and a select few."

"Of course," Daniel said dryly. "Very kind of you to make an exception for me."

"Your decade in America thinned your blue blood. And building Curtis Shipping from the ground up, your hands now carry the stains of trade. No erasing that, my friend."

Daniel nodded. "I also dress myself and can do a simple sum in my head—that is unless Julia is nearby. It is the damnedest thing, but when that woman is in the room, all coherent thought goes right—"

"Then you tend to think with another part of your anatomy. It is why you are no longer a full partner in the firm."

"Touché." Daniel smiled. "However, I do not know how Melody maneuvered Emily to extend the invitation to you and your sisters, but Julia is pleased with this turn of events. And when my wife is content, I am—"

"Not sleeping in the guest quarters," Brett said.

"Exactly." Daniel grinned.

Brett took another sip of his whiskey, pondering Emily's reason for avoiding society, and if Melody was truly responsible for changing Emily's mind. The East India House, the company headquarters of the East India Company, was located on Leadenhall Street in London. Drummond had refused to assist Emily, and she had rejected Brett's offer of help. But if Emily sought clarification for the questions she had in regard to her fiancé's work, it would be difficult to do so with his sisters in tow.

As a businessman, he was used to having everything add up into neat, logical sums. This invitation did not add up. He was missing information. With his sisters joining Lady Emily in the city, Brett had a vested interest in ferreting out what was missing. Lady Emily might be in need of a better chaperone than the absentminded Agnes, but he refused to allow his sisters to step into that role. Not when it involved clandestine meetings with men of Mr. Drummond's ilk.

"So you will go?" Daniel said.

"I will. Far be it from me to be the source of so much distress. Besides, while you are a lousy shot, Melody is not. She would shoot me and not shed a tear." Brett could not resist adding, "And when have I ever turned down an invitation from a beautiful woman?"

"Having seen Emily fend off your attention over the past year, I am confident of her success in continuing to do so. As I said, she is a good judge of character."

"Everyone has their blind spots." He must be standing in Emily's. It was time he shifted to a more favorable position.

Daniel shook his head, but refused to comment. "Since I have been distracted with the festivities, we have not had a chance to catch up properly. What is this business in London? I know there was something else on your mind. What is it?" Daniel walked over to an English Tudor cargo rack where mahogany cue sticks polished to a gleaming sheen were neatly stacked. "Game?"

Brett followed Daniel to select a tapered cue and chalk.

"This particular business does not concern Curtis Shipping. I am on a personal errand for Aunt Beverly."

Daniel tipped his head to the side as if contemplating the matter. "Let me guess. She has sent you to retrieve something for her in Seven Dials, thus satisfying her lifelong wish for you to disappear?"

Seven Dials, near Covent Garden, named for its convergence of seven streets and its signature column with six sundials on it, was synonymous with abject poverty and all manner of craven vice. With its overcrowded slum dwellings and dark alleys, it would be an easy venue into which a gentleman could disappear, never to be heard from again. "Let us hope that is not where my search takes me."

"You are serious," Daniel marveled. "What has she lost?"

Brett smirked. "Your good friend, my beloved idiot of a cousin, Andrew Winslow Reynolds, now the Duke of Prescott, has disappeared, and I am tasked with finding him."

Surprise crossed Daniel's features. "You did ask when you arrived if I had heard from Drew recently. Do you fear foul play? God knows, the family never wanted Drew to claim the title." His eyes hardened. "Drew wrote and requested that I not give his father and brother the honor of my presence at their funeral, a snub I was happy to execute on Drew's behalf, but that is the last I heard from him. How long has he been gone? And why the devil are you tasked with finding him? Your aunt Beverly never trusted you with her crockery let alone her good silver, so why has she suddenly entrusted you with finding her lost heir?"

"About three months." Brett rubbed his neck, which burned like a brand of guilt. "And . . . well, his last night was spent drinking with me."

"Ahhhh," Daniel said as if that explained the matter. He leaned against the bar and folded his arms across his chest. "I understand. You encouraged him to flee and seek his freedom in America, rather than don his ducal crown of thorns with all its aristocratic trappings."

Brett tossed Daniel a black look, and took a sip before answering. "I might have said words to that effect. Hell, we were both deep in our cups. Toasting his freedom from his father and Gordon's tyranny. Drew was in shock. As you know, being the fourth son, he never expected to inherit. Add to that, Prescott's mantle is not an easy one to bear, his father's legacy staining it black. Drew understands the full import of what becoming the Duke of Prescott entails."

"But his friends know Drew for the man he is, as we know you to be more than a provincial American clod," Daniel pointed out. At Brett's withering glare, Daniel held up his hands in defense. "However, I do understand that the name comes with a reputation that no man should have to carry. I remember that Drew rambled on about the year he spent painting in America after he visited us. The freedom that came with not being stamped as *that bastard's youngest son*. You can well imagine how he is grappling with taking the title, particularly when he has carved out an identity for himself as the artist A. W. Grant.

"His paintings did well in America, and those you brought over here garnered more admirers. In fact, his last picture sold for over two hundred pounds. If he does follow your advice and flee his ducal trappings, thanks to you, he has the funds to subsist independent of his inheritance. And his family has no inkling of this income. Probably a good thing, because his last picture of the delectable nude was risqué. Aunt Beverly would not approve, but I do." Daniel grinned.

"It was Aphrodite, the goddess of love and beauty." Brett shook his head. "And all these years, Drew was believed to be the simpleton in our trio. Glad you find this amusing. At least someone does." But he had to concede Daniel's point. "I am aware that I have to accept some of the responsibility for his flight."

"Some?" Daniel arched a brow. "You planted the seed and engineered the means for Drew to fund his escape."

"Fine. More than some, but Drew is his own man, responsible for his own decisions." He decided against showing Daniel the note his cousin had left his aunt. She had delivered the damning missive to Brett paired with a tongue-lashing that still had his ears ringing. Best to keep its contents quiet until he had discussed the matter with Drew. That is, once he found his errant cousin. While Brett could not force Drew to return home, he hoped to deter him from pursuing the madcap course of action spelled out in his parting missive, and which now burned a hole in Brett's jacket pocket.

"As we both know how canny Drew is, I suspect his disappearance is shoving a thorn up your aunt's arse," Daniel said. "She is probably in bed now calling for her smelling salts or laudanum. I say, well done, Drew. The woman deserves every torturous moment he can squeeze from the bitter old bat. However, his younger sisters do not. Drew knows this and would never abandon them. My guess is that he will return when he feels your aunt has sufficiently suffered."

Brett relaxed enough to grin. "I surmised the same, so I told Aunt Beverly I will find Drew. However, I have no intentions of dragging him home until I determine his intentions. Or until Drew has played out whatever hand he has chosen to deal the woman."

"Fair enough. When he does return, he will be the Sixth Duke of Prescott, making him another member of the peerage. You, my friend, might be forced to revise your opinion of our aristocracy. And"—he lowered his voice—"finally realize that not all of us are of the same ilk as the Earl of Wentworth."

Brett's eyes snapped to Daniel's, the name like a fist to his gut.

"Just think on it, Brett. It is past time," Daniel added.

Brett tossed his drink back. He only wished it could drown out the memory of the man whom Brett held responsible for nearly destroying him and all he sought to build.

Daniel cleared his throat. "Now then, to cheer you up, I will let you attempt to best me in billiards and win back the first of A. W. Grant's works. It is a generous offer, considering its stock is poised to increase with Prescott's ducal rise."

Brett's gaze lifted to the nautical portrait over the hearth. A majestic oil painting, it depicted the *Bostonian*, the first freight carrier he and Daniel had purchased upon launching Curtis Shipping.

In painstaking detail, Drew had captured the lumbering ship with the fog-enshrouded Boston Harbor in the distance. The piece had been a gift to them both and once proudly graced their Boston office. When Daniel had settled in England, the painting's residency had alternated between the two of them numerous times with various wagers determining its ownership.

The *Bostonian* reminded Brett that he was more than an untitled American, but a man of wealth and influence in his own right. The Earl of Wentworth would learn that, should their paths cross again—which was a possibility if he escorted his sisters to social engagements in London. And accompanying his sisters would be Lady Emily Chandler. Picturing her flashing blue eyes, he forgot Wentworth and his errant cousin, and the tension gripping him eased.

For the first time that he could remember, he looked forward to attending a gathering of the ton. Lady Emily Chandler may have a hidden agenda, but so did he. He vowed to determine her motivation for extending her enigmatic invitation to him and his sisters. And of course, he had to find his wayward cousin.

But first he had a painting to win.

Chapter Five

❧

EMILY savored the cool breeze that whipped the skirts of her walking dress about her legs. She trailed Jonathan, her seven-year-old brother, his sword bobbing against his leg as he bounded over the vast acreage belonging to Tanner Stables. The sword was a gift from Brett, who had sacrificed one of his cravats to fashion a belt to secure it against her brother's hip.

Brett Curtis had a diversity of clever talents, and as they walked, she used the time to formulate a plan to win him to her cause. In approaching any worthy adversary, one had to proceed with caution. No doubt, Brett would oppose the idea of her pursuing a murder investigation and might be a tad difficult about the matter. To counter his protests, she needed to arm herself with an arsenal of facts and stay resolute in her goal.

"Hello there!"

She nearly stumbled to a stop. *Brett Curtis.* The man needed to wear a warning bell, because he had an irritating habit of sneaking up on her.

She summoned a smile and turned to greet him. Good lord, she was a fool. There was no way a woman could ever be prepared for *this* man.

His navy blue jacket hugged his broad shoulders and slim waist, while his smile was slow and easy. "I hope you do not mind my joining you. I have a few matters I wished to discuss about our trip."

"No, of course not." She could not avoid the man forever, particularly if she hoped for his assistance.

Jonathan withdrew his sword and pointed it down a rough-hewn dirt path. "This way. I will lead because I am armed and you are not."

"Brave man," Brett said, his lips twitching. "You have a formidable guardian to protect your honor. I shall have to tread carefully."

"Very wise of you," she said solemnly. They fell into step behind her brother's darting figure. "Jonathan has been talking nonstop about visiting this new stallion that Robbie Tanner recently acquired. He is quite wild, not unlike Daniel's Black Angel before Robbie broke him to saddle." The Tanner family stabled the best bloodstock in the county, most of which they sold at Tattersall's in London.

She glanced askance at Brett, annoyed when he made no response. Her words did not need a comment, but to offer one was to partake in the polite ritual of social discourse. Then again, his silence should not surprise her. The man never followed the rules.

The lane ascended a hill and beyond its rise, the countryside unfolded before them in an expanse of lush green grazing meadows. Brushstrokes of black, brown, and gray horses dotted the landscape.

"It is beautiful here."

She nodded. "Yes, it is lovely. The Tanner family has owned this land for well over a century."

"You and your English love of exalted bloodlines, particularly as it roots you to the land."

She raised a brow at his cynicism. "Your mother is

English, and her late brother was the Duke of Prescott. That makes you *half* English, does it not?"

"True," he conceded. "That is the half in me that recognizes the beauty here and why the Tanners would never abandon it." He grinned.

Intrigued, she pressed him further. "And the other half? The American half, what does it see?"

"Roots that bind." His grin faded. "Tethers holding you to your *precious stone set in a silver sea* so you never venture beyond your shores, thus neglecting a wider world with riches to be explored, or as the businessman in me would say, to be exploited."

She recognized the *Richard II* Shakespearean reference, and tipping her head to the side, she studied him. "So you feel no kinship with any *blessed plot* of land? Not even in America?"

"I do not." He shrugged. "I am free to roam where my work or the new trading routes take me. Do not misunderstand me, I love my family's home in Boston, but my schooling was in England, and I spent the term's holidays at my uncle's, only traveling home for the summer recess. So my affinity to my family estate is not as entrenched as yours or Daniel's. Perhaps bridging two countries, both very different, I was never able to grow roots in either."

"I can understand that," Emily said, marveling that she did. While she had planted herself in the country, it was not due to an affinity for the land, but rather an escape. A sanctuary she sought due to similar feelings of displacement, or rather, of no longer belonging anywhere else, Jason's death unmooring her so.

Disturbed at this unsettling connection between them, she reminded herself that she had her family, had recently become an aunt, and had a purpose. Those ties did bind, and they were enough.

"Will you two stop squawking and dawdling!" Jonathan bellowed. "We need to get to the stallion before dark so we can see him." He brandished his sword at them.

Annoyance flared through Emily, but Brett simply laughed.

"Aye, aye, Captain. We will posthaste dispense with our dawdling and pick up our paces." Beneath his breath, he added. "Will he stab us if we do not comply?"

Her laughter surprised her. "Best not to risk it. As he has pointed out, he is armed and we are not."

"Not true. I have my cravat. We could tie him up." He winked at her.

She stared at the white muslin fashioned in a neat Gordian knot around his neck. It was a mistake, because her gaze then shifted to his lips, which were curved in a devastating half smile. Warmth flooded her, and she dismissed her concerns over Jonathan's sword. Brett Curtis carried far more dangerous weapons.

They crested another ridge to the field where the stallion was paddocked. Jonathan dashed ahead to clamber up the tall fence rail and lean over the top. "Cor, he's splendid, isn't he?"

Emily silently agreed. The horse was a sleek black beauty, tall and regal. He lifted his head, and studied Jonathan with eyes dark as coal. After emitting a disdainful snort, he cantered away from them.

"Robbie has done it again. Where does he find these prizes?" Brett said.

"They breed many, and his brothers scout for new stock. Robbie then travels to assess their finds. It is also my understanding that you let him know when purebred stock arrives at the docks." She pulled her attention from the horse to look at Brett, whose gaze remained on the horse.

He shrugged. "It is the least I can do after he saved my life. If not for his adroit handling of the reins of the curricle, I would have suffered more than a broken arm. However, then you would not have been recruited to draft my correspondence, which might have saved me a few headaches and a lot of time," he said.

"I think you would be facing far graver problems if you

had been shot." She said the words lightly, but her stomach curdled at the memory of the thugs who had attacked Brett and Robbie.

A startled laugh escaped him. Clearly the reminder did not disturb him. "True again." He glanced back at her. "Good thing I was not. Or were you hoping otherwise?"

"Oh, no. I am glad you survived. As you well know, I had need of your assistance the other day." She drew in a deep breath, and took the first step in her dance with the devil. "In fact, I was thinking about your offer of assistance and—" She got no further.

"I knew it!" Ignoring the stallion, he strode away from Jonathan's perch.

To her annoyance, he left her no choice but to follow him.

He lowered his voice to an excited hiss. "I knew there was more to your invitation."

"I beg your pardon?"

"You have an ulterior motive for wanting my sisters and myself to stay with you in London. Do not deny it. Contrary to Melody's prattle, you have no interest in escorting them to society events," he declared, his expression triumphant.

"Do not be ridiculous. I am pleased to—"

"No, you are not. Daniel says you have been avoiding the social affairs of the ton for years, have not extended any invitations to friends, and stunned Julia with your sudden, gracious offer. So it begs the question, why?"

"Why what?" Her anger flared. Tamping it down, she cursed Daniel for his breach of confidence, and Brett for digging into wounds he could never see. He thought he knew something, but he did not.

He understood nothing of the fears she fought to keep at bay.

That her will faltered in the crush of crowds. That the murmurs sweeping the room were like a strong current threatening to drown her—again.

He folded his arms across his chest. "Do not deny it. You

need my sisters as decoys while you arrange clandestine meetings with men like Drummond and—"

"That is enough! You have no idea what you are talking about," she cried, advancing on him. "It is not your sisters' help I need, but yours, you arrogant, obtuse man."

His lips parted before he snapped his mouth closed. "My help?" he blurted inanely, recovering his voice.

"I hoped we could perform a mutual service for each other. I have decided to accept the assistance that you offered me the other day. In exchange for your help, I am offering you mine with your sisters."

"Calling me obtuse when I did deduce you had an ulterior motive is rather rich." He arched a brow.

"Fine. But arrogant still stands."

He shrugged. "I have been called worse."

His words reined in her own temper, and the tension gripping her eased. "I understand that while in the city, you will need time to search for your cousin. Your sisters confided your aunt's worry over his recent disappearance."

He scowled. "My sisters are not known for their discretion, Melody in particular."

"Neither is my brother-in-law."

Brett made no response, but warily studied her as if he could extract her true motives. "So you wish for me to speak to my contact at the East India Company?"

She glanced over at Jonathan, who held his sword above his head as the stallion stood majestically, eyeing her brother with distrust. She and her brother faced dangerous adversaries and needed to proceed cautiously. "No, I need your assistance with a matter of a little more delicacy."

He frowned, but did not question her. He let the silence unfold, not rushing to fill the void with speculations, as most men were wont to do. It was one more trait of his that she appreciated.

"It is about those answers that I am seeking. You see my questions, or rather, my suspicions arose when I reread some of my late fiancé's letters." She repeated what she had told

Drummond about the discrepancy in the ledgers. "Accounts were not adding up, supplies were disappearing, and monies used for payment on items delivered were missing. He feared he had found evidence of foul play."

Neither surprise nor interest crossed Brett's features. She needed to give him something more. "Jason's clerk and his valet accompanied Jason's casket home. During Jason's funeral, his clerk left me an address for me to contact him. He asked that I do so to discuss a matter of vital importance. He would not say what, and I . . . I did not press him at that time because I was . . . I . . ." She faltered and heat burned her cheeks. "I was . . ."

"I understand," he intervened. "The viscount was your betrothed; you were grieving."

She *had been* grieving. In the darkest depths of despair, but he need not know that. "Yes. Well, this past year I recalled his request, and I wrote to him at the address he had given me. He has replied and agreed to meet with me in London, and I wish to do so because I believe the matter he wished to discuss concerned Jason's death."

"You want me to escort you to a meeting with your fiancé's former clerk?" He rubbed his neck, looking uncomfortable. "Shouldn't your father escort you? Have you asked him—?"

"No, I have not. And you must not mention any of this to my father or Julia. Please, I need your word on that."

He frowned. "Lady Emily, he was your fiancé. You do have a right to allay whatever misgivings you have regarding his passing. I am sure your father would understand—"

"No, please. I have put them through enough the last few years; I will not put them through any more. You must give me your word that what I share with you will remain in the strictest confidence. That you will not breathe a word of it to anyone." Desperation had her near begging.

After a prolonged stretch of silence, he nodded. "You have my word—with one caveat. Should they become cognizant of whatever it is that you wish to discuss, and ask me directly, I will be honest. I will not lie to your family or Daniel."

"Of course not. I am not asking you to do so. But until that situation arises, I am requesting that you keep my confidence because they would not approve, particularly after all that happened to Daniel and Julia two years ago when they pursued a similar course."

"I understand," he said.

"Thank you." She lifted her chin and stared him straight in the eye. "I believe Jason was murdered, and I need your help in proving it."

Brett stiffened with a curse. His eyes darkened and he shook his head. "No! No more murder mysteries. Absolutely not." He spun away from her and stormed off in Jonathan's direction.

That was it? Her mouth opened and closed like a fish tossed on land and left to dry. *Of all the arrogant, insensitive . . .* She caught up her skirts and started after him. When he suddenly stopped and spun around, he nearly collided with her. She stumbled back and blinked up at his thunderous expression.

"Blast and damnation!" he barked. He leaned low, crowding her as his voice spilled out in an angry hiss. "Do you know the dangers inherent in investigating a murder? Daniel almost got killed. Julia almost got killed. More important, *I* nearly got killed! I have no interest in dying young. Or watching you kill yourself in this quest. Not to mention your father would murder me. Then we would *both* be dead. So do you see why I cannot assist you? And why I cannot allow you to continue along this dangerous journey?"

She fisted her hands. "You cannot stop me! You gave me your word. You said you would not mention this to anyone, so you can make your own decisions in regard to your involvement, but you cannot speak for me. You said that I deserve answers. Well, I aim to get them and do not need your approval *or* permission to do so." She cursed her voice for hitching at the end.

"Devil take it! This is the East India Company. The largest mercantile company in the world, synonymous with malfeasance and unbridled corruption. You will not get justice because half of Parliament is in their pocket, and their charter was recently renewed for another twenty years." He closed his eyes, clearly struggling for calm. When he opened them, he gentled his tone. "Listen to me. I understand that you are upset. That you have a right to your answers. But at what expense? Your life? You fiancé is gone, and I am deeply sorry for that. But *this*, this will not bring him back."

She tugged down her jacket hem and straightened her spine. "You tried to talk Daniel out of his course, too. But he persevered and he prevailed, as will I."

He gave an incredulous laugh. "You are mad, stark raving, bats-in-the-belfry mad."

She was. It was her deep, dark secret. Had been since she had received word of Jason's death, but for the first time since acknowledging it, she did not care. If madness was going to be her driving force, so be it. She would embrace it.

An enraged bellow rent the charged silence. "Do not call my sister mad!" Jonathan barreled toward Brett, sword raised and aimed with deadly intent for his gut.

"I told you one of us would get killed," Brett muttered beneath his breath as he made a timely pivot out of Jonathan's path. He stripped the sword from her brother's hand, and swung him up and over his shoulder. "You are right. She is not mad."

He imprisoned Jonathan's legs against his chest. Holding her squirming brother tight, Brett executed a shallow bow. "My apologies," he said to her. "It is not you that is mad, but rather your course of action. Before you embark upon it, I simply ask that we discuss the matter more thoroughly." He slapped a hand on Jonathan's rump. "As for you, young man, I applaud your coming to your sister's defense, but next time give the poor fool a chance to apologize before you dismember him. Not all of us are unrepentant blackguards, and a man has a right to redeem himself." His gaze met Emily's.

She pursed her lips, but did not respond.

"Fine. I won't stab you. What's Emily's going to do?" Jonathan said.

Brett shifted Jonathan around to perch him on his

shoulders. "Go to a ball in the city where she will be forced to dance with a bunch of stuffed-up, overdressed popinjays. They will step on her toes and pen poor poetic tributes to her beauty. Is that not mad?"

"She will not! She never goes to balls. She doesn't like them."

Emily flushed, feeling exposed. Brett did not need to know these private details that Daniel and her brother were so cavalier in sharing. She glanced away from Brett's scrutiny. Let him make of their words what he would.

"Well, she has changed her mind. She appears to be intent on her course this time around," Brett said.

"You will have to go with her. I will loan you my sword, and you can protect her feet from all those popin . . . who-ever they are."

Brett's eyes met Emily's. "I will do so if it is the only way to protect her. However, I have a similar aversion to balls, so I am hoping I can persuade your sister from her course."

She bristled at the glint in his eyes. He did not understand her or what this quest meant to her. It put them on equal footing, because she never knew what he was going to do next—even as she desperately wished that in this matter she did. That she would not be venturing forward alone. "My mind is made up. But by all means, take all the time you need to form your own decision."

"Your sister is nothing if not determined." Brett shook his head. "But then, so am I."

Her confidence momentarily wavered, but she shored it up. Brett Curtis might be able to persuade most people to do his bidding, but she was made of sterner stuff. Had to be for Jason's sake.

She would not fail him again.

Chapter Six

B RETT pressed his knees into the horse's flanks and leaned low. He let the wind whip over him, cleansing the rage vibrating through him. He had asked her to wait, and she had not. It was a simple request. But she was not a simple woman.

Lady Emily was complicated and conniving.

He urged Remington, the handsome chestnut he had procured from Daniel's stables, into a gallop. If she continued on her quest, she was going to get her fool self killed. And *then* he could say that he had warned her.

He gritted his teeth, well aware that he sounded like a petulant boy who had not gotten his way. Well, he had not. She had left without him to visit her fiancé's family.

His ears rang with Julia's voice prattling on about how pleased she was that Emily had reconnected with the late viscount's brother and younger sister because before Jason's death, they had been close to the family. Julia surmised that enough time had passed so that Emily felt strong enough to rekindle old friendships.

He snorted. Did Emily think him a fool? She wanted something. His bet was on assistance from the brother. *What was his name? Tristan? What kind of fool name was that for a man?* Clearly, Emily never intended to discuss anything further with Brett, but he refused to be deterred.

His work forced him to deal with truculent mill owners and cantankerous customs officials. This provided him the experience needed to deal with one stubborn, feisty beauty. She might look like a delicate, porcelain doll, but she was Athena—which put him at cross-purposes with the goddess of warfare, strategy, and heroic endeavor. It did not bode well for him.

He crested a ridge and a short distance down the road, he spotted the blue and gold of Taunton's sleek four-wheeled coach. A footman in Taunton's blue livery sat on the back rumble seat.

"Whoa, there! Halt the carriage!" He slowed Remington to a canter and then to a trot as he shortened the distance between them. He drew abreast of the coach and reined in to dismount while the carriage rumbled to a stop.

"Mr. Curtis! Sir?" The driver's eyes widened.

"My apologies for the abrupt interruption, but it is imperative I speak with Lady Emily before she continues her journey."

"Yes, sir. Of course. Is anything amiss—?"

"No! My apologies, I should have said that straightaway. There is nothing wrong—"

"You! What do you think you are doing?" Lady Emily demanded. She had flung open the carriage door and beneath her bonnet, her eyes blazed. "Henry, ignore this man and continue on!"

She made to slam the door, but Brett caught the handle, yanking it open.

"Devil take you! What are you about?"

"Joining you," Brett said and seeing Taunton's footman circle the carriage, he tossed him his reins. "Please hitch Remington to the back. I shall be riding in the carriage." He made to vault inside, but Emily's hand was firm and hard against his chest.

"No, you most certainly will not!"

He heard a giggle, and peered around Emily to see Agnes, her hand covering her mouth as she struggled to suppress her laughter. At least someone found this amusing. "Ah, Agnes, my dear, would you mind exchanging places? I am sure there is room for you on the rumble seat with that strapping footman . . ."

Emily gasped and now both hands slapped his chest. Warmth surged at the intimacy of her touch. It was as if a lit candle were pressed to dry wood, so sudden did the heat ignite.

Emily inhaled sharply and then yanked her hands away and addressed Agnes. "Remain where you are. Mr. Curtis is mistaken. He will not be joining us and is leaving posthaste."

"On the contrary. The mistake was yours in not speaking to me before you left this morning. Agnes can stay, but we have unfinished matters to discuss and you did demand my discretion on this subject." He waited for her to respond, and when she did not, he continued with a shrug. "If you insist on my not riding with you, then I shall be obliged to continue the conversation here. Now, I do not think I made myself clear yesterday about why I opposed your—"

Gasping, she clapped her hand over his mouth.

The scent of a floral perfume wafted from the teasing strip of bare wrist that peeked out between her leather glove and her jacket sleeve. He inhaled deeply, and a madcap desire to laugh bubbled up within him. His lips curved and at the intimate movement, Emily snatched her hand away, her eyes wide pools of blue.

Flushing, she turned her back on him and murmured to Agnes. After a moment, an amused Agnes slid forward to exit the carriage. He stepped aside for the maid, but caught the delighted smile she flashed the footman, who withdrew the carriage steps and offered her his assistance.

Agnes retained the footman's hand in hers while he escorted her to the rumble seat. Brett grinned and made to step into the carriage, but Emily still blocked him, her brow furrowed and lips pursed.

They were at a standoff. Through sheer force of size, he

could resolve the matter, but being a gentleman, plowing through her was not the most civilized course of action. Not that he would not like to toss her over his shoulder and carry her home.

"Henry, please continue. Mr. Curtis will be joining us for a portion of our journey." She eyed him like the interloper she clearly considered him to be, and then withdrew to settle in the forward-facing seat.

He climbed in, and took the seat opposite.

She arranged her skirts around her, folded her hands in her lap, and regarded him with a look of strained patience.

"Let me again offer my apologies for my choice of words yesterday," he said, keeping his tone conciliatory. "As I said to Jonathan, you are not mad, because it is not madness to seek to redress a wrong that you believe happened to Jason." When she opened her mouth to correct him, he lifted his hand and amended his words. "Fine, *know* happened to him. That is an honorable quest, and I admire your desire to pursue—"

"Good, then I suggest you allow me to do so unimpeded. We have both made our opinions clear, so I do not see that we have anything further to discuss."

He clenched his jaw to bite off his sharp retort, his temper rising. "You think I am a hindrance to your plan?" he scoffed. "Aside from the dangers inherent in a murder investigation, do you have any idea of the obstacles you face should you present your accusations to the East India Company? Do you have a plan? Or are you going to blithely waltz up to their offices and demand answers to your questions? Call for an inquest into a death that is now nearly four years old?"

She stiffened, and a mottled flush stained her cheeks.

Undeterred, he continued. "Do you think you will get anywhere without evidence? You cannot possibly have thought this through. I am only asking you to do so if you want my assistance."

After a moment, her reply was delivered in a tone that dripped with honey sweetness, and her expression was a mocking portrait of wide-eyed innocence. "You mean I cannot simply bat my eyelashes and ask nicely for the answers I demand? What if I shed a pretty tear or two? Are you certain they would deny me then? The daughter of an earl? Even if I pleaded ever so politely?"

He narrowed his eyes. "Sarcasm does not become you."

Her expression cleared, and she shrugged. "Then stop patronizing me. It does not become *you* and insults me." She eyed him with scorn. "With three sisters, you should know that as much as men like to believe otherwise, women do have a brain in their heads, and we are quite capable of using it. I have had a year to consider this matter, and I do not take it lightly. I am well aware of the obstacles, and the . . . the dangers that I face."

She lifted her chin. "But perhaps I have made a mistake. Not in continuing this discussion with you, but in initiating it in the first place, because I refuse to spend time with someone who condescends to me. More important, who believes I am a vacuous, featherbrained female. One who would confront the East India Company without a thought, a plan, or evidence to back up my accusations. I have given this matter serious consideration. It has been all I have thought of over the last twelve months. Keeping me company when no one else would." Her voice finished on a hitch, and she turned to gaze out the window and draw deep, even breaths.

He opened his mouth to protest, and then closed it. She had a point, and he had to concede it. He had been an arrogant arse, but it irritated him to be called on it. Sighing, he lightened his tone. "Featherbrained female? I was thinking more along the lines of obdurate, headstrong, and stiff-necked." *Athena, goddess of war*—but he kept that to himself.

She turned to him and after a moment, she, too, relented. "Omit headstrong, replace obdurate with determined and stiff-necked with strong, and I accept your apology."

"Obdurate. One who stubbornly refuses to change one's opinion. Obdurate stands."

She eyed him silently, and then shrugged. "It does not matter. Your opinion is of no consequence to me."

He laughed. "You have made that clear. However, if I am going to assist you, you are going to have to be prepared to hear it. In business, the best alliances are forged when there is an equal exchange of ideas. When two people can express their opinions in a constructive manner that is beneficial to both parties."

As the import of his words sunk in, a flash of hope blazed in her eyes. "You . . . you are considering assisting me?"

"If I cannot change your mind, you leave me no choice. Who else is going to make sure you do not get your beautiful, obdurate head lopped off?" She might be intelligent and have a plan of action, but she was still a doe waltzing into a den of foxes. Such confrontations never boded well for the doe.

He could swear that he saw the flame of hope flare brighter. Then her lips curved into a smile that stole his breath.

Her smile was disturbing for its rarity. Like a falling star, you had to catch it quickly before it disappeared. At least, it was rare for her to shine it on *him*. The surprise of it had turned him as addled as Daniel was when Julia entered a room. It could prove problematic, because he needed to be sharp-witted to stay one step ahead of her. Silence settled between them, with only the rumble of the carriage wheels and a distant giggle from Agnes filling it.

"Thank you. I accept your gracious offer of assistance . . . and . . . and the dubious compliment."

Her words shattered his thoughts, and he cleared his throat. "Just one question: *Why me*? Why not Daniel?"

"Julia would never forgive me if I involved Daniel in this. Not after all they have been through to arrive where they are."

"Ah, now I understand. I am expendable."

She flushed. "Of course not. You built Curtis Shipping from the ground up. That demonstrates determination, ingenuity, and intelligence. You also supported Daniel when he needed your help, even when, as now, you were aware of the dangers in doing so. More important, you are canny, persuasive, and clever. I can use those attributes in pursuing my goal."

Pleased that she had given him a thought after having spent the last year dismissing him, he found himself straightening in his seat.

"You can wheedle, connive, bully, and—"

"Thank you. I think," he said dryly. She had been talking to his sisters.

"And you are an American."

That caught him off guard. "And that is helpful to you because . . . ?"

She waved her hand airily. "Americans are arrogant optimists who are not cowed by our peerage. That is, your reverence stops short of letting a high-ranking title interfere with your goal . . . or rather, my goal." She beamed.

"And Daniel always cursed my lack of respect for your aristocracy. Little did he know it is an asset. Thank you."

"You are welcome."

"I take it that you have a plan?"

"Of course. I am going to do as you suggested and obtain the evidence I need to prove my case before I present it to the proper authorities."

"And where exactly do you plan to get this evidence? Jason's family just happens to have been safeguarding it for you all these years?"

She sighed. "I agree to hear your opinion, because you recommend that it is in my best interest in cultivating an alliance. I will defer to you on that, as you are more experienced with collaboration on business matters. In return, you must agree to curtail your patronizing tone. It offends, and you would be wise to defer to *my* expertise on this matter, as I have too often been at the receiving end of it."

There was a glint of warning in her voice. She looked so prim and proper in her cornflower blue spencer jacket, but her soft exterior hid a spine of steel. He dipped his head. "I will try. So this evidence?"

"When Jason . . . when he . . . ah . . ." She wavered, but then cleared her throat and forged ahead. "When Jason passed, his valet escorted his personal effects home. There was a trunk that contained his business ledgers, journals, and documents, as well as his correspondence. I believe that in this material, and with the letters I have, we will be able to glean more information about Jason's investigation. It should tell us which accounts are involved, and allow us to determine the name of the person or persons responsible for overseeing those accounts."

He nodded. "That is a good beginning. His family has this trunk and will be willing to relinquish it? Or at least allow you to peruse its contents?"

"I do not see why not. You see, upon his death, it was delivered to me, so it is rightfully mine." She lifted her chin and dared him to refute her ownership.

"I see." But he did not. If it was given to her, how had it come to be in the viscount's family's possession?

"My father had it turned over to the Bransons," she said, answering his unasked question. "He thought the sight of it upset me." She glanced out the window again. "I was . . . I was not home to stop him. After Jason's death, Julia took me to the Lake District for a few months. She thought a change of scenery would be a good idea. You see, Jason grew up in Bedfordshire, so there were . . . there were many memories—"

"I understand," he rescued her, hating to see her flounder. Steel was strong, but if enough heat or duress was applied to it, it could bend or break.

He was beginning to grasp how deep her grief had been. She had reforged herself, but there were still cracks. She hid them beneath her poised veneer, but if one looked closely, they were there.

More buried secrets.

Brett regretted he had not viewed them earlier. Her triumph over her grief added to her courage—and strength. She would need both to achieve her goal. But perhaps having already conquered her demons, she feared no more. Admiration for her suffused him, and something else. *Desire.*

He tamped it down. He could not go there. They had enough with which to deal without further complicating matters. "Fine. Then we shall find out if they are willing to let you recover the trunk."

"Yes, that is where I am heading now. I will let you know what—"

"No."

"No, what?" she said, bristling.

"I am going with you. That is another one of my stipulations if you want my assistance. I agree to help you *and* not breathe a word of your agenda to your family, even though when they learn what you are up to—which, if you succeed, they will—I am putting my life at risk. Your father has a handsome set of Manton dueling revolvers that he—"

"I understand," she said.

"I am willing to risk my life twofold, and all I ask in return is that you agree not to pursue any lines of inquiry, travel anywhere, or do anything in regard to this investigation without me. Those are my terms and they are nonnegotiable."

"Do not be absurd. Nothing is going to happen to me on a visit to the Bransons. How on earth am I to explain your accompanying me? You have never met them!"

He shrugged. "You comment on my talents. Well, one of yours is that you are adept at weaving tales. In one of the addendums to my business letters, you convinced a customs official I had a disfiguring pox, despite the man having seen me the prior week. I am sure you have spun some fabrication for your family that enables you to go on your merry way unchecked. You will think of something. I have complete faith in your ingenuity and imagination."

At her truculent expression, he hardened his tone. "Listen to me. As you dig deeper and others are alerted to what you are doing—as they will be when you start asking questions and prying into treacherous matters—then you will no longer be safe. Because if you are right, and someone is responsible for your viscount's death, your quest to have that individual strung up at Newgate will not please them.

"Your goal of justice is a worthy one, but your adversary is fighting for his life, and that goal trumps yours. People become desperate when their lives are threatened and will stop at nothing to thwart you—including murder, which you believe they have proven themselves capable of committing.

You would be wise to remember that." He gave her a searching look, as if he sought to assure himself that the full import of his words had registered.

Her lips had parted and her face had paled. After a moment, she nodded curtly. "Fine. I agree to your terms."

"Good. Then as I always say after completing a successful business alliance, I look forward to working with you. To justice."

"Justice for Jason." She paused before adding more softly, "Thank you. Thank you for assisting me when I know you . . . you would rather not."

"You left me little choice." Then he grinned. "As I said, obdurate."

"Determined." She lifted her chin.

Chapter Seven

❧≈❧

B RANSON Manor was built in the sixteenth century in the
Tudor style. It boasted a Tudor arch entrance complete
with the Weston heraldic crest above the door.

Brett paused to study the ferocious-looking dragon
carved into the gray stone frontage. "I never excelled at
Latin. If the motto reads 'beware of fire-eating dragons,'
perhaps we should retreat?"

"You are not amusing," Emily said and tossed him a
reproving look. Before he could respond, the door opened,
and they were ushered into the drawing room to await Jason's
brother, Tristan Branson, now Viscount Weston. When she
had first come to call after Jason's death, the pain of it had
nearly dropped her to her knees. With each subsequent visit,
the agony had lessened until it settled into a dull ache in her
heart.

She crossed to the large French windows and stared
unseeing outside, fighting back the siege of memories. Whispered words of love, stolen kisses, a forbidden passion and
much more. She curled her arms around her waist.

"Are you all right?"

She blinked at the burning in her eyes. It was time to stop looking behind her, and to look ahead. Having a goal and someone to assist her helped her to do so. She faced Brett, still marveling over his agreeing to work with her. "You need not worry about me. This is not my first visit. I am fine."

"That does not necessarily make it easier. Do you want me to speak—?"

"No. Certainly not. I appreciate your concern, but just because I agreed to your escort, it does not mean that I agreed to relinquish everything to you. That is not the assistance I am looking for. I am quite capable of—"

"Using the brain you have. Yes, I have seen you do so. Admirably." He grinned. "You know, I am not your enemy. I am on your side. I give you my word of honor."

She arched a brow. "I did not know we were at war."

He laughed. "Oh, we have been from our very first meeting. You had your weapons drawn, defenses fortified, complete with a moat surrounding you. Believe me, my dignity still carries the scars from having a beautiful woman rebuff my attentions over the past year when our paths crossed."

A beautiful woman. He was casual with his compliments. He should not be so in a business alliance. "Perhaps we did get off on the wrong foot. If I promise to lay down my weapons, can we call a truce? It might be wise if we are to be on the same side. Agreed?"

"Agreed." He smiled.

He stood so close that she caught the scent of his sandalwood soap. She tamped down the impulse to draw a deep breath. A throat being cleared broke the silence, and she whirled.

"Lady Emily, what a pleasure, as always. I was delighted to receive your note saying you were coming to visit."

The viscount was a tall, lean man, whom Jason had groused kept his head buried in academic tomes, hence the indoor pallor. The lenses of his wire-rimmed spectacles illuminated blue eyes that mirrored Jason's, and she had to brace herself to meet them. "Lord Weston, the pleasure is mine. I had been meaning to make a visit earlier, but time slipped away from me."

"Since you've become an aunt, I am sure that your time is not always your own. My sister has met the twins, and I hope to pay a visit soon. All is well with your family?"

She responded, making the obligatory inquiries after his mother and sister, and then turned to Brett. "Allow me to introduce Bedford's former business partner, Mr. Brett Curtis."

"Ah yes, of Curtis Shipping," Weston said, studying Brett. "Viscount Weston, at your service." He bowed. "News of your company fills the *Times*. I have been looking for a sound investment and Bedford highly recommends your firm. Perhaps we can find time to discuss the matter further."

Brett returned the bow. "Of course, but I am confident that Bedford's opinion as my former partner is thoroughly unbiased," Brett said straight-faced, causing Weston to laugh. "Lady Emily mentioned she was making this visit, and I hope you do not mind my intrusion. She has told me that we share a mutual interest, so I insisted on joining her." As Weston turned to her in question, Brett surreptitiously cocked a brow at Emily, encouraging her to respond.

"Yes, he was quite insistent. In fact, he gave me little choice in the matter." She stalled, scrambling for a reason until inspiration struck. "What the financials neglected to share about Mr. Curtis is that, like yourself, he is an avid ornithologist." She almost giggled when Brett's attention snapped to her, his expression appalled. "Just last year, he and Daniel visited Bedford's cousin, Lord Bryant, and viewed his extensive collection of skins."

"Is that so?" Weston beamed. "Bedford neglected to mention that."

"Well, Bedford has been tied up with estate matters and the birth of the twins, so he has probably forgotten about our shared interest," Brett said, recovering. "I shall have to take him to task for that. That is, when I have a chance to update him on all I have been up to recently. We have much to discuss." Brett gave her a deliberate look.

She simply smiled at him, undaunted. He would not dare give her away to Daniel. He had given her his word. To an Englishman, their word was everything. It was tied to their honor. Brett may be American and while upstart colonials did not stand by king and country, she had faith in Brett to stand by her.

"Oh, my apologies. Please sit," Weston said, motioning them forward. "Let me arrange for refreshments."

Brett waved a hand for her to precede him, and she swept over to the settee, taking a seat. The room was a mixture of yellows and greens, the wallpaper peppered with a variety of birds perched on or peeking out from vines that climbed the wall. Weston had done some redecorating; the bird prints were new.

Brett eyed the paper and prints, and with Tristan distracted in flagging down a footman, he grimaced. "Ornithology?" he hissed under his breath, and dropped into the chair adjacent to her. "He couldn't natter on about foxhunting? Or be an avid horseman? Like most *normal* Englishmen?"

"Unfortunately, no," she whispered back. "But you did insist on joining me."

"My mistake," he said. "I seem to be making a lot of them lately."

"Now then," Weston said, returning his attention to them. "I am delighted to show you my collection of skins but it is not as extensive as Bryant's. Some of his specimens are on display in the British Museum."

"Yes." Brett shifted on his seat. "They are, ah . . . impressive. Distinct."

A housemaid entered the room, bearing a platter of coffee and tea, which she set on the table before them. Emily slid forward to do the honors, both men accepting coffee.

"Distinct? Unusual phrasing. How so?" Weston said.

"Yes, how so?" Emily asked as she handed Brett his coffee, her lips twitching.

Brett paused, and then snatched his saucer so abruptly

that the china cup rattled, spilling some of the coffee. "How careless of me. I did not burn you, did I?"

"No, I am quite all right." She bit her lip to stifle her laughter.

Brett turned to Lord Weston. "Ah, what I meant is that they looked so real."

Weston laughed. "They do indeed. However, that is the purpose of skinning the birds rather than mounting them. It maintains their shape so much better. As an ornithologist you must recognize the difference."

"Yes, do you not agree, Mr. Curtis?" she politely inquired, unable to resist. For some perverse reason, she found his aggravation appealing.

Brett's eyes narrowed at her. "I do agree. However, perhaps we can discuss this further at another time. Lady Emily is not as eager an ornithologist, and so . . ."

"Oh, no, I find it fascinating. Is there a particular species that you are enamored of when you observe birds?"

Before Brett could respond, the maid returned with a tray of tea sandwiches. She posed a question to Weston and while he was distracted, Brett hissed at Emily, "Tread carefully, lest you find your lovely hide mounted with the rest of his fine-feathered friends."

She glanced at him with wide-eyed innocence. "We cannot very well dive straight into a discussion about Jason's trunk. Civilities have to be exchanged first. It is proper etiquette. Or as I am sure you have learned in your business dealings, diplomatic."

Incredulity crossed his features and Brett simply blinked at her, unable to respond as Weston's attention returned to them.

"Please help yourself." Weston pointed to the array of sandwiches. "And that is a good question Lady Emily presents."

"Lady Emily is very clever indeed." Brett's smile did not reach his eyes and he fell silent, as he appeared to ponder his response. "My cousin, now the Duke of Prescott, visited me in America one year. He introduced me to a friend of his, John James Audubon, who was traveling across the country, rendering detailed paintings of birds for an anthology he was compiling. He shared with me his picture of a peregrine falcon in full hunting dive. I've always been partial to falcons, having studied them in school and observed them hunting here in England. Audubon explained that the bird is believed to be the fastest on earth. An admirer of hunters who catch their prey, I find the falcon is a particular favorite of mine." He narrowed his eyes on Emily.

"Extraordinary. I would dearly love to see his paintings," Weston said.

Emily frowned. Brett thought she was the clever one, but it was he who was quick-witted. She had wanted to point out the absurdity of his insistence on accompanying her on this visit. Brett had missed her point, but she had received his. Like the peregrine falcon, she was now convinced that they would catch their prey.

"Hopefully he will publish his anthology so that you can," Brett said, turning back to Weston. "However, I do not mean to distract from the true purpose of Lady Emily's visit. As much as I appreciate her allowing me to join her, she has a more pressing matter to discuss."

"Oh, Lady Emily?" Weston's expression was curious.

"I admit that I did come with an agenda." She bristled that Brett had opened the subject that was hers to introduce. She would have to speak to him on that matter. "I have avoided this subject on my previous visits because I was not certain how to approach it. You see, it is about Jason's trunk." She read the surprise in Weston's eyes, and a stillness settled over his frame as if he, too, had to brace himself to hear his brother's name. "I know this is difficult for you, as it is for me. That is part of the reason my father turned his trunk over to you in the first place. He believed it would be hard for me to sort through Jason's personal effects. At the time, he was right. However, it has been over three years, and I was wondering . . . well, I was wondering if there was a reason Jason had the trunk delivered to me in the first place. If there was something in it that he wanted me to have."

Weston set his coffee down. "I understand. Admittedly, I

did wonder why it was originally given to you, rather than brought straight home. I thought it unusual, and so I did go through the contents, studying the items carefully to see if there was anything that I believed Jason would want you to have. Mementos, personal letters, or something of that ilk."

"And?" she asked, leaning forward.

He splayed his hands, looking rueful. "It was all ledgers, memos, and correspondence. There was little in the way of personal effects."

"Perhaps I might take a look at the items?" She struggled to not betray her eagerness. Mundane business papers might be of no interest to Tristan, but they were vital to her. "You never know, there could be something that I might view differently? That is if it is not too much of an imposition."

"Oh, no, not at all," Weston hastened to assure her.

"Thank you for understanding. I was not . . ." Her words trailed off as she noticed his furrowed brow.

"There is only one problem with your request. You see, the materials are no longer in my care," he said, chagrined. "When I realized it was all related to his work with the East India Company, I turned everything over to Lawrence Drummond. You remember Mr. Drummond. He worked—"

"With Jason. Of course, I remember. How could I forget?" Her smile was brittle. *Drummond.* The dratted man appeared to thwart her at every turn.

"Yes. He came to pay his respects a month or two after the funeral. You must understand that Jason's death was difficult for him. In Calcutta, the two of them were working closely together." Tristan fell silent, as if he needed to summon the energy to continue. "Drummond asked if there was anything he could do for us. If there was unfinished business that he could take care of for Jason. Jason was very meticulous about tying up loose ends, so Drummond worried that there might be some incomplete paperwork that he could finish on Jason's behalf. He offered to look over the material to ascertain if anything was outstanding, knowing we were unfamiliar with Jason's work or his accounts."

"I am sure he was more than eager to take Jason's papers off your hands," Brett drawled.

"Yes. He was. I explained to him about these business papers. I told him I would see that the material was delivered to him—once I had removed those few personal items."

"Did Drummond agree to wait?" Brett said. "Or did he offer to sift through the items with you? To save you the trouble of having to do it alone? That is, he must have understood and been sympathetic to your pain in undertaking such a task."

Emily frowned, wondering at Brett's intent. Drummond was many things, but a murderer he was not. The man was not single-minded enough. Jason used to quip that Lawrence, like Narcissus, often missed what was unfolding right outside the window, his own reflection distracting him so.

"You are quite right. He did offer to assist me, but I felt that for Jason's sake, I had to do the job myself." Weston turned to Emily, his smile wistful. "He must have been confident that you would have done so as well. That is, once you were ready to tackle the project, so I could not let him down."

"No, of course not," Emily said, smiling reassuringly. After all, it was not entirely his fault that he had let the evidence slip from her hands.

"Then you sent all Jason's papers on to Drummond?" Brett pressed further.

"Yes. But I am sure if you wrote to him about this matter, he would be amenable to your request. That is, if he has not already dispensed with the contents."

"In his efficiency to be of service to your brother, I am sure he has long since taken care of this outdated business," Brett said, his eyes dark.

Weston furrowed his brow. "You may be right, but there is no harm in asking. I could speak to him on your behalf."

"That is kind of you, but not necessary," Emily said quickly. "I agree with Mr. Curtis that Mr. Drummond has long taken care of the items by now, so please do not trouble him further with this matter." The last thing she needed was

Drummond alerted to the fact she was still worrying her pretty little head over Jason's business.

"I am sorry I could not be of further help, but your trip is not in vain. Unfortunately, Patricia is residing with friends at present. She will be sorry to have missed your visit, but my mother is home. Would you mind seeing her before you leave? That would mean much to her."

Emily smiled. "Of course, I would enjoy that."

"Let me send for her." He stood. "While you do so, Mr. Curtis and I can step into my study. I would like to get his opinion on MacLeay and Vigors's recently introduced Quinarian system of classification." Weston bowed. "I will collect their paper on the system in case you are not familiar with it. If you will excuse me, I shall return shortly."

When he had disappeared, Brett turned on her. "I ought to wring your delicate neck! *The Quinarian system of classification*? What the devil is he talking about?"

A sputter of laughter escaped her. "I have no idea. But your opinion on it should be edifying," she said, struggling to keep a straight face. "Oh for goodness' sake, just look wise, nod your head, and murmur in a scholarly tone, *very interesting, most complicated,* or *not really up to date on all its details.* You will be fine."

"*Very interesting? Most complicated?*" At her laugh, he scowled. "I will be edifying indeed."

"I did say that you did not need to make this visit with—"

"Yes, yes," he cut her off, and then arched a brow. "It appears Drummond has confiscated your evidence. Very interesting. Most complicated," he teased, smiling at her frown. "Did he mention this when you met with him, or was he too busy trying to kiss—?"

"No! He did not mention it. But he worked with Jason and they *were* friends. It is not surprising or out of the ordinary for him to make this offer. In fact, the company probably directed him to do so."

Brett emitted a noncommittal grunt. "We should determine if the sympathetic Mr. Drummond was acting on his own recourse or if it was at the request of the East India Company.

But for now, do you have another plan?" He arched a brow. "Any other source of incriminating evidence?"

She lifted her chin. "We will go to London and meet with Jason's clerk as planned. Determine what he knows. And then we will proceed from there."

Brett nodded. "Fine. But *together*. I concede that you may not have needed me here, but in London things are different. We work together. And please, no more birds."

"No more birds," she agreed with a smile.

Chapter Eight

⟊⟋

"ACKERMANN's Repository of Arts? This is a print shop?" Melody said.

Brett almost laughed at his sister's woebegone expression, which she gamely tried to hide. He, Emily, and his sisters were strolling the length of the Strand, one of London's busy shopping districts. The spell of April rain that settled in at the beginning of the week had finally abated and the clear skies beckoned, so they'd had Taunton's coach let them out to continue on foot.

He and his sisters had joined Emily and her father at Keaton House over a week ago. True to her word, Emily had shifted through the stack of invitations she had received, selecting those she thought his sisters would most enjoy. She had drawn up a calendar, alerted Brett to those events at which his attendance was expected, and set about contacting Jason's former clerk to arrange a meeting. Lady Emily Chandler was nothing if not efficient. However, the present excursion was added to their itinerary per his request.

Emily was not the only one with a mission.

"Do not worry, Melody," he said. "Ackermann's also publishes illustrated books and sells master paintings, art supplies, and sundry other decorative items. I am confident you will find something on which to toss away your allowance—that is if you have any left after your shopping excursions." He grumbled the last as he weaved through a group of pedestrians on the busy thoroughfare. "I can point out some clever political and social caricatures that might amuse you."

"You are too kind," Melody said sarcastically.

Emily laughed. "Pay him no mind, because what he neglected to add is that Ackermann is best known for a monthly periodical he publishes. Its arrival is eagerly anticipated because it covers the current trends on everything from art, literature, commerce, and politics to fashion."

"Yes, he did choose to omit that part," Miranda said, casting a reproving look his way.

"So I did," Brett said, unrepentant as he winked at her. It was his job to tease his sisters, and over the years, he had become rather adept at it.

"We can examine the newest styles and determine what best suits your taste. Some periodicals provide patterns and fabric samples." Emily cocked her head to the side and peered at Brett. "In fact, the shop has become a popular gathering place for Londoners. I am surprised your brother knew of it, let alone recommended it."

"What? Do you not think I like to mingle among the sophisticated set?"

"No." All three women answered simultaneously.

They knew him too well. "You may be right, which explains why I am already regretting my decision to escort you here." He had forgotten about the fashion section in the magazine. His purse would be paying the price for that. He frowned as Melody caught Miranda's hand and pulled her ahead to point out an item in a shop window. "They're going to be broke by week's end," he muttered.

Emily laughed. "London does come at a price. So do you have business at Ackermann's? Melody was telling me that your cousin Prescott was an accomplished painter. Did he purchase his supplies here? Ackermann manufactures much of the art materials that he sells."

He needed to remember Emily had a good memory and a clever mind. "I thought it would be a good place to start."

"Have you had a chance to speak to any of his friends, while I have been keeping your sisters busy spending their allowance?"

He smiled. "You have upheld your part of the bargain, occupying my sisters too well. Unfortunately, I had some business matters to attend to and have not had a chance to make any social calls. But I will." He took her arm, guiding her around a puddle as they continued down the street.

"Melody said you hired a new business manager. Is he not able to handle most matters?"

Melody again. His sister was a veritable leaking font of information. If he did not plug up this breach, Emily would become as well versed as he on the affairs of the Curtis family. And there were subjects he preferred to remain private. Emily was not the only one with secrets. "Yes, he is efficient, but I still need to be consulted. It is my company, therefore my responsibility. However, I did hold a meeting on another matter that might be of interest to you."

She glanced at him. "Oh?"

"I spoke with that contact I mentioned to you, a friend who works at the East India Company."

She stopped short and cast a glance at his sisters before she spoke. "You asked me not to do anything in regard to this matter without you at my side. Well, in return, I ask that you—"

"The man is discreet," he said quickly. "And loyal to me because if not for my assistance, he would be in debtor's gaol. As you say, London can exact a price, and that price is high indeed if one gets sucked into its gaming clubs. I promise you, he has climbed out of trouble, has no wish to sink back into it. He will find out what we need to know without creating a ripple."

She stared at him and finally nodded. "Fine. What did you ask of him?"

"To find out what he could about what Jason's work entailed and what he knew about Drummond."

She frowned. "You are making a mistake about Drummond. I know the man, have for years. He is vain, arrogant, and does not like his attentions to be rebuffed, but those character flaws do not make him a murderer. He does not have the mettle for it."

"You may be right. But I find it curious that he is an obstacle we keep tripping over. As you say, he *is* a dandy. In my experience, most fops are not known for altruistic deeds that do not benefit their person or feed their vanity. Drummond's offer of assistance was a quiet act of virtue. If the company did not direct him to collect Jason's papers, it makes me wonder if Drummond had an ulterior motive in doing so of his own volition."

She pursed her lips and appeared to mull over his words. "Fine. You can follow that lead."

"Thank you," he said, amused at her officious manner. As if he needed permission to protect her.

"I have arranged to meet with Jason's clerk at the end of the week," she said.

"Let us hope it progresses more smoothly than my meeting with Weston."

"It should." Her lips curved "After all, he is not an ornithologist."

"Good. I am quite birded out." He lifted his arm for her.

"I understand." She smiled, and after a slight hesitation, she curled her hand around his elbow. They ventured forward to catch up with his sisters, who had wandered ahead. "I believe he is a medicinal herbalist."

He stumbled to a stop, appalled. "Surely you jest?"

"I do," she said with a laugh. "I could not resist." Her cheeks colored to match the bell-shaped skirts of her rose-colored walking dress.

Good lord, she was lovely. He drank in her bright features and swallowed.

"Here we are. The Repository of Arts."

Miranda called back to them, shattering the spell holding

him transfixed. Pedestrians tossed them curious glances, forced to weave around them. He found his voice. "Shall we continue?"

Her laughter had faded, and she dropped her eyes from his. "We shall."

They caught up to his sisters, who waited for them before the front doors. The sight of another stone heraldic carving above the entrance restored Brett's humor. A crowned lion and a unicorn stood on their hind feet, their front legs propping up the crest. The beasts were perched atop Ackermann's name in large block letters etched deep into the stone. "Latin again. I think it says, 'Ye who enter, be prepared to pay a high price.' Perhaps we should leave."

Laughing, Melody shook her head, and shoved him forward.

They entered the elegant shop, where patrons milled around the floor, studying the paintings and prints gracing the walls, while others flipped through the large racks of prints. Stacks of paper and other decorative items littered shelves. There was a long table with stools before it, where customers could sit to study his illustrated books.

"Come, let us grab those empty stools and devour his most recent fashion plates," Emily said.

"Will you be all right?" Miranda said, turning to Brett.

He smiled at her worried expression. "I will be bereft without your company, but have no fear. I shall heroically persevere in an effort to entertain myself." He bowed low. "All I ask in return is that you enjoy yourselves, and of course, that you do so without spending a farthing."

Emitting an inelegant snort, Melody stomped off, while Miranda rolled her eyes before turning to follow.

Emily and his sisters settled themselves, their heads soon bent over fashion plates. Brett scanned the premises. A friend of his had directed him to the shop after Brett had mentioned having some paintings he was interested in selling. Brett later met with one of Ackermann's clerks and arranged for the shop to be the sole distributor of A. W.

Grant's works, with Brett acting as the liaison between the shop and the reclusive artist.

Now more than ever it was imperative that his cousin's identity be kept secret. It was one matter for the dispensable fourth son of a duke to dabble in trade, but it was an altogether different matter for Drew to continue to do so as the Duke of Prescott. The English aristocracy had strict guidelines about crossing class boundaries, and they took umbrage at those who defied them. Drew's lucrative artistic career not only ignored their rules but also shattered them all. More so, in selling the mythological nudes, he ventured well into scandalous territory.

Ackermann's clerk, Mr. Greenfield, being tall and lean as a flagpole, was easy to spot, towering a foot over most people. He usually could be found peering down at the patrons through a pair of gold-rimmed pince-nez spectacles perched on the end of his imperious nose. Always impeccably dressed in austere black, with a gold watch fob tucked into his pocket, he was a difficult man to miss.

Brett located Mr. Greenfield at the back of the shop, his hands folded behind his back, head bent toward a man who gesticulated toward something in a glass case. Brett walked toward the pair, stopping to idly study a series of decorative hand-colored prints depicting fashionably dressed young women. A few minutes later, a voice interrupted him.

"These prints are showcased in the latest edition of our periodical. This ball dress of tulle over pink gros de Naples is lovely. Notice the detail in the satin leaf ornaments and the décolletage is trimmed in pearls. Exquisite work."

"I am not a student of fashion, but I recognize high-quality goods when I see them. It is my job to do so. My sisters have accompanied me here. Please steer them clear of ball gowns lined in pearls or any other priceless gems."

Mr. Greenfield bowed. "Of course. I shall see if we carry any prints of gingham. Is that not popular in America?"

Brett studied Mr. Greenfield's straight-faced look and grinned. "Perhaps we can meet in the middle? If you keep me out of debt, I will be in yours."

"Fair enough, sir. So how can I be of further assistance to you? Dare I hope you carry news of the enigmatic A. W. Grant? We sold the last three paintings you delivered, but that was nigh over four months ago, and a few patrons have inquired about the artist. How do you wish me to respond?"

"Unfortunately, I am not certain of the artist's plans, because he has recently gone into seclusion."

"Ah, yes. An artist's temperament can be capricious." Greenfield nodded. "Understandably, it can make them difficult to work with."

Brett suppressed a snort at the understatement. "At present, I am finding that is the case. You mentioned some patrons had inquired about his work. Was there someone in particular who showed interest? My friend was mulling over the idea of doing some commissioned work," he lied glibly.

"I did have an unusual encounter a few weeks ago. A gentleman came into the shop who appeared to be visibly upset. He demanded to see our collection of A. W. Grant's paintings. I informed him that we had sold out of all our pieces, but hoped to get more in shortly."

"Did he wish to purchase some?"

"He did not say. He inquired if we were the only distributor of Grant's work. When I explained we were, he pointed out that if that were the case, how had a friend of his acquired one of Grant's pieces in an antiquities and consignment shop in Kent. He insisted the shop vowed this particular work was an original, not a resale." Mr. Greenfield spread his hands helplessly. "He was not pleased when I could not explain the matter and had no knowledge of the shop or the transaction. However, it does beg the question: Are we still, as contractually agreed upon, the exclusive purveyor of A. W. Grant's works?" His amiable expression had disappeared, his coal black eyes piercing.

Brett stiffened, bristling at the implication. "I have not authorized anyone else to sell A. W. Grant's works, nor have I delivered any other paintings to be sold since the last four I placed in your hands. You are Grant's sole distributor. I give you my word."

"Very good, sir." Greenfield dipped his head, appearing to be pacified.

"This gentleman was certain the piece his friend purchased was one of A. W. Grant's?" Brett said.

Greenfield shrugged. "I asked the same. He said the painting had Grant's signature on it." Greenfield paused, but after a moment, he lowered his voice. "It is not our policy to divulge information about our patrons or their interests in a particular item, but in light of your friend's choice to remain anonymous and his inventory is slim, I will make an exception in this case." Greenfield glanced around the shop as if to ensure they were not being overheard.

Brett frowned, wondering at the man's manner.

"You might wish to inform the artist that interest in his work has reached another level. This gentleman who visited us is from one of the most prominent families in England. In fact, he himself has come into a dukedom."

Brett froze.

Reverence dripped from Greenfield's voice as he continued. "His father and his heir recently died in a tragic accident, so this gentleman has suddenly found himself holding the title." He lowered his voice further. "It is the talk of the ton as he was originally fourth in line."

"Prescott!" Brett muttered.

Greenfield blinked. "Yes, well, as I said, I do not like to mention names, but I see that we understand one another. Needless to say, when an exalted member of the peerage deigns to sponsor an artist, a fashion, or a sport, it does tend to set a trend." He shrugged. "Look at the impact Beau Brummell made on fashion. You would be wise to tell your artist friend that it is in his best interest to increase his output."

"I will do so. Without naming names, this esteemed customer visited the shop how recently? A few weeks ago? Sometime last month?"

"I believe it was a few weeks ago, early March."

"Did he happen to mention the name of his friend who had purchased one of A. W. Grant's paintings in Kent?"

Greenfield tapped his fingers to his lips, considering the

question for a moment, and then nodded. "I suppose I can divulge that as the individual was not a patron of ours. He said Lord Haversley had bought the painting. I believe he said it was an oil of a four-rigger lost at sea."

"Thank you. This has been most interesting." Brett dipped his head.

"Please do remember to pass this information on to the artist. And do let Mr. Grant know we are most honored to carry his paintings, and hope to continue the relationship. I will leave you to your sisters. Should they or you have any further questions, I am, as always, at your service." Greenfield bowed, and then left Brett with his churning thoughts.

How the devil had one of Drew's paintings ended up in a shop in Kent? Of course, Drew would be concerned over the question as there was the small matter of payment for the purchase. The shop in Kent would have no way of giving A. W. Grant his portion of the sale because they did not have his address—or his identity. Drew did not need the money, but he would not appreciate being fleeced. Nor did Brett. He frowned, disturbed at this turn of events.

"I saw you talking to Mr. Greenfield. Was he helpful?"

He turned, finding Emily had stolen upon him. "He was a wealth of information. In fact, do you think that at any of your scheduled events, we might, perchance, encounter a Lord Haversley?"

Emily thought for a moment, and then nodded. "He is engaged to Lord Dayton's daughter, so he should make an appearance at the earl's ball, which we are attending tomorrow night." She lowered her voice. "Is he a friend of your cousin?"

He wondered why everyone had this sudden compulsion to lower their voice. Feeling perverse, he leaned toward her and dropped his own. "I am not sure, but I would like to speak with him and determine that."

Emily scowled. "Is this another one of your stipulations? You demand to know all my plans, but I cannot inquire anything of yours?" She made to turn away, but he caught her arm.

"My apologies. I was teasing. My cousin visited here recently. He was interested in a painting that Haversley has recently purchased, and I want to hear more about it. And learn if Haversley has any information about my cousin's whereabouts."

"A painting." She looked intrigued. "Any particular artist?"

"He's an American. A. W. Grant."

Her eyes widened. "I know the artist. Daniel owns one of his paintings. It hangs in his billiard room."

"Not anymore." Brett grinned. "I won it off of him in a fair wager."

"But Daniel said he had won it off of you in a game of cards," she said.

He shrugged. "Cards are not my forte. Billiards are."

"I shall remember that," she said, amused. "So you, Daniel, and Lord Haversley all are collecting this A. W. Grant's works. They must be very valuable."

"You have no idea. Pity the artist is a temperamental pain in the . . . ah . . . neck. Or so I have heard. Now then, have my sisters narrowed down their selection of gown styles to a mere hundred?"

"Miranda has. She has wonderful taste." Emily smiled. "As for Melody, we may be here awhile yet. Returning to another matter, when your friend from the East India Company sends word that he has the information that you requested, I would like to meet with him as well. You stipulated that I do not pursue matters without you. Well, that is . . . that is my stipulation as well. That you do not pursue anything without me."

"I do not—"

"If you do not agree, I must advise you that your sisters have a fitting with Madame Duchard, the French modiste, next week. I might find myself too busy to escort them, so you would have to schedule the time to do so."

He had to admire her audacity in getting her way. She was very skilled at it. "I was going to say that I do not have a problem with that. Now threatened with a trip to the dressmaker's, I surrender to your terms. As I said, I am on your side. For now—or until things become dangerous and your lovely neck is threatened with—"

"I understand. And I can agree to that."

When she smiled at him, something tightened in his chest. He resisted the urge to run a finger around the soft curve of her cheek and across those beguiling lips. He tamped down the wayward yearning and cleared his throat. "Shall we collect Melody? I think she should be ready—or not."

"One can hope." Emily grinned.

It was wise that his sisters had accompanied him on this trip to London.

While he was protecting Emily, they could keep him safe—from her.

Chapter Nine

～≫≪～

EMILY sidestepped a pile of manure that polluted the unswept street lining the Thames. She lifted her handkerchief to her nose as the stench of raw sewage and other debris that littered the river wafted up to them. The cacophony of sounds provided another assault to her senses.

Costermongers peddled their wares, horses' hooves clacked on the pavement, and carriage wheels rumbled over rutted roads. Harried men bent on their destination weaved through it all, while boys, ragamuffins in tattered clothes, bellowed to one another. A nearby group of them kicked a ball.

Her arm was looped through Brett's, and the warm, solid strength of it was reassuring. They were heading toward the dock area where the offices of Curtis Shipping were located. It was a far cry from the posh environs of Mayfair and the Strand and as alien to her as a gentlemen's club, because one never ventured south of the Tower of London. But Emily refused to be left behind while Brett met his contact from the East India Company. For this clandestine venture, she decided against taking a chaperone. Instead, she wore a cloak with a concealing hood. In light of the unique location, she was confident that the chances of someone in her social milieu seeing her alone with Brett were slim to none.

"We can turn back if you would like," Brett offered. He dipped his head, studying her face as if he could see her nerves jumping like skittish rabbits. "I asked him to meet us at our other offices on Craven Street. That is where we meet with our investors and clients, but he refused to venture out of the Wapping district, not wanting to leave the environs of the docks—"

"It is all right. I insisted on coming," she said. She refused to retreat because beneath her nerves, something else stirred. Excitement. This was a far cry from her usual environs, and its contrasts fascinated her. The area was gritty, alive, and pulsated with vibrant energy. It was a glimpse into the churning wheels of industry that powered working London and which was forbidden to women of her class.

"There is not much to them—" He broke off as a leather ball came hurtling toward them.

With an agility that startled her, Brett lifted his foot and deflected it with his Hessian boot. It landed harmlessly on the ground, and he sent it sailing with a hard kick.

"Baines, how many time have I told you to keep your lot away from the banks of the river? I am not replacing another one of these."

"Righto, Guv. Right sorry, I am. We was on Broad Street, but we might 'ave lost our ways." The lanky youth with a shock of unruly black hair spilling out of his cap had the gall to wink.

"I am sure you did," Brett said dubiously. "See that you find your bearings and move along."

The boy tipped his hat, and with a piercing whistle that rent the air, he gathered his cronies and headed off with a jaunty wave.

"A saucy one, he is," Brett muttered. "But he is an enterprising lad. And, of course, a former thief. Turn here, the offices are up ahead on the left."

"Thief I can believe," Emily said. "Enterprising?"

"Oh, that he is. At low tide, he and his grime-faced friends scour the mud looking for items to sell such as coal, rope, copper, and nails." He shrugged. "Dubbed mudlarks. More often than not, they pilfer from the river traffic," he groused.

Fascinated, Emily furrowed her brow. "How do you know his surname?"

"Caught him in the act of nicking my wallet." His grin slipped from his lips and his eyes darkened. "He was not working in the mud because he had sliced his foot on glass. After I got a surgeon to stitch him up, I offered him a safer job sweeping the offices. Injuries such as his are the hazards of their occupation, but poverty drives them back to the mud because it is the only living his lot can scrounge up. Perhaps when enough of them die, your aristocracy will be moved to find other means of employment for those born beneath their class, or more so, their attentions."

She noticed his clenched jaw and held her silence, having no argument against his accusation. Her peers preferred to insulate themselves from poverty and its harsh ramifications plaguing those who suffer from it.

"Here we are," Brett said, stopping before a nondescript, two-story, red brick building. He opened the front door and gave a shallow bow. "Welcome to Curtis Shipping or rather, one of our more humble and cluttered offices."

Emily stepped eagerly inside, pushing off her hood as she did so. The room was a long rectangular space with desks filling the floor and entrances to offices lining the back wall. Clerks occupied the desks, while groups of men studied nautical maps tacked to the wall. Charts covered one wall and prints of square-rigged vessels hung on adjacent ones. A few bookcases and racks stood in the back beside cabinets, a few with drawers jutting open and bursting with files.

The energy was palpable. Men moved between offices, a few firing directives to the clerks, while others dug through files, and conversation flowed with a fierce animation. She had entered another world, and it riveted her.

As the men became aware of their arrival, like a ripple rushing across a lake, silence spread over the room.

"Gentlemen, we have a visitor," Brett announced, stating the obvious. "This is Bedford's sister-in-law, Lady Emily Chandler. Forgive our intrusion and continue on with your work. However, with so lovely a distraction, I'll settle for your maintaining the appearance of looking productive because with luck, you might succeed in being so."

His words elicited laughs and grins, until a gentleman cleared his throat and bowed deeply. There ensued a mass movement of dips and bows as all men followed suit.

"Perhaps it is a good thing that your aristocracy disparages work in trade," Brett said beneath his breath. "Your set would be so preoccupied with paying the proper obeisance to each other's rank, that they would never get a thing accomplished."

She refused to snicker, but her lips twitched. "Today the fault is yours. Work stopped when you introduced a woman into a man's domain. Quite scandalous," she said, her words for Brett alone as she nodded to the men. It was a shame that women were banned from business environs, because this was far more entertaining than any ladies' gardening club, community service, or the mundane domestic activities to which her sex was relegated.

"My company, my responsibility, my rules. However, I was given no choice in the matter, as you did insist on joining this meeting. Obdurate."

"Determined. This man is discussing Jason's work. My fiancé, my responsibility, my rules—despite your stipulations."

He glanced at her, his expression amused. "Fair enough. But do not smile at anyone. They will never recover."

Before she could respond to the offhand compliment, a man separated himself from the group. Young and sandy-haired, his hazel eyes brimmed with laughter. "Lady Emily, it is a pleasure." He dipped his head. "Curtis, your arrival is fortuitous. I was looking for an excuse for them to do nothing and be compensated for the lost time. I could not have found a lovelier one."

Brett clasped the man's shoulder. "Well, then, consider this an opportunity to prove your stellar management capabilities by keeping the men on task."

The young man appeared to ponder Brett's words a moment before he responded. "Fire me now because failure is the inevitable conclusion in all futile undertakings."

Laughing, Brett turned to her and introduced Owen Jenkins, his office manager. "I cannot do without the man, so I lured him away from our Boston offices and put him in charge here."

Their teasing banter surprised her. They appeared more friends than owner and manager. English kept a respectful formality between employer and employee. However, she identified Mr. Jenkins's accent as American, so perhaps business relationships in America were more casual—or they were so under Brett's employ.

After greetings were exchanged, Mr. Jenkins lowered his voice. "Your friend sent word that he is running late, but should arrive shortly. I advised Baines and his boys to keep an eye out for him."

"So that is what they were doing along the banks," Brett said.

Mr. Jenkins then begged Emily's pardon and requested a few minutes to discuss matters needing Brett's attention.

The manager's questions ran the gamut from shipping schedules to the inventory on one of their packet ships. His head bowed, expression serious, Brett listened, occasionally interjecting a comment or giving a response to one of Mr. Jenkins's queries.

She followed them over to a wall chart that listed the names of various packet ships, their tonnage capacity, and departure timetables.

Noting her interest, Mr. Jenkins nodded to the chart. "This here changed the course of passenger travel."

"Due to its accounting of tonnage capacity?" She frowned, bemused.

Brett laughed and shook his head. "After the war with America ended in 1813, the increase in shipping lines crossing the Atlantic caused ship owners to experiment with regular timetables to deal with the increase in traffic. Before the war, passengers traveling on packet lines had to wait until the cargo holds were filled before departing. This meant passengers often had to wait weeks to travel. That is no longer the case with the implementation of these schedules. With the advent of steam, travel will become even more efficient, no longer being at the whim of the wind."

"However, that is still years away," Mr. Jenkins said.

"But it is coming," Brett said with conviction. He pointed to a print of a vessel hanging nearby. "This is the *Savannah*, the first steamship to cross the Atlantic. She left Savannah, Georgia, on May 26, 1819 and arrived at Liverpool twenty-five days later."

There was wonder in Brett's voice, excitement lighting his eyes as he admired the full-rigged ship. Following his gaze, she frowned. "But it has sails."

Brett pointed to the hull of the ship. "It also has a ninety-horsepower steam engine which powered the trip for eighteen days, while the sails were used for the remaining seven. The paddle wheels could be folded up when they were not in use—"

A cough interrupted them and Brett turned to Mr. Jenkins, whose expression was amused. "I am not sure Lady Emily appreciates your love affair with speed. Curtis Shipping's interests may rest upon it, but alas, no one else's does."

To Emily's wonderment, a light flush stole across Brett's cheeks. At his boyish chagrin, something moved in her chest. Like a window she had shut had been blown open. It was little wonder that after Jason's death, she had never responded to any other man until Brett Curtis stumbled into her life. He was like no one other.

He rescued mudlarks from working in the Thames, waxed effusive about his work, and had a casual, almost jocular relationship with his employees.

He was different. Irreverent, intelligent, driven, and . . . passionate.

If he expended this much passion toward steam engines, she could only imagine what he would be like if he applied equal zeal in his attentions to a woman's body. The steam they could unleash would power the *Savannah* across the ocean and back.

Good lord. Where had that come from?

A shiver swept through her body.

Brett dipped his head, and a sheepish grin curved his lips. "My apologies. Thank you, Jenkins. I tend to forget my audience. Admittedly, I cannot fathom why no one else is equally enamored with steam-powered vessels."

"It does boggle the mind," Mr. Jenkins said, a teasing glint in his eyes.

Emily found herself rising to Brett's defense. "It is fascinating, and if it is the wave of the future, then Curtis Shipping will be at the forefront of it. I assume you have plans to invest in steam-powered vessels?" She sincerely hoped he pursued . . . steam. As both men stared at her, she flushed and clasped her hands before her. "Because as you say, it is lucrative to do so, speed being vital to making timely shipments."

Brett tossed back his head and laughed. "Careful, Jenkins, if she grasps the import of this innovation so quickly, your job could be in jeopardy."

Mr. Jenkins smiled. "I stand forewarned. Perhaps I should prove my mettle by prodding our audience back to work. Lady Emily, it has been a pleasure." He bowed and quietly departed.

At his words, Emily looked around, catching the men's gazes shift and heads quickly dip. Grinning, she turned back to find Brett speaking with another man.

When the man left, Brett addressed Emily. "While I was rhapsodizing over steam engines, I have been advised that my friend came in through our back entrance. He is waiting in my office. Shall we?"

She followed Brett through one of the closed doors. The

room was not large or ostentatious, which surprised her as she had imagined the owner's workspace to reflect the prosperity of the company. His was more serviceable, with a sturdy oak desk and a pair of chairs before it. Similar to the outer room, charts, bookcases, and more pictures of ships vied for space on the walls.

Her gaze fell to the man rising from one of the chairs. He doffed his cap, crushing it in his hand. A foot shorter than Brett, he was a lean wiry man. His dark eagle eyes and sharp features held a cunning look as he shook Brett's hand.

"Caleb Little is the fourth son of Baron Little, and is a junior clerk, known as a writer in the East India Company. As such, he is familiar with the company and its operations." Brett made the introductions. "Lady Emily Chandler."

Little's features narrowed on her, but he dipped his head in greeting.

"Mr. Little, thank you for agreeing to meet with us," she said. Brett took her cloak from her and hung it on a hook behind the door. He then gestured her to a seat and circled his desk, both men waiting until she was seated before taking their own seats.

A rush of excitement spiraled through her. She neatened the skirts of her carriage dress and clutched her gloved hands in her lap. After so long a wait, she desperately hoped that Little had something that would bring her closer to her goal.

"Have you any information?" Brett asked, diving right into the point of their meeting.

Little glanced at Emily and shifted uneasily in his seat, his brow furrowed.

"It is all right, Little. You can speak freely," Brett added.

At Brett's prodding, Mr. Little gave a shrug and spoke in a gravelly voice. "Well, it took a while to find someone familiar with the viscount's work. Files under Weston's name and his colleague, a Mr. Drummond, have been purged. I did some snooping and could find nary a one, not even when I doled out a few bribes to look into classified material. Despite all Parliament's regulating acts to clean us up, enough quid lining the right pockets still gets the job done." He tipped his chin to Brett. "I will give you an accounting of monies spent, and you can deduct it from my debt. All in a good cause, of course," he added soberly.

"Of course," Brett said dryly.

Emily wondered if Drummond had a hand in the lost paperwork. After all, he had dispensed with the documents in Jason's trunk.

"But you met with a man familiar with the viscount's work?" Brett pressed.

Little nodded. "I did. The viscount was overseeing the sale of opium to the Agency Houses in Calcutta and arranging for the shipments to Canton."

"Opium?" she said. Stunned, her lips parted. Jason had not mentioned opium in his letters, and the idea of him being involved in this sordid business disturbed her.

Little gave her a curious look. "Opium is our most lucrative trade now. Parliament renewed our charter, but they dealt us a bad hand when they took away our monopoly of the Indian trade routes. Those venues are now opened up to competitors like Mr. Curtis here." He nodded toward Brett. "We then had to change our game and deal with the cards we had left—the monopoly over the tea trade with China. But it is a winning hand, because there is a fortune to be had in trading opium to the Chinese in return for the tea," he boasted.

Brett shook his head. "China has banned the purchase of the drug, yet you still profit in selling it to them. Your company never ceases to astound me with its innovative means to circumnavigate the law."

"Please, we do not use *our* company ships," Little protested, his eyes wide, his expression one of cunning guile. "No, sir. We do not want to be caught selling a contraband drug. That would jeopardize our trading rights in Canton, which in turn would jeopardize our tea purchases."

"Far be it from you to be caught doing something illegal," Brett said, shaking his head.

"Exactly. So that's where your viscount and his man Drummond come in. The opium is produced in Bengal, sold to the Indian Agency Houses in Calcutta so the East India Company is not buying or selling the product directly, and from there merchant vessels sell—"

"You mean smuggle," Brett corrected, arching a brow.

Little shrugged. "I suppose, if you want to get particular about it. They unload the cargo in Canton where it is sold in return for tea, which is England's addiction, so it be a fair trade and everyone be content." He splayed his hands.

"Particularly those in your company who are once again lining their pockets," Brett said. "You do leave a destructive wake in your path, first plundering India's wealth, and now flooding China with opium addicts."

Little smiled. "Now, then, being in trade yourself, you must understand there are winners and losers in every risky venture. It's a roll of the die."

Brett narrowed his eyes. "You play a dangerous game that I doubt will end well."

Emily edged forward on her seat. "Of course, it is dangerous. Viscount Weston was involved in illegal smuggling activities and is dead. Do you think the Chinese authorities sent agents over—?"

"He was not directly involved in the smuggling per se. The merchants that off-loaded the opium in the factories in Canton handled that aspect." At Brett's arched brow, Little shrugged. "Might be splitting hairs and all that."

"What happened to the viscount?" Emily asked. "They said he got ill, and it was very sudden. And then . . . then he was gone."

Little again turned to Brett for guidance.

"I suggest you answer her," Brett said. "That is, if you want me to forgive your debt. I should get what I purchased. My clients do."

Little frowned. "I do not know the details. The information I have comes from a friend and cost a fair bob to get. The viscount's death was hushed up because it would be difficult for his family. But a select few in the company heard that he got ill. Ill from the opium, that is. Rumor has it that the drug killed him."

Shocked, Emily froze while her mind screamed in denial, and a wave of dizziness gripped her. Darkness hovered at the edges of her thoughts, threatening to engulf her.

No! Not Jason. Never.

Every fiber in her body protested it, and her conviction gave her the strength she needed to push forward. She violently shook her head. "No! That is a lie. It is not true. I *know* Jason. I *knew* him. That is not something of which he would partake."

"Lady Emily—"

"No!" she cried. "You did not know him. It is a horrid, vicious lie, and the company has some nefarious reason for spreading it, but it is not true." She glared at Little as if she could force the man to take back his words.

Brett stood and circled his desk. "Thank you, Caleb. I appreciate your assistance." Brett escorted the man to the door, and turning back, he came to kneel before her. "I am sorry, Emily." He caught her hands, enfolding them in his.

She lifted her eyes, blinking furiously through her tears. She clung to his hands. "You do not understand. A year before Jason sailed, he was thrown from a horse and broke his arm. He refused to take laudanum when the doctor came to reset it. Not one drop. He barely imbibed alcohol. He liked numbers, coherency, said liquor addled his brain. That is why he agreed to pursue this investigation, to apply his accounting skills. The government was looking for men with public educations to better the company's reputation." She was babbling, but could not stop. "He—"

"Shh, Emily." Brett's tone was gentle, soothing.

In the back recesses of her mind, she noted that he had dropped her title.

"This is *one* account from one man," he continued.

"Well, it is the wrong one!"

"Then we will get the right one," he said simply. "We will find out the truth. I promise you." His eyes bored into hers, reassuring and warm.

She held his gaze, and when he squeezed her hands, she believed him. She drew a deep, shuddering breath.

"I am on your side. And for what it is worth, *I* believe you," he said as he tucked a stray strand of hair behind her ear. "We will get your answers."

She caught her breath at the intimate gesture, dropping her gaze from his as her heart pounded.

She did want answers. Now more than ever she needed the truth to combat this slanderous lie blackening Jason's memory. Until today, that quest had been enough for her, but as her eyes lifted to Brett's, she feared that was no longer all she wanted.

Another need arose. The need for something more. *Someone* more. Someone who was passionate and . . . and who believed in her.

Someone on her side.

Chapter Ten

BRETT met his sisters, Emily, and Taunton in the foyer of Keaton House. Brett and the women were dressed in their finery to attend Lord Dayton's ball. The women's gowns were a bright mosaic of color, but Brett only had eyes for Emily.

She was a vision in blue satin that had some intricately embroidered lace net overlay. He swallowed as his eyes dipped to the pearl necklace that draped almost provocatively over the creamy swells of her breasts, teasing him above her décolletage. .

He had to clear his throat before he could speak. "Ladies." He bowed deeply. "Your beauty humbles me. You will be the belles of the ball and put every other woman to shame. Perhaps you should stay home, thus saving them from being ignored."

Melody laughed gaily, and moments later, someone poked him in the back.

"Pray tell, dear brother, what color is *my* gown?" Melody teased from behind him.

"Green?" Brett guessed, winking at Emily, who covered her mouth to stifle her laughter.

"Just as I suspected." Melody circled back in front of him and grinned. She wore an off-white frilly thing, embroidered roses sprinkled over it, and a pink sash cinching her waist. "Your eyes never left Lady Emily, but I forgive you, because she is stunning."

"You may be right. I find that I am rather . . ." He paused and looked at Emily again. "Distracted this evening." He admired the flush coloring Emily's cheeks and seeping down the slim column of her neck. He yearned to press his lips to the alabaster skin there and feel her pulse race. To let his mouth slide further over the rise and fall of her . . . Taunton cleared his throat, and damned if Brett's face did not burn.

"Ladies, you all look lovely and will be sure to turn every gentleman's head," Taunton said. "Fortunately, my heart is weathered enough to withstand such a siege of beauty, but I do pity the young bucks. They will be undone."

Brett frowned at his sisters' shared looks of delight, not liking the idea of a roomful of men's attentions on the pair, nor on Emily. Conflicting emotions warred within him. He was torn between his protective instincts toward his sisters and a spurt of possessiveness toward Emily.

Mine.

The word ached to burst from his lips, so he was relieved when Burke, Taunton's ever-efficient butler, appeared with the woman's cloaks and curtailed this train of thought. However, after spending so much time with Emily, it was inevitable he would feel protective toward her.

They had become allies, if not . . . *friends.*

A nagging voice pointed out that a friend did not imagine kissing the pulse at the base of her throat, or caressing the round curves of her breasts, or—

He should remain home and put some distance between himself and Emily. After all, he rarely participated in these formal affairs of the ton, aware it was not his name that garnered most of his invitations, but his bank account. He blamed his sisters for corralling him into playing chaperone, and wished, not for the first time, that he had brothers.

"Shall we go? I believe our carriage awaits," Emily said.

Alas, as her *friend*, he should keep an eye over Emily, particularly as she braved a roomful of randy bucks. It was the least he could do. He stepped forward to offer her his arm. After a brief hesitation, she accepted his escort and allowed him to guide her out.

He glanced quickly behind him to see Taunton escorting his sisters. Devil take him, he had completely forgotten them! He was no better a chaperone than the absentminded Agnes. Guilt stabbed him.

It was going to be a long night. He prayed to God he survived it.

❦

AFTER ARRIVING AT the Earl of Dayton's and dispensing with their cloaks, they moved to join the receiving line. Brett dismissed the curious looks directed their way along with the rising tide of murmurs, more interested in the change that had stolen over Emily during the carriage ride. She had become unusually quiet, and a white pallor had replaced the lovely flush that had stained her cheeks earlier.

He frowned when her eyes drifted over their audience, a slight tremor in her fingers as she neatened her skirts. She then clasped her hands tightly before her. He caught a flicker of wide-eyed panic before she dropped her gaze.

The display of raw nerves was at complete odds to everything he knew of her. She was his strong, brave goddess of heroic endeavors. *His Athena.*

Emily lifted her chin. "These affairs can be overwhelming. I do hope your sisters enjoy themselves."

He frowned, disturbed at her show of bravado. Similar to yesterday when he had witnessed her pain, he wanted to shield her from whatever darkness shadowed those luminous blue eyes. Unable to act on that forbidden instinct, he changed course.

"You have a point," he said. "Melody?" He tugged on his sister's sash. She tossed him an impatient look, but he spoke in an avuncular tone. "Lady Emily was commenting that these affairs can be overwhelming. As you are a shy, retiring thing, I wanted to let you know that there is still time to turn around—"

"Ah, Brett, you have such a droll wit." She waved her hand airily. "I now understand why the ladies are always tittering behind your back. Isn't that right, Miranda?"

"Yes, he is endlessly amusing," Miranda drawled, looping her arm through Melody's. "Let us hope it keeps him entertained far, far away from us."

"Droll?" Brett furrowed his brow. "Is that a new vocabulary word you have learned? I am surprised it is in your primer."

"Children, children," Lord Taunton interceded. "You are worse than Jonathan at war. Please, weapons down and best behavior."

"Of course." Melody smiled sweetly, then narrowed her eyes at Brett and mouthed, *Behave.*

He stuck his tongue out, earning a horrified laugh from her, before she turned her back on him.

"I see my concerns are for naught," Emily said, shaking her head. "But I am glad that you have a care for their welfare. They are lucky to have such a concerned older brother."

Her sarcasm delighted him, but the return of color to her cheeks pleased him more. "I tell them so, but they do not appreciate me. Cannot fathom why." Emily's laughter was a sweeter note than any the orchestra had played. She was better, but he would monitor her closely, make sure those shadows stayed away.

The Earl of Dayton was a jovial, big barrel of a man, and was charmed to have them as his guests for the evening.

"Thank you." Emily dipped into a curtsy. "I look forward to catching up with Charlotte. Dare I hope I can steal her away from her fiancé, Lord Haversley, is it?"

Brett's attention perked up at the name, and he caught Emily's knowing glance. He had forgotten about Haversley and his betrothal to Dayton's daughter, but she had not. He gave her a grateful smile.

"Of course. Haversley is in one of the gentlemen's card rooms, so Charlotte should be somewhere about. She mentioned that she has not seen you since your triumphant first Season a few years ago. She will be delighted to know that you have finally abandoned your country hiatus, as am I. It was much too long, my dear. Much too long." He smiled at Emily.

Emily's smile wavered briefly at the light chiding, before she lifted her chin and moved on.

The introductions finished, they made their way into the ballroom. The room was awash in light that danced over the glittering gems adorning the women's gowns and their elaborate hairstyles. An orchestra played a lively quadrille, while couples whirled and glided as they executed the intricate dance steps. Clinking glasses, rumbles of conversations, and trills of laughter accompanied the music.

Miranda and Melody wore matching expressions of awe and delight. He ignored them, his attention on Emily, having noticed her pursed lips at Dayton's reference to her hiatus. He recalled her absence from society, and her flight to the Lake District to flee all that reminded her of Jason.

Her fiancé had been a fortunate man—to have been loved so very deeply. Years ago, Brett had believed a woman had felt as strongly for him, but he had been proved wrong. Resentment toward the viscount flared, a man who'd had everything, but turned his back on it to travel to India. The man had been a fool.

"While I chaperone your sisters, you can steal some time to speak to Haversley," Emily said, interrupting his thoughts.

"Maybe I should stay. Melody can be—"

"Exactly. While she is being so, she does not need your scowl scaring away potential dance partners." At his wary look, she added, "My father is here. I promise, his scowl can rival yours should the need arise. Please. It is the least I can do to aid you in your search."

He hesitated, but his need to speak to Haversley tugged at him. He would return quickly. He needed to keep an eye on his sisters, but as the music washed over him, he yearned for something else. He wished to hold Emily in his arms. Refused to let the evening end without partnering her on the dance floor. For a few moments, he could pretend that he, not Jason, was the fortunate man.

⋙⋘

A FILM OF cigar smoke permeated the card room, and the chorus of masculine voices drowned out the music. Brett had met Haversley at a few other social events, so his gaze shifted over the players looking for his bright shock of ginger hair. Finding his target, he wended his way toward Haversley's table, nodding to acquaintances and snatching a drink from a passing footman.

Fortunately, he did not have to wait long for Haversley's luck to run dry and his hand to fold. "Haversley, a drink to drown the bitterness of your loss?" Brett said. He handed Haversley the tumbler of whiskey as he moved away from the table. "Fifty pounds is steep."

"Curtis." Haversley greeted him with a nod and accepted the drink. "Which is why it was time to leave."

"Smart man."

"No, a cowed one. My fiancée will have my head if I remain. I have a fondness for my head, prefer it attached to my neck," he quipped.

Brett laughed. "Actually, I wanted to speak to you about my cousin Prescott and your mutual interest in a painting."

"Ah, yes," he drawled, smiling. "A. W. Grant's *Adrift at Sea*. I gave it to my brother, payment rendered to cover a portion of an outstanding debt I owed him."

A gambling man. Little wonder his fiancée did not want him overstaying his welcome in the card room.

"Your cousin learned of it and tracked me down, demanding to know where I had purchased it. He did not believe I had picked up a Grant original in an obscure antiquities shop in Kent. Said it was nigh impossible." Haversley snorted. "Had the gall to accuse me of paying for a forgery and offered to buy it off my brother."

"A forgery?" Brett said, unable to mask his surprise.

"Indeed. I told my brother, but Thomas refused to sell to Prescott. You see, my brother sees himself as a connoisseur of art, and so your cousin's claim was of grievous insult to him." Haversley shrugged. "Admittedly, my brother can be a pompous arse."

"Have you heard from my cousin since then?"

Haversley shook his head. "I am sure he is busy with his estates now that he inherited the title. Who would think it, fourth son and all? Mind you, I did give him the name of the shop in Kent. Damned if he did not vow to pay them a visit, so you might look to find him in *Once Upon a Time Antiquities and Consignment Shop*; I believe that was the name of it. Small town in Gravesham called Buxom. Let me know if he discovers a Rembrandt." Haversley winked and thrust his glass at Brett. "My thanks for the drink." He bowed and made to turn away, but Brett's hand on his arm stopped him.

Brett dropped his arm. "I inquired about the painting because I, too, am a collector of Grant's works, as he is a fellow American. This one sounds intriguing. Makes me wonder why my cousin was interested in it. Do you think your brother would be amenable to another offer, if the price was right?"

He needed to buy the damn painting. He owed his cousin that, because if not for Brett, Drew would be painting for pleasure, not profit as Brett had pressed him to do. For the first time in his life, he cursed his enterprising initiative.

Haversley looked intrigued. "I could speak to him."

Brett bowed. "Thank you. Before your brother speaks to me, I suggest he has the painting authenticated at Ackermann's. It is my understanding that they are the sole distributors of Grant's works and would be able to assess its value." Knowing Haversley was a gambling man, Brett was betting on the fact that Haversley and his brother would not confide Ackermann's findings to Brett. Instead, they would sell him a forgery for a reasonable price, satisfying all parties.

Haversley nodded and turned away.

Brett now somewhat understood Drew's disappearance.

He was on a quest to locate an art forger.

The information lightened Brett's burden. He would try to assist Drew in acquiring the forgery, but Brett trusted his cousin to find the forger on his own. Brett had enough answers for now, would collect more when his cousin returned. Only if Drew did not resurface would Brett continue his search.

Emily was his priority now.

He needed to assist her, not only to save her neck, lovely as it was, but also to catch a murderer. He now believed her claim. But if Jason did not die from opium abuse, it meant he had uncovered something incriminating and been killed because of what he had found.

Due to the East India Company's unscrupulous business practices, Brett was not surprised to learn that one of their employees was a murderer. However, it was now more imperative than ever that they find their answers before someone learned that he and Emily were investigating matters and decided Jason was not the only one who needed to be silenced.

Tomorrow he would consider how to proceed without their arriving at the same grisly end.

But not tonight.

Tonight, he had a dance to claim.

Chapter Eleven

❧❦❧

EMILY knew the minute Brett returned to the dance floor. Her whole body was attuned to his presence, like a violin responding to a bow. She recalled the comforting grip of his hands when he had held hers in his office and stared intently into her eyes.

I believe you.

The three simple words gave her the strength to face friends she had avoided for too long, as well as to ignore the murmurs of surprise over her return. More pleasing was to see her father's delight when she had accepted an offer of a dance—something she had not done in years.

She had thought conquering her nerves would settle so many of the emotions that churned within her. But when Brett returned, she knew that was not enough. Other feelings that he evoked still percolated within her. He awakened old yearnings. One did not need love to feel desire, and it simmered in her.

Her gaze followed Brett. The man was always striking, but in his formal black evening attire, he was devastatingly so. He walked with long, purposeful strides, without the haughty nobility that stamped the aristocracy. He ignored everyone moving from his path, his gaze locked on her.

Her heart thudded as he neared, drowning out the orchestra and the voices surrounding her.

"May I have this dance?" He bowed low and flashed that blinding white smile of his.

It had been so long since a man had looked at her as Brett did. Like she was stunning and he wanted her and *only* her.

She gave him her hand, dipped into a curtsy, and smiled back. His arm slipped around her waist and he led her over to join the quadrille.

He bowed again and she curtsied, and they glided forward and back in the rhythm of the dance, her feet light. Her body brimmed with awareness, an instrument coming alive with sounds she had not played in years, but a tune she knew well.

Her gaze met Brett's and his look was warm, intensely focused, and . . . intimate. A shiver suffused her. She laughed as he twirled her around. She did so for the sheer exhilaration of it, the sound of her abandon stunning even her.

Brett's eyes sparkled under the shifting light of the chandelier, and his smile lightened her heart. Beneath her hand, his shoulder provided a sturdy anchor. His arm around her waist, combined with the warmth of Brett's body heating hers, fanned the small flutters in her chest.

Brett was a good dancer; tall and lean, he moved with an athletic grace.

Her breathing became shallow, her pulse quickening. She lost track of time, place, and everyone else surrounding them. They were alone . . . until the music stopped, the dance wound to a close, and the magic ended. She stood before Brett, unable to draw a steady breath or move away as she should.

A low cough shattered the moment, like ice water tossed on a roaring fire. She stepped back, and turned. Her breath caught at the sight of Drummond so close beside her. She wished the dratted man would do as she had requested and leave her alone.

In contrast to Brett's austere black, Drummond's waistcoat

was a rich emerald green, his neck cloth tied in another knot that must have taken his valet too much time to fashion. A glimmer of light reflected off the diamond pin piercing the lapel of his jacket.

His eyes dipped disdainfully over Brett. "Curtis. Surprised to see you here. However, Lady Emily, I am delighted to see *you*. Your beauty renders me speechless."

"Not quite," Brett muttered.

A tic vibrated in Drummond's cheek, but otherwise, he ignored Brett and bowed. "May I have this dance?"

"No." Brett snatched her hand and tucked it around his arm, holding it securely in place. "The lady is quite parched, needs a lemonade. I was going to escort her when you interrupted us. Another time."

Brett turned his back on Drummond and practically dragged Emily off, oblivious to Drummond's expression. The man looked positively apoplectic.

She emitted a horrified giggle. "That was very bad form. Very bad indeed."

"Did you want to dance with him?"

"No, but—"

"Now you do not have to. No thanks are needed."

"I should not be surprised to see him here, but I had forgotten that Drummond is related to the Earl of Dayton via his mother's side of the family. However, Drummond appeared surprised to find you here." In the receiving line, others had scrutinized Brett with the same look that Drummond wore, as if sizing up how an American had received an invitation to their elite club. It provided a hint into the reasons for Brett's impatience with the aristocracy.

He shrugged. "There are some in the ton who do not condescend to acknowledge me. In their eyes, my work in trade supersedes my relationship to the Duke of Prescott and my friendship with Bedford. In America, while many genuflect over English titles, success in business garners equal respect and opens as many doors. Our peerage is wealth. The more you have, the higher you rank." He turned to Emily and seeing her expression, he grinned. "You need not worry about me. I decline to attend most of these events by choice, not due to lack of invitations."

She nodded. "Me, too. I had my debut, enjoyed my Season, and got engaged to Jason. But I have learned that after losing someone you love, you can never recapture the past or return to who you once were. I feel like a stranger at these affairs, so I stopped coming to most." She emitted a small laugh. "I am also older now, practically an old maid at three-and-twenty."

"Older and wiser. And I find that it is better to have a few very good friends, than many shallow acquaintances."

"True, and a wise observation. I will keep that in mind."

"You do that, particularly the point about my being wise." He winked.

She smiled, but it faded as she became aware that they were leaving the ballroom. "Where are we going? We cannot leave. Your sisters—"

"Are fine. They are holding court with some other young women. A few vultures were circling, but your father's vigilance has them waffling. We will return shortly." They moved further down the hall. He peered into the library, and then drew her inside, leaving the door open.

"What are you doing?" she hissed, tugging at his grip. "We cannot go in here."

"Just for a minute, one minute." Once he ascertained the room was empty, he led her between two rows of bookcases. He released her hand and paced to the length of the aisle and back. His stride was agitated, his expression conflicted as he ran a hand through his thick hair, leaving it looking attractively disheveled.

"What is it?" Apprehension gripped her.

He returned and stared at her intensely. "It is this. There is no help for it." He slid his arm around her waist, yanked her against him, and swallowed her shocked gasp with his mouth. His lips closed over hers, devouring, kissing her with a thoroughness that stunned her.

Her mind reeled with the taste and the feel of him as she lifted her hands to clutch his upper arms. His kiss elicited a rush of long-buried emotions, passion and desire, and . . . something more. Much more. Good lord, she wanted him. She tasted whiskey on his tongue as hers parried with his. She groaned as his hand splayed over her back, drawing her closer. The hard, solid length of his body pressed against hers, burning her like a welcome brand.

He abruptly released her, as if his own behavior appalled him. He held up his hands. "I apologize. I never should have—"

"Please. You strike me as a man who goes after what he wants without apology. I find I am a woman who likes to do the same." She nearly laughed at his wide-eyed look when she looped her arms around his neck and pulled him down to kiss him again. There was something to be said for experience. She made sure to apply it.

She plundered his mouth as if searching for buried treasure. Her tongue ran over his full lips, and her fingers threaded into the golden curls that teased the collar of his jacket. She arched against him, liking the feel of his chest against hers, the thundering beat of her heart matching his. Pleasure suffused her, but she wanted more.

He yanked away and gaped at her, his hair boyishly mussed, his eyes dazed. "*What are we doing?*"

She laughed and flattened her hands on his chest. "Laying our weapons down," she murmured.

He shook his head and caught her wrists, stepping back, as if he needed the distance to collect his thoughts. "No. This is a full-frontal assault, with all weapons fully engaged. That was dangerous. Inflammatory. Any more and we will be burned alive."

"Perhaps you should surrender, and I will ensure your survival."

He grunted. "I thought I already did."

"Mmh, perhaps we should negotiate the terms."

He arched a brow, his attention caught. "Terms? I thought it was my assistance in keeping you alive, for your agreeing to not go off alone and do anything foolhardy. Was there more?"

"That is our original arrangement, but due to your stringent stipulation that we do everything *together*, we will be spending a lot of time in each other's company. Due to the nature of our relationship—"

"The *nature of our relationship*?" He looked bemused. "I thought we were becoming friends, but now I am not so sure."

"Friends do not kiss each other senseless," she pointed out.

"Very true." Brett grinned. "You are rather good at that. Whatever new scheme you are plotting, perhaps we should discuss it when my wits have not been burned to cinders."

"No. Now is the perfect time to discuss this matter, but we haven't much time. I was going to suggest that due to our obvious attraction toward each other, we—" She stopped at his snort of disbelief.

"You think I am an overbearing, arrogant arse."

"And you think I am an ornery, meddling, obdurate female. Are you not familiar with the idea that when two people spar with each other, it is often a symptom of a deeper attraction?"

"No, but I am familiar with chemistry. I know when two combustible elements come in contact with each other, they tend to ignite. I believe we just got singed," he said, his eyes teasing.

"We did." She beamed at him. "So there is little point in fighting such formidable forces of nature. I say that we concede defeat to a higher power."

Brett stared at her for a moment. "Lady Emily, exactly what are you proposing?"

She folded her hands together, lifted her chin, and stared him straight in the eye. She was prepared to do more than collude with the devil . . . far more. "I propose that for the duration of our arrangement, it would be difficult and rather silly to dance around this attraction that is simmering between us. I suggest, instead, we simply enjoy it."

"Enjoy it?" Brett's lips curved into a smile. He rubbed his chin, as if pondering the matter seriously. "And how do you propose we do that? A few stolen kisses?" He peered around the near vicinity. "Behind bookcases in libraries or garden shrubbery?"

Was the man really this obtuse? She had thought he had a way with women, but saw no sign of it now. "With an affair." She tossed up her hands and glowered at him. "A very discreet one, of course," she hastened to add, considering he was being so dim-witted.

He swiped his hands down his face, and gave his head a sharp shake, opening and closing his mouth but emitting no sound.

Perhaps she had made a mistake. Perhaps the man was simply a good kisser, and he did not feel any of the things that he made her feel. Then she would . . . She would simply arranged to have him killed and buried in the corner pasture of Robbie Tanner's paddock. The one that was reserved for inferior or diseased stock. She would have no other choice.

"You cannot be serious," he sputtered when he had recovered his voice. He leaned forward and practically growled at her. "Your father would kill me. If he does not, Daniel would. I would not survive a day."

"Do you plan to tell them? For goodness' sake, what part of *discreet* eludes you? Men and women carry on affairs all the time. Pity Americans are so puritan. I thought your kiss said you were a man who did what you wanted, damn the consequences. Unfortunately, I thought wrong." She shrugged, and made to turn away.

Brett caught her arm and swung her back to face him. "Do not be absurd. The consequences of this is marriage. That is damning indeed. You are the daughter of an earl. Sister-in-law to a duke. I am an untitled American who works in trade. There can be no alliance between us. Not in your world."

"I am not looking for marriage. Have no plans to enter that contract. The last one nearly killed me." She ignored the piercing in her chest and lifted her chin.

He nodded. "I understand. I, too, have no plans to offer for another woman. I did that once . . . and, well, death is not the only means of losing someone you love." He hardened his jaw.

She paused, stunned. She knew only one facet of Brett, the glib, self-assured businessman. This was another, a vulnerable side. Melody had mentioned his failed engagement. She should have realized it might have left some scars. Again, she wondered what sort of woman had rejected him—particularly after that kiss. "I am sorry," she said softly.

"So was I," he said tightly, and then shrugged. "It was a long time ago. Not everyone is fortunate to have what you had with your fiancé. He must have been a very special man."

"He was. Very special." She swallowed, disconcerted to have Jason enter this conversation like a third party interrupting an intimate tryst. For the first time, a flicker of irritation arose within her.

Jason was dead, and she was alive, very much so. She had not felt this alive in a long, long time.

But Brett did not want her, or rather, like herself, was not willing to take the risk of loving another again *or*—he feared Daniel and her father would kill him should he become involved with her. There was *that*. She gnawed on her lower lip.

She would never again have what she had with Jason. This had to be enough for her. Passion. Desire. A man to hold her . . . to touch her. To remind her that she was alive and a desirable woman.

Not any man, but *this* man.

This strong, vibrant man who was turning her down. And he thought *her* stubborn. There was only one course of action left to her. She would simply have to remove his reservations.

To seduce him.

She caught her breath at the brazen thought, waiting for her conscience's appalled protest to erupt. The denials never came. *Well then*. Brett had said she had too many hidden weapons at her disposal. It was time to deploy them.

The man would never know what hit him.

A small smile curved her lips.

Brett held up his hands and stumbled back a step. "Now what are you planning? As I have said before, I have three sisters; I recognize guile when I see it."

She laughed. "You poor man, always under siege from women. I do not know how you weather it." She turned her back on him, speaking over her shoulder. "We should return. If you have no plans to offer for my hand, we cannot be caught alone in here. You would not survive the scandal of *that*. As you know, my father does have a pair of Manton revolvers and would be delighted to use them if it meant seeing me married." She grinned at his groan, but did not wait to see if he followed her when she headed back toward the ballroom.

She kept her smile in place, but prepared for battle. She anticipated an easy conquest. Then she would seize all his assets and demand a full surrender. Heat suffused her at the memory of the strength of his muscular body flush with hers. She sighed.

He had fine assets indeed.

Chapter Twelve

❧ ❧

W HERE are we meeting this clerk?" Brett asked Emily, refusing to shift or fidget in his chair despite the unfortunate fit of his trousers. He should be immune to the torment as it was a permanent affliction ever since Emily had presented him with her ludicrous proposition. His hand tightened on his knife. The woman was going to be the death of him if her father did not kill him first. He valued his life, or did so when his body was not in this pulsating state of pain.

He reiterated to himself what he had been repeating like a child reciting a rote passage. *It was the right decision. And an honorable one.* Despite unleashing all sorts of carnal images in his dreams, in the light of day, he was a gentleman, or was raised to be one. And she was a *lady.* He could not dishonor her so—even as his body screamed for release from a prison of his own making.

She looked so angelic in a lovely yellow day dress. The sun streamed over her and created a halo effect above her golden hair. Who would have thought there was a conniving she-devil beneath her prim and proper exterior?

They were seated at the dining room table as they broke the fast, alone except for Jonathan and the bustle of footmen. Petie, Taunton's eagle-eyed housekeeper, was also flitting about somewhere. She made her presence known with an occasional throat-clearing, do-not-forget-that-I-am-near warning. His sisters were having a lying-in after their exciting evening, and Taunton had eaten earlier and retired to his study. Brett was grateful for the reprieve, feared his lustful thoughts were branded on his brow.

Jonathan had abandoned his meal to engage his toy soldiers in a battle beneath the table. His occasional cries of gunfire were the only noise to break the silence that had settled between them. As he regarded her, Emily ever so slowly licked crumbs from her mouth. He was mesmerized by the slow and sensual movement of her pink tongue sliding over her full lips until she . . . smiled.

The blood drained from his head. She had done that on purpose! He stiffened, or the parts of him that were not already in that particular condition did so.

Jonathan's soldiers should shoot him now. Put him out of his misery.

"He said he would meet us in Hyde Park," Emily said, answering the question he had posed earlier.

Having no recollection of what it was, he prudently held his silence and nodded curtly. Better to look the fool than to open his mouth and remove all doubt.

She glanced at his untouched plate. "You are not hungry?"

"I do not have much of an appetite." He cursed the hoarse croak in his voice.

"Pity. Cook's sausages are delicious." Emily's eyes never left his as she speared her fork into one, lifted the succulent meat to her mouth, and bit in.

Bloody hell. He gritted his teeth, swallowing his protest as she slowly chewed.

"Surrender or die!"

Jonathan's bellow shattered his immobility. He dropped his knife. *Enough.* "Look, I surrendered, and it is time you did the same. You need to lay your weapons down, because if you are not careful, one is going to misfire and get both of us killed."

"Weapons?" Jonathan's tousled head poked up from beneath the table, and he scrambled to his feet. "Do you have weapons?" Disappointment clouded his features as he surveyed the table. "I do not see any."

"Oh, they are here all right," Brett said.

Jonathan looked perplexed. "Where?"

Emily intervened. "Nowhere. Mr. Curtis has an active imagination. In fact, maybe he will play war with you? Oh, my mistake, he prefers not to battle, is wary of engagements that involve an element of risk, even if the rewards of victory might be worth fighting for." She aimed a challenging look at Brett.

Damn her. Was she questioning his bravery? Or his masculinity? He feared it was both. "My apologies, Jonathan. I am already engaged in a battle of a different sort with your sister, and it is not wise to engage in a war on two fronts at the same time."

"What sort of battle?" Jonathan frowned. "She doesn't have a sword."

"But Mr. Curtis does," Emily quipped, a spurt of laughter escaping her. At Jonathan's blank look, she relented. "Mr. Curtis believes he is at war with me, but he is mistaken. I am not his enemy."

"Then who is?' Jonathan scratched his head.

"Himself." Emily rose to her feet, forcing Brett to his. "Enough talk of war. We need to go change, because Mr. Curtis has offered to escort us for a brief sojourn to Hyde Park before his sisters awaken."

"Can I bring my sword?" Jonathan asked.

"Of course," Brett answered before Emily could respond. "I might have need of it. But do not attack anyone unless we give you permission."

Emily steered Jonathan to the door, and Brett overhead Jonathan pose another question.

"Is Mr. Curtis bringing his sword?"

Emily glanced back at him, her eyes brimming with teasing lights, while his narrowed in silent warning.

Amused, she wrapped her arm around Jonathan's shoulders and practically shoved him from the room. "We will see."

"But I want to see his sword."

Emily's trill of laughter was her only response.

To think, the lyrical wave of it used to be music to his ears.

With a groan, he dropped into his seat, set his elbows on the table, and rested his head in his hands. She was formidable. He might have to call in reinforcements. He would write to Daniel and Julia to see if they could manage a visit. With the House of Lords in session, Daniel must be needed to cast a vote on some matter of national importance or other.

Emily would be forced to behave with her sister around. Wouldn't she? He did not know. He had no idea what crossed through the woman's mind.

He would draft that letter to Daniel.

Reinforcements might not save him, but they could not hurt.

⭠⭢

THE APRIL DAY was brisk and overcast. March's chilling bite lingered, belying the advent of spring. Being late morning, Rotten Row was quieter than the midday hour when Londoners, willing to brave the less than temperate climate, promenaded near the roadway encircling the park. As they watched the carriages and riders, they made sure to *see* and *be seen* in their fashionable attire.

They left Hyde Park Corner and headed east toward the Serpentine River. Jonathan skipped ahead, his nurse quickening her pace to keep up. Brett glanced behind to see Agnes following at a leisurely pace. He surmised she was seeking sights of more interest to her, no doubt something in long pants and a tall hat.

Brett kept his head down, his hat tipped low, not wanting

to run into any acquaintances, particularly with Emily looking so fetching in a lavender carriage dress, a becoming blush staining her cheeks. He had no interest in sharing her. Despite his intentions to keep his hands to himself, that did not mean he wanted to steer her anyone else's way.

"There he is," Emily said, catching his arm. "He . . . he looks unwell." Worry furrowed her brow beneath the brim of her bonnet.

He glanced up to see a gaunt man walking with a cane, his gray overcoat dwarfing a diminutive frame. Brett gave her hand a squeeze before it fell to her side, and they awaited the middle-aged man's approach. There was a wan pallor to his skin, and an air of weariness as if he had walked too many miles on meager rations.

The man removed his hat and bowed. "Lady Emily."

Emily dipped her head. "Mr. Marsh, thank you for taking the time to meet with me."

"It is my pleasure. It was an honor to work with Viscount Weston." His gruff voice gentled. "He was a good man." His eyes set in deep sockets drifted to Brett, his expression wary.

Brett was not inclined to set the man's mind at ease. Aware of the lack of scruples inherent in the men of the East India Company's employ, Jason's former clerk might be looking to sell information as a means to climb out of his poverty. The man looked as if he had fallen on hard times and could use a few pounds.

As if sensing the mutual distrust, Emily hastened to make the introductions. "This is Mr. Curtis, a friend of my brother-in-law's."

"I am familiar with Brett Curtis, or rather, his company. Curtis Shipping is a competitor of the *Honourable* East India Company." A sneer curved the man's thin lips as he evoked the full title.

"I doubt the East India Company views any firm as competition to its *venerable* enterprise," Brett said evenly. "However, I am here to assist Lady Emily. That is my only business today. Please, will you walk with us and give her a chance to explain her purpose?"

Jonathan's shouts as he scampered ahead filled the silence that lengthened as Marsh assessed Brett. Marsh appeared to have assuaged whatever misgivings he harbored, because he dipped his head and fell into step beside them.

"Mr. Marsh, you asked me to get in touch with you after the viscount's death," Emily began. "You said you had important matters to discuss with me. I was not prepared to hear what you had to say then, but I am now, and I hope . . . I hope it is not too late."

Frowning, Marsh's gaze dropped and he fingered his cane. "There were issues that I thought you should be aware of at the time. That were important to the viscount . . ." His voice trailed off, and he lifted his eyes. "But now I do not know what could come of dredging this all up again. I do not see the point, only the dangers inherent in doing so."

Emily's lips parted before her now-familiar look of determination settled on her features. "Viscount Weston is the point, Mr. Marsh. You cannot in good conscience believe what the company has been circulating about him behind closed doors."

Marsh stopped short, and a flicker of surprise lit his dark eyes before they darkened.

Emily faced him down. "Please, you know he did not die an"—She faltered, but forced herself to continue—"an opium addict. I implore you, help me to uncover the truth. If you believed him to be a good man, then I know you will not turn away from getting him the justice he deserves." At his conflicted expression, she pressed further. "I believe you are the only one who can."

His gaze shifted between them, his eyes sad. "Lady Emily, please, you do not need this kind of trouble. Let it rest."

"What kind of trouble?" She frowned. "What is it that you still fear? It has been nearly four years. Surely no one—"

"A tarnished reputation does not heal with the passage of time. Once lost, it can never be redeemed. Because I cannot repair my good name, I cannot get work. No one will hire a *thief* and a *liar*," he bit out bitterly. "As a bachelor, I did not have much to lose, and I reside with an elderly aunt. She appreciates my company and my care. But you, you are a lady and the daughter of an earl. You cannot afford to lose your reputation."

Brett nearly snorted. He and this Marsh agreed on one matter.

"Lord Weston would not care for any slander to harm you," Marsh said. "I made a mistake in approaching you at his funeral. Please do not make another one." He made to turn away, but paused at Emily's plaintive cry.

"I cannot," Emily cried. She stared at him through a sheen of moisture blurring her eyes. "I let Jason down when I did nothing after you first approached me. His memory is all I have left of him, and I refuse to fail him again by allowing innuendoes and lies to blacken it. I am sorry for the injustice that has befallen you. Jason wrote of your work, and of you, with great respect. I believe you are no thief, nor a liar, but someone needed to sully your name, and thus call into question the veracity of your word."

Wide-eyed and still, Marsh simply stared at her.

"Lady Emily is right," Brett said. "We would like your help, and it would not come without a reward. Consider it an exchange of sorts. My company has need of honest and loyal men, particularly clerks who are valued in their work." He extracted his silver card case from his jacket pocket, and gave Marsh his card. "Owen Jenkins manages my London offices. Tell him I sent you. The late viscount's testimony on your behalf is reference enough. We can give you time to settle in, but I hope that when you do so, you will be ready to speak with us."

Marsh eyed the card as if he feared it was something offered in a dream.

"Thank you for seeing us." Brett bowed and turned away, silencing Emily's protest with a warning look.

"Wait." They turned back, and Marsh gestured for them to continue on their walk with him. "You are right. The viscount deserves justice. And as the Good Book says, *'When justice is done, it is joy to the righteous but terror to the evildoers.'* It would be nice to evoke fear in the individual responsible for these slanderous lies. Were you aware of the viscount's mission?"

"Jason told me he had been directed to clean up some discrepancies found in the accounts tied to a factory house in Calcutta," Emily said. "I thought that was his mission, but I learned recently that he was overseeing the company's opium trade to China." She shared what they had learned from Little.

Marsh nodded. "He was doing both, but his true mission was investigating the discrepancies in the accounts. Lord Roberts hired the viscount. Roberts is one of the ministers of the crown overseeing the company, and he had learned of money missing from funds used to pay for the opium delivered to Calcutta. Despite opium being a contraband drug, our government sanctions its trade with China because we have a vested interest in its sale. Merchants selling the opium are making a fortune, and our Exchequer relies on the revenue that the tax on opium brings. Its income alone practically covers our expenses for the tea we purchase from China, so Parliament is not partial to anyone interfering with that enterprise. It was Jason's job to ferret out the culprit who had the audacity to do so."

"I take it the viscount succeeded in his investigation?" Brett said.

Marsh hesitated, then gave a curt nod. "I believe he did, but after a series of suspicious accidents that nearly cost him his life, he began to fear for it. To safeguard what he had uncovered, he copied the incriminating information into a smaller ledger, which he kept locked in a leather portfolio along with his diaries and personal letters. He then secured these items in a false bottom of his trunk."

Emily drew a sharp intake of breath, and Brett squeezed her arm, giving her a furtive shake of his head, again warning her to silence.

"The viscount had made arrangements to sail home when his valet discovered his body," Marsh said, and nodded to Emily. "It became my greatest honor to escort both the trunk and the viscount's casket back to England. I directed his valet, Winfred, to deliver the trunk to you, where I believed it would be in safekeeping, or rather, where the East India Company would not think to look."

Visibly shaken, Emily drooped at his words. Brett ached to slip his arm around her waist and give her his support, but he could not. He cleared his throat. "The identity of the man who was embezzling, did the viscount confide it to you?"

Marsh looked bleak. "That is the rub. He did not. I only know that it deeply disturbed him."

"What of Lawrence Drummond, his colleague. Did he confide in him?" Brett pressed.

Marsh shook his head. "The viscount kept his own confidence. He said he was not to administer justice himself, but turn over his information to Lord Roberts. I do not believe Mr. Drummond knows any more than I. However, it was Drummond who convinced the viscount that his life was in danger. After the viscount was wounded in a skirmish with some disgruntled sepoys, Drummond urged him to return home."

"Wounded?" she breathed.

Marsh waved his hand dismissively. "A discharged rifle winged him. It is a common occurrence in a volatile environment. It was not serious."

"So Drummond did not know about the trunk's false bottom?" Brett said.

"Drummond? No, only myself, and of course, Winfred, as he had access to the viscount's trunk and his belongings."

"I see," Brett said, mulling over Drummond's role.

They stopped and Marsh splayed his hands. "You have my address, but that ledger should be enough to at least raise questions about the viscount's death. With them, Lord Roberts might give you the audience that was denied to me. I do believe he is suspicious over the viscount's death, but without evidence of foul play, there was nothing he could do. People believe what they see, and an English surgeon verified he died from the opium."

Emily gasped, her hand covering her mouth.

"All Lord Roberts could do for the viscount was to prevent the cause of death from becoming public outside the company. In deference to the family, he ensured the files referencing him were sealed. I was surprised to learn you had discovered the true manner of his death. I am sorry word of it reached you, and I can only hope it goes no further."

Emily's chin jutted out. "It will not."

"Thank you for your time, Mr. Marsh. You have been most helpful," Brett said.

"No, the thanks are mine for your confidence in me. I will not forget it. I am sorry I do not have more information, but if I remember anything else, I will write to you. I do hope you can clear the viscount's legacy in the company. As I said, he was a good man, and he deserves better."

Emily nodded.

Marsh bowed deeply, tipped his hat, and left them.

Brett gave Emily a moment to collect herself, glancing around for Jonathan. He located him a short distance ahead, his sword held aloft as he darted along the edge of the lake, his nurse and Agnes nearby.

"There is no other course of action," Emily said, breaking the beat of silence.

He turned back to her and noted her fierce expression. Athena, his warrior, had returned.

"Jason's reputation is at stake, so we must act."

"His reputation within the company, that is. Thankfully, they were able to ensure the viscount's name was not tarnished outside of its hallowed walls."

"Lord Roberts safeguarded Jason's name, the Honourable East India Company did not," Emily corrected fiercely. She applied the same derisive sneer to the company's name as Marsh. "In addition to the ledger, we now know that Jason kept a diary. No doubt, he would document his investigation and confide all he had learned. It is imperative that we acquire that portfolio and all its contents."

"I take it you have a new plan?"

"I do." She lifted her chin. "We must steal the trunk from Drummond."

A fit of coughing gripped him, and he struggled to tamp down the string of curses that rose to his lips.

Oblivious to his struggle, she continued, Athena in full battle. "We will bribe one of his servants or hire someone to break in." She waved a hand airily. "What about that boy, the mudlark? You said he tried to steal from you?"

"And got caught doing it," Brett said, incredulous.

"Fine, but he could find someone willing to do the job. We will have to figure out the particulars, but we need that trunk. And I intend to get it."

"Listen to me, there will be no stealing of anything."

She ignored his words and began to pace. "Perhaps I could cry prettily and tell Drummond that the trunk had sentimental value to me, that it was in my family for generations, and—"

"Now you are sounding ridiculous. A trunk is not a family heirloom, nor does this trunk even belong to your family. Even you with your talent for weaving tales cannot spin that one without arousing suspicions."

She stopped, looking crestfallen. "You may be right."

"Surprising as it is, I am sometimes," he said with strained patience. He rubbed his hands over his face, and sighed. "Let us discuss this more thoroughly and rationally, after you have time to absorb everything Marsh has confided. It must be upsetting to you to hear that Jason knew he was in danger, that he escaped a series of accidents. I am sorry, Emily. He sounds like a brave and honorable man."

She blinked her eyes, looking away. "Yes. Yes, he was."

"We are not retreating, but reassessing matters in light of this new information and taking the time to determine a rational course of action. That is, a path that will not land us in Newgate for theft."

"You are right again," she sighed. "Landing in gaol will not help Jason."

He caught the slight twitch to her lips, her amusement

belying her tone of resignation. That was his Athena. "Nor would your father be pleased."

She winced, and they lapsed into a companionable silence as they continued walking, both lost to their thoughts. No doubt Emily to her scheming, while he wondered if Burke had posted his letter. He hoped to reclaim the missive. He had changed his mind. He did not need witnesses to his demise.

He had told Jonathan it was not wise to fight a battle on two fronts, yet here he was, struggling to fight off Emily's advances and his own attraction to her. In addition, he needed to assist her in clearing Jason's name. And do so before whoever embezzled from the East India Company, murdered the viscount, and destroyed the reputation of the one man who could have spoken on the viscount's behalf, discovered what he and Emily were up to. Add to that, he also had to stop Emily from committing theft and landing in Newgate. Lastly, all this had to be done before the Earl of Taunton discovered what they were up to and murdered him.

He could not win all these battles, and he did not need Daniel here to call him a bloody fool for agreeing to assist Emily in opening Pandora's box.

Hell, his being a fool was the only thing of which he was certain.

Chapter Thirteen

꧁ꗃ꧂

EMILY peered down the corridor leading to the guest quarters. The passage was cloaked in darkness, which was good because it meant no one was afoot. It was also bad, because she was walking nearly blind with the thin glow of moonlight her only guide. She wished her father had retired earlier, cursed him for keeping Brett in his office so late. Her father had probably been nattering on about some business issue on which he sought Brett's advice.

She had her own matters to discuss with Brett and did not appreciate his avoiding her over the last three days. She sidestepped a table, tugged Agnes's mobcap low over her hair, and counted the doors to Brett's room.

Over a year ago, while a guest of theirs, Brett had cajoled her into reading to him while he was briefly bedridden after his carriage accident. During that time, Agnes had sat nearby sewing, and the door had remained open. This visit would be different. Heart pounding, she braced herself to breach all levels of propriety and enter a gentleman's bedroom.

Should she be caught, she *would* be signing her name to a betrothal contract neither of them wanted.

Well then. She would have to ensure they did not get caught.

After knocking quietly, she held her breath. A clock chimed in the distance, but time crawled, inexorably slow, as she awaited an answer.

The door finally swung open and Brett stood framed in the candlelight. "What the . . . ?" He peered down the corridor, and then unceremoniously yanked her into the room, closing the door behind her. "What is it? What are you doing here? Are you mad? We need to get you back to your room before anyone sees you."

He started toward the door, but she broke free and stepped beyond his reach. "Most Englishmen would be pleased to have a woman visit their bedchamber."

"Those Englishmen have nothing better to do than flaunt their titles and gamble away their estates, so they can afford to lose their frivolous, debt-ridden lives," he snapped back. "I happen to—"

"Yes, yes. So you keep reminding me. You value your life, have a company to run, responsibilities, et cetera, et cetera," she finished with a sigh. At his scowl, she shrugged. "So you best lower your voice before someone hears you talking to yourself and comes to investigate. Then you will be the one deemed mad, not I."

He glowered, but spoke more quietly. "You cannot be here. Whatever you have to say, it can wait until the light of day. I will—"

"No, it cannot," she said, dodging his advance and holding up her hands. "We have things to discuss, and you have been avoiding doing so." She kept her eyes on his face, but his state of dress, or rather undress, was distracting. He had removed his boots, cravat, jacket, and waistcoat. The top buttons of his white dress shirt were undone, the tails untucked and hanging loose. She fought, admittedly not very hard, to keep her gaze averted from the teasing strip of skin along the column of his throat and the V opening to reveal his bare chest.

"It is difficult to ignore your father, Jonathan, and my sisters when we are guests in your household," he said defensively. "Besides, *you* invited the girls to Bess's Bonnets and . . . whatever that blasted shop was. I assure you, I had no interest in them purchasing more accessories, and I have no need of a bonnet."

"I thought while they were trying on items, we could speak privately, but you chose to escape."

"I did not *choose to* escape. I had an appointment to speak to someone about a painting. Lest you forget, your part of our arrangement was for you to entertain my sisters so I could attend to some of my own business."

That quieted her. "Was it in reference to the A. W. Grant painting in which your cousin was interested?"

He nodded, eyeing her warily as she moved deeper into the room. "Do come in. Ignore all my warnings, and make yourself comfortable," he said dryly.

"Oh, please, it is not as if you have never had a woman in your room before. I am sure that I am not the first and—"

"But you will be the last if we are caught," he snarled, but hastened to amend his words. "Not that I am admitting to entertaining any women in my room—" Swearing beneath his breath, he began again with strained patience. "We will not discuss this. Or rather, *I* refuse to discuss this."

She simply laughed. He was adorable, rumple haired and bad-tempered. A half-filled glass with a decanter beside it caught her eye. She strolled over to the table on which they sat and picked up the crystal tumbler. "Why don't you finish your drink? It might relax you. You know, it is usually the other way around, with the woman needing her nerves to be calmed." When he refused to rise to her bait, she shrugged and took a sip. It was port. "There are other means to relax a man—"

"Devil take you!" He stalked over to her, grabbed her by the upper arms and yanked her close, his face but inches from hers. "You are a wolf in sheep's clothing. But you forget, you are in a lion's den now, and you'd best be careful or . . ." He released her as if her skin had burned and staggered back, his expression appalled.

"Or what?" Intrigued, she sidled closer to him, laughter bubbling up within her.

"Never mind," he bit out between clenched teeth. He snatched the drink from her, drained it, and then strode to the hearth—across the room from her. "If you have something to discuss, I suggest you do so before—"

"I know, I know. Before we are discovered and my father shoots you." With a sigh, she slipped off the ridiculous mobcap, plopped into the large easy chair beside the table, and curled her legs beneath her.

This seduction business was proving more difficult than the murder investigation. It was ironic that when she had lowered her defenses, he had shored up his, complete with his own moat. His contained a snapping male dragon. A boat *and* a battering ram might be necessary if she wanted to approach him. Her eyes drifted to the tantalizing strip of bare skin, and she swallowed. And she did want to . . . get closer. *Much closer.*

He narrowed his eyes and folded his arms across his chest. "Do not get comfortable. You are not staying."

His voice sounded husky to her ears, which was progress—of a sort. "Pity." Her gaze strayed toward the large four-poster feather bed.

"Emily!" he barked.

"Fine, fine." Perhaps she had gone too far. At least he had used the intimacy of her name, rather than the more formal address of *Lady* Emily—despite its being barked in exasperation. It was still progress of a sort. "Are you sure you do not want another drink . . . ?"

That drew a reluctant grin from him. "It would take a lot more than two drinks to get me drunk."

"Alas, I will not be able to take advantage of you. You could always take—"

"Yes, you have made that clear." A laugh escaped him, and he shook his head. "And I have made it clear that I want to live, so we are at an impasse. Now as to other matters, I suggest you begin before my patience ends."

"What patience?" she muttered.

"Emily!"

"I told you to keep your voice down. I want to know how we are going to acquire the trunk from Drummond. If you are opposed to having someone steal it, how else do you suggest we obtain it?"

"We do not need to steal it because as I was mulling it over, I realized that Drummond probably does not have it."

She furrowed her brow. "But Tristan said that—"

"He gave the *contents* to Drummond—the ledgers, correspondence, and business items. Tristan said he was keeping all personal property belonging to his deceased brother, and I am assuming that would include the trunk itself."

She smiled. "You may be right. He would do that. So we will rob the Bransons?"

He snorted. "There will be no robbing of anyone. Tristan mentioned his sister. Are you close with her? If you are, and she has not come to town yet, you can write to her before she does so and inquire about the trunk. You can spin her one of your yarns, something about Jason having hidden your letters in a portfolio secured in this false bottom, and you wish to reclaim them. That should at least determine if they still have the trunk."

"That is brilliant," she said, excitement lacing her tone. "And she is still in the country, because her mother mentioned during my visit that they planned to come to town at the end of the month. I am sure Patricia will assist me, and more important, she is discreet." Patricia Branson had chaperoned many of her and Jason's trysts. Like Agnes, she deliberately got "*distracted*" or "*lost*" for short periods of time.

"I will mention Jason's diary is in the portfolio as well," she added. "She will understand that I have a vested interest in safeguarding any intimate confidences he might have disclosed in regard to our relations. I am sure she will turn the portfolio over to me, and as it is locked, she cannot tamper with it—even though I trust her not to do so. Once we reclaim the items, we can deliver the incriminating ledger to Lord Roberts."

"Before we do so, we need to speak to Jason's former valet. We need to find out if he has any additional information and if he, too, has been threatened. Jason's ledger might prove embezzlement and hopefully identify the guilty man, but we need more if we want to accuse this man of murdering Jason."

Unconsciously, she drew in a sharp breath.

"I am sorry, Emily. I spoke harshly—"

"No, it is all right. The truth of his death still pricks, but it no longer draws blood."

"So this Winfred?" he prodded, gentling his tone. "Do you know his address or his new position of employ?"

She shook her head. "Tristan's sister will, because the family would have given him a reference. Winfred was devoted to Jason, was with him for years. He taught Winfred to read. The poor boy thought he was incapable of learning, but Jason taught him otherwise. I will ask Patricia when I inquire about the letters."

To shake the memories of Jason and Winfred, she stood and restlessly strolled the room. Brett had made use of the secretary desk, and its surface was buried in scattered papers. Always the businessman.

"While you contact Tristan's sister, I will see what I can learn of Lord Roberts," Brett said. "More important, I will try to determine who was responsible for ruining Marsh, branding him a thief and a liar."

Surprised, she glanced up. She had not thought of that. Brett was better at this strategizing than she, but his words reminded her of something else Marsh had shared. "Do you still believe Lawrence Drummond is involved? Marsh said Drummond urged Jason to leave. Drummond's real failure was in not convincing Jason to flee sooner."

"Was he urging Jason to leave to protect Jason—or himself?" Brett countered. "If Drummond is guilty of embezzling the funds and feared the viscount implicating him, it would be in his best interest to get rid of Jason, as well as to collect any incriminating evidence, hence his taking possession of Jason's papers."

"You may be right," she said, but remained dubious. Brett had understandably taken a disliking to the man, but she could not fathom the fashionable dandy killing his friend.

"So we have a plan that will keep us out of Newgate," Brett said. "Discussion over. Let me ensure the corridor is empty before we are discovered and end up in deeper trouble than we are already in."

"I suppose I have done enough to upset my father once our investigation comes to light." She laughed at Brett's grimace. Unable to resist, like a predator on the prowl, she advanced toward him, amused to see him retreat a step. "Do not worry. I will protect you, I will vouch for your behaving like the perfect gentleman—despite my wishing otherwise."

"Emily," he said softly. He did not bark her name this time, and it sounded like a whispered caress on his lips.

Delighted, she paused but inches from him, so close she could see the rise and fall of his chest, hear his shallow breathing. He was not immune to her. It was further progress, but more important, he could not retreat further—or he would land in the fire. She smiled. She had him just where she wanted him.

Trapped.

Now she needed him to surrender. "But it does beg one more question," she said softly.

He swallowed. "Oh? What is that?" His voice sounded as if it were scraped over sandpaper.

"If we are already in deep trouble, what harm can come from stealing a few moments together? A fleeting interlude of pleasure?"

His eyes fell to her mouth.

"You forget, I was engaged. I am not a young girl or an innocent. I am very, very mature," she practically purred the words in her most seductive murmur.

He laughed uneasily. "Ah, that has not escaped my notice."

She smiled. "Good. I like an observant man." Unable to resist, she swept her finger down the strong column of his bare throat, watching his Adam's apple bob as he swallowed. "So I promise you, I know exactly what I want and how I want it." She grasped his open shirt, ignoring his fingers that closed over her wrists. He blinked at her, looking a little dazed.

Emboldened, she stood on her toes and leaned close, dropping her voice to a breathless whisper. "You are a smart man, so listen carefully. If you are so convinced that my father will kill you, it might be in your best interest to grasp whatever pleasure you can before he does so. A man deserves to live life to the fullest, to—"

"Hell. I give up," he growled and yanked her to him, his breath warm against her lips. "I am an idiot."

"You are," she whispered. "But I will give you a chance to redeem yourself."

His laugh was low and sultry, pouring through her body in a delicious wave. Then his mouth was on hers, hot, demanding, and kissing her senseless. Every thought drained from her head, replaced with a flood of desire and need.

With a moan, she arched, vised her arms around his neck, and kissed him back. Giddy in her success, she reveled in his surrender. More so, she relished the hard strength of his body against hers, the wet and warm softness of his mouth, and the scorching heat of his kiss. She parried her tongue with his, wanting more. Wanting him. She caught his lower lip in her mouth and nibbled.

A deep, masculine groan rumbled out, and then his arm lowered to slip beneath her knees. She was swept off her feet and into his arms.

A laugh escaped her as he tossed her onto the bed, but then her amusement fled when he whipped off his shirt. She caught her breath. The flickering light of the fire danced over his body, and she drank in the hard contours of his chest, his taut waist, the lean, strong muscles of his abdomen. He was masculine beauty personified. She sighed.

But while he carried his own weapons, she had come

armed as well. She sat up and with a languid shrug of her shoulders, she let her wrap slide down her arms.

His eyes flared and his lips parted as his gaze roved over her gossamer night rail.

The groan of pleasure escaping him ignited a slow, burning fire in her body. Heat slid down the column of her neck and over the curve of her breasts bared above her plunging décolletage. The gown was from her trousseau, and she was glad she had worn it. After all, it was bought for this purpose . . . to drive a man mad.

"Christ, Emily. You are killing me." He lifted a knee and climbed onto the bed, a sleek, well-toned cat stalking her. He dropped his body into the welcoming cradle of her arms. "But you are worth dying for."

"You are not dying." She wiggled her hips against his, feeling the heat of his arousal. "On the contrary, you are very much alive."

He grunted and then lowered his head, his tongue moving over the swell of her breasts. She threaded her fingers through his hair and opened herself up to the passion he unleashed in her. But the intimate touch of his mouth on her burning skin had her yearning for more. She freed her arms from her sleeves and shoved her gown down to her waist.

There was a sharp intake of breath before his hands moved to her breasts, caressing and molding, his lips following. With a gasp, she arched against him, digging her fingers into his shoulders. His skin was hot and sweat slicked against hers. She moved her hands over the planes of his back.

She had waited so long for this. The smoldering rush of heat. Of need. She had been so alone, but had never been lonely until Brett had stumbled into her life and stirred up these forgotten yearnings. Cravings for the simple comfort of being held. Being touched. Memories of intimacy and passion resurfaced. Her heart might have been broken, but the rest of her body remained whole, responsive, and very much alive.

She lifted her leg and planted her foot against the edge of his bedside table, his hard arousal settling intimately against the juncture of her legs where moisture pooled. When his mouth closed over a nipple, she couldn't suppress the cry that sprang to her lips. Good lord, the man was good with his mouth—or his mouth was good on her. She dug her fingers into his shoulders, and clutched him close.

She braced one foot against the bed, and the other on the table, and arched. The table moved, teetering and then tipping over with a resounding crash. The unmistakable sound of glass shattering shortly followed.

Brett jerked back.

She stared blankly at the empty space where the bedside table had stood.

Brett surveyed the debris on the floor. "I hope that vase was not a family heirloom."

Grunting, she ignored his jest and scrambled to the edge of the bed beside him. Broken shards of china, the remnants of a white vase and a mug, lay in pieces over the floor. A pool of water was edging its way toward the oriental carpet.

"Looks like there were some casualties in our battle. Perhaps we should retreat for the evening. Things are getting dangerous," he quipped. He stood and snatched a towel from a nearby rack, using it to sop up the water.

Emily couldn't help it; she buried her face in the bedding to suppress her laughter. When she lifted her head, she found Brett standing with his hands planted on his hips, a grin curving his lips.

"I take it that is a *no*, it was not a family heirloom?"

"No, it is but a small sacrifice," she said and shrugged a bare shoulder. "I was distracted by the spoils of war. I will be more careful next time."

He laughed and tossed the wet towel at her. "You are shameless."

She grabbed the cloth and launched it back at him. He caught it against his chest and smiled. She returned his smile, but when his eyes met hers, dark and dangerous, her smile wavered. Something lurched in her chest, and she swallowed. Good lord, he was beautiful. She couldn't move. Couldn't breathe.

The sound of someone knocking on the door shattered the spell and she gasped. Quickly scrambling to her feet, she yanked up her gown and snatched her robe to her. She turned to see Brett frantically tugging his shirt over his head.

"In a minute," he bellowed from behind its folds. "The wardrobe," he hissed. He grabbed her arm and whipped open the door to the large cabinet. Shirts and jackets were shoved aside as he hefted her inside the cleared space. "Quiet," he warned before slamming the door in her face.

The pitch-black darkness silenced her protests at his dictatorial manner, and she clamped her mouth closed. Once her eyes adjusted, she caught a shadow of white and fingered the sleeve of one of Brett's linen dress shirts. As if against her will, she brought it to her nose, inhaling deeply. It smelled of starch and soap. Appalled, she shoved it away. She was acting like a love-struck fool, and that she was not.

Tonight was about desire, passion. Sex. Satisfying a need. Nothing more.

She heard the low murmur of voices, and unable to resist, she pried open the door a crack.

"But however did you knock the table over?"

Miranda.

"A restless dream," Brett said, and continued when Miranda made no response. "Ah . . . I was fighting a losing battle. There were casualties."

Emily slapped her hand to her mouth to stifle her snicker.

"Are you worried over Drew? Have you learned anything? He will return, won't he? He does not believe Aunt Beverly's horrid accusations that he is unfit to assume the title? That he is incapable of learning—"

"No, of course not. He will return. I am certain of it. Not for Aunt Beverly's sake, but for Olivia and Elise's. He will never abandon his sisters. Now stop worrying, and go back to bed. All is well here."

She nodded. "Are you sure you were not worried over our spending all our allowance?"

He laughed. "That was last night's nightmare. But, Miranda, your money, your responsibility. Spend it wisely."

"Yes, but spending it frivolously is much more fun!"

"And my nightmare continues," he muttered. "Good night, Miranda."

Miranda's soft laugh carried to Emily, and she waited a minute before moving.

"She has gone, and you need to leave as well. Now."

She shoved the wardrobe door open and slipped out. He was right. They risked discovery should they continue their *battle*. She wanted to ask about his cousin and his aunt's aspersions, but that would have to wait for another day. She crossed to where he stood near the door and paused before him. "A kiss good night?"

"Hell." He stared at her, then snatched her against him, giving her a hard, scorching, and quite thorough kiss.

When he set her from him, she was weak-kneed and blurry-eyed.

He opened the door, ensured the corridor was empty, and then shoved her unceremoniously into it. "Good night." He winked before firmly closing the door.

She grinned when the lock clicked in the latch. He did not trust her, but she had breached his defenses and felt confident she could do so again.

Brett was right again. It *was* a good night. But for the first time in years, she looked forward to tomorrow.

Chapter Fourteen

❧

A WEEK had passed since Brett had surrendered to Emily. There had been a few stolen kisses since then, but a crisis at his company had kept Brett working to all hours. The forced separation gave him time to come to his senses. The problem was, he was not ready for either common sense or self-preservation to prevail, particularly when images of Emily stole into his dreams at night.

He recalled the passionate abandon of her response, the feel of her in his arms, her lips warm and locked with his. Each night, he had awoken tangled in his sheets, a sheen of sweat filming his body, his loins aching. No, he was not ready to abandon the reckless path on which he was treading. Not if it meant giving Emily up. After all, she was right. A man deserved to live before he died. And Brett was going to die. If her father did not kill him, Daniel would.

He confronted his friend's sharp, green-eyed scrutiny from across the table at White's and cursed himself for being too late to intercept his letter inviting Daniel and Julia to

London. Their arrival yesterday further complicated any clandestine trysts with Emily.

Brett sipped his whiskey and pointedly ignored Daniel. The man did not know a bloody thing, and Brett had no plans to enlighten him.

"You look guilty as hell. Who is she?"

Brett sputtered, nearly choking midswallow. He coughed and straightened in his seat. "I do not know what you are talking about. My hands and my time are tied up with my sisters and . . . and . . . Lady Emily," he stuttered, cursing his trip over her name. "Even I, with my considerable gifts of persuasive charm"—he ignored Daniel's snort—"cannot juggle more than three women at a time, regardless of the activity."

Daniel waved away his protest. "No. There is something. You could never carry off a bluff. It is why I trump you at cards. You get edgy, shift in your seat, and avoid eye contact—exactly as you are doing now. It is a telltale sign that you are hiding something."

"You beat me at cards because Robert Shaw is a wily cardsharp who taught you all his tricks. You never should have—"

"Now you are hiding something *and* prevaricating. What is your interest in Lord Roberts? Why did you ask about him? Is he interested in investing in Curtis Shipping?" His eyes widened. "Christ, the East India Company is trying to buy us out." His voice rose, and he slammed his glass on the table. "Do not dare consider—"

"They are not moving to buy us out! I asked because a friend mentioned that Roberts was responsible for recruiting Emily's fiancé to work for the company, and I—"

"I was right!" Daniel cried. "There is a woman." He studied Brett with that narrow-eyed scrutiny.

"What are you talking about?"

"Emily, not *Lady* Emily, but Emily. So I take it that you no longer want her lovely neck in a noose?"

Brett made to shift in his seat, and then froze, cursing Daniel for reading him so well. The man was like a hound on a scent, and Brett had no intention of being sniffed until Daniel extracted the truth. He did what he had learned made Daniel and his sisters stop hammering at him. He confessed—minus a few details.

"After all *Lady* Emily has done for my sisters, it would be my neck in the noose, feet dangling, should I not behave myself around her. I am grateful to her for squiring Melody and Miranda around town. I am also quite capable of exhibiting a modicum of civility, even when the woman is just as capable of driving me mad." In the bedroom and out of it.

Daniel simply laughed. "It is a God-given gift those Chandler sisters have. Take it from me, smile, nod, and do not fight them. I will admit, I was surprised Emily extended the invitation to you when she made a point to disappear when you visited, or to ascertain your departure date when she could not avoid you. Then when in your company, the two of you always sparred."

Brett kept his expression neutral, but at the mention of sparring, heat crept up his neck. He and Emily were still sparring. It worked for them. Very well—a detail best kept to himself—along with his assistance in a murder investigation. Definitely under the "detail to omit" column. He cleared his throat. "Perhaps seeing me with my sisters made her reassess her opinion of me. After all, they love me."

"No. That is not it," Daniel said. "Emily is not swayed by others' opinions, particularly biased ones. She makes up her own mind."

Annoyed, Brett shrugged. "As they say, it is a woman's privilege to change her mind. After spending more time in my company these last few weeks, Lady Emily appears to have changed hers. It was inevitable." He smiled, having moved to familiar ground. "After all, I have a way with women, I have three sisters and—"

"Please, spare me," Daniel warned and then sighed. "I had hopes for Emily. She seemed such a bright, young woman."

"Oh, Lady Emily is a clever woman, of that, there is no doubt." She had roped him into dancing attendance on her like a bloody marionette doll—again, in bed and out. He took a sip of whiskey before he said anything damning.

"Then I trust her to take care of herself. As for your inquiry about Roberts, I was not aware he was responsible for recruiting Viscount Weston, but Roberts is one of the ministers loyal to the crown who sit on the Board of Control. Pitt created the board to oversee the East India Company and its directors, and to give the government greater control to regulate the corruption riddling the company. To do so, the ministers recruited upstanding young men from public schools, even some of rank, to work in the company, hoping to redeem its reputation." Daniel's eloquent grunt revealed his opinion of the futility of that venture.

"But if Jason was engaged to be married, why would he accept a position that would send him to another continent?"

"I believe the plan was for Jason to get settled over there, and Emily would follow later. Jason always yearned to travel to India. His father had been a clerk in the company. He had taken the post because he was the second son and did not expect to inherit the viscounty, but did so later in his life due to his elder brother's death. Most Englishmen who worked for the company and held stock in it made fortunes over there and returned home to flaunt it. Regular *nabobs*."

"*Nabobs*?"

Daniel smiled. "The English's pronunciation for a Mogul leader."

Emily had neglected to mention that Jason's father had worked for the company. It could explain why the details of Jason's death had been kept quiet. If it was in deference to his late father, a former company man, that made the company's hushing it up admirable rather than suspicious. He puzzled over it, finding the empathy to be at odds with the company's more unscrupulous practices. "How long was Jason over there?"

"Not long. He sailed March 1818 and died in December of that year, suffered a fever of some sort. There are frequent outbreaks of cholera, and many officers have died over there. It is not a soft posting."

And some were murdered in others' pursuit of a fortune. Brett clenched his jaw.

"Emily discussed Jason's work with you?" Daniel's gaze narrowed on Brett.

Once again, his friend appeared to be on the scent of something. "I might have asked about his time there, or Miranda and Melody expressed an interest," he glibly lied, keeping his gaze level with Daniel's and nary one shift in his seat.

Daniel nodded. "I ask because as I have warned you before, Emily does not usually discuss that period in her life, so tread carefully down that path. If Emily is upset, Julia will have my head and if Julia has my head, then—"

"Yes, yes, my own is forfeit. Tell me about the period following Jason's death. As you have said, it was difficult. I know from Emily and you, that with a few exceptions, she has been on a self-imposed country hiatus for the last three years or so. Her friends and acquaintances appeared surprised, albeit pleased, at her return. I was wondering why her reentry in society took so long."

He recalled Emily's words, *You can never fully return to who you once were.* He was curious about who she had been before tragedy had transformed her into the determined, single-minded woman whom he knew now. He wanted to know the young girl she had been, and perhaps better understand this beautiful, complex woman.

It was Daniel's turn to look uncomfortable. "When I returned from America, it was two years after Jason's death. I do not know—"

"Now you are prevaricating."

"It is not my story to tell."

"I understand, but I will not betray your confidence. You do not need to give me all the details, just those you are willing to share. I have come to consider Lady Emily a friend, and I simply wish to better understand her."

Daniel stared at Brett for a drawn-out moment before arriving at his decision. "Emily was very young when she and Jason met. Her mother had died the year before her debut, and she became engaged during her first Season. I think she was seventeen. Julia said Emily and Jason were inseparable once they were betrothed, quite besotted with each other. First love and all that.

"So it was hard enough for Emily when Jason accepted the post, but she knew what it meant to him, and hoped to sail over and join him. When she received word of his death, Julia said it was as if Emily had died with him, as if a light in her had gone out. She became but an empty shell of her former self. Julia feared Emily would never emerge from her grief." Daniel paused to sip his drink. "Julia took her to the Lake District to separate her from memories of Jason, as well as to squash the whispers that were beginning to circulate. It was the best thing to do. With time and Julia's care, Emily made her way back."

Not all the way back. *I am not looking for marriage. Have no plans to enter that contract. The last one nearly killed me. I . . . I will not go back.*

Suddenly, Brett understood Emily's proposition more fully. She had not lowered all her defenses; a fortress still encased her heart—and it was securely locked, the key destroyed. She was willing to indulge her passion, to flirt with desire, and to fill the emptiness of Jason's loss, but she refused to open herself to love again.

Well, they made a pair.

"Now that you understand how far Emily has come, I suggest you stop poking at her unless your intentions are serious."

"I understand."

"I am serious, Brett." Daniel gave him a hard look.

Brett nodded. "So am I. I have come to care for her, too. Very much."

He did not need Daniel to tell him that he and Emily were playing a dangerous game. Hell, he already knew that. But he understood Emily, something Daniel could not do, secure in his marital bliss. This arrangement worked for him and Emily. They might have to proceed cautiously, but Emily was worth the risk.

They both were getting exactly what they wanted, nothing more.

⇒⇐

EMILY GAZED INTO her nephew's face, mesmerized when Colin's tiny hand curled around her finger, clutching it so tightly, so trustingly. Pity that trust given so freely in the young had to be earned as they matured.

She glanced up to see Julia smiling at her, her daughter, Emma, in her arms. They were waiting for Melody and Miranda to change before they departed for an afternoon concert. "How long are you in the city?" Emily asked, keeping her voice neutral, despite being desperate to know.

"A few weeks. We need to visit the town house and ensure the work is progressing on schedule. And of course, I wanted to see you. See how you fared."

When in town, Daniel and Julia usually resided at Daniel's town house, but its rooms were undergoing renovations. Daniel's late brother's taste ran to the ostentatious. Julia, like most wives, had decided it was time to put her own stamp on the town house.

Julia and Daniel were settled in Julia's former room at Keaton House, which was across the corridor from Emily's bedchamber. The proximity to her sister's keen-eyed scrutiny put a damper on Emily's investigation, not to mention curtailed any assignations with Brett. If cognizant of either activity, her sister would urge her to abandon both courses. And that she would not do. Frowning, she hoped that when everything came to light, Julia would understand—at least about the investigation.

She jumped at the touch on her shoulder. Lifting her eyes, she found Julia had moved beside her, her gaze one of concern.

"We do not have to go out if you do not wish to do so. I am content to stay in and play cards here."

She blinked, recalling the many invitations Julia had declined or outings she had forgone to keep Emily company at home. Guilt pricked her. "No, it is all right. I promise you,

I would not have returned if I was not ready." It was the truth.

The nerves were still there upon first arriving at an event, but the urge to flee had disappeared. Melody and Miranda's company helped to distract her. Then there was Brett. He was never too far, teasing his sisters or ready with a witty quip. There were moments that she worried he saw her fear, that he had discerned there was more to her unease in society, but he could not. She had buried her deepest secret very deep. And if one kept up appearances, others rarely dug further.

"And lest you forget, this is not my first time in town," Emily continued. "Admittedly, I did not go out much, but coming here was the first step. Accepting invitations was the last one, so now my recovery is complete. You need to stop worrying about me, Julia. You have your own family now, and I am quite all right."

"You are my family, too," Julia said softly. "I so wanted to come with you when you first left for town, but we had too many dratted guests staying with us after the christening. I got rid of them as fast as I could."

"How rude of friends and relatives to overstay their welcome, wishing to linger and celebrate your happiness."

Julia smiled. "Exactly. Quite unpardonable. I am glad that Brett wrote to say that all was going well, and suggested we come to town. I was biting at the bit to do so for your sake, and thankfully, Daniel wants to vote on this upcoming agriculture bill."

Emily froze, heard no further than Brett had invited them to town.

Why had he extended the invitation? And without mentioning it to her?

He must know it would hinder their plans. She pursed her lips. Just when she thought they were fighting the same battle, or at the very least moving in the same direction, the man does an about-face. She did not like him going behind her back. It made her wonder—what else had he kept from her?

"Emily? What is it? You look upset."

She shook her head. "It is nothing. Nothing at all. I was surprised. Brett did not mention that he wrote to you."

"Oh? And you and *Mr. Curtis*, *Brett* that is, are now on civil speaking terms?" Julia appeared amused—and intrigued.

Heat crept up her cheeks. "*Mr. Curtis* has been behaving himself, so we have been able to converse with civility. For his sisters' sake, that is, and of course, they provide us with a buffer."

"Of course," Julia said. "I am glad. For his sisters' sake, that is."

She caught the teasing gleam in her sister's eyes, and bristled. "It would be difficult to chaperone his sisters if we continued to be at odds with each other."

"I do not disagree," Julia said, obviously struggling to suppress her laughter. "So he no longer wishes to decapitate you? And you no longer wish for one of his ships to go down with him on it?"

She had forgotten that she had confided to her sister her irritation with Brett. "We have made amends. In fact, we have laid down our weapons and have a temporary truce."

Julia studied her, and Emily cursed the heat burning her cheeks. She should not have mentioned weapons and truce. Like a spark, it ignited a burst of intimate battle images. She resisted the urge to fan her cheeks.

"I am glad to hear that. I like Brett Curtis very much, and I always hoped you two would set aside your differences." Julia appeared to hesitate a moment, before continuing. "Was there any other young man of interest at the balls you attended? Anyone else worth mentioning?"

What on earth? Something in her sister's searching look gave her pause. As if she dangled a hook, Julia was clearly fishing for something. Emily had been in town but a fortnight; were there already whispers circulating about her? And worse, *Brett*? "No, absolutely not. Really Julia, at three-and-twenty, I am no longer a debutante with a line of beaus clamoring for my hand."

"Emily, my love, you forget the mercenary working of our

aristocratic marriage market. You may no longer be a debutante, but you are the daughter of an earl, an heiress in your own right, and beautiful—whether or not you choose to acknowledge it. Those are coveted assets. Many a gentleman will ignore your being in your *dotage*"—she rolled her eyes—"if it means gaining access to your inheritance."

Emily grimaced. "I understand, but I have no intention of letting a fortune hunter, nor any other man, ensnare me. I promise you, that should be the least of your concerns." She gentled her tone. "Julia, please, you need to stop worrying about me. I may not be on the shelf, but nor am I a naïve, innocent girl."

"Yes, well, it is an older sister's prerogative to worry over a younger one, so you cannot argue me out of it."

"Fair enough. Then your questions about gentlemen I have met are out of sisterly concern? You have not heard anything? It is your turn to alleviate my worries."

"No, of course not." Julia paused, and then sighed. "That is not completely true. Tristan's sister stopped by Bedford Hall. She said that you had visited recently, and she was sorry to have missed you, so was delighted to have received your letter."

"Yes, well, I was sorry to have missed her as well."

"Patricia mentioned that Lawrence Drummond had visited her and Tristan but a week after you left for London."

"Mr. Drummond?" she echoed, wary of Drummond paying a visit to the Bransons so soon after hers. Emily did not believe in coincidences.

"Do you remember him? He was posted with Jason in India. Very personable young man."

"Yes, I am familiar with him." She struggled to keep her expression neutral, while her pulse raced.

"Apparently he asked of you."

"Of me?" Emily said, not pleased to hear that.

Julia laughed. "Yes, you. He told Patricia that he was heading to London, and he had hopes of seeing you here. He asked if she knew of your plans. Patricia was under the impression that the man is carrying a tendre for you." Julia's eyes danced with teasing lights. "Patricia is a friend of Drummond's younger sister, Clarise, and I think Clarise confided her brother's feelings to Patricia. Do you know Clarise? She had her debut at the beginning of the Season. The Earl of Dayton hosted a lavish ball. Drummond's mother is—"

"A distant cousin of the earl's," Emily finished. "I did see Mr. Drummond briefly at another ball the earl held, but I did not have a chance to speak with him." She had no choice in that incident, but Brett's rebuff of Drummond was not the first, and her own rejection of his overtures had been quite firm.

So why was the man persisting? Unless . . . Did he have something to confide in regard to Jason's death or had he changed his mind about assisting her? Perhaps her query had him intrigued enough to study anew the business papers that he had.

Her questions convinced her that she would have to speak to him, which might prove difficult. With Brett intent on tossing Drummond into Newgate, she doubted Brett would give the man a fair hearing, and she did not dare meet him alone. She had given Brett her word, and the memory of her ill-fated meeting with Drummond precluded that option.

"Patricia said Clarise sang her brother's praises," Julia continued. "Apparently, their father died years ago, so Drummond is head of the family now. He allowed his sister to buy her gowns for her debut at Madame Duchard's, not that I countenance such extravagant indulgence. That is right, Emma, no spoiling for you. That is, if I can rein in your father, which is proving problematic."

"I am sure Mr. Drummond and I will cross paths again," Emily said. She would be sure to keep an eye out for him. There must be a way to speak to him without Brett murdering him.

"Yes, and as I said, he is a very nice young man," Julia pressed, her eyes gleaming.

Emily held up her hands. "I cannot stop you from worrying, but please, no matchmaking. *That* I will handle on my own."

Julia sighed. "Emma will allow me to pick out her husband. You will listen to your mother, won't you, my love?

Mmh, she has nodded off. That does not bode well for future mother-daughter discussions."

Emily's smile faded seeing her sister's features soften as she smiled at her daughter, her face transformed into a portrait of maternal serenity. Something twisted in Emily's heart. In forgoing marriage, she had lost so much more.

Her chest tightened. She would never cradle her own child in her arms or experience the protective tug of motherhood. Once upon a time, to see Jason's blue eyes reflected in their child's gaze was all she had coveted. But it was not to be.

Despite the pain of it, seeing this beautiful, innocent child reaffirmed her conviction.

She refused to pass on the darkness within her—as her father had passed it on to her. It was carried in their blood, nearly destroying her father after her mother's death, and then Emily when she had lost Jason. Julia was strong, but Emily could not guarantee that her own child would be so, because Emily had been strong, too—until tragedy broke her. No child should have to fight their way back from . . . *madness*.

She swallowed back her pain. She had made her decision and did not regret it. What she had with Brett, the give-and-take of passion and pleasure, was all she had to offer. She just hoped Brett had not changed his mind, considering the invitation he had sent to Daniel and Julia behind her back.

If he had, well then, she would have to change it back. Better yet, seduce him again. She looked forward to the challenge.

Chapter Fifteen

❧

Emily smiled at Melody, who glided across the dance floor. They had all left town and journeyed to Hertfordshire to attend a house party at Lord Sutton's. As he was a mere baron, his estate did not boast the grandeur of the Earl of Dayton's town house, but being a jovial and popular member of the ton, invitations to his parties were coveted.

"Is that her second dance with the *same* partner?" Brett grumbled from beside her.

"It is not," Miranda said with strained patience. "For goodness' sake, he is fair-haired and her last partner had black hair. All gentlemen look alike to you."

Brett grunted. "How the devil am I to notice hair color, when all I see is the wolf in black evening attire? This one is drooling. I should intercede."

"Don't you dare," Emily said quickly before he could move. "Melody is capable of handling herself. Let us just hope she does not break another fan in doing so." Worry laced her tone.

"How many fans has she broken on you, Brett?" Daniel said, amused.

"I do not keep count."

"Up to a full score," Miranda supplied, and shook her head at Daniel who arched a brow, a challenging glint in his eyes. "Absolutely not," she said shaking her head and struggling to suppress her laughter. "You cannot talk me into placing another wager on Melody breaking one more fan. I can no longer afford to place losing bets."

Daniel smiled. "Wise decision."

"The dance is over," Brett said. "Her partner is smiling, and I see fangs. I need to remind him that refreshments have been provided, but Melody is not one of them."

Miranda caught Brett's arm. "Stay. Do not move. Bedford and I will intercede and switch partners. You and your black scowl are to remain here."

Daniel bowed to Julia, his expression solemn. "I am off to rescue a fair damsel from a predator. Pray for me."

"How brave you are," Julia said solemnly but her lips twitched. "Try to refrain from shedding blood."

"I will do my best." Daniel winked at a snarling Brett before following Miranda.

"*Stay? Do not move? Remain here*? Does she think I am a dog to obey her bidding?" Brett muttered.

Julia laughed and turned away to respond to a question from a young woman on her other side.

"She would be foolish to think that," Emily said, "because you do not follow anyone's bidding but your own."

Brett turned on her. "What the devil are you talking about? I have traveled to this infernal house party, clearing my schedule for three days, all at your insistence that my sisters would enjoy it, but more important, that Jason's sister planned to meet you here. Once you retrieve the portfolio from her, feign an illness so we can escape early."

"Stop whining. There will be no early escapes. Many of the exalted guests here, whom you like to dismiss and disdain, are investors in Curtis Shipping. Far be it from you to condescend to socialize with them once in a while."

Brett opened his mouth to protest and then snapped it closed, for once having no ready retort. After a moment, he grumbled, "I do not whine, and the dismissing and disdaining is mutual."

"I understand. On another matter, you neglected to mention that you wrote to Daniel and Julia, inviting them to town. Did you not stop to think how that might complicate things? I would have appreciated your discussing the matter with me before making a decision that impacts my plans." She lifted her chin and dared him to refute her.

He studied her expression, and he appeared to move from irritated to amused. "Truth be told, I tried to retrieve my invitation, but was too late. As for complicating matters, I believe we passed complicated when you visited my bedchamber—"

"Keep your voice down!" she hissed. Mortified, she cast a furtive look around, heat suffusing her cheeks.

"As I said, we have sailed beyond complicated and are now heading into dangerous waters." His eyes dropped to her lips and his husky tone sent shivers down her spine as he leaned toward her. "But I must have a penchant for danger, because I—"

"Did I overhear someone mention danger?"

At Julia's interruption, Brett straightened abruptly.

Emily lifted her fan to cool her cheeks. He was right. Ignoring their audience veered too close to dangerous for her peace of mind.

Oblivious to their reactions, Julia's attention remained fixed on the dance floor. "I see Daniel and Miranda, but Melody and her partner have disappeared. Perhaps it is harmless, but—"

"I will find her," Brett spoke through clenched teeth. "If you ladies will excuse me." He gave a stiff bow before striding off.

Emily could not resist following his tall figure as he wended his way through the crowds. She was not the only woman whose attention he held. Heads turned, feminine gazes roving over his body with an almost predatory gleam in their eyes. Brett was right. There *were* wolves out there—and some of them were female. She fought the urge to snap their mouths closed. Ridiculous. She held no claim on the man.

"I lied. Melody is quite safe. She is heading over to the refreshment table with Miranda and Daniel," Julia said, flashing an unrepentant grin. "But I needed for Brett to leave because I have news."

Surprised, Emily turned to Julia, noting the excitement brimming in her eyes. "Oh? What is it?"

"Mr. Drummond is here."

"Drummond?" Emily echoed, her heart pounding. She glanced around, but could not locate him in the sea of black and white jackets flooding the floor.

"If Patricia is to be believed and he has feelings for you, I am sure he will find you. If you wish to speak to him, I thought it best to do so without Brett and Daniel hovering."

No, that would not do. Brett would not be pleased, but not for the reasons Julia surmised. Guilt stabbed Emily as she met her sister's eager gaze. "Yes, that . . . is most helpful. Thank you." She had promised Brett she would do nothing without him, but she did not have the heart to put a damper on Julia's excitement. Should they encounter Drummond, Emily doubted he would share confidences in a public venue with Julia as chaperone. Thus if nothing transpired, she kept her word to Brett.

"We should stroll the perimeter of the room to be sure to be seen."

Julia was clearly enjoying herself, no doubt, pleased to see Emily express an interest in any man, whatever her reasons. Pity her sister had the wrong man. Emily's guilt deepened, but she gamely lifted her chin and looped her arm through Julia's.

They nodded to acquaintances, pausing to chat with those who offered Julia congratulations on the birth of the twins. As friends swarmed them, Emily released Julia's arm, no longer needing her support. During her rare appearance in society, Julia's arm had provided a lifeline she had clung to as Julia cleaved a path through the crowds, like a ship's masthead breaching stormy waters.

It helped that the murmurs carrying Emily's name had tapered off to near silence. From the comments she had overheard, the ton had moved on to a more scintillating absence than her own—such as the mysterious disappearance of a higher ranking personage than she. Her ears perked up as she overheard another mention of Brett's cousin.

"No, I have not seen Prescott since he came into the title," a gentleman drawled. "Probably busy running the estate into the ground. Flunked out of a string of schools, you know. Gordon said his brother was practically illiterate, had little use for him."

His companion snorted. "Gordon was a colossal arse. Do not believe half the rot he uttered. Loaned the bastard blunt to cover a substantial wager, and he never repaid a farthing of it. Even if Prescott is a mutton-headed half-wit, he is a better sort than his brother."

Their voices faded as they drifted away. Her eyes widened. *Illiterate*? Could that be why Brett was so determined to locate his cousin?

She recalled Melody mentioning Prescott flunking out of a few schools before landing at Dunbar with Brett and Daniel. Was Brett concerned about Prescott's competence to manage the ducal estates? Then again, as the gentleman had said, these could simply be rumors that Prescott's late brother had circulated. Acrimony between brothers was not uncommon. And lord knows, she had learned the damage that unchecked rumors could inflict.

"Emily, you remember Mr. Drummond, do you not?"

Julia's introduction broke through her train of thought. "Of course. Mr. Drummond. It is a pleasure." She dipped into a curtsy, noting his flamboyant attire.

Only a liberal application of hair wax could have achieved

the wild and unruly look of his fine auburn hair. She doubted Brett's thick golden locks needed assistance in achieving the casually disheveled style that was the men's fashion of the day. No doubt, Brett simply did not bother to brush it. Women studied Drummond with interest, but unlike Brett, she surmised that to be Drummond's intent.

He executed a deep bow, and as he straightened, his golden eyes glowed warmly. "The pleasure is always mine. Your beauty steals my breath. This evening my pleasure is twofold, for the Chandler sisters, like the most stunning gems, enhance every setting they deign to grace."

Emily bit down a madcap urge to sputter out a laugh, and quickly waved her fan in front of her face. She had forgotten the ritual of flattery and flirtation. It had been so long since Jason had showered her with compliments, and Brett was more frugal with his.

She pondered that. Did Brett not find that she enhanced a setting like the most stunning gems? *Obdurate* and *determined* appeared to be his adjectives of choice for her. She frowned. Perhaps Americans courted differently—not that they were courting. Far from it. They were . . . she did not know what they were, and certainly did not have time to ponder the matter at present.

"How you flatter, Mr. Drummond. You are too kind." Julia ostensibly fanned herself, while from behind it, she flashed Emily a *behave yourself* glower. Drat Julia's acute hearing. Emily's snicker must have escaped her before she fully stifled it.

"As I have told Emily, that is candor, not flattery." Drummond grinned. "Now then, the evening is a temperate one, and they have opened the doors to the terrace. May I escort you ladies outside? I see you fanning yourselves, and concede it is rather warm in here."

"That sounds lovely. Would you care to take a turn outside?" Julia sent a pointed, *will you say something* look on Emily.

"Yes. Yes, a stroll. Lovely idea," she blurted inanely.

Drummond offered them each an arm, and as they moved toward the French doors, he asked about the twins.

Julia followed with an inquiry about Drummond's sister, easing them into the smooth rhythm of social discourse. "And Clarise, is she enjoying her Season thus far?"

"My sister would dance the night away if given the opportunity. Alas, it appears the gentlemen are delighted to assist her in achieving her goal. All well and good for Clarise, but you must understand, it is trying for a protective and doting older brother."

"Believe me, you would be finding her far more difficult if she were sitting out most of the dances," Julia pointed out. "Isn't that right, Emily?" Julia said as they stepped onto the terrace.

Drat and blast. She had lost track of the conversation. Something about dancing? "Yes, the nights pass much faster when one is dancing." Julia gave her an odd look, and Emily hastened to clarify her words. "That is, they can be far more enjoyable when one spends it on the dance floor with a handsome partner such as yourself, Mr. Drummond."

There. She could dredge up her flattery when forced.

"Thank you." Drummond dipped his head in acknowledgment of her compliment. "As for dancing, I hope I can claim one from you, Lady Emily. We were rudely interrupted the last time I asked."

She knew she shouldn't smile, but her lips curved. "Yes, well, ah . . . Mr. Curtis is American, so you have to excuse him. He is not as familiar with our rules of proper etiquette," she lied glibly.

As they headed toward the yard benches, Julia paused, forcing them to stop. "Oh, dear. I fear I have a pebble in my slipper. Please, do continue. I will catch up once I remedy the matter."

Caught off guard at Julia's subterfuge, Emily hastened to voice a protest. "No, really. I am happy to wait—"

"Come, Lady Emily, we are well chaperoned," Drummond said with an inviting smile, waving a hand to draw her

attention to the pockets of guests who had also ventured outside. "And I recalled some information on that topic you
brought up the last time we spoke, which would be of little
interest to your sister."

Emily's eyes widened. *Drat and blast. Now what?* She
resisted the urge to swipe clammy hands down her skirts.

"Go ahead," Julia prodded. "But I trust you not to venture
too far." She gave them a stern *chaperone-like* look.

"If you insist." Drummond bowed to Julia, and turned
to Emily. "I believe we have been summarily dismissed.
Shall we?"

She cursed Julia's sudden penchant for matchmaking,
because short of giving Drummond the cut direct, and then
later having to explain to Julia her reasons for doing so, Emily
was left with no choice. "We will not venture far. Just down
this path." She still had no intention of disappearing with the
man, and it was best to make that clear at the onset.

It was early evening, that indecipherable time of twilight
that defined the breach between daylight and darkness. Tall
lanterns were interspersed along paths leading into the gardens, like patient sentries poised to illuminate the paths
when the final light faded.

She fell into step beside Drummond, careful to keep a
safe distance between them. She did want to hear what he
had to impart, but refused to pay a price for it.

"The last two times we crossed paths, Mr. Curtis interrupted us. I am relieved to find you alone," Drummond said.
"I understand he is Bedford's former business partner and
godfather to his twins, but speaking as a friend who has borne
witness to his boorish behavior, not once, but twice, it might
be wise to limit your exposure to his sort. I only presume to
caution you because you have been absent from society for
some time. You forget that one is judged not only by their
character but by the company one keeps. I would hate for you
to be viewed poorly due to your naïveté," he finished, his tone
apologetic.

What a pompous arse.

Bristling, she opened her mouth to scathingly inform him that as an earl's daughter, she was well versed in knowing whose company to avoid, but then paused. If she wished him to speak openly with her, she should not begin their conversation with a chastisement. With difficulty, she bit back her retort. "I will keep that in mind."

As they continued, he offered up the usual platitudes on the balmy evening, following with tidbits on shared acquaintances. She listened with half an ear, hoping he broached the subject soon before her patience wore thin.

"I am glad we are alone because I have something important to discuss with you." He paused beside a marble statue of some Grecian robed personage, hands raised in a plaintive plea.

"And what is that?" She braced herself, wary of his seeking to rekindle the sentiments he had proclaimed in their last encounter. She glanced back to ensure Julia was within calling distance, and took another step back from Drummond.

"I paid a call on Viscount Weston and his lovely sister a couple of weeks ago, and he mentioned your visit."

"Yes, I saw the viscount and his mother just before I left for town."

"That is kind of you to stay on good terms with the family."

Why would I not? she wondered, but held her silence.

"The viscount mentioned some documents he had turned over to me. These papers belonged to Jason and concerned unfinished business matters from his time in Calcutta."

"Oh?" She kept a neutral tone, while silently cursing Tristan for blundering into areas she had asked him to stay out of. She had no patience for another of Drummond's lectures on keeping her pretty little head out of men's business matters.

"Those papers were placed in my care shortly after Jason's death, and over the years, Tristan has never mentioned them. You must understand that I found his interest, coming on the heels of your own inquiry about Jason's work, well, curious at the very least, but more so, alarming."

Her eyes widened, and she feigned surprise. "Do you think the viscount has come upon the same information that I did in rereading Jason's letters? Could he possibly—?"

"Certainly not!" Drummond snapped, but hastened to gentle his tone. "Lady Emily, the viscount did not discover discrepancies in accounts or any other evidence of malfeasance because he did not review the papers. He left that for me to do because I am familiar with Jason's work. Mind you, had the viscount studied the documents, he would not have found anything of interest because as I told you once before, there is nothing to discover."

She frowned. "Are you sure? Because in Jason's letters—"

"For God's sake, you cannot believe anything Jason wrote!"

Startled, she studied his flushed features, the barely controlled anger, and wondered at his words.

Drummond pressed a gloved hand to his brow. Lowering it, he paced away, but then turned back with a sigh. "You must understand, I had my reasons for trying to deter you from your course when you first approached me for assistance. I did not want to cause you pain, pain that I know what I am about to confide will inflict, but you leave me no choice."

A chill suffused her. "Please, if it involves Jason, whatever it entails, as his fiancée, I have a right to know."

"Jason was not himself toward the last few months of his life. I do not know if you know this, but his work for the East India Company involved overseeing the opium trade." He reiterated Caleb Little's explanations of Jason's work. "It is not uncommon for, well . . . It is a difficult posting in that infernal country, so it is not unusual for men so far from home and separated from friends, family, and those they love . . . to suffer loneliness. To alleviate their despair, some seek an escape, or rather, find solace elsewhere," he said softly.

She had to moisten her lips before she could speak, feeling the blood drain from her face. *This was Jason's friend.* "I do not understand. What are you saying?"

"Lady Emily, a lot of men posted over there sought their comfort through the oblivion provided in smoking opium. And for some unfortunates who partake, they become dependent upon the drug."

She fought to draw deep and steady breaths. She wrapped her arms around her waist and clung tight. If she did not, she would lunge at the lying, deceitful bastard and gouge his eyes out.

A noose was too good for this man. He deserved to be drawn and quartered. She swallowed the pain his words inflicted. "So like one addicted to laudanum, Jason was . . . delusional? Is that why I should not heed anything he wrote in his letters? Is that what you are saying?" she pressed.

Drummond held up his hands plaintively. "I am sorry. I did not want to tell you this, but I worry that you are digging into matters best left buried. Let us forget I said anything. Please, as your friend, allow me to leave you with the memory you have of Jason and not tarnish it with things we cannot change."

"I am trying to understand. Please, help me to do so. Laudanum is readily available here. People take it all the time. It is prescribed as a remedy for sniffles. I do not understand how—?"

"Laudanum is but a tincture of opium," he interrupted impatiently. "Opium in its purest form is far more dangerous. If consumed in large qualities, one sees things that are not there. Imagines things that are not real. Those who fall under its spell . . . well, it is not a pretty picture, so let us not finish drawing this out. Jason would not want you going down this path. Let him rest in peace."

He reached out to her, but she retreated, evading his treacherous touch. "Yes. I now understand why you did not want me to pursue my course."

Because it would implicate you.

Had Jason identified Drummond as the embezzler? It would explain why Marsh had said Jason's findings had disturbed him. To learn a trusted friend and colleague was the culprit would be upsetting indeed. It was easy to jump from lying bastard to embezzling thief—but from there to murderer?

She pressed her hand to her temple. Uncertainty and confusion battled within her, making it difficult to think clearly. Not with Drummond standing so close, hovering over her, feigning solicitous concern.

But she had one more question, and once they were answered, she would be quite finished with the man. "His clerk, Mr. Marsh, and his valet, Winfred, must have been aware of Jason's . . . ah, his affliction and chose to keep quiet. I suppose I should be grateful for that. It is a small comfort that his reputation was protected."

Drummond did not immediately respond, but something hard flared in his eyes.

"What? What is it?"

"Allow me to give you another warning. Stay away from Marsh. The man is no good." He paused, as if battling with himself how much to confide. "Just *who* do you think helped Jason to procure the opium? To prepare it? Helped to keep his secret?"

"Mr. Marsh?" She remembered the sadness, the pain, and the bitterness that darkened the frail man's eyes. Jason was not the only one deserving justice.

"Marsh," Drummond confirmed, spitting out the name as if it was toxic.

"And Winfred?"

Drummond waved a hand dismissively. "He always had his head buried in his books. Never understood why Jason taught that boy to read, because when he finally lifted his eyes to notice what was going on around him, it was too late."

"I see," she murmured. *Lies. Malicious, slanderous lies.* Winfred had been ready with a bandage before Jason cut himself. Yes, he loved his books, but he had cared for Jason more. His teaching Winfred to read had sealed the young man's devotion. She recalled the tears Winfred had manfully fought to stifle, and the agonizing grief they shared over the loss of a man they had both loved. "I understand." All too well.

"I hope you do. Lady Emily, I tell you these things because I am your friend. But . . ." He stepped closer to her, his eyes locked on hers.

She again retreated, wary of the warmth in his gaze.

"But you must know I continue to hope that someday, we can be something more to each other."

She nearly shuddered. "Please. I have explained to you—"

"Yes, you have. You loved Jason. But in light of what you have now learned, you must understand that the man I knew those final months was no longer the man you loved. He never should have left you. I would not have done so."

Good lord. The man was mad. There could never have been anything between them before. Now all she wanted from this man was his head in a noose.

She could not hang him for his slanderous words, but she would find the evidence to drag him before the magistrate on charges of embezzlement. And perhaps . . . just perhaps murder.

"Mr. Drummond, it is too soon. I have much to think about, and need the time to do so."

"Of course. Forgive me, but you must understand that I have waited a long time, and—"

"Patience is an admirable virtue, and I appreciate yours." She sounded like a veritable prig, but did not care. "Now we must find Julia and return," she said, raising her voice as she evoked her sister's name.

"Emily—"

"There you are. I was on my way to join you, when look who found me," Julia said, materializing before them as if she had been awaiting Emily's call, which thankfully, she had been.

· Emily followed her sister's gaze to the group standing behind her, and froze as her eyes locked on one man.

Brett.

She really needed to get him that damn warning bell.

When she met his eyes, they blazed with an icy blue rage, chilling her to the bone. She forgot her nerves and every thought in her head but one—she had made a grave mistake. She swallowed, fearing what price she would be paying for it.

Chapter Sixteen

❧❧

THEY had come full circle. Brett gritted his teeth to keep from lashing out at Emily as he fell into step beside her. Once the introductions were finished, Drummond had made his excuses and slithered away like the snake he was, but not before tossing Brett a triumphant look.

What the bloody hell had he meant by it?

Brett vowed to find out, even if he had to shake the information out of Emily. She *had promised* him. Had given her word that she would not investigate matters alone. That should include clandestine meetings with bastards like Drummond, a would-be embezzler, murderer, or just plain slithering snake. Something twisted in his gut. The betrayal was all too familiar.

Like a hapless fly stuck in a web, he wondered if he had once again become entangled with a woman he could not trust.

"Stop scowling. You will scare the ladies—not that you do not already do so," Melody grumbled. "I mean really, it was not like I had disappeared into the shrubbery with the man. We had gone for refreshments in full view—"

"Yes, Melody, so *you* have explained," Brett said with strained patience. "And *I* have explained, while I trust you, that does not mean I trust every gentleman here." He gave Emily a pointed look. "I warned you about the wolves. You cannot let fashionable dress and a posh accent deceive you."

Emily flushed and her jaw tightened, but she made no response.

Melody sputtered out a laugh. "Please. Lord Phillips is harmless," she quipped to Miranda beneath her breath, "but I wouldn't mind him nibbling on my . . . neck."

Brett whirled on Melody. "I heard that!"

"Oh, for goodness' sake. There is something sour in your punch. Perhaps you should try the champagne. I hear it does wonders in lightening one's mood."

"Leave him alone," Miranda said, intervening. "Abandoned to his own company, he will eventually annoy even himself. Maybe you can cheer him up, Lady Emily. Brett's mood always improves when conversing with a beautiful woman. At the very least, it will force him to be civil." Miranda ignored Brett's growl and caught Melody's arm to draw her ahead to join Julia and Daniel.

The silence stretched taut as he and Emily trailed the group, but Brett would be damned if he would break it. *She* owed *him* an explanation.

They approached the terrace where more couples had congregated outside to savor the balmy temperatures. Snippets of conversation and laughter drifted over them, while red-coated footmen balanced trays with tall, crystal flutes.

"Melody is right. Champagne is needed," Emily said and gestured to a footman.

"A drink will not improve my mood—"

"No? Well, perhaps it will soothe mine." She thanked the footman as she collected a brimming glass of champagne. "But I doubt it."

For the first time, he noted the pallor and the shadows

clouding her eyes. A slight tremor shook her hand, and she spilled some champagne before she steadied the glass and brought it to her lips. Whatever Drummond had confided, it had shaken her. Some of his anger shifted from Emily and onto the bastard.

He itched to curl his hands around the whoreson's slimy neck and squeeze.

Emily finished a sip, and met Brett's gaze. "I understand you are upset to find me with Drummond, but I encountered him with Julia, and I could not rudely dismiss him when he asked to have a word with me. Julia was nearby at all times and it was in a public venue. You must understand that after your behavior toward him at Lakeview Manor and again at Dayton's—"

"*My* behavior?" he scoffed. "You cannot be serious! You are taking me to task for *my* behavior? After the way that man was mauling—"

"Keep your voice down," she hissed in warning, casting a furtive look around.

He swore as he noted the curious glances directed their way. "Wait a few minutes and then follow me." Without obtaining her consent, he strode from the terrace. He took the steps to the lawns at a brisk pace, then turned down a path that led into a hedge maze adjacent to the main yard.

While not as elaborate as the maze at Hampton Court, it turned and twisted in an elaborate spiral. Luminous mythological statues carved out of white marble were placed in strategic pockets throughout the maze. Flickering torches interspersed in the yews helped to light the dirt paths as daylight waned.

During one of his school holidays, Brett had spent a drunken evening stumbling around the maze with Sutton's son, Daniel, and Drew. It gave him the advantage over other couples seeking a clandestine refuge within its natural walls. He knew the location of most of its secret haunts.

He stood just inside the entrance, waiting for Emily. When she entered the shadowy enclosure and cast a wary glance over her shoulder, he caught her arm. She swallowed her cry upon recognizing him, and did not resist his towing her along, moving quickly lest they be seen together. "It took you long enough," he muttered.

"Will you stop! I cannot just disappear. Julia would worry. I had to let her know my whereabouts. I told her I was going to view a new statue with you and Lady Eloise. But where, pray tell, *am* I going? Are you mad?" she hissed at his back.

"Undoubtedly." But one could not very well discuss murder and embezzlement amidst a prying audience.

It was a dangerous game they played, but hearing the giggles, rustles, and twitters emerging from the maze, they were not the only ones who dared to risk scandalous consequences. "Heed your own advice and keep your voice down." He neared a statue of a goddess in a flowing Grecian gown, wearing a formidable helmet and holding a staff. She reminded him of the heroic Athena, and he found it fitting that they seek refuge with her. He pulled Emily around the statue and into the intimate space carved out behind her. "Who is Lady Eloise?"

"The only woman nearby whom I recognized," she said impatiently as she eyed the area, and then arched a delicate brow. "This definitely crosses the boundaries of complicated and moves deep into dangerous."

He shrugged. "As I said, we did that when you visited my bedchamber. Then again when you ducked into the shrubbery with that—"

Emily tossed her champagne into his face. "You go too far!"

He snatched his handkerchief and furiously swiped at his face. Blinking, he caught a flash of lavender as Emily moved to sweep around him. He bit off a curse, grabbed her arm, and hauled her back. He crushed her close, cinching his arms around her slim waist. The impact of her soft body against his had every thought draining from his head—but one.

Her breath hitched and her eyes dropped to his lips, and then he closed his mouth over hers. The touch was like striking a match to tinder. The mixture of tension, rage, and frustration that had simmered within him burst into flames.

Her lips were velvet soft and melded to his. She tasted of champagne and Emily and he practically inhaled her. He took and took some more, desire coursing through him.

Her glass slipped from her hand and dropped unheeded to the ground as she curled her arms around his neck and arched her body into his. A moan escaped her, and she slid her fingers into his hair as her tongue parried with his.

He savored the feel of her breasts crushed to his chest, the warmth of her body seeping into his. Holding her settled his temper far better than the richest champagne. Their ragged breaths mingled as he kissed a pink cheek before returning to claim her mouth.

A distant cough snapped him back to his senses. Horrified, he released her and stepped away. Christ.

He may not trust her, but by God, he wanted her. His body cried out in protest, his loins aching. While he yearned to snatch her back into his arms, he refused to let desire lead him astray again. He shook his head to clear it of its lust-driven haze and, with unsteady hands, he returned his handkerchief to his jacket pocket.

Emily regarded him warily, her breathing ragged.

He straightened. "You gave me your word, and you broke it. How am I to trust you—?"

"*You* talk of trust? You wrote to Daniel and Julia behind my back. After I asked you to keep them out of things. How am *I* to trust *you*?"

"That is not the same thing! I told you, I made a mistake. I tried—"

"As did I . . . of sorts."

That gave him pause. Against his will, his lips twitched. "*Of sorts?*"

She tossed up her hands in exasperation. "As damning as it appears, I had no desire to speak with Drummond alone. But as I have explained, I could not very well refuse *his* request to speak to me—not without making explanations to Julia that I am not ready to make. And truthfully, he would not have spoken as freely as he did with your black scowl accompanying me. Lawrence Drummond thinks you are rude and boorish, and has warned me to avoid your company lest I be judged no better. In light of your recent behavior, he may be right."

"*My* behavior? Again, it is *you* who disappeared—"

"Will you stop?" she hissed. "A few kisses shared with you does not make me a light skirt that couples in the shrubbery with every man that I meet. You are the *only* man I have kissed, let alone looked at, since Jason." Her eyes narrowed. "Do not make me regret it."

The warning in her tone distracted him, and it took a moment for the import of her words to hit him. Stunned, his lips parted and he studied her jutting chin. Damned if her confession did not take another bite out of his anger, and like a ship cut free of its mooring, he floundered.

And then he blinked. Damn, she was good. "You are trying to distract me. The fact is that you met with Drummond when I expressly asked you not to—"

"I did not go alone, Julia accompanied me. I had but to say her name, and she would be at my side."

She had a point, despite his reluctance to concede it. She was tying him up in knots, making him want to thrash her one minute and kiss her the next. It was little wonder he could not think straight. He blew out a breath. "Fine, but that does not mean I have to like it," he grumbled.

"I do not expect you to."

He heard the amusement in her voice, and sighed. "So what did he have to say for himself? Did you learn anything new?"

"Oh, yes," she said and lifted her chin to stare him straight in the eye. "I learned you were right about Lawrence Drummond. I learned that he is a lying, traitorous bastard, and I intend to find the evidence that implicates him in embezzlement and—" She hesitated briefly before adding, "Perhaps murder."

His eyes widened. Whatever the hell Drummond had said, it had been damning. "Is that all?" He couldn't suppress his wry smile. "You plan to accuse a friend of your fiancé, who has family connections to the Earl of Dayton, of slander, embezzlement, and potentially cold-blooded murder. Is that your plan?"

"It is." She frowned. "I am simply confirming all you believed, while I defended the man. Are you having second thoughts? Because I assure you—"

"No. I have no doubt the man is a lying bastard. And if guilty of these charges, I hope he hangs until he rots. But hoping and having it happen are two different things. Until we procure evidence implicating him in anything, we have nothing."

"I will find it." She fisted her hands at her sides. "He dared to tell me that Jason was an opium addict. That Jason was lonely and sought solace in the drug. Drummond claimed to be his *friend*." She sneered the word. "No friend of Jason's would utter such slanderous lies."

Damning indeed. A sheen of tears glistened in her eyes, sparkling in the twilight. He enfolded her in his arms, feeling the tension vibrating in her rigid frame before she relaxed against him. He pressed his cheek to the crown of her hair and spoke softly. "I am so very sorry, Emily. Such betrayal is unpardonable."

They stood in silence, and he breathed her in, marveling at her determination and resolve.

She tilted her head back to meet his eyes, blinking back her tears. "He will pay. He will not get away with it. For Jason's sake, I will not give up."

He had no doubts that Emily would keep this vow on behalf of Jason, and he almost pitied Drummond.

He stared into her fierce expression and admiration swamped him. That was what he sought from a woman. *Unwavering loyalty.* Faith forged in steel and that withstood friends, foes, or any other force that sought to bend or break it. Something sliced through him. The long-taloned claws of a green-eyed monster.

Jealousy.

He was jealous of a man dead and buried nearly four years. It was a sobering thought. Jason had been a lucky man, and Brett was merely his substitute. A warm body to warm a grieving heart. A partner to assist in a murder investigation.

He stepped back, needing the distance between them. "So we find Patricia and the portfolio, which she hopefully will be able to retrieve from Jason's trunk."

"Yes. She should be arriving tomorrow," Emily said, eagerness lacing her words. "Do you think it could be all over then? That the ledger and Jason's diary will be incriminating enough? That we can bring them to Lord Roberts? Have you had a chance to speak with him?"

"I hope so. And no, I have not had a chance to speak to Roberts. But I will. Perhaps he is here, because half of London appears to be."

"Lord Sutton's house parties have always been popular with the ton. Invitations to his events are coveted."

"I have an idea as to why." Unable to resist, he drew her back into his arms. He heard the worry and uncertainty in her voice despite her attempt to hide it, and he wanted to distract her as she did him. To give her all she wanted from him.

He dipped his head to the slim column of her neck and pressed his lips to the throbbing pulse there.

"Why?" she breathed, tilting her head to the side to give him better access.

He laughed softly and lowered his voice to a seductive murmur. "He has an elaborate maze, and rumor has it that those who dare to enter never emerge the same. I spent a school holiday here once." He spoke between the nibbling kisses he rained along a rounded shoulder. "Sutton warned us that all sorts of dangers lurked in its hidden corners and crevices. He said they emerged only after dark, so we boys best stay clear of it when the sun set. And you know, he was right." He kissed the silken curve of her breast where the lace décolletage teased him. He inhaled deeply, smelling the subtle fragrance of lilacs.

"Yes, I believe he was." She arched back against his supporting embrace.

He lifted his head and caught her lips in a plundering kiss. As his mouth devoured hers, he pressed his body full length to hers, easing her backward until she was braced against the marble base of Athena. He leaned in and deepened the kiss, savoring the sweet taste of her.

He liked the fashion of the new gowns with their straight lines, lack of hoops, and thin-layered petticoats. He eased off his glove, needing to touch her skin to skin. To feel the heat that radiated from her body. To feel her passion. He drew up the embroidered hem of her lavender satin gown, sliding it up a silk-clad calf to cup his hand below her knee. He lifted her leg to his waist, moving his hand along the strong muscle of her thigh, squeezing and caressing.

She drew a ragged breath as his hand slid further. "This danger of which you speak . . ." Her eyes were heavy-lidded, her voice breathless. "Did . . . did you heed Sutton's warning and avoid it?"

"Of course I did." He smiled, resting his gaze on her swollen lips. "As a boy," he added and lowered his mouth to the curve of her ear, his breath stirring the soft tendrils of hair. He finished in a whisper. "Then thankfully, I grew up." A groan escaped her when his hand closed over the juncture between her legs, cupping the moist center of her.

Her lashes lowered as his fingers moved intimately against her.

He slid aside her silken pantaloons, separating her moist folds and slipping a finger inside.

Gasping, she gripped his shoulders. "Yes, well . . . Oh lord, you do have a way with . . . with danger."

He laughed, the sound husky even to him, for his mouth was spit dry, parched from the need of wanting her. He closed his lips over hers as he pleasured her. Soft strokes that teased and taunted. She pressed herself against him, moving in rhythm to his thrusts.

He struggled to ignore his own pulsating need that was near the breaking point.

When a soft whimper escaped her, he swallowed the sounds with his mouth. She broke their kiss and tossed her head back in her abandon, lost to the desire sweeping her. Good lord, she was exquisite. Passionate. Responsive. Exotic.

Her body eventually shuddered and then sagged against him. He gently removed his hand and caught her about the waist, supporting her limp body.

It was a while later that her words, barely audible over the pounding of his heart, drifted to him.

"I think . . . I think it was wise you did not venture into the maze as a boy."

He grinned. "Alas, there would not have been much of interest to me then. No toy soldiers or guns."

"Yes, but lots of intense engagements and some clever swordplay." She slid her hand down and pressed her palm against his arousal that strained against his pants.

"Too true." He smiled and leaned toward her just as a loud, hacking cough erupted and shattered the moment. With a groan, he reluctantly removed Emily's hand and stepped back, allowing her to regain her footing. "Alas, that skirmish will have to wait."

She straightened her skirts with an unsteady hand. "Yes. We should vacate the area before we are discovered. I . . . I will go first." She tucked a loose curl into her coiffure, and nodded to his head. "Your hair is standing on end. Best see to yourself before you depart." She then slipped around the statue, and in a flash of lavender skirts, disappeared.

Nonplussed, he blinked at the space where she had stood. Sutton had been right. One who entered the maze did not exit the same. An unfilled hunger tugged at him. He raked his hands through his hair and regretted that he could not heed Emily's advice further and take a moment to see to himself. To find his own release.

Hell. He was in trouble. However, as Emily had once so sagely said, a man deserved to live before he died. And by God, he hadn't felt this alive in a long, long time.

Chapter Seventeen

❦

L ADY Sutton drew out the last plaintive, discordant, note on
her violin and finally deigned to put her audience out of their
misery. Emily blinked at Brett who exploded from his seat to
give a resounding round of applause. She stood more slowly,
wondering at his enthusiasm. The man must be tone deaf. It
was the only explanation. She was not a connoisseur of classical
music, but if that was Bach, she would eat her new bonnet. And
that bonnet boasted at least a dozen ostrich feathers.

"You enjoyed the performance?" she said beneath the
thunderous clapping.

"Despised it. God-awful. Worse butchering of Bach I
have ever heard." His smile was unwavering, his tone cheer-
ful. "Sounded like a cat under torture. But that is maligning the pitiful beast who is doing no more than what this audience yearned to—lamenting his fate."

Bemused, she pressed him further. "Then why the enthu-
siastic response?"

"Surely the Egyptians celebrated after the tenth plague
and their suffering came to an end?"

"You cannot equate Lady Sutton's solo to a biblical calamity," she admonished, but her lips twitched.

"No? Would you not prefer frogs, lice, or locusts for an encore?"

She laughed, but changed the subject lest they be overheard. "Is Melody musically inclined? I wondered, considering her name. If so, she might have played this afternoon."

They were in the Suttons' music room, where a handful of guests had been invited to provide afternoon entertainment. They had attended the performance because Patricia and Viscount Weston were seated up front. Fortunately, most of the performers played with a mastery their hostess lacked. Guests were now making a hasty exit, no doubt hoping to avoid being put in the awkward position of showering false compliments on Lady Sutton, a charming hostess, but a truly dreadful violinist.

Emily followed Brett down the row of chairs, hoping to catch Patricia before she disappeared.

"My name is a product of my mother's admirable, albeit futile optimism," Melody said in answer to Emily's query. "She harbored the misguided conviction that I was destined to be a pitch-perfect prodigy. After numerous instructors informed her that I did not possess an iota of musical talent and my tenth instructor quit, my mother finally put her hopes to rest and my listeners out of their misery." Melody's smile was wry.

Clearly she did not suffer lingering guilt over her failure to live up to her name *or* her mother's expectations.

"But I am sure Melody could manage our hostess's rendition of caterwauling. Couldn't you, Melody?" Brett said, smiling at his sister.

"Probably," she sighed. "But you scooted me off the stage before I plumbed the full range of my potential. Miss Sutton needs an overbearing older brother to whisk her from center stage under the auspices of protecting her from misunderstood critics."

"I prefer protective to overbearing," Brett said. "No one would dare interrupt Lady Sutton's performance. A benefit your aristocracy enjoys is the privilege to indulge their pro-clivities, regardless of whether or not it is at another's expense—such as the loss of their audience's hearing, wallet, or patience."

"I fear you may have a point," Emily said. They had wended their way to the back of the room, and when Melody turned to converse with another, Emily took the opportunity to address Brett privately. "You need to distract the viscount so I can speak to Patricia alone."

"What? Absolutely not. I have been tortured enough for an afternoon. No birds. I will speak to Patricia with you."

"Do not be absurd. You cannot accompany me. I am supposed to be inquiring about long-lost love letters. How do you propose I do so with you hovering like a hulking shadow? Or address an intimate subject in mixed company?"

"*Hulking, hovering shadow*? Shadows do not hulk. I will hover. Quietly. If I am a shadow, she will never know I am there. People give little heed to shadows."

She fought to keep her voice level. "I understand you are still upset over my meeting with Drummond, but you have to learn to trust my judgment. I promise to keep an eye open for anyone wielding suspicious instruments. But I assure you, Patricia will not sit quietly should someone attempt to strangle me with their violin strings."

"You do that so well. 'Tis a gift," he said dryly, a teasing light in his eyes.

"What?"

"Making me feel like an idiot so that I have no choice but to agree with you, lest I prove the point by arguing otherwise."

"You are not an idiot. You are, as you recently admitted, protective. But Melody is right. That well-meaning trait tends to veer toward overbearing. I think it is due to having three younger sisters. If you only had one, things might have been different."

He looked surprised, then he laughed. "That is another talent of yours. I think there is a compliment in there until I realize you are using them to distract me from the point at hand." When she only grinned, he blew out a breath. "Fine. I will discuss the *edifying* and *most interesting* Quinarian system of whatever with the viscount. *For you.* But you will owe me. And I *will* collect. I am tempted to ask Lady Sutton to give you a private performance."

She narrowed her eyes. "You would not dare."

"Well, there are other ways in which you can thank me for my sacrifice," he drawled. He dipped his gaze meaningfully to her lips, and then over the red flush she felt spreading over her breasts and up her neck. "One more thing. You would be wise to remember that the most dangerous instruments are not musical—or in plain view."

When Brett winked at her, she found herself tilting toward him before she straightened. "Go. Now. They are almost here."

"The Egyptians could not have suffered more than I," he groused.

"Poor you," she crooned to his back as he stomped off.

"Why *poor Brett*?" Melody said. "Where is he off to? He does look rather disgruntled. Is he worried about Miranda? She is with Julia and Daniel taking a turn of the gardens. Shall we join them? Or stay and rescue *Brett*?" Her eyes gleamed, clearly anticipating a sweeping rescue plan for her beleaguered brother.

Emily had dispensed with one Curtis, surely she could deal with another. "Brett is fine. I promise, no rescuing is required."

Melody was still eyeing Brett. "He is looking more glassy-eyed than disgruntled. I can fake a swoon. I have used it before when he needs extricating from a woman's . . . ah, that is, when he needs to excuse himself to attend to a pressing business matter." Flustered, her eyes shot to Emily's.

"I understand," Emily said. She had no doubts that Brett Curtis needed to be *extricated* from many a woman's pressing *business* interests, but she did not feel sorry for him. The man dispensed charm like bees cultivating flowers, thus he created his own difficulties with women. She dismissed

Brett, needing to concentrate on Melody, or rather getting rid of Melody.

As Patricia paid her respects to Lady Sutton, Emily looped her arm through Melody's and lowered her voice to a conspiratorial tone. "Can you head to the gardens without me? My friend, Miss Patricia Branson, is about to join us, and I need to speak with her privately. You see, the man with whom Brett is conversing is her brother, Viscount Weston. I believe Brett seeks to garner the viscount's good-will because he is interested in Patricia."

Intrigued, Melody eyes widened. "What makes you think *that*?"

"The viscount is an avid ornithologist"—at Melody's blank look, Emily clarified—"a bird-watcher. As we both know, Brett has never given birds any heed. I suspect he is feigning an interest in them to get in the viscount's good graces in order to court Patricia."

"Brett has not shown an interest in women of late, but you may be right," Melody said, wide-eyed. "He is clever like that, and he definitely has no interest in birds. Daniel's cousin is an avid bird-watcher, and Brett called the man a nice enough chap, but a bit of a banal bird-obsessed bore."

Emily bit her lip at Melody's indiscretion.

"Her brother is a viscount?" An odd look crossed Melody's features, and she gnawed worriedly on her lower lip.

"Yes, Viscount Weston. He was my late fiancé's younger brother."

"That makes his sister *Lady* Patricia?"

"No, she is *Miss* Patricia Branson. Only the viscount holding the title goes by lord and his wife will be lady, but his offspring go by miss or mister."

"Goodness. I cannot keep all this straight. I would be in a horrible muddle if I lived here," Melody said.

"Then perhaps it is a good thing you do not. Is her title or lack thereof a matter of concern to you?" She glanced at Patricia. Their hostess appeared intent on holding her sole admirer captive, because she was now pointing out something on her violin.

"It is just that . . . well, Brett vowed to never give his heart to another English aristocrat. He said that if the feather-brained female . . . ah . . ." She flushed and hastened to continue. "That is, if a woman cannot accept a man on his own merits, rather than judging them on their ancestral pedigree, he wants nothing to do with the shallow-minded lot. I believe those were his words. I overheard him muttering that to Daniel years ago. Despite his slurred words, he was emphatic. Of course, he did not notice me, being under the influence of strong drink. Daniel was half dragging him, half carrying him upstairs to his chambers." Melody wrinkled her nose.

Emily doubted Brett would feel as protective toward his sister if cognizant of this breach of confidence. But it did explain Brett's deep-seated disdain for the English peerage. Not only had an aristocrat trampled his heart, but the woman had also rejected him for being an untitled American. Her rejection was cruel, shallow, and most damning of all, unforgivable.

She recalled the words he had tossed at her in the Earl of Dayton's library when she had sought to seduce him. *You are the daughter of an earl. Sister-in-law to a duke. I am an untitled American who works in trade. There can be no alliance between us. Not in your world.* Bitterness had been etched in them. Her heart twisted.

Brett was right. There could never be an alliance between them, but not for the reasons he stated. The true reason had nothing to do with who *he* was, but all to do with who *she* was. *A damaged woman.*

Their alliance was no longer just about getting caught. It was about not hurting each other. About protecting each other so that when this wonderful interlude that they shared wound to an end, they could walk away unscathed. She and Brett carried enough wounds.

"You do not have to look so worried," Melody said. "If Patricia is amiss all is well. Brett is only averse to getting involved with a member of the aristocracy."

Melody snapped Emily back to the present. She frowned at Melody's reminder, but Patricia was heading toward them, so she had little time to contemplate them—or if they held a warning. "Let me handle matters from here. I will meet you in the gardens later." Melody had a gift for the dramatic, but she was a terrible actress and Patricia would see right through any glib excuse she gave to leave them some privacy.

"Oh, I wanted to meet—"

"Later. I promise."

Melody looked conflicted, but then with a wink that was so like her brother's, she dashed off.

"Who was that? I did not mean to interrupt you," Patricia said. She approached slowly, her gaze following Melody.

"Brett Curtis's sister. I shall introduce you later, but she was overdue to meet the rest of our party," Emily said and caught Patricia's hands in hers. She held her smile steady as she stared into Jason's blue eyes and such heartrendingly familiar features.

Jason and Patricia shared the same spun-gold hair, a distinctive catlike slant to their eyes, and full lower lips. Jason used to quip that Patricia was his softer side.

"It has been too long," Patricia said and smiled wistfully. "As I missed your visit, I was delighted to receive your letter. Truth be told, I was perishing from boredom, waiting for Tristan to leave his books and birds long enough to escort me to town." She rolled her eyes. "I was plotting to travel on my own when your letter arrived and gave me something to occupy my time instead of nagging Tristan to get organized. You averted fratricide. Do not laugh, it was a near thing."

"I am glad for my sake, but more important for Tristan's, that you have arrived safely," she said, and then glanced around the room, ensuring they had it to themselves. "Let us sit." She directed Patricia to one of the rows of chairs.

Once they dispensed with the social inquiries after family and mutual friends, Patricia's eyes gleamed, and she leaned forward. "So about those missing letters, dare I presume they are love letters?"

"Why else would I wish to retrieve them?" Emily said, and bit her lip, hoping she looked appropriately abashed.

For good measure, she cast another furtive glance around the empty room.

"Jason was such a romantic," Patricia sighed. "They must have been quite delicious to warrant a hidden compartment in his trunk." She stared off dreamily into space.

Delicious? Emily recalled pestering the ever-patient Burke for the mail, her heart racing at the familiar slant of Jason's hand on the envelope. He was not a demonstrative writer, but in the beginning, they had been lovely—until they segued into the business about the discrepancies in the accounts.

She frowned. Jason clearly wanted to share with her what he was involved in. If Jason had discovered Drummond was the guilty party and found friend to be foe, she wondered if Jason had questioned whom he could trust. She could only imagine his despair—and loneliness. The thought chilled and shamed her. Searching only for words of love, Emily had ignored any warnings of danger that Jason had voiced.

She wondered if Jason had felt betrayed when she did not respond to his shared confidences. Perhaps *betrayal* was too strong a word. She could only hope that her present course of action could make amends for her thoughtlessness.

"Emily, are you all right? You look pale." Patricia caught her hands and squeezed them. "Forgive me. This must be painful for you."

Emily's smile was sad. "It is, but I do wish to reclaim Jason's letters because I will always cherish them, as well as all he shared of us in his diaries." To lighten the moment, she added wryly, "Admittedly, I also would be mortified should they fall into another's hands." She grinned, but paused when Patricia did not share her amusement, but shifted in her seat, looking uneasy.

"That is true. However, the thing is . . ." Patricia began, but then paused, and worried her lower lip.

"Is what? What is the thing?" Patricia's unease transferred to Emily, and she tightened her grip on Patricia's hands.

"Do not worry," Patricia said, hastening to reassure her. "All is not lost."

"Patricia, please speak plainly. Do you have the portfolio or not?" Emily struggled to keep her voice even, but her voice climbed with her increasing disquiet.

"I am so sorry, Emily. There was nothing there," Patricia said sadly.

Devastated, Emily's lips parted. Her grip fell limp and she drooped in her seat.

"It is all right, Emily, all is not lost," Patricia said quickly. "I have a plan to find out where they might be."

Emily could only stare blankly at Patricia, blinking at the excitement that brimmed in her friend's eyes.

"I have enlisted help. Someone who worked with Jason at the East India Company and who already possesses most of the contents of Jason's trunk. More important, he can gain access to any files, ledgers, or a portfolio which he does not already possess but which might still reside at the East India Company."

"Who?" Emily breathed. But God help her, she knew.

"Me."

Chills suffused her, and she froze.

"See? Mr. Drummond is here. He will help you to find this missing portfolio. I promise you. All is not lost." Patricia stood and clasped her hands together. She beamed at Drummond as if he was the answer to their most fervent prayers.

Once Emily could hear herself think over the roaring in her ears, she summoned a wan smile for Patricia and braced herself to face her nemesis.

Chapter Eighteen

⊱⊰

"Lady Emily, we meet again." Drummond dipped his head, appraising her coolly.

"It must have been fate that had Mr. Drummond crossing my path," Patricia said. "I was worried about telling you I could not find your letters. Then I ran into Mr. Drummond, and I recalled Tristan asking him about some business papers of Jason's that Tristan had turned over to Mr. Drummond. Mr. Drummond called on us a few weeks ago and was kind enough to inquire after you. Is that not providential?" Patricia beamed approvingly at Drummond.

It took Emily a moment to recover her voice, and she had to moisten her dry lips to respond. "Yes. In fact, Julia and I ran into Mr. Drummond yesterday." She rose on unsteady legs.

"Yes, and we discussed Jason's posting in India," Drummond said. "Lady Emily appears quite determined to understand all that his work entailed, despite my advising her that it is best to let the past remain where it belongs—safely in the past."

"So you are aware of the particulars of what Lady Emily seeks?" Surprised, Patricia shifted her gaze between them.

"My apologies, but this revelation about *missing personal correspondence* must have eluded me," he said coldly.

Emily refused to cower under his narrowed-eyed scrutiny. She did not know if she could salvage this situation, but she had to try. There was no need to feign the flush that rose to her burning cheeks, but her trilling laugh was forced. "Really, Mr. Drummond, a lady dare not share such personal confidences with a gentleman." She paused, challenging him to contradict her. "And aware of your concerns about my queries, I turned to Patricia for assistance on this trivial, but more delicate matter. I hope you can understand my predicament and can forgive me for not being completely forthright with you." She spread her hands helplessly, looking suitably chagrined.

Drummond paused, no doubt struggling to discern whether or not he was being played for a fool. The man was either obtuse or his vanity saved him from drawing such a disparaging conclusion.

"You are nothing if not persistent in your quest, soliciting both of our assistance, unbeknownst to each other," he said.

"You did suggest I remember Jason as the man he was. These letters are all I have left of the man I knew, so you must understand my desire to reclaim them." Let the scoundrel challenge *that*. She omitted reference to the diary for fear of Drummond seeing that as possessing more incriminating information.

He furrowed his brow and pursed his lips, appearing to still be weighing her sincerity. She lifted her chin and met his gaze.

"So now we must work together," Patricia said, oblivious to the undercurrents swirling beneath their exchange. "Surely this portfolio can be located so that Lady Emily can retrieve her correspondence. After all, these letters belong to *her*, not the company. This portfolio must be gathering dust in a filing cabinet. Can you not search through a few?

That is not too much to ask. As Jason's friend and former colleague, how can you refuse to assist his fiancée?"

Emily bit her lip at this appeal to Drummond's chivalry. Patricia had no way of knowing the man had no loyalty. *Or honor. Or morals.*

Drummond left Patricia's plea to hang suspended for a minute before he emitted a beleaguered sigh. "Lady Emily, you leave me no choice, because I see you are most determined to have your way. Miss Branson is right. Perhaps it is time we worked together. If I promise to pursue this matter and review all the items I might still possess, as well as locate any files of Jason's that reside at the East India Company, will that alleviate your mind? Will you then promise me that you will let this matter rest? And not burden anyone else with your request?" he said, his gaze locked on hers.

Was the man so vain that he truly believed she was blind to his duplicity? And so ignorant that he was oblivious to hers?

Drummond's features were composed, his expression unreadable.

She summoned a smile of relieved gratitude, clasped her hands together, and lied through her teeth. "I would be pleased to accept your offer of assistance. Thank you." The man had left her no choice. She could not refuse him before Patricia, but neither could she ever work with the villainous bastard. Nor would she abandon her course—not until the traitor was rotting in the deepest, darkest bowels of hell.

"Consider me your faithful servant." He caught her hand and brought it to his lips. "But please, do not give this matter another worry. Leave it entirely in my hands."

"You are too kind," she managed. His mouth was like a Judas brand on her silk glove. She tamped down her revulsion, and practically yanked her hand from his, sliding her thumb over the area, desperate to erase all remnants of his traitorous touch. Later she would wash the area thoroughly.

Oblivious to her recoil, he straightened. "Good. I am departing tomorrow, but should you wish to reach me,

Clarise and I will be residing with the Earl of Dayton." Drummond paused briefly to give his esteemed connection his proper deference.

"Is Clarise here with you?" Patricia asked.

"Of course. As her only male relative, she is stuck with my escort. She is about somewhere. No doubt taking advantage of her older brother's lapse in vigilance, but alas, I can only rescue one beautiful damsel at a time."

Patricia's laughter rang out, delighted with the turn of events.

Emily's smile was so brittle, she feared it might crack. "Perhaps she is in the gardens where I am due to meet my family. I should head there now, before they deem me lost and send out a search party, or you are forced to do the same for your sister."

"Shall we venture down together?" Patricia suggested. "Sutton's gardeners are gifted, and he does have that intriguing maze."

"He does indeed. Allow me." Drummond smiled at Emily, and gestured for them to precede him.

Emily refused to meet Drummond's gaze, lest her flustered expression at the mention of the maze give him mixed signals. But she had a far more pressing concern. She needed to find a quiet, secluded place to explain Drummond's offer to Brett. Somewhere that no one could overhear his explosive reaction.

❧❦

"HE DID WHAT? Is he playing you for a fool?" Brett blurted, looking thunderstruck.

Solitude and quiet reigned supreme in the library, but Brett's booming voice shattered that sanctity as it resounded in the room. She could never depend on the dratted man to behave as he should. "Keep your voice down," she hissed.

Brett glanced around Sutton's plush library with its inviting green and gold brocade couches, wall-to-wall rows of books, and the mammoth world globe planted in the center of the room. They were alone at present, but the open door was an invitation to anyone's interruption. He caught her arm and dragged her behind a tall potted plant. He selected a leather-bound volume from the shelf and shoved it into her hands. "Look studious."

She rolled her eyes. "Yes, because no one can see us standing behind this greenery. Or if they do, our literary pursuits will put to rest any nefarious suspicions they might harbor."

"Exactly. Stop smiling. I gave you a tragedy."

She glanced at her book, *Antigone*. "So you did. What is yours, a farce? That should adequately sum up this situation."

He grunted. "True. The villain offering his assistance in finding evidence that potentially implicates himself is ripe for Drury Lane. You would be adept at penning an amusing tale; have you ever considered trying your hand at a comedy?"

"Melody was right; you are so very droll. Drummond is obviously convinced we have no suspicions of his role in the embezzlement and perhaps even in Jason's death. I can only assume his offer of help is an attempt to prevent me from turning to someone else. After all, it makes sense when you consider that he shares your opinion about my persistence."

"You mean your obduracy—"

"Persistence. I think he now understands I will not stop searching until I receive the answers I seek."

"We could turn this matter over to Lord Roberts and ask him to investigate, now that Patricia no longer has Jason's portfolio. Marsh did say Roberts was suspicious about Jason's death. As the bereaved fiancée, you might be able to persuade him to—"

"Are you abandoning me?" she said, narrowing her eyes. "This is an ironic turn of events. Drummond pretends to assist me and you beg off."

"I am not!" he snapped, then lowered his voice. "You say I should trust you; well, you need to do the same. I will not abandon your cause, but remember what happened to Sophocles's poor *Antigone* when she sought justice for her dead brother." He nodded toward her book.

"I am breaking no unjust laws, so unlike poor Antigone, no one should hang me. But if you remember, *Antigone* succeeded in what she set out to do. She gave her brother the honorable burial he deserved. I seek no more than to restore Jason's good name within the company, and of course, to see that Drummond meets his own just ends should he be found guilty."

His eyes gleamed. "I expected no less than that very answer." He tucked a loose strand of hair behind her ear.

Nonplussed, she frowned. His lips curved, and he brushed his fingers over her cheek in a featherlight caress. Her breath quickened and a heat suffused her. He trailed those nimble fingers over her lips, making her forget her retort.

He caressed the contour of her lower lip. "I surmise you are right and that Drummond does not wish you seeking help from anyone who might truly assist you. Someone whom he considers to be bad company, like myself. No doubt he fears my trade-blackened hands will tarnish your stellar reputation. I wonder what he would think if he knew where else they have wandered," he said softly.

She blinked at the smoldering look in his eyes, and a knot of desire tangled within her.

His fingers lowered to caress the curves of her breasts. "What would he say to their roaming over every inch of your delectable body and—"

"Shh. The door is open," she breathed against his hand. Where he touched, her skin burned.

His smile was slow and dangerous. "So it is. Perhaps I should stop talking lest someone hear me." His hand fell, and he leaned forward.

Despite the threat of discovery, she could not summon the will to move or protest. She had become rather reckless of late. *Why stop now?* He caught her lips with his, and she let herself sink into his kiss for one blissful moment.

She savored the comfort, the touch, and the familiar taste of him, letting him settle emotions that Drummond's proposal had disturbed. She wanted to lean into Brett's strong body, to trust him as he asked her to do. The kiss deepened, a slow tangle of tongues and mingling breaths before she returned to her senses and drew back.

He sighed and dipped his forehead to hers. "Who would have thought the library can be almost as dangerous as the maze? Imagine that." He straightened and wiggled his eyebrows.

She opened her mouth to respond, when laughter interrupted them.

"Is it empty?" a female voice spoke in a loud whisper.

"Just as I said," Brett spoke loudly. He quickly retreated to a safe distance, while Emily sought in vain to fade into the potted plant. "Antigone's most notable trait is her loyalty," Brett continued as he peered around the plant. "Ah, Winspear, fancy meeting you here. I did not know you were an avid reader."

"Nor I you," a masculine voice drawled, more amused than offended. "However, I believe you will agree with me that there are other reasons one is enticed to seek the inner sanctum of the library. While I do not presume to suggest that you have found one, allow me to give you the privacy to do so, or carry on with your edifying *literary* pursuits. *Antigone* is a fine selection."

"What? But that is not fair—" the feminine voice protested.

"It is. They arrived first. Come, my dear, we can do our literary plundering elsewhere. Pray tell me, have you visited Sutton's maze?"

A lilting laugh answered the suggestive tone and then, "Who is *Antigone*?"

Brett laughed, but mortified, Emily skittered out from behind the plant. "This is madness. We cannot hide in here. What was I thinking?"

"It is all right. He did not see you, only me."

"And that makes it all better?" She shoved *Antigone* into his hands and frantically neatened her hair and her skirts. "How do I look?"

"Like a woman who has been thoroughly kissed." At her

groan, he held up his hands and laughed again. "I am jesting. You look as beautiful, as serene, and as unattainable as you always do. But you need not worry, no one would dare accuse the daughter of an earl of impropriety behind a potted plant," he teased.

She frowned at his choice of words. *Unattainable.* Is that how he saw her? After her breakdown, it was the portrait she had sought to paint of herself.

So why did Brett's words upset her?

Because she now knew his opinion on aristocratic Englishwomen. It should not matter, because she did not want him to look deeper or expect more from her. Of course not. Unattainable was more tolerable than shallow, broken, or worse—*mad.*

"We should leave." Disturbed at the heaviness that settled over her like a wet blanket, she strode to the door. She did not wait for him to follow, but with his long-legged strides, he quickly fell into step beside her.

"We still have the advantage over Drummond," he said.

"How so?" she said as they walked down the corridor leading away from the library. A wealth of oil paintings hung in multiple rows and plastered the towering walls. Her gaze drifted over them.

"While Drummond is *supposedly* playing hero to your damsel in distress, he is doing so under the mistaken belief that you will be waiting patiently to hear from him. Your being the well-bred daughter of an earl, he will expect you to do as you have been raised, that is to quietly attend to your embroidery or your social obligations."

"You are mocking me. I happen to have a fine hand at embroidery."

"I have no doubt you excel at everything you set your mind to, and *that* is Drummond's failing, or rather one of his many failings, considering he is a potential embezzler, traitor, and dirty, rotten—"

"I understand. But how does Drummond's ignorance of my gift with a needle and thread constitute a fault in his character?"

"Because he does not *know* you. He does not know that beneath your calm façade lurks a combination of Athena, the goddess of heroic endeavors, and Antigone, avenger of her fiancé's honor."

The man was nothing if not well read, and he carried a little of Melody's dramatic flair. Still, she rather liked the comparison, and a responding flutter arose beneath her breasts. "What is your point?" she said.

"After a period of time passes, I predict that Drummond will apologize and look pained when he delivers the heart-rending news that he has found nothing. Which is hardly surprising, of course, since Drummond is likely responsible for the files' disappearance in the first place."

"Again, Drummond's inevitable failure helps us because . . . ?" Exasperation laced her words.

"It gives us time to search for the portfolio ourselves without Drummond hovering over your every movement. He will not watch over you if he thinks he is handling matters while you are occupied embroidering pillows or chairs or whatever you embroider." He waved a hand airily.

"Chairs?" Her lips twitched. "Drummond has not been hovering over me. *You* have been doing that," she teased.

"I have not. *I* have been trying to *protect* you, and—" He paused, blew out a breath, and started again. "Drummond *has* been following you. He visited the Bransons, where he inquired about you. He met up with you at Dayton's, and then appears at this house party where he knew Miss Branson had plans to meet with you."

Disturbed at the idea, she curled her hands around her waist. "Will he stop now that he is pretending to assist me?"

"I do not know, but I think it is time for us to begin monitoring *his* movements. I have some men under my employ that I can hire to do this. I will speak to them."

"I want to find Winfred, Jason's valet, but I did not have a chance to ask Patricia his new address. Drummond interrupted us. But now I am worried that Drummond might follow us to Winfred's place of employ. If so, he might threaten Winfred as he threatened Marsh."

"All the more reason to monitor Drummond's movements. And Emily, should Drummond seek to meet with you again, I need your promise that you will not meet with the man alone. I cannot be with you because he does not trust me, but the lack of trust between us is mutual."

"Of course," she said, furrowing her brow. "I did not think this would become so cloak-and-dagger."

"Well, let us hope we have better luck than this poor fellow." Brett tipped his head toward a still life of a skull perched on a pile of books. Its hollow-eyed black sockets stared ominously back at them. At her indrawn breath, he laughed. "I was jesting. Do not worry, we will prevail. How can we not, with Athena leading the charge?"

"With her protector at her side."

When he smiled, she managed to return it. They would trounce Drummond at whatever game he played. After all, the odds were against him.

Chapter Nineteen

❧❧

BRETT slid his gaze past Miss Patricia Branson to narrow it on Drummond, who stood beside her on the opposite side of the dance floor. The snake was known to be the craftiest of all the beasts, so he and Emily needed to stay one step ahead of him.

He gritted his teeth, Drummond's offer irking him. No doubt the bastard imagined himself the hero to Emily's distressed damsel. He snorted. His Emily was a charging bull and woe to the misbegotten matador who blocked her path. He almost felt sorry for the ignorant whoreson. *Almost*, but not quite.

His attention shifted to Emily, who stood beside Julia and a few yards down from him. Her hair was tucked up in a neat chignon, threaded with violet flowers, and small ringlets framed her face. She was lovely. As if aware of his eyes on her, her gaze met his. He should look away, rather than stand staring like a lovesick fool, but he could not bring himself to do so, not when she moistened her lips and drew an unsteady breath.

He wished everyone in the ballroom would magically disappear. He needed them gone, because the dance he yearned to perform with Emily was not a quadrille. It was intimate, scandalous, and involved minimal to no clothing.

He dipped his eyes to the lace edging the neckline of Emily's emerald gown. Its plunging décolletage teased him with the rise and fall of the creamy swells of her breasts, and his pulse raced. He imagined pressing his face there and breathing in the lavender scent that she dabbed in the valley between her breasts. She must have read his intent, because a rose-colored blush suffused her fair skin and she abruptly whirled away—but not before she tossed him a narrow-eyed *behave yourself* warning.

He chuckled softly. Needing a distraction to douse the flare of desire, he searched for his sisters—then froze. A frigid green-eyed gaze met his, spearing him in place.

Daniel.

Well then. He did not need his sisters after all. The blast from his friend's glare was akin to jumping into a frozen lake. He swallowed.

"The card room. Now."

Without a by-your-leave to his startled wife, Daniel turned on his heel and stormed off. Like the parting of the Red Sea, couples scurried from his path lest they be plowed down.

Julia studied Brett. After a beat, her eyes widened. "Oh, dear. Who is she?"

Devil take her, and Daniel, too!

They deserved each other. Both were like bloodhounds keen on a scent and right now he reeked. *Of lust. And need. And thwarted desire.* He nodded curtly to Julia and fled before he lost more than his dignity.

He had barely stepped through the doors to the card room when a tight-lipped Daniel accosted him. Daniel tipped his head in the direction of the back corner, away from the card tables, prying eyes, and sharp ears. Rumbles of masculine voices and barks of laughter filled the crowded room. Surely Daniel would not kill him before an audience of so many?

Daniel was pacing. When Brett joined him, Daniel whirled and caught Brett by the lapels of his jacket and shoved him against the back wall. "What the devil are you up to? And do not repeat Melody's blather about Patricia Branson, because you looked straight through the woman. Not so with Emily." He stepped back and folded his arms across his chest.

Patricia Branson? What mischief was Melody brewing now? Brett dismissed the query. He had far more pressing problems to address. He straightened his jacket and opened his mouth to respond, but Daniel spoke over him.

"Do not deny it! I saw the look you gave Emily. Have you no decency? Can you at least leave her clothed in public?" His eyes raked the room, and seeing curious gazes turned their way, he lowered his voice to a furious hiss. "It was bad enough when you two were snapping at each other like rabid dogs. I thought I would have to rescue one of you. Now what am I to do? She is my sister-in-law, do you understand that?"

"Yes, I do, and I can explain—"

"You best hope so. More important, those explanations better involve a marriage proposal."

"Listen to me . . . *What*?" Brett staggered back.

"You heard me. What did you think would come of this? She is not one of your doxies, but gently bred. If your future plans do not entail begging on hands and knees before Taunton, you are a bloody cur, a scurrilous blackguard, a debaucher of innocents, a sodding—"

"Oh, for God's sake, it is *not* like that," Brett snapped. "You have it all wrong. *She* sought out *my* help and that is what I am doing, assisting her with a matter that she is investigating." It was the partial truth, but the best he could offer.

Daniel arched a brow. "My pardon, but that look you gave her is assistance she does not need. You cannot deny that something passed between you. My jacket is still smoldering from the sparks of—"

"That is enough!" he snarled, fist clenched. "You have made your point in reminding me that Lady Emily is gently bred and lest we forget, sister-in-law to an arrogant arse of a duke. She deserves to be spoken of with the respect you believe, and I *know*, she bloody well deserves."

Daniel closed his mouth, and his eyes narrowed. After a moment, he uncrossed his arms and the scowl contorting his features eased. "So it is like that, is it? I knew it! Like a pair of damn magnets, were the two of you. Just facing the wrong way. In my book, that makes you the bigger arse."

Brett blinked. Daniel never did hold his temper for long, but this abrupt face in the opposite direction had Brett struggling to keep abreast of him. "What the deuces are you talking about? What the devil has this got to do with magnets?"

"It is basic physics," Daniel said, waving a hand. "Like poles repel each other, opposites do not. Once the magnets are correctly aligned, they fit together—so to speak."

"So to speak," Brett repeated and stepped away from Daniel. Turning his back on him, he swiped his hand through his hair. Hell. Daniel's innuendo unwittingly forced Brett to face the one truth he could no longer ignore.

There could never be a consummation to this dangerous dance in which he and Emily were engaged. He could not make love to Emily as he yearned to do, nor cradle her in his arms the whole night through, or roll over and kiss her awake in the morning. Something tightened in his chest.

Daniel's reference to magnets was apt. Inherent in the principle of attraction between two magnets is that they be polar opposites. And there it was. The inescapable truth. It always circled back to who she was and who he was not. No matter what they felt for each other, or what forces pulled them together, neither could change who they were.

"But explanations are still needed," Daniel said, and waited until Brett turned back to him. "What is this investigation of which you speak? And what are your intentions in regard to Emily?"

Brett blew out a breath. "I need a drink." He waved a footman over, grabbed a tumbler of whiskey, and drained it neat. He returned it to the tray, snatched another, and sipped more slowly. He ignored Daniel's arched brow as he struggled with his response.

In speaking to Daniel, he was not betraying his word to Emily. He had warned Emily that if confronted directly, he would not lie. And he would not. He could fob him off, but Daniel was his oldest friend, and he trusted him implicitly. More important, he could use his help. As a duke, there were resources and people that Daniel had access to that Brett did not. He could only hope that Emily understood.

"As I have told you, Emily has been through a difficult time. I will not stand by and see her hurt again," Daniel added.

Brett's eyes shot to Daniel's. He wanted to growl that he cared about Emily's heart, too. If he did not care for her and who she was, he would not willingly let her go.

Conflicting emotions roiled through him, and he struggled to put them into words. "I have a care for her, too. Do not think I do not. I promise you, I would never hurt her. She may be family to you, but she means something to me, too. But things are complicated. I cannot ask you to understand, but I do ask you to trust me. I promise to protect her even if it is at the expense of *my* heart."

Brett was certain of only one thing—he was not ready to sever this magnetic force that drew Emily and him inexorably toward each other. It had been there from the very beginning. He feared it always would be. He hoped when he had to break it, he survived being alone again.

"I trust you. That is, until you bloody well muck things up. And if you do—"

"I understand. It will not be pleasant."

"As long as we understand each other," Daniel said. "Now then, about this other matter. What, pray tell, is Emily investigating? And does Taunton or Julia know about it? More important, why the devil did Emily turn to you and not me for assistance?"

More questions without answers.

Daniel collected his own drink from a passing footman. He moved to a nearby table and drew out one of its chairs. Sitting, he leaned back, and settled in to wait Brett out.

Brett cursed his friend, who never had any patience, but chose this particular moment to find some. Before he confided in Daniel, he had one stipulation. "I need your word that what I tell you stays between us. Emily has a right to share her story when she so chooses—without pressure from you. Understood?"

Daniel paused, but then nodded. "You have my word, but if there is a body that needs burying, you best explain quickly before it putrefies."

Brett's lips twitched. "Ah, it has not come to that quite yet. And this might take some time."

"Fortunately, I happen to have some to spare," Daniel said, all vestiges of humor gone.

Brett slid back another chair and dropped into it with an air of resignation. "Shortly after the twins' christening, I ran into Lady Emily at Lakeview Manor." The tale unfolded slowly, interrupted with Daniel's inevitable curses and rants.

"Devil take you! Lady Emily is two times a fool, and you no better. You almost got killed the last time we tried to capture a murderer. Have you forgotten that? Have you gone daft?"

"Should I have left Lady Emily to pursue her course on her own? Or allowed her to seek assistance from the very man whom she is trying to implicate?" Brett rejoined and waited until Daniel snapped his mouth shut and glowered into his drink.

He was having second thoughts about confiding in his friend. In the past, Daniel's support had been unfailing ever since he had rescued Brett from one too many beatings at Dunbar Academy. Daniel had been the only English boy to befriend the lone American. But when Daniel launched into a tirade about Brett and Emily opening Pandora's bloody box, Brett had had enough. *This* was help he did not need. He slammed his drink on the table and opened his mouth to tell Daniel to sod off, when suddenly Daniel fell silent and emitted a long, suffering sigh.

"Fine. What do you need from me? How can I help?" At Brett's expression, which was nothing short of jaw-gaping surprise, Daniel shrugged. "I know Emily, too. She is a dog with a bone when she sets her teeth into something, and there is no talking her out of it. As you say, she would have proceeded alone and could have become more entangled with this Drummond bastard. You may have been right to assist her, but wrong to not confide in me. I—"

"I had no choice. That was her stipulation before she confided in me."

Daniel grunted. "I still cannot believe she did not turn to me, regardless of her concern for Julia and the twins. It does rankle." He tipped his glass toward Brett. "You must be dispensable."

"No doubt," Brett said, taking no umbrage at the comment. Daniel only echoed his own thoughts when Emily had first approached him. "But I could use your assistance, and I am glad that I can rely on it."

"Of course. Julia will have my head if she discovers what Emily is up to and learns that I did not try to stop her—or failing that, did not assist her. Besides, another thought crossed my mind. Perhaps, just *perhaps*, mind you, this quest of Emily's has not been detrimental. In fact, it might be beneficial. That is, now that both of us are looking out to see that she is safe."

Blinking, Brett froze in the act of lifting his drink to tug at his ear. "Pardon?"

Daniel laughed. "Emily has changed. Just look at her." He waved his hand in the direction of the ballroom. "She is participating in the Season, dancing, *and* reconnecting with old friends like Patricia Branson. My wife is damn near giddy. Taunton walks with a ridiculous new spring in his step, and even Jonathan senses the good moods and is behaving himself. No, I take that back. Wishful thinking on my part. He stabbed one of the footman the other day." He frowned, but then continued. "Maybe having a quest or a purpose is the impetus Emily needed to step back into her life. And that is not all bad."

Nonplussed, Brett mulled over Daniel's words. He wanted to take credit for Emily's transformation, but it belonged to

Jason. Emily was risking everything for him. The familiar prick of jealousy pierced Brett, and he hardened his jaw.

"Maybe having you snarling at her, rather than treating her like fragile heirloom china, as we all have been doing the past few years, has been medicinal. Perhaps, again with a heavy emphasis on the *perhaps*, having someone look at her as if she will not break and more so as an appealing woman, does not hurt her either." His hand shot up to silence Brett. "Absolutely not. Not repeating that either. *Ever.*"

Something heavy slid off Brett's chest. Maybe Jason could not take all the credit for Emily's transformation. He remembered her response when he touched her, her abandon, and her passion. He beamed at Daniel.

"Wipe that smile off your face," Daniel snapped. "This quest may have done her some good, but for God's sake, it is still dangerous. She is trying to prove embezzlement and potentially hang a man for a murder committed over four years ago without a lick of evidence. This is a tangled web you have woven. Do not lose sight of that."

Brett cursed Daniel for tossing a cold dose of reality onto his euphoria. *Bastard.*

"So what is Drummond's motive? What drove him to embezzle the money? And move from embezzlement to murder? The man must have been desperate," Daniel said.

Brett blinked. He had not thought to ask these questions, and he wished they were rhetorical because once again, he had no answers. When Daniel was not being a bastard, he was useful.

"Embezzlement is about money," Daniel continued. "The man must have been in dire straits to cheat the largest mercantile company in the world—and then, if Emily's accusations are confirmed, to kill a man to protect himself."

"Maybe he is in debt? Is he a gambler?" Brett asked.

Daniel shook his head. "I do not know, but I will be sure to find out. To build a case against the man, it is wise to determine his motive. I can also assist you with another matter. An agriculture bill that I am supporting is coming up for vote, and I am meeting with a few men to garner their support. Lord Roberts is one of those men."

Daniel's words reinforced Brett's decision to confide in him.

"I take it you had a reason for inquiring about him the other day," Daniel continued. "What is your true interest in the man? Do you think Jason wrote to Roberts, revealing his suspicious about Drummond?"

"I doubt Roberts is aware that Drummond may be the culprit in the embezzling," Brett said. "But within the company, Marsh's reputation was blackened so well that his word became suspect when he sought to speak out to defend Jason. Roberts knows who lodged the allegations against Marsh and sullied his name. I want to link Drummond to Marsh's downfall."

"And how exactly do you propose to accomplish that?" Daniel said, his brow furrowed.

"With your help, actually, now that you've offered." Brett leaned forward. "I need you to ask Roberts about Jason's former clerk. Pose your interest under the guise of being concerned that your former partner has recently hired said clerk without any references. Mention that you had heard troublesome rumors about the man and wished to substantiate them because of your concern for me."

Daniel smiled. "I can lament your American naïveté in believing in a man lacking pedigree and reference, but armed with will and gumption, can rise above any misfortune to make something of himself if given a chance." He winked at Brett.

Brett shook his head. "It took more than will and gumption to toss off the British's yoke of tyranny—"

"And once again, we digress." Daniel laughed and held up his hand. "I will speak to Roberts and look into Drummond's financials. In the meantime, what are you planning to do, besides keeping a chaste eye on Emily?" He gave him a pointed look.

As if that was an easy job. Brett explained about finding

Jason's former valet. "It is the next logical step. After that, I fear the trail grows thin."

"If it does, let us hope Emily takes comfort in knowing she did all she could for Jason, and that his reputation outside the company has been safeguarded. Dare we hope that will be enough for her?"

"One can hope." Brett shrugged, his expression reflecting Daniel's doubt.

On that bleak note, they both drank. Brett might not be able to stop Emily from pursuing her course, but with Daniel's support, the odds against Drummond tipped in their favor.

Brett's greater concern was Emily's reaction to his speaking to Daniel. He may not have broken his word to her, but he had taken a small sliver out of her trust. Brooding, he drank some more. He had done so to keep her fool head safe, but he doubted she would see it his way. Well, he would just have to make her do so.

An image of Emily's blazing blue eyes flashed through his mind. Perhaps it was the alcohol dulling his wits, but damned if he did not anticipate the challenge.

Sparring with Emily was almost as enjoyable as scheming with her, or best of all, making up and kissing her senseless and . . .

Daniel slammed his glass on the table. "Stop grinning like a besotted, daft idiot before I lose my drink!"

Chapter Twenty

❦

"N ooooooo!"
What in the world? Emily quickened her pace in response to her brother's high-pitched shrieks.

Over the past few days, Jonathan had unleashed an onslaught of whining and begging to visit one of Brett's ships, so they had plans to visit the London Docks later that morning. Had her brother finally inflicted real damage with that wretched sword of his, thus forcing the excursion to be postponed? She furrowed her brow, surprised to find herself disappointed at the prospect.

She had agreed to join the excursion, ostensibly to save Brett from her sword-wielding brother, but truthfully, she had yearned to get another glimpse into Brett's world and had been looking forward to the venture. So when she rushed into the library, she was relieved to discover her brother in a precarious position, but otherwise unharmed.

"But I need my sword!" Jonathan cried. He was flapping like an upside-down fish against Brett, who had Jonathan's legs imprisoned against his chest. "Fine, fine. I promise not to stab anyone again," Jonathan grumbled.

"Good man. I will hold you to your word," Brett said and lowered her brother to the ground.

Jonathan scrambled to his feet, his hair tousled, shirt askew. "So can I have my sword back?"

"You may, but remember a sword is a weapon. As such, it should be used with proper respect and wielded only in fair combat," Brett said. He retrieved the item from where he had tucked it into his trousers behind him and returned it to Jonathan. "A man's word is his solemn vow, so if I learn that you have broken yours, your sword will be confiscated and fed to the Queen's Pipe at the docks. Do you understand?"

Jonathan scrunched up his face. "No. The Queen's Pipe?"

Brett smiled. "It is the name for the kiln in the Queen's Warehouse. Goods that are spoiled, damaged, or that the customs officials have confiscated are burned in this furnace. It runs night and day, and its ashes are sold for manure. That is, after they have sifted out the nails and other pieces of iron, as well as any valuables."

"What do they do with the nails and iron?" Emily found herself asking.

"They melt them down and use them to make other items, like gun barrels."

"Gun barrels? Cor, then they can shoot the thieving pirates!" Jonathan shouted.

"Ah, we are more civilized these days. Thieves and other miscreants go before the customs officials, who . . ." At Jonathan's crestfallen expression, Brett's voice trailed off. With a wink at Emily, he bent close to Jonathan's ear and spoke sotto voce. "Actually, I heard there might be a secret ship upon which they force the no-good, rotten blackguards to walk the plank at sword point. They call the ship *the Skull and Crossbones*."

"*The Skull and Crossbones*?" Jonathan breathed. A beaming smile split his face. "I knew it! The British Navy will not let any no-good thieving blackguards get away with anything." He lifted his sword and jabbed it in sharp thrusts toward a foe only he could see.

Emily rolled her eyes.

Brett simply laughed. Straightening, he ruffled Jonathan's hair.

At the affectionate gesture, something constricted in her chest. He was good with her brother. He had rescheduled a meeting with Owen Jenkins to accommodate Jonathan's pleas to see the ships.

He would make a wonderful father—and he deserved to be one. When their strange, wonderful interlude wound to a close, she had to let him go. To free him to find another woman who could give him the life she could not. And she would.

Just not yet.

Her brother dashed from the room, and she cleared her throat. "*The Skull and Crossbones* is a fine touch. His grisly imagination will feast on it for some time."

He laughed. "I thought so. He is a brave lad. Your father must be proud."

"My father believes that like Job, he is being tested. Then he makes me promise to have only daughters." She pressed her hand to her stomach, covering another stab of pain. She changed the subject. "I am looking forward to visiting your ship. What is this one importing?"

He smiled. "The *Waveny* delivered a shipment of timber. Our imports are predominately timber, cotton, and tobacco."

"Why only those?"

"Those are the products England coveted during the war. Your British Navy blockaded our ports stretching the length of the eastern coast. Unable to export these goods, it opened a market for them here when the war ended. During the blockade, Daniel and I cultivated relationships with mill owners, southern plantations, and logging companies, enabling us to fill the demand for these products."

"Very clever." She smiled, and was unable to resist questioning him further. "I was curious. How did you acquire the capital to finance your venture? To purchase the fleet of ships? If you do not mind my asking."

Business matters, particularly money or finance, were not discussed in polite company, nor were they a proper conversation topic for a young woman, but curiosity overrode etiquette. Besides, Brett was an American, and often gave little heed to stodgy etiquette. He was different. *Like her.* The unbidden thought crossed her mind, closely followed by another—she was beginning to prefer different. Very much.

"My father is a partner in a prominent Boston law firm, so he assisted us with legal matters and provided us a loan of capital. We then courted private investors, both English and American." He shrugged. "The war had ended, and nationality is irrelevant when one is begging on bended knee for their livelihood, so to speak."

"*So to speak.* It must have been difficult to set aside your opinions of our pampered, haughty aristocrats." She cocked her head to the side, amused.

"What opinions?" Brett rejoined.

"It appears business trumps prejudices," she said, smiling at the teasing gleam in his eyes. "And now you are expanding into Bristol and hoping to move toward steam. It is an impressive success. Admirable. You should be very proud."

Brett gave her a sharp look, and she marveled at the flush that stole over his features before he glanced away.

Interesting. The man must not be used to compliments, at least not from her. It was something to ponder. After all, he was good at so many things. She thought of his kisses and the interlude in the maze and—

"My pardon, sir, but this message was delivered for you. I was advised that it was important." Burke entered the library and handed Brett an envelope.

Flushing, she watched Burke depart, cursing her train of thought. "Anything amiss?" she asked Brett, who was reading the note.

"It is from Jenkins," Brett said, and then cursed, his expression thunderous. "Devil take it! Bertram Marsh was viciously attacked on his way to work."

She gasped. "No! Is he all right? What happened?"

"Jenkins says he is bruised and battered, but the surgeon he sent for assured Jenkins that Marsh will make a full recovery."

"Thank goodness," she breathed. "How did Jenkins learn of it?"

"Baines and his mates stumbled upon two ruffians assaulting Marsh on Ring Street. The boys chased them off, Baines retrieved Jenkins, and he then helped Marsh into a hackney and escorted him home. Marsh has requested to speak to me. Jenkins says he was quite insistent on the matter." He handed the letter to her, his face grim. "Apparently Marsh's rooms were ransacked. The only fortunate news is that his aunt was not home at the time, because she was paying a call on an ill friend."

"We must go to him," she said, skimming Jenkins's note. "We need to ensure that he is all right and learn what he wants to speak to you about."

Brett nodded. "Yes, *I* will visit him and—"

"I am going, too!" she protested, glaring at Brett. "This is my fault. I dragged him into this matter, so it is because of me that—"

"I understand you feel responsible and are concerned for Marsh's welfare, but you cannot visit a single man in his rooms," Brett said.

She bristled. He spoke with measured calm, as if reasoning with an unruly child, forgetting that moments earlier he had been explaining the intricacies of his company to an intelligent adult. She might have to revise her earlier opinion of him. Perhaps he was not that different from most men after all. "Marsh resides with his aunt," she reminded him, "which is very respectable. I am going. I will wear that concealing cloak that I wore when we visited your office. No one can identify me in that, but it is a risk I am willing to take. His aunt will be distressed and will need a woman's empathy. I am going."

The muscle worked in Brett's cheek as he gritted his teeth. "I cannot take you into a situation that is dangerous as Marsh's condition attests to, and which—"

"It says here that Jenkins has posted Baines and his boys to guard Marsh's rooms." She pointed to that section in Jenkins's letter. "That should give us fair warning of any pending danger."

"I told you, *we* are not do anything . . ." Brett began, but at her expression, he tossed up his hands. "What am I thinking? If I refuse, no doubt you will simply go on your own. Fine. Come. But you tell Jonathan about the change in plans."

She grinned. "Fine. Now that he has given his word about not using his sword, I shall be quite safe. Do not look so bleak. You asked me to trust you. Well, I do. I trust in you to keep me safe."

"Mmh. Why do I feel like my own words are coming back to haunt me?"

She simply laughed, and dashed off to brave Jonathan's temper tantrum.

❧❦

BRETT FOLLOWED MARSH'S aunt to her nephew's room. She was a diminutive woman, rail thin, her gray eyes matching her wan expression. Upon meeting them, Mrs. Marsh had dabbed at her tears with a lace handkerchief, lamenting the damage to their rooms and the assault on her nephew. Emily had tossed him a reproachful *I told you so* look.

Emily might be right about the aunt, but he still wished he could have assessed the situation first. He should have insisted on it, but her jutting chin and *you cannot tell me what to do* look had silenced him. He shook his head, baffled to feel a smile curving his lips. She would not be his Athena had she meekly ceded to his demands. Truth be told, her capitulation would have disturbed him far more.

He shook his head, marveling at how easily she was maneuvering him to her way of thinking. Like leading an ass to water.

Brett stopped short when Emily froze on the threshold of Marsh's room, but her reaction saved him from contemplating the indignity of the analogy. Marsh's battered face gave him pause as well. One eye was swollen shut, his lip split and twice its normal size, and a multicolored bruise distorted one cheek.

Marsh moved to sit up, and his aunt rushed to his side to rearrange his pillows behind his back. "I do not think you should—"

"It is all right, Auntie." Marsh's swollen lip gave his words a slight slur. He patted her arm while she bent to tuck his blankets around him. "I promise you, I look worse than I feel. Auntie, would you be so good as to bring us a cup of tea?"

She straightened. "Of course. How remiss of me."

"Tea sounds lovely. Thank you, Mrs. Marsh," Emily said.

Brett's only interest in tea was that it secured the privacy they needed, which is what he surmised Marsh intended.

Brett noted Mrs. Marsh left the door wide open, and a maid appeared to settle in a chair just outside the room. He grunted, wishing Emily gave equal care to her reputation.

Emily had adjusted to Marsh's appearance and had crossed to his bedside. "Mr. Marsh, please let me offer my most sincere apologies. You warned me not to dredge up matters better left buried. I feel responsible for this horrid attack, and I am wretched over it."

He brushed aside her concerns. "No apologies are necessary. You believed in me when no one else did. For that, I shall be eternally grateful." He echoed words his aunt had said to them upon their arrival. "As to the other, well, we know what the culprits were after, but they searched the wrong place. Now with the ledger safely in your hands, we can identify who is behind these attacks. Justice will prevail, and the blackguards will rot in Newgate." He spoke with a strength that was at odds with his battered appearance.

Emily visibly cringed, as if their failure would be another blow to his face.

Brett broke the silence. "Yes. That is exactly what they will get. However, it might take a little more time for justice to be meted out."

Marsh's good eye darted between them. "The portfolio? You do not have it? Was it stolen? The trunk lost?"

"They were not in the false bottom of Jason's trunk," Emily said, and splayed her hands helplessly. "Jason's sister, Miss Patricia Branson, said the compartment was empty."

Marsh closed his eyes and sank back into his pillow.

"All is not lost, Marsh. We will recover it. And . . ." Brett trailed off, a sudden idea striking him. He turned to pace, caught up in his excitement. "If Drummond is behind this attack and is responsible for destroying your reputation, I believe he made a crucial mistake in attacking you a second time, this time physically—"

"What?" Marsh sputtered, wide-eyed. "My pardon, but do you mean *Lawrence Drummond*, the viscount's former colleague is behind this attack? And you suspect *him* of maligning my reputation? I do not understand. He urged the viscount to flee, sought to protect him after the attacks on his life." Marsh pressed a frail hand to his temple.

Brett stopped and arched a brow at Emily. He left the decision on what she wished to confide to her.

She drew a deep breath and forged ahead. "We have reason to believe Lawrence Drummond is the man whom Jason identified as having embezzled from the East India Company." She briefly summarized how they had arrived at their suspicions.

"But why would he betray the viscount? They were friends. What is his motive?" Marsh said.

Bloody motive again. Devil take it, he should have examined Drummond's motivation earlier. Hoped that Daniel was successful in his search to do so. "Greed is usually behind embezzlement," he echoed Daniel's response.

Marsh nodded solemnly. "As the Good Book says, 'The love of money is the root of all evil,' *Timothy* 6:10."

"Yes, err, very true." Brett could cite scripture as pathetically as he could read Latin, which is to say, hardly at all.

"You were saying earlier that if Drummond is responsible for this attack on Marsh he made a mistake? What do you mean?" Emily said.

"Because why search Marsh's house if Drummond has all the incriminating material in hand? Why take that risk?

I think Emily's persistence in searching for Jason's ledger has Drummond fearing that there may be something still circulating that could incriminate him. That is, if he is indeed the guilty man we believe him to be."

"And Mr. Drummond is offering to assist me to thwart my finding this evidence?"

"What is this about Mr. Drummond's offer of assistance?" Marsh grimaced as he sought to frown.

Brett apprised Marsh of Drummond's offer, and then continued. "We knew that already, but we assumed Drummond had no plans to search himself, while assuring you that he was working diligently on your behalf." He again paced as if to stay ahead of his churning thoughts.

He summarized Drummond's movements to date. "We believe that Drummond first collected all the business papers in Jason's trunk and destroyed any files pertaining to Jason's work at the company. Drummond then ostensibly tarnished your reputation, preventing you from speaking for Jason or against Drummond should you have had any damaging information. In essence, Drummond took care of anything or anyone potentially harmful to him."

He stopped and grinned at Emily. "Then you came along and began digging into his buried secrets. Now he is afraid. I think he fears Jason's letters have steered you toward new information that only you are privy to, and he is desperate to acquire this information before you."

"So we are now searching for the same incriminating information, but are at cross-purposes with each other?"

"I think so, which raises the stakes, as you are now competing against the other." He frowned, remembering another race for information that he and Daniel had found themselves engaged in—and the dire consequences of that. Unconsciously, he rubbed his now-healed broken arm. At least he and Emily knew what they were searching for, an advantage he and Daniel had not had. It was something.

"But where *is* the portfolio? Drummond does not have it, it was not in the trunk, and I do not have it," Marsh said, frustration lacing his words.

"There is one more lead to follow," Emily said. "You did say Jason's valet was the only other person cognizant of this false bottom in the trunk?"

"Winfred!" Marsh's good eye locked on Brett. "You must find him and warn him that he is in danger. The thugs who waylaid me might go after him next. If you are thinking of speaking to him, Drummond might have similar thoughts, particularly if he is monitoring your movements."

Emily gasped. "Of course. We should have considered that." She shot Brett another chastising look, as if he should have had the foresight to know that as well. "I forgot to tell you that Patricia Branson gave me Winfred's address. Patricia told me her brother had procured a post for Winfred with Lord Halford's eldest son. Halford is hosting a ball tomorrow evening. I hope to speak to Winfred then, but I will send a note of warning to him immediately."

"Another ball." He sighed and grimaced.

Ignoring him, Emily addressed Marsh. "Winfred also tried to talk to me at Jason's funeral. I think he wanted to confide something that I was not ready to hear."

Brett frowned. "You did not mention that either."

Her eyes lifted to his and then away. "Yes, well, I do not like to revisit that time, so I have not done so until recent discoveries have forced me to look more closely. I should have recalled—"

"No," he said, cursing himself for being obtuse. "Do not punish yourself for not being able to process information at your fiancé's funeral. For grieving," he added softly. "We will speak to Winfred. He can then share whatever it is that he wished to confide to you all those years ago."

Her brow furrowed, but she nodded. "Yes, you are right."

"I remember something as well," Marsh said. "Winfred mentioned to me on the voyage home that he saw Drummond leaving Jason's rooms shortly before Winfred had found Jason . . . er . . . ah, Jason dead," he stammered, glancing uncertainly at Emily before forging on. "Winfred had forgotten about it in the chaos of the ensuing events. Winfred also

said that Drummond's valet had told him that Drummond
had supplies of opium."

"Good lord," Brett breathed. "That is damning indeed."

Emily's lips parted and she looked wide-eyed. "I need to
get Winfred to confirm that." She turned to Brett, excitement
brimming in her eyes. "We need to convince Winfred to speak
to Drummond's valet, to convince him to come forward. To
give this statement to a magistrate and see what other information he may have."

Brett smiled. "We do, and we will."

"Do you think Drummond might have given the drug to
the viscount, pressed it upon him?"

Emily cleared her throat and looked at Brett, as if she
sought his support. He gave her an encouraging nod. "I think
that is exactly what he did. And it is now even more imperative that we speak to Winfred."

His Athena.

Marsh audibly swallowed. "I see. Mr. Drummond will
have much to answer for come Judgment Day, breaking two
of the Lord's commandments." He met Emily's gaze. "I trust
you shall prevail. However, allow me to offer my services
as well. What can I do? There must be something."

Before they could respond, there was a knock on the door,
and Mrs. Marsh returned carrying a large tea-laden tray.

"Tea and biscuits. Oh, thank you, love," she said to Emily,
who had hurried over to relieve Mrs. Marsh of her burden
and assist her in setting it on a corner table.

Brett answered Marsh. "There is something that would be
of great assistance to me. If you can provide the names of
anyone else who worked with you and your late colleague on
that troublesome project, that would be most helpful. It might
be wise to speak to them, or to those who have returned from
their posting abroad."

Marsh nodded. "Right, sir. I will think on that. They
might have information I do not."

"My thoughts exactly," Brett said.

"Mind you, Mr. Curtis assured me that you are to take

all the time you need to recover. Is that not right, Mr. Curtis?" Agatha Marsh said as she handed Brett his cup of tea.

Brett hated tea, preferred coffee, but accepted it with a smile. "Of course. Marsh, do not return to work until you are fit to do so. That is an order. That is another nonnegotiable point."

Mrs. Marsh beamed. "See, Bertram. Mr. Curtis wants you to take care of yourself, and I shall be seeing that you do just that." She fussed over his pillows, and then handed him his cup of tea.

Brett used her distraction to toss his tea into a nearby plant. It was mostly water, and the plant thirsted for it, appearing as beaten down as Marsh. He caught Emily's frowning rebuke and shrugged, unrepentant. Emily might maneuver him to do many things, but he would be damned if she turned him into a tea drinker.

The small act of defiance reminded him that he remained in control of certain parts of his life. That was a good thing, because she was wearing his defenses down and eroding barriers he had erected years ago. It left his battered heart exposed—and worse, vulnerable.

He did not want to fall in love with Lady Emily Chandler, but it might be too late.

Chapter Twenty-one

❧❦

"I CANNOT believe that you have talked me into this," Brett grumbled.

Emily lifted her skirts to descend the narrow, dimly lit stairwell ahead of him. The flickering light cast from a maid's lantern was all that illuminated their passage. She tossed Brett an aggrieved look over her shoulder. "Should I have arranged for Winfred to meet us outside in the shrubbery? Or in the library where anyone could stumble upon us?"

When she reached the bottom, she turned to face him. "Besides, I needed to separate you and Melody. If she mentioned *the good Mr. Jenkins* again, you might have throttled her."

Brett hurried down the last steps, but paused at her comment. "She was doing that deliberately."

"Of course she was. And as amusing as it was, the steam pouring out of your ears looked dangerous. Really, you need to trust Melody to take care of herself." Jenkins had delivered some papers to Keaton House yesterday afternoon. He had stayed to take tea with Daniel and Brett's sisters, all whom he knew from his time in the Boston office.

"I have no choice, do I?" Brett muttered. "She never listens to me. Reminds me of another young woman I know. Perhaps you two should be separated. I think . . ." he began and then broke off. "We digress. Shall we continue?" He flashed the maid one of his disarming smiles.

"Ah . . . er . . . yes, sir," the young girl stammered, and then turned to lead them down a corridor lit with a single oil lamp that was perched in a nearby sconce.

Emily rolled her eyes, bristling at the gleam of amusement in Brett's.

The maid stopped and knocked on one of the doors lining the corridor. When the minutes crawled by without a response, she knocked again. "Mr. Winfred?" Silence answered her.

Emily frowned, quite certain that Winfred's note had directed them to meet him at his rooms at eleven o'clock. He had even solicited the help of a footman to locate them at the ball and direct them to this downstairs maid. She had been waiting to escort them to Winfred's rooms in the basement, where he lodged with the other male servants.

So . . . where is he? Had Drummond already gotten to him?

She had not seen Drummond at Halford's, despite keeping a vigilant watch for him, even soliciting Julia's help to do so. Her sister's delight gave Emily a twinge of guilt, which deepened when Julia assured her that if Drummond was present, he would not escape her notice.

But why was the valet not answering his door?

She struggled to keep her worries at bay as the silence echoed.

"If you will excuse me, may I?" Brett nodded to the door.

"Of course, but I do not think he is here. Perhaps Master Halford required his services," the maid said apologetically.

Brett bent and ran his finger along the doorframe.

Only then did Emily notice the slivers of splintered wood that surrounded the lock. She drew a sharp breath.

Brett inspected the scraped area and his glove came away

with fine splinters. He straightened. "We are too late." He gestured for them to step back and barred their advance with his arm. His expression somber, he turned the brass knob and gave the door a gentle prod, but it swung open easily. "Winfred's not here, but someone else has been." He opened the door wide to reveal the upended room.

The maid gasped, and Emily groaned. Winfred's room did not contain the bric-a-brac of the Marshes' drawing room, being more sparsely furnished, but the few possessions belonging to the valet, predominately books, were scattered across the floor. The drawers of two bureaus jutted out, clothes spilling over them. The bedclothes looked riffled through, their pillows on the floor.

She had wanted justice for Jason, but at what cost? Winfred's life? Or threats to Bertram Marsh and his aunt?

Or . . . to *Brett*?

She lifted her gaze to his handsome features, and her knees weakened. The price was too high. Perhaps it was time she slammed Pandora's bloody lid closed and locked it. Jason had been dead and buried for nearly four years, his reputation outside the company was safeguarded, and she had no evidence implicating Drummond. Was she on a fool's quest that was endangering everyone who became involved? What about her family? Or heaven forbid, the twins?

"Emily?"

She blinked, struggling to calm her runaway thoughts. Brett took one look at her expression and guided her to a chair in the corner of the room, sitting her down. He disappeared, but soon returned to press a glass into her grip, cupping her hands around it.

"Drink this." He pressed his fingers beneath the tumbler and urged it toward her.

It was water and refreshingly cold. It slid down her throat and washed away her grim train of thought. She finished every drop, lowered the glass, and drew a shuddering breath. "I am all right."

"Yes, you are." He tucked a strand of hair behind her ear, his smile so sweet it nearly brought tears to her eyes.

Her momentary lapse annoyed her. She would not falter. How could she with Brett at her side? He was a safe harbor, or a sturdy anchor that, at the very least, she could use to pull herself to safety.

"Hold on to that." He winked and turned to step out into the hall.

She strained but failed to decipher the low murmur of voices. She clenched her jaw, determined to remind Brett that she may have faltered, but she had not fallen. She was quite capable of hearing whatever news was being imparted. In a minute, she would tell him that in no uncertain terms. Maybe a few minutes. She cursed herself for being a coward masquerading as a brave crusader.

"Winfred is all right."

"What?" she gasped, her gaze searching Brett's.

He carried the maid's lamp, its light casting flickering shadows on the wall. He set it on the bedside table and closed the door. "A colleague of Winfred's, another footman who shares this room with him, said they were together when they discovered the room had been broken into. Winfred had asked this young man to meet us and convey Winfred's apologies for needing to flee."

"But where did he go?"

"Therein lies the rub," Brett said, frowning. "His friend did not know, but said Winfred would get word to him when he could. Winfred's only instructions were to not report this incident until the footman had given us Winfred's message and time for us to leave his room unseen.

"I gave the gentleman my card and instructed him to contact me as soon as Winfred resurfaces, and the footman promised to keep his confidence about our visit. I asked for a quarter of an hour before he reports this to the housekeeper, so we have a few minutes. But if there was anything to be found, I am sure whoever did this has located it," he finished, his gaze shifting over the disarray.

Worry segued into annoyance. "For goodness' sake!" she huffed. "Winfred could not take a few minutes to give us a by-your-leave himself? If the culprits had already left his room, why did Winfred have to flee so soon? I did tell him what I had to discuss was important." She slipped off the chair and snatched up a handful of books, irritably shoving them into the bookshelves. "I do not think that is too much to ask after all that Jason has done for him. I do not—" She snapped her mouth closed when Brett caught her hand and extracted the novel she held.

"Have a care. These poor tomes are innocent. But you are right, it is not too much to ask," he gently agreed. Disregarding his pristine black evening clothes, he settled on the floor beside her. He set the book on the shelf. "Do not worry. Winfred cannot disappear entirely. I have tried to do so when Melody has been harping at me, and it is impossible. I promise you, he will turn up somewhere."

She scowled and handed him another book. The quiet task of restoring the shelf calmed her. They worked in companionable silence. "Do you think whoever tossed this room found Jason's ledger? That Winfred had Jason's portfolio after all?"

"I do not know. We will have to wait until we speak to Winfred."

She nodded, struggling to overcome her frustration and disappointment. "I am not good at waiting," she muttered. When Brett did not respond, she turned to him. He was fingering a book in his lap and smiling as if he had discovered a long-lost friend.

He glanced up and grinned. "It is Dafoe's *Robinson Crusoe*," he murmured. "In it, Crusoe refers to his island as the *Island of Despair*. When I was first shipped back here for school, I wrote to my mother and told her that was what I thought of England, and I pleaded for her to send a ship to rescue me with all due haste."

Her heart twisted at the image of a young boy shipped a continent away to attend school in a foreign country—without family, friends, or . . . a title in a world where rank reigned supreme. *The Island of Despair.* "You must have been very homesick."

Her soft tone caught his attention, and he snapped his

eyes to hers. In that typically dismissive way men had about displays of emotion, he shrugged and hastened to assure her that he carried no lasting scars. "It was not as bad as all that. I met Daniel and soon after Drew arrived. I read this aloud to Drew, and it was his favorite book. That is, until Daniel and I started calling him Friday." Grinning, he returned the book to the shelf.

"You read the book out loud to him?" She again questioned Drew's intelligence, or lack thereof, and wondered if his cousin *was* illiterate. Her suspicions grew when Brett avoided her eyes, and his lips compressed into a tight line.

"I did. Hasn't Julia ever read to you?" There was a challenging edge to his query.

Surprised, she did not immediately reply.

He swept to his feet and held a hand out to her. "We should leave. Each minute we stay, we court scandal should we be discovered."

The chance to respond had passed. Clearly, he was done reminiscing. She pondered his reaction to the innocuous question as she allowed him to assist her to her feet.

Prescott's disappearance was part of a larger picture, and the details about why Brett sought to find him were missing with his cousin.

"Speaking of Prescott. Have you located him? Or received any word from him?" she said lightly. "I fear I have not upheld my end of our original bargain in giving you time to look for him. You have been too busy assisting me. But while we are forced to wait for Winfred to reappear, you will have time to renew your search."

"That is not necessary," he said. "Like Winfred, Drew will be in touch with me when he is ready." He collected the lantern, opened the door, and waited for her to precede him.

"What makes you so sure that he will do so?" She fell into step behind the maid, who had waited to escort them back.

"Because I have something he wants. Badly."

"Haversley's A. W. Grant painting in which your cousin was interested?" she prodded, waiting for him to ascend the narrow staircase. He glanced at her, clearly surprised that she had remembered the painting.

"Exactly." He grinned, and then climbed the stairs.

"You bought it for him? Why?"

"Because he was unable to do so himself."

At his enigmatic response, she pressed him further. "Why will he contact you about *that* particular painting? Is it valuable?"

Brett's snort drifted down to her. "Hardly. It is worthless. In fact, I am certain it is a forgery."

"I do not understand. Why on earth would your cousin contact you over a forgery?" she said, baffled.

"Because it is in his best interest to do so."

He stopped at the top landing. "We should not come barreling out together. I will go first, and you should follow a few minutes later—once the maid determines that no one is about."

He opened the door and returned the lantern to the maid. The maid wisely held her counsel before she followed Brett out. Halford trained his servants well.

Emily exhaled an exasperated huff. Brett was finished with the subject, or had finished telling her what he wished to share. *Secrets.* She thought she knew the man. Seeing him at his office, the docks, with her family, and intimately with her. She was discovering she did not. Or rather, there was so much more she did not truly know.

She knew nothing of his past. Of the young boy tossed into a sea of aristocrats and forced to swim—or drown. He had loved and lost an Englishwoman. And this mystery surrounding his cousin. They had shared some passionate moments, but nothing more. She frowned.

Wasn't that all she wanted?

It was the stipulation to their alliance and the seduction that she had embarked upon. It annoyed her that she should now be questioning it.

Emily blinked at the blaze of light when the door opened.

"It is all right, mum. You can slip out now," the maid said.

Emily was grateful for the interruption, her thoughts confusing her. "Thank you, I appreciate your assistance. If you do hear anything, anything at all from Winfred, it is very important that you let him know that I am most anxious to hear from him."

"Yes, mum. I will do so." The maid bobbed a curtsy and then disappeared.

The footman had Brett's card, and Emily now had the maid's assurance. Between the two, they should soon receive word of Winfred's whereabouts.

To return to the ballroom, Emily had to cross through a portrait gallery lined with Halford's ancestors, an austere and grim-faced group. She was scowling back at one dour-looking fellow when the click of boots forced her to recompose her features.

She struggled to place the identity of the man approaching, but like a distant object, his name eluded her. Due to her absence from society, this was not uncommon, but it still frustrated.

The man carried himself with a rigid aristocratic bearing, his head tilted slightly back. He was dressed in uncompromising black, his evening jacket and matching waistcoat beautifully tailored, and the knot in his silk cravat a rival to Drummond's. He could have alighted from one of the portraits, because his heavy-browed expression mirrored that of the ancestor with whom Emily had been exchanging scowls.

He stopped short as he caught sight of her, and his austere features softened. "Ah, Lady Emily, 'tis a pleasure," he drawled as he dipped into a bow.

Wentworth! The Earl of Wentworth. "Lord Wentworth," she greeted him as she curtsied.

"I hear congratulations are in order, and your lovely sister and Bedford are the proud parents of twins. Taunton must be so proud—as must you be."

"Of course. I take my role as the doting aunt seriously, and my sister agrees. She assures me I have turned spoiling into a fine art."

"I am sure you jest. As I advise my daughter, indulged children may be excused, but they quickly grow, and spoiled adults are not so amusing." He spread his hands in a *there you have it* gesture.

Yes, he definitely could join the ranks of Halford's humorless portrait gallery. His daughter had Emily's most sincere sympathy. "I shall keep that in mind. Thankfully, I have a few years before the damage is irreversible."

He nodded, her wry tone clearly eluding him. "Quite right. They are young yet. Please convey my felicitations to Bedford and your lovely sister. I have not had the . . ."

Once again, the clacking of boots on the hardwood floor echoed, and she turned to see Daniel and Brett enter the corridor.

"Emily, Julia sent me to find you, and now I have. Pity all of her requests cannot be resolved so easily," Daniel said, his amused voice ringing out.

"It appears you can do the honors yourself, Lord Wentworth," Emily said, grinning at the earl.

The earl turned to greet Daniel. The smile curving his lips wavered and then froze. It was like watching a warm lake ice over, so cold was his expression. Emily resisted the urge to rub her hands down her arms. "Have you met Mr. Curtis of—?" she began.

"Spare me the introductions," Wentworth rudely interrupted. "We are well acquainted. Unfortunately, our history goes back a long way."

Brett's eyes flared and a muscle vibrated in his cheek, but if one did not know his features as well as Emily had come to know them, his reaction would have been missed. He did not deign to greet Wentworth or respond to the insult.

Wentworth addressed Daniel, dipping his head. "Bedford. I had heard you and Curtis still kept company, but I refused to believe it. Now that you have come into the title, I had hoped you had outgrown your youthful transgression into trade. Thought you had refined your taste in confidants, considering those whom you solicited to support the agriculture bill. It appears I was mistaken," he said with scathing contempt.

"On the contrary," Daniel drawled and crossed his arms. "My taste is impeccable, particularly in regard to choosing my friends, so the mistake must be yours."

Mottled spots of red suffused Wentworth's features, and a sneer contorted his lips as he regarded Daniel and then Brett, who had crossed his arms as well. The silence stretched taut before Wentworth managed to reply. "It appears I am too late to warn you against trusting *this* man. Do not say I did not try."

"I have trusted Mr. Curtis with my life. As I am still breathing, that makes your warning groundless, rather than belated. Wouldn't you agree, Curtis?"

"I do, but considering *my* life was almost lost in saving yours, *I* should have been warned about keeping company with you."

"You have a point," Daniel conceded, and then appeared to consider his words. "But I saved you from being pummeled to death in school, so we are even."

"You may jest, but heed my words," Wentworth said coldly. "This man is not to be trusted, and you may rue the day that you chose to do so." Wentworth vibrated with barely controlled rage, before he whirled and stormed from the room.

Wide-eyed, Emily's lips parted as his imposing figure receded.

What in the world?

She and Brett had had their battles in the past, but *this*, this was an all-out war. She turned to study Brett, noticing the crack in his calm façade. He dropped his arms and balled his hands into fists, his jaw clenched, eyes hard.

"I forgot what a pompous arse he is," Daniel said, breaking the silence.

"You have an enemy in Wentworth. What in the world did you ever do to cross him?" She blurted out the question before considering the impropriety of it.

Brett snapped his gaze to hers, and she nearly recoiled

from his fury. "What did *I* do? I had the audacity to fall in love with his daughter. I then compounded that infraction by asking for her hand in marriage." He turned and with long, agitated strides, strode from the room.

Stunned, she moved to hurry after him, but Daniel caught her arm, holding her back. "Let him go. Give him time."

She wanted to protest, to follow Brett and apologize, but Daniel was right. She, of all people, understood the difficulty in weathering the painful siege of memories. Like a strong current, they could catch you unaware and sweep your feet out from under you. It took time to claw your way back to solid ground. "I cannot recall Wentworth's daughter. I do not believe I have met her." It was an inane comment, but she did not know what to say.

"Lady Janice Wentworth. You might not. She came out about a decade ago," Daniel said. "I do not know if their feelings for each other would have lasted, but Wentworth never gave them a chance. And Janice Wentworth was not strong enough to stand up to her father—even though she was of age and had her own inheritance, so she was at liberty to make her own choice."

Emily frowned, because once upon a time, she had possessed that strength. When she had fallen in love with Jason, she would have done anything, risked anything to be with him. Devil take the consequences. Brett had deserved better than this Janice, but Wentworth's reaction was no surprise. "As an earl, Wentworth had some lofty duke destined for his daughter, I take it?"

Surprised at her bitter tone, Daniel glanced at her.

She shrugged. "Our aristocratic marriage market is like Curtis Shipping, an exchange of lucrative goods. I was fortunate that our father did not feel compelled to barter Julia and me away. Julia married for love, and I would have as well," she said softly, her smile wistful.

"I forget that not everyone is as fortunate as I," Daniel said, and then he turned serious. "If you recall, I was not Julia's first love. I like to think I would have been had I not been an ocean away, so I did not have the chance to stop her from making the worst decision of . . . Well, she eventually came around to my way of thinking. It took some convincing because Julia can be . . ." He stopped and looking abashed, began again. "The point I keep losing is that broken hearts mend. So there is hope for Brett and you. However, I suggest you do not give him too much of it. Hope, that is, unless you are serious."

She froze, not sure that she had heard him correctly.

"I do not know what is between you, but tread carefully. I do not want to be picking up the pieces of two shattered hearts." He gave her a wry look. "Do not stay too long. Julia will worry." And then he left her alone.

She pressed an unsteady hand to her temple, her thoughts swirling in a maelstrom of emotions.

If Daniel had seen something between Brett and herself, had Julia noticed it as well? And if Daniel was right, was she giving Brett false hope? She recalled his embittered expression, and curled her arms around her waist. Lady Janice Wentworth was responsible for that—not Emily. But the woman had etched a scar into his soul, and Emily could not bear to add another.

She did not want to hurt Brett, but was not ready to give him up.

She . . . she needed him. And . . . he needed her.

He needed her to show him that not all women were as weakhearted as Janice.

Chapter Twenty-two

❦

BRETT slid his pen into the inkwell, leaned back, and swiped his hands down his face. What time was it? He glanced at the ormolu clock on the mantel. It was nearing midnight. He sighed. He should retire. Despite Taunton's loan of his office, he was getting little done. It was difficult to concentrate on the present while trapped in the past.

He could almost feel the dampness of that long-ago night seep into his bones. The rain had been intermittent, but it had eventually soaked him through. How long had he stood on that blasted street corner, waiting like the daft love-struck idiot that he had been?

Lady Janice Wentworth.

Good lord, he had loved her so. He had been but three-and-twenty, and Janice had been three years younger and so lovely. She had remained unwed at age twenty, because her domineering father had refused to let her go, and so Brett had planned to rescue her from her father's tyranny. He had thought she loved him, and she had, but not enough—or not enough to defy her father.

"Stupid, besotted fool," he muttered into the empty room, unable to summon sympathy for his younger self.

In the past, work had rescued him from that street corner. It had carried him through those early years and the last few days, but had failed him tonight.

Damn Wentworth.

Damn the bastard for rising like Lazarus to surprise him. Brett had vowed to be prepared when he confronted his nemesis again. To be the confident, successful man of business that he was. To be the bastard's equal, despite all Wentworth had done to destroy him.

He snatched his drink from the desk and crossed to the hearth to glower at the dying embers of the fire. Grabbing a poker, he stabbed at the coals, needing to chase away the chill of that damp street and the shock of Wentworth.

He returned the poker to its stand, draped one arm over the mantel, and brooded into the fire.

"What is all this?"

Jerking, he whirled, sloshing brandy over the cuff of his dress shirt.

Emily.

He cursed as he patted at his wet sleeve. "What the devil are you dong here? And dressed like *that*?"

She wore a light pink robe over what clearly was her nightgown. The dancing light of the fire cast a warm glow over the beauty of her features. She looked like an ethereal angel—until she opened her mouth.

"You have been avoiding me. Do not deny it." She brushed aside his concerns like a pesky interruption and speared him with an accusatory glare. "I do not appreciate it."

She was more she-devil than angel anyway. "I was working. If you remember, I do have a company to run."

"Yes, yes," she sighed. "Your company, your responsibility." She studied the plans and furrowed her brow. "These look like the interior of a ship. Are you building another ship?"

He blinked at her. The woman had no boundaries, did not give a fig for propriety, and was now nosing about in his business. And it was nearly midnight! He stormed over to snap up the plans, but the excitement in her voice stopped him.

"These must be the improvements to the staterooms on your packet ships. Melody said Jenkins was nattering on about this to her. He wants to increase the size of the staterooms and make them more luxurious."

"Melody said that Jenkins was *nattering* on?" he echoed. His sister had played him well. He could imagine Jenkins's enthusiasm, because God knows Jenkins had been nattering on about his idea *to him*—and unlike Melody, he shared Jenkins's excitement. His mood improved at the image of Melody's eyes glazing over.

He nodded to the sheets of paper. "Jenkins has a sound idea, and has hired an engineer to render detailed plans. We can charge higher fees for the plush accommodations and entice passengers into booking on our ships over a competitor's."

"So this plan has returned Mr. Jenkins to your good graces?"

"Sometimes the man proves his worth," he conceded. "But I will mention Melody's interest in his plan to him. I may suggest he discuss the advent of steam the next time they meet. Melody would be riveted." He lifted his glass in a toast and drained it.

Emily laughed. "You are too cruel."

"She deserves it, after singing the good Mr. Jenkins's praises to me for the past week. She is lucky I did not wring her neck." Their eyes met, and lost in the amused warmth of hers, it took him a moment to pull his gaze away. "I was just cleaning up here." He set his drink down to gather up the plans. He ignored Emily as she picked up his discarded glass and disappeared with it.

Papers tucked under his arm, he turned—and froze. Emily had settled herself on the burgundy settee, her skirts like a billowing cloud around her. She sipped from his now-refilled crystal tumbler.

"My father called this office his oasis of solitude. We were warned not to disturb him when he was within. But we always did, so he started locking the door," she said, smiling at the memory and fingering the key she held. "He soon discovered that he missed Julia and me making forts beneath his desk or my mother pestering him with tea. He demanded to know how a sane man was expected to get any work done in a silence that echoed. After that, he only locked it during particular times—and with my mother on his side of the door." She wiggled her eyebrows.

He leaned against the desk, wondering at her game. "So I take it that I am trapped?"

"As I have said, you have been avoiding me, and there are things that need to be discussed." She lifted the key that hung on a slim rope and slipped it over her neck. It disappeared down the collar of her robe.

"Do you think it is safe there?" he drawled. He was good at games, and this one intrigued him.

"Maybe not, but you will not be getting it until I am ready."

"Is that a dare?" He nearly laughed.

"Behave," she warned. "Now come sit by me." She patted the space beside her, tucking her skirts around her.

He glanced at the clock, and then sighed. Whatever Emily was up to, as usual, they had to play by her rules. "Can this not wait until the morning?"

He did not know if he could focus, having been unable to concentrate on anything all evening. Then again, a feminine distraction would get his mind off Wentworth. Perhaps the night was not a complete waste. That is, if he could convince her to play . . . *with him.*

His mood lifted, he set aside his papers and quickened his steps to join her on the settee. Once seated, he grasped her by the arms with the intent of pulling her onto his lap.

Her palm, flat against his chest, stopped him. "Not yet."

She was going to be the death of him. Or at least certain parts of his anatomy. He exerted a little more pressure.

"Stop that! I told you to behave."

"I do not think you are in any position to comment on *my* behavior, when you flout all the rules." He pressed his lips against the soft underside of her chin because she had lifted her face to strain away from him. "Good thing I never cared for your English rules. Find them tedious." He rained a trail of kisses down the slim column of her neck, inhaling the scent of some floral soap. "Your skin is soft as satin."

"You need to listen. I want to discuss something with you."

"You have my undivided attention," he murmured. His position forced her to lean back against the curved arm of the settee, and he moved his body over hers. He supported himself on one hand and threaded the other through her hair, sending pins scattering and dismantling the chignon holding up her hair. The freed strands tumbled about her shoulders.

"What are you doing?" She slapped his hands away.

He laughed. "If you have to ask, I am not doing too good a job of it." He dipped his head to give her a scalding kiss, but she turned her face away. "I am finishing what you have started."

"I did not start anything—"

"On the contrary. You locked the door," he teased. He would have preferred her lips, but he settled on a curved cheek.

"Stop it!" she cried, and pressed against his chest with more force.

The aggrieved tone cut through his passionate zeal, and he drew back. At the sight of her distressed features, he immediately sobered. He shifted away, allowing her to sit up. "What is it? Has Drummond—"

"For goodness' sake, it is not about Drummond. Not everything is about him and the blasted portfolio!" She belted her robe tight around her slim waist.

Incredulous, he gaped at her, unable to believe he had heard her correctly. "Hang Drummond and the ledger with him for all I care. That is *your* goal, not mine. Mine is to keep your fool head safe, so do not accuse me of being single-minded when you have clenched that bit between your teeth, and woe to anyone who seeks to remove it." His voice had risen, but seeing her stricken expression, he relented and gentled his tone. "What is this about, Emily? If it is not about Drummond, then what or whom does it concern?"

"You! You imperceptive, blind man," she blurted, her features flushed and furious.

"Me? What have *I* done?" *Daniel*. Damn the man. He had asked him to keep his confidence. He swiped his hand through his hair. "Look, I can explain. He—" He broke off when she jumped to her feet and paced before him.

"Our situation. It needs to change. It is not right. You have held me in your arms, kissed me, and we have been intimate, yet there is this chasm between us. Gaping holes filled with all we do not know about each other."

Not Daniel. His tension eased. "I have hidden nothing from you. You have seen me almost as naked as Adam in the Garden of Eden, but I am happy to rectify that," he teased, moving his hands toward the buttons on his trousers.

"Do not be obtuse. You are not usually, but being a man, and this being a discussion about a relationship and feelings, it might be out of your realm of understanding."

That was *not* a compliment. He was not sure if it maligned *his* intelligence or the ignorance of his sex as a whole. He feared it did both. Worse, she could be right. "What is it that you would like to know?" The question was out of his mouth before he could snatch it back, for he knew. *Wentworth*. The man was a wretched plague on his life.

She returned to the settee and sat beside him. "You must have loved Janice Wentworth very much to have asked for her hand in marriage."

This was *not* the distraction he needed. He nodded curtly. "I did."

"Do . . . do you love her still?"

He stared at her, reading the concern in her somber expression and marveling at the shadow of worry clouding her eyes. Did she believe he was still that daft fool pining away for his forsaken love? "Of course not. It was nearly a decade ago. She is long married by now, no doubt with a brood of children."

Emily furrowed her brow. "I do not understand. If you do not care for her, why were you so upset—?"

"I did love her and I asked her to marry me. She accepted,

her father declined. We planned to flee to Gretna Green, but at the last minute, she lost her courage." He shrugged. "It is a familiar and trite story. She was of age and the choice was hers, but her father was overly protective. I expected too much of her, because her family would have disowned her. At the time, I did not have anything to give her but an uncertain future. I expect she came to her senses before I did."

"You gave her your love. That should have been enough. It would have been enough for me," she said earnestly.

Surprised and oddly touched, her words dispersed the remnants of the chill that had gripped him earlier. "That is very romantic, but over the past decade, I have learned that one cannot eat on love. Nor can love put a roof over your head."

"Could she not wait for you to accomplish your goals? You think that I am a naïve romantic, and that I expect too much from her. Maybe so, but she has turned you into a cynic and that is worse. If she claimed to love you and had agreed to marry you, you had a right to expect everything from her. I planned to follow Jason to India. I would have followed him to Hades if need be."

She was magnificent. He had stood on that bloody street corner waiting for the wrong woman. He swallowed, and with a rush of tenderness, he brushed loose strands of hair back from her forehead, letting his hand linger and then sweep down her hair. "I believe you would have. Good thing India is not that far south," he teased.

"You mock me, but you are wrong to be so forgiving of her. She did not have the strength or the loyalty to stand by you, and that failure is hers alone."

He stared at her fierce expression. She was his warrior, Athena. And for once, she was fighting for him—or the injustice she believed had been done to him. Something rolled over in his chest. He feared it was his heart, giving up the fight against her.

He froze, rattled. Denials sprang up fast and furious. How could he love a woman who had promised to save herself for a man dead and buried? It was difficult to compete with the dead, particularly one who appeared to be a saint.

But perhaps, perhaps, it was time he did so.

His heart thundered. It was a novel thought, would change everything between them. Of course, Emily would fight him. She was brave, but a coward in love. She feared loving and losing again.

Well, then he would have to change her mind. He had always liked a challenge, and the rewards at the end would be well worth this one.

Because I love her.

And that was the truth in all its complexity. He loved everything about her. Her strength. Her fierce resolve. Even her thickheaded obduracy.

And he was keeping her—forever. There was only one way in which to accomplish this goal. He would have to seduce her as expertly as she had seduced him. It was only fair.

Quid pro quo was the one Latin phrase he had learned well.

Emily was giving him an odd look. No doubt because he sat grinning like a besotted fool. At least this time, he was doing so over the right woman. He cleared his throat. "I was not fortunate in love the first time around. Jason was lucky to have found you," he said. *As am I.*

"Yes, we were fortunate to have shared something special." Her gaze fell, and she bit her lip.

"You do not have to worry about me. I promise you, I am quite recovered from Lady Janice Wentworth's rejection."

"But then . . . then why are you still so angry at her father? Your response to him did not look like someone recovered from past injury."

He scowled. After his recent epiphany, Wentworth was the last person he wished to think about, but he owed her an explanation.

He caught a long coil of her hair, needing a moment to settle himself. "That is a different injury. Wentworth did not stop at thwarting our elopement. When Daniel and I first sought investors in Curtis Shipping, Wentworth steered potential backers away from us. When our goods were imported, we learned he had bribed a customs official to confiscate a shipment of our tobacco. He declared it rancid and it fed the Queen's Pipe, costing us a small fortune when we were barely turning a profit."

Her eyes widened. "How did you tie the corrupt customs official to Wentworth?"

"Not all customs officials are corrupt. Another heard our grievance, and investigated matters until he found the guilty man."

"What about Wentworth?"

"A corrupt customs official's word pitted against a respected peer of the realm would not hold up, so we did not pursue the matter. Another of your aristocratic privileges is often immunity from liability. But I am not worried about Wentworth. I usually keep an eye out for the bastard, but he caught me off guard at Halford's. Other matters distracted me. And speaking of distractions . . ." He let his voice trail off suggestively as he slid the long strand of hair through his fingers. "There is a far more pressing matter that requires my attention."

"Oh? Such as?" Emily's eyes gleamed.

"I appear to have lost a key."

"So you have." She laughed, and the trilling sound of it rolled over every inch of his body. "Wherever can it be?"

He turned in his seat and leaned over her. This time, she did not resist. "It appears a clever young woman has taken charge of it. She is cunning, fierce, and loyal. I am her prisoner until I can locate that key."

"She sounds formidable." She smiled into his eyes and looped her arms around his neck. "Perhaps you should make the best of your confinement."

"What did you have in mind?"

"Oh, I can think of something," she practically purred. She slid her hands into his hair and with a yank, she brought his head down to hers and crushed their lips together.

He kissed her back, his body melting onto hers. She roamed her hands down his back and beneath his linen shirt. Earlier he had discarded his jacket, waistcoat, and tie. Impatient to feel her hands warm against his skin, he broke the kiss, sat up and whipped his shirt over his head, tossing it to the floor.

Her gaze roved over him slowly, a languid smile curving her lips. The heat of her look was almost as arousing as her touch. When she splayed her hands over his abdomen and up his chest, his breathing quickened. He bent to plunder her mouth again, kissing her as if he could not get enough.

The taste and feel of her was like his own opium. He understood how a man could become addicted. His feelings for Emily were all consuming. He kissed her cheek, the tip of her nose, and drawing back, he stared into her eyes as they fluttered open, heavy-lidded and passion dazed.

"About that key . . ." His voice was hoarse as he grasped the collar of her robe and wrenched it apart with one quick tug. He caught his breath. Her nightgown was but a sheer veil over her body, and he eagerly feasted on the teasing view of smooth, creamy skin. The key was nestled in the valley between her breasts, gently rising and falling as she drew shallow breaths. He wondered if one could be jealous of an inanimate object.

He gathered her in his arms, burying his head between her breasts and inhaling deeply. Her body was soft and warm—but clothed. He grunted, craving more. He sat up and moved to the end of the settee. He caught the hem of her gown and with deliberate slowness, he began to ease it up her body.

It was like unveiling a sinuous nude carved in luminous white marble. He feasted on each tantalizing piece of skin he exposed. He spread featherlight kisses over her slim ankles, calves, and knees. His hands followed his lips, sliding up her legs, molding and caressing the long length of them.

When he reached her thighs, her hands gripped his shoulders, her fingers digging deep.

Slowly, inexorably he tortured her, inching toward his intended goal.

Suddenly aware of his intent, Emily grasped him by the hair and yanked up his head. "No! You cannot. Stop!"

"But we can. The door is locked. Have mercy on this poor besotted prisoner, who only seeks your pleasure. Do not torment me."

Her eyes widened and she bit her lip. After a moment, she loosened her grip. He held her gaze as he slowly eased up her gown, watching her eyes darken. Her lashes fluttered and then lowered. He dipped his head to the junction between her thighs, to her most intimate spot. His breath brushed her legs, and he kissed the satin-soft skin of her inner thigh. A moan escaped her and then she fully surrendered.

He pleasured her with his tongue and his fingers, finding the sweet spot that had her writhing. He claimed her with the same desperation that a true prisoner would devour a meager ration of food. A soft whimper escaped her. Her hands fell to the settee, fingers digging deep as she arched against him.

She was better than the richest brandy or the most potent opiate. The small sounds she emitted were music to his ears. A gasping cry escaped her as she found her release, and her body shuddered beneath him. When the last spasm eased, he sat up and folded her into his arms, holding her against his heart, where he hoped to keep her.

"I think I could grow accustomed to having my own prisoner," Emily whispered.

He smiled against her hair. Forget the key. There was no escaping her hold on him. She had enslaved him heart, body, and soul. He loved her.

Chapter Twenty-three

⋙ ⋘

EMILY slammed her book closed. She had reread the same paragraph numerous times and could not recount a thing. She set it on the nearest table, tipped her head against her chair, and closed her eyes. Instantly, she was transported back to her father's study. Brett was doing things to her, magical things, things that only a sorcerer should know. With his hands . . . his fingers . . . his mouth. Decadent things. Erotic things.

Wonderful things that Jason had never done.

Her eyes flew open. She shot to her feet and paced the library. It was the truth.

Brett had led her down a path that she and Jason had never ventured, but that was not what disturbed her. What bothered her, or what rattled her to the core, was her response to his touch . . . to *him*.

Like a maestro, Brett waved his wand, and her body became an instrument that sang under his direction. It was as if all her emotions had been in a deep sleep, and Brett was awakening her to the full chorus of them. Passion. Desire. Excitement. Unleashed yearnings sang within her, and she doubted she could silence them.

That frightened her most of all, because while she knew she could not keep Brett, she did not know how she could let him go.

She pressed her hand to her throbbing heart. A knock on the door caused her to jump, so frazzled were her nerves. She frowned, having coveted a morning to herself. Brett was at his office and Julia had taken the girls and Jonathan to the British Museum. Emily had begged off with the excuse of a headache, and to her relief, Julia had not questioned her.

After calling out a response, Burke poked his head into the room.

"Pardon me, mum. There is a Mr. Drummond here, who wishes to speak with you."

Her lips parted. *What could he want?* Well, he could go to Hades. Then again, once there, she would not know what the duplicitous bastard was plotting next. Conflicted, she gnawed on her lower lip. She could claim to be indisposed, but dismissed the idea. She was quite safe under her father's roof— but she had promised Brett she would not meet the bastard alone. She would keep her word.

"Show him into the drawing room," she answered Burke, who patiently awaited her response. "And send for Agnes."

There was no impropriety in having a gentleman caller visit her at Keaton House while her father was but a short distance away, working in his . . . office. A rush of heat suffused her cheeks when a fleeting image flashed before her of Brett in that studious enclave, his hair tousled from her fingers and him leaning over her body.

She pressed a hand to her temple. She needed to stay focused, because Lawrence Drummond was dangerous. With Agnes close and the servants about, Drummond would not dare to risk another murder. She shook her head. She was being ridiculous.

It was Brett's fault for keeping her awake to all hours. It

had dulled her wits, but it was too late to beg off now. Truth be told, she was interested to hear what story Drummond would weave today.

≫≪

IN THE DRAWING room, Drummond stood with his hands clasped behind his back while he studied a portrait of her family that hung above the hearth. Dressed in his usual impeccable style, his dark burgundy jacket hugged his broad shoulders.

She directed Agnes to a chair in the corner and waited until the maid was settled with her embroidery before addressing Drummond. "That is my father's favorite, despite Jonathan's absence," she spoke to his back. In the painting, her father stood behind her mother, who was seated. She and Julia framed her, leaning on opposite sides of their mother's chair.

When Drummond turned, she directed him to a portrait on the adjacent wall. "My father had this one commissioned of Jonathan. It was only recently finished." Jonathan was a belated surprise, joining their family a decade after the completion of the first portrait. Sadly, their mother had not survived his birth. "Lord knows how the artist got Jonathan to sit still long enough to pose, but I think it captures his impish grin perfectly."

Drummond studied the likeness. "I believe you are right. I am sure Jonathan was plotting his escape while the artist was distracted with brush and pallet."

"No doubt," Emily said. Not for the first time, she wondered how this man could be a cold-blooded murderer and what had driven him to it.

"Please have a seat. I will see about refreshments." She turned to have Agnes summon a maid, but Drummond stopped her.

"That will not be necessary. This is not a social visit. I did not come to discuss the finer points of family portraits or to exchange social niceties over tea," he said tightly. He braced his feet apart and crushed his fine leather gloves in a balled fist.

It was the stance of a common boxer, and she braced herself for battle.

"I have learned that you have been continuing your own search, independent of mine, after I expressly asked you to leave this matter in my hands. That I would take care of it for you." He waited for her response, and when she did not deny his accusations, he continued. "I know that you and Mr. Curtis sought to meet with Winfred, Jason's former valet, the evening of Halford's ball."

Her eyes widened. She recalled Brett's conviction that Drummond was following her. Had he trailed them then? She had not seen Drummond at the ball, and not for want of looking. "Pray tell, how on earth did—?"

He dismissed her question with an impatient jerk of his hand. "It is not important how I came by my information. The point is, not only are you still doggedly pursuing this matter, but you are doing it against my professed wishes and with the very man I warned you against keeping company with. More important, I have come to learn that Mr. Curtis and his sisters are your guests at Keaton House. I cannot fathom how Taunton has been duped into sanctioning this, but as I have shared my concerns with you in regard to Mr. Curtis's character, I find this arrangement untenable. I must press upon you the need for you to find them alternative lodging. You must have a care for your reputation."

Just who did he think he was?

Bristling, Emily drew herself up to her full height. This man was not her father, husband, nor anyone else whom she was obligated to honor and obey. It was a struggle to respond with civility. "Mr. Drummond, as I have told you, Jason's letters are dear to my heart. They are all I have left of him, so while you have agreed to assist me, for which I am grateful, I never said I would sit idly by while you did so. I see little harm in my desire to speak to Winfred."

She ignored his frown. "As for Mr. Curtis, your

introduction to him was not under the most favorable of circumstances, nor did his behavior improve upon a subsequent meeting. For those reasons, I understand your reservations about the man. However, as you know, he was my brother-in-law's partner and is godfather to the twins. Bedford would not bestow such an honor upon a man he did not respect *or* trust, nor would my father sanction having him as a guest in his home. Those credentials are also enough for me. Now I do hope that we can—"

"I see. So that is the way it is." His mouth pressed into a disapproving line.

"I beg your pardon?"

"Once again you have formed an attachment, and your choice has not favored me."

She blinked. This was how rumors started. They began with an incendiary comment, and if not snuffed out immediately, they ignited and spread. "Mr. Curtis is a family friend, nothing more," she said firmly, praying that her burning cheeks did not betray her second bald-faced lie.

"Let us hope that you speak true, because I did not have the chance to warn you about Jason's weak character, but heed my words. I have warned you about Mr. Curtis, but will do so again. I do not know how he has managed to mislead your brother-in-law or the earl, but I have it from a reliable source that the man is not to be trusted."

Wentworth. The man was nursing his ancient vendetta like it was a treasured heirloom. "And would that source be the Earl of Wentworth?"

A flicker of surprise crossed Drummond's features. "So Mr. Curtis has been honest in regard to one area. You know then that he tried to abduct Wentworth's daughter?"

"It was far from nefarious. Mr. Curtis asked for Lady Janice Wentworth's hand in marriage, and he was accepted. There was no abduction. Furthermore, the lady was of age, had her own income, and was free to change her mind. She chose to do so. No harm done."

Drummond visibly struggled to digest her defense of

Brett. He looked as if were choking on it. "Once again, it is evident that your mind is made up. I could not compete against Jason, so I sailed to India. But I thought with Jason's death, I might have another chance. I hope that I am not too late."

Her lips parted. She had not realized that was why Drummond had taken the post abroad, sailing to India a full year before Jason. "Mr. Drummond, I—"

His hand shot up, forestalling her response. "I could not protect you years ago, but as I said, I hope I am not too late to prevent you from making another mistake. If your relationship with Mr. Curtis is but a friendship forged through family connections, I suggest you reconsider it. You need to distance yourself from the man and see that he lodges elsewhere. Rumors are afoot, and I would be remiss if I did not warn you against him."

"What are you talking about? What rumors?" The cunning look in his eyes gave her pause.

"I can say no more at present. However, if you promise me that you and Mr. Curtis will curtail your alliance and leave me to find your letters, I might be able to intercede and speak up on his behalf. Otherwise, I cannot help him," he said and let his hands unfold in a helpless gesture.

Stunned, she stared at him. Surely, she could not have heard him correctly. She had to moisten her lips to respond, her mouth bone dry. "Are you saying that if I do not stay away from Mr. Curtis, he could find himself mired in some scandal or trouble of some sort? And that you can prevent it from unfolding should I heed your words? Let us speak plain, Mr. Drummond. Are you threatening me, or Mr. Curtis?"

Drummond's brows snapped together and his nostrils flared. "Interpret this information as you will. I am simply informing you that this matter is best left in my hands. I have promised you I will handle it, and in exchange, all I request is your word that you and Mr. Curtis stop poking into areas best left alone. The East India Company does not appreciate outsiders snooping into its business. If you continue to do so, there could be repercussions."

"I see," she said, her heart pounding. Good lord, he *was* threatening her. She folded her clammy hands in her skirts.

"I hope that you do," Drummond said. "I cannot stand by and watch you endanger yourself as Marsh was endangered, and God knows what has happened to Winfred." He narrowed his eyes on hers as if to gauge the impact of his words.

She did not disappoint, unable to suppress her start of surprise at his reference to Marsh.

"Yes, I have heard about the clerk's injuries. I do not know what has precipitated these incidents, but I believe it has to do with Jason's incoherent ramblings about conspiracies and embezzlement that he foolishly imparted to you. So you see why it is understandable that the company does not want these old accusations to be dredged back up. It is dangerous to dig up cold graves."

Heat climbed her cheeks, and her body vibrated with her barely contained rage.

How dare he threaten her!

Then again, the man fought for his life. If she found the evidence convicting him of being the vile, contemptible blackguard that he was, he would be ruined.

He planned to destroy Brett's reputation in the same manner that he had destroyed Marsh. He had played his hand well.

Devil take him!

She struggled to keep her voice level. "I certainly do not wish to endanger myself—or anger the East India Company. Nor do I want Mr. Curtis to run afoul of the company either. I promise you that much. I just want . . . I want my letters returned to me. They are all I have left of Jason," she finished softly. She clasped her hands before her, feigning the contrition the bastard expected.

Drummond visibly relaxed, his shoulders loosening and the gleam in his eyes nothing short of triumphant. "So then we have an understanding?"

"Of course. But will you not be in danger yourself?" She widened her eyes.

His features softened.

It took every vestige of her strength to step back slowly rather than flinch in horror from the hand he lifted toward her.

He paused, glanced toward Agnes, and whatever he saw in the maid's expression had him dropping his hand. Regrouping, he gave Emily an understanding look. "I think you have had enough loss in your life. I will tread very carefully. I have worked for the company and know how to navigate its dangerous labyrinths without arousing suspicion."

She summoned a wan smile. "I am relieved to hear that, because I really want those letters," she said sweetly, unable to resist aggravating him.

Drummond's smile faltered, and he stepped back and cleared his throat. "Of course. Well, then I best be on my way and locate them for you. Perhaps once I deliver your coveted prize, I can claim an award for doing so." He grinned.

He must be interpreting the flush on her cheeks for a fair maiden's blush, being the dolt that he was. Did he truly believe he could threaten her, and then expect her to flutter her lashes at his heroics? He was a bigger idiot than she had originally surmised.

When she did not respond, he relented. "It is early yet, and I have obstacles to clear first," he quipped as he slipped on his gloves. "But I shall not return until I am triumphant." He tossed her another grin before departing.

When the front door closed behind him, the anger bolstering her drained from her limbs. She practically stumbled to the settee and collapsed into it.

"Shall I have Sully follow him and pummel the scoundrel?"

Her head shot up, and she blinked at Agnes. Sully was one of her father's most imposing footmen. "Tempting as that is, Agnes, I will handle this. Thank you."

She could not dismiss Drummond's threats. More so, she

could not let Brett continue to assist her at the risk to his reputation—or his company.

His company was everything to him. *His company, his responsibility.*

She recalled the investors he mentioned cultivating, both here and in America. They could be financially ruined as well, or at the very least, lose their investments. Brett could be destroyed.

Rattled, she rubbed her arms, her body cold, so very cold. It was one thing for threats to be implicit in pursuing a murder investigation, but it was something altogether different when the murderer delivers those threats in person.

She refused to endanger Brett.

Her heart thundered at the thought of anything happening to him. She bit her lip, tasting blood. The pain of it cleared her head. She needed her wits about her to think. To formulate a plan to keep him safe. She had lost Jason, and refused to lose Brett because she . . . she couldn't.

There was not time to unravel her tangled feelings or ease the throbbing in her heart, because it was not only Brett she had to consider. There was Melody and Miranda. Any libelous scandal enveloping Brett would tarnish them all. Scandals had a ripple effect, spreading over whole families and sucking everyone under.

Brett had warned her against her chosen path. She had lured him into this poisonous web, so she must extract him from it. If she shared Drummond's threats with Brett, she had no doubt that the man would fight. He would never abandon her. She could not let that happen. Her mess, her responsibility.

She only hoped that Drummond did not act rashly until she gave him cause. Thankfully, with Winfred's disappearance, there was nothing for her and Brett to act upon at present. She would send Agnes to speak to the Halfords' staff and determine Winfred's whereabouts. Drummond was following her and Brett—not her maid.

If Drummond was found guilty, Emily would see to it

that he was tossed in gaol, where he could never again endanger anyone she loved.

She wished she could ship Brett and his sisters back to America, but would settle for getting them out of London. Away from her as Drummond had demanded—but safe. She would deal with the keening cry of her heart later.

Chapter Twenty-four

❦

BRETT turned Winfred's note over in his hand, guilt pricking him. Jason's former valet had agreed to meet with them the following week. Brett dared not contemplate Emily's reaction if she discovered he had withheld this information. It threatened the tenuous trust he sought to build with her.

In his defense, he fully intended to do so, but had delayed because she had been so out of sorts the last two days, having taken to her room with some ailment. Julia had assured him Emily was fine, but something nagged at him.

Emily may look like a delicate flower, but she was a tenacious vine. She did not wilt or waver, but he had to concede that lately her color was off. Deep shadows underlined her eyes as if she had not been sleeping well, and he had caught her studying him, worrying her lower lip. More disturbing, she was not snapping or sparring with him, so distracted was she. But when he had sought to determine what was amiss, well, she had snapped at him *then*.

He surmised that the stress and tension of their search was finally catching up with her. He paused and then snorted. No, that was not it.

There was something else. He had glimpsed a glint of determination simmering in her gaze. She was planning something. Hell, the damn woman was always planning something.

What the devil could it be?

He ran a hand through his hair, frustrated he could not give the matter his undivided attention. One of his ships, the *Bostonian*, was due to arrive at week's end, importing a large shipment, and he needed to ensure his paperwork was in order.

Daniel had promised to alert him if Emily escaped—or rather, left Keaton House. Enlisting Daniel to spy on Emily took another chip out of that trust they were building. Brett sighed. He really needed to work on that. It was crumbling fast.

Suddenly, he swore and frantically shoved aside the papers cluttering his desk, searching for the envelope that had arrived yesterday. With more pressing needs demanding his attention, he had set it aside to address later. Then like the idiot that he was, he had forgotten it.

The envelope contained the report from the agent he had hired to trail Drummond and alert Brett if the bastard was up to anything of interest. He located the item, tore it open, and extracted a single sheaf of paper, avidly reading it. *Bloody hell.* He shot to his feet. The conniving whoreson had paid a visit to Keaton House on Monday—two days prior. Christ. That was what had sickened Emily. He was feeling queasy himself.

What had the slanderous snake said to her?

And why has she kept it from me?

He shoved Winfred's note into his trouser pocket, snatched up his jacket, and gave the corner tall clock a quick glance—eleven o'clock. Emily would have retired, but she might still be struggling with sleep. It did not matter. She would awake when his hands closed around her shoulders, and he started shaking the information out of her thick, hardheaded skull.

≫≪

HEART THUNDERING, BRETT stood beside Emily's bed. He had locked the door behind him. There would be no escape. The dim light of his oil lamp illuminated Emily's slumbering figure. She lay on her back, one hand curled beside her cheek. She looked so angelic, so innocent. But he knew her to be the she-devil she was. He set his lamp on the nearby table and eased onto the bed beside her.

This was not going to go over well, but he did not give a damn. There were answers to be had, and until he got them, he did not want her screams bringing the household storming in on them.

He brushed his lips against her ear and whispered her name. She moaned and shifted, swatting at his face to push him away. He shook her shoulder less gently, and when her eyes flew open, his palm closed over her mouth. "Do not scream . . . Ow!" He yanked his arm back. "You bit me!" he said, surprised, shaking his injured hand.

Emily shot to a sitting position and pulled the covers to her, but his perch on half of them hindered her attempts. "What are you doing here? Good lord, Daniel and Julia are right across the hall. Do you have a death wish?"

Definitely not ill. No case of the vapors here. More spitting viper. "I am here for answers. And I am not bloody well leaving until I get them."

Her expression turned truculent. "I do not know what you are—"

"You do. Do not lie. What the devil did Drummond want?"

Her lips parted, and her face drained of color, but she remained mutinously silent.

He bristled at her defiance, but when she looked away, her body curling inward, he paused. Whatever the hell the bastard had said, it had her more frightened than the whole damn murder investigation.

The only other time he had seen Emily this rattled was after hearing the opium allegations leveled against Jason. His eyes widened.

What further accusations had Drummond leveled? And against whom? "Christ," he muttered. Because he damn well knew.

With a surge of protective tenderness, he drew Emily's into his arms. "It is all right. Whatever Drummond said, threatened, demanded, or wants, he will not succeed. Do you hear me? He will rot in gaol. I promise you that. If not for embezzlement or murder, then for upsetting you. I will see to it. Hang me, if I do not."

She remained stiff in his arms, but when his lips brushed her temple, her body slowly relaxed. She slipped her arms around him and clung tight. "No, we cannot. It is too dangerous."

He almost snorted. "And when has a little danger ever stopped you before?"

She drew away, her expression appalled. "Do not jest. This is different."

"More dangerous than a murder investigation?" he said dryly.

"Listen to me. You need to take Melody and Miranda and leave town. You must—"

His blood ran cold. "Did he threaten them? By God, I will—"

"He did not threaten them. He threatened you! He plans to ruin you in the same manner that he ruined Marsh. I do not know how, but he made it clear that if I do not sever my connection with you, abandon my search, and leave him to find my letters, that there would be repercussions. He said the East India Company did not like people probing into their business, and that . . . that you were not to be trusted. He dared to allude to your history with Janice Wentworth, implying you had attempted to abduct the woman. I should have stabbed him with the fire poker when I had the chance." She grumbled the last. "Agnes is loyal to me. She would have helped me dispose of the body."

Brett nearly smiled at that. "We will keep that as an option should he visit again. He is scared. We are closing in on him, and he knows it. That is not all bad. It might make him do stupid, reckless things, like tip his hand with this warning."

"A warning you need to heed! You cannot stay here," she implored. He had discarded his cravat and jacket before seeking her room. She grasped his shirt. "You are not listening. Any slander to your name tarnishes Melody and Miranda by association. It could have repercussions that harm your company. Think of your reputation, of your investors, and the loss in profits. You need to disappear before that happens. Promise me that you will get far away. I cannot . . . I will not be responsible . . ."

He pressed his fingers to her lips, quieting her flood of words. "Of course, I will heed this threat. I am not dismissing it, but unlike Drummond, I am not a fool, nor am I a coward. If he flings any of his slander, I will deflect it at that time. It is all I can do, but you need to trust in me to handle it, because I will not leave you or abandon your cause. I gave you my word, and I refuse to break it." He dropped his hand, and then nodded to her. "Move over."

"I knew you would be difficult," she muttered. After a moment, she sighed and slid aside. "You do know what will happen if you are found in here?"

He laughed softly. "I seem to be courting danger wherever I go." He slid off his boots and climbed into the bed, still wearing his breeches and shirt. Emily curled against his side, her head cradled on his shoulder.

Despite the threats to him, his family, and his company, for this moment, he was content. He rested his chin on her head and savored the feel of her in his arms. Warm. Safe. She was soft, but so strong. And conniving. "So how did you plan to get rid of me?"

"What?"

"Come now, you have had two days to devise a plan. I know the way you think, and faking an ailment has given you the time to retire and do so."

"I have been ill!" she protested indignantly, slapping his shoulder. "Ill with worry over your arrogant hide, but no more." When he simply waited her out, she huffed out a breath. "Fine. Patricia Branson mentioned that Lord Farnsworth is having a house party, complete with a masquerade ball at his estate in Kent."

He groaned. "Melody would love that."

"Yes, so you can take the girls while I recover here, and Drummond will think—"

"No."

"What?"

"When I first agreed to assist you, my one stipulation was that we would work *together*. Admittedly, in the beginning, I agreed because I knew you would proceed on your own, and I wanted to keep your fool head safe. But it is different now." He shifted her body beside him, needing to see her face. He propped his head on his arm and gazed over her features. They had all become so dear to him—even the wary look she was currently giving him.

Her eyes met his. "How so?"

"Now your goal has become mine. I want justice for Jason as much as you do. He was an honorable man and deserves it. But more important, if Drummond is guilty, I want to see him face the magistrate and see justice meted out. You said you sought my assistance because you believed I am a man who achieves what I set my mind to; well, then allow me to do that. I will not run away from these threats or leave you."

"I see," Emily murmured.

"I hope you do because I still plan to keep your fool head safe as well as the rest of you." Unable to resist, he caught a strand of her hair and wrapped it around his hand. "Because I have come to value your life more than my own."

"Brett . . ." Emily's eyes widened, two beautiful pools of blue. When her lips parted, he drew her to him, closing his mouth over hers. His soft, strong warrior. His love.

"Brett . . . ?" she breathed, pulling back.

He smiled, nuzzling her cheek. "Yes?"

"You have on too many clothes. You should take them off."

He laughed, delighted. "Another good plan." She knelt

and began to undo the buttons on his shirt, but he brushed her hands away to whip it over his head.

She splayed her hands across his chest, caressing his bare skin. Her lips followed her hands and she kissed his chest, leaning down to draw his nipple into her mouth.

He groaned at her touch and threaded his fingers through her hair, sliding the long strands through his hands. "I take it that you have recovered from what ails you."

She shifted to lay the full length of her body over his. The feel of her breasts crushed against his chest was a delicious torture. She cradled his head in her hands and lowered her mouth until it hovered above his, her breath teasing his lips. "Perhaps, but I know how I could feel much, much better."

"I did offer to assist you," he said and smiled.

Her eyes gleamed in the dim light. "You did, and I know you will keep me safe. After all, you carry a sword." She wiggled her hips against him.

He snorted out a laugh. Her gown and his trousers were the only barrier separating her from his aching arousal. Another sweet torture.

"I am sure you wield it very well because, as you say, you are a man who accomplishes what he sets out to do."

"I am. However, there is one impediment to your plan."

"Yes?"

"You, too, have on too many clothes."

"So I do." Emily eased off of him. Then his wicked seductress gave him a slow, knowing smile and in one fluid motion, she shucked off her gown.

She sat there in all her stunning, naked beauty. The light danced over each silken curve, and every thought drained from his head but one.

Good lord, he was keeping her.

"*Emily*," he groaned.

⇒⇐

EMILY SWALLOWED AT the smoldering look in his eyes, the sweet whisper of her name on his lips. Her heart pounded so hard she feared it would burst from her chest as he drew her into his arms. His body was warm against hers, all angles and planes that fascinated her. She had always admired the grace and strength of his body. She pressed her lips to the hollow of his throat and caressed the firm-knit muscles of his arms, the sweeping dip to his hips, and then over his lean, taut abdomen.

She was no innocent and had no regrets over it because her experience made her bold. She smiled as she lowered her hand to his hard arousal straining against his trousers. "I think you need to unsheathe your sword." Her voice sounded husky even to her ears. Brett grunted, but shed his trousers so quickly she barely had time to blink before he was back beside her and yanked her into his arms.

"Dear God, I love you," Brett said, warmth and laughter in his voice.

Her world stopped. Then toppled on its axis.

Heart hammering, she fought to draw breath.

Could he . . . ? Did he . . . ? Or was it the heat of the moment?

A myriad of emotions suffused her. Surprise. Confusion. And pure joy. A stunning jolt of it. Her heart swelled with it. She grasped on to that, pushing back the doubts and allowing herself to cherish the moment. To savor the pleasure his words and his touch gave her. To let this beautiful man love her.

She reveled in the touch of his hands as they moved over her. Slowly, tenderly, almost reverently, he caressed her. She curled her fingers over his shoulders, reaching up to twine her fingers in his hair. He gently cupped her breasts and then inched his hands down along her waist, her taut stomach, and over her hips. The butterfly-light touches left a burning trail in their wake.

He lowered his head, and she moaned as his mouth closed over a taut nipple. *Oh God.* He was clever with his mouth. And his tongue. Her passion flared anew, and her body shivered with exquisite pleasure. She writhed, recalling the moves to a familiar dance. Of passion and lust. She had never perfected the rhythm of all its intricate movements, but it had been exciting to experiment. But it was . . . It was better now.

He lifted his head and kissed her deeply, plundering her mouth. She lowered her hand to curl her fingers over his warm erection, gasping at the soft velvet heat of him. She slid her hand along the firm length of his arousal, smiling when he groaned, reveling in the power her touch had over him.

Yes, much better.

The sound of his response, his breath quickening, was almost as arousing as his touch. Her own moans escaped her when Brett's fingers slipped between her legs and between her moist folds. She was ready, his caresses having built an aching hunger in her. For him. She moved her hands to clutch his shoulders, needing to hold on to him.

Dear lord, he knew moves she had not experienced before. Her lips parted as he deftly continued his strokes, teasing and thrusting. A rush of heat suffused her, and her body shuddered in a spiral of need. She again reached down and grasped the smooth, warm length of his straining erection, caressing him with more urgency. He was as ready as she.

"Brett."

His name escaped her in a breathless plea. It had been so long, and she was ready. She needed him. Desperately.

"Emily," he murmured, and then he gently removed her hand from him and rolled with her so that she lay beneath him. He lifted his head and his eyes met hers, his heavy-lidded with his passion. He held her gaze as he grasped her hips and settled himself deeply within her, sliding into her welcoming warmth.

He paused and she saw his eyes widen slightly. Not wanting to lose the exquisite moment to questions about her innocence, she reached up and drew his mouth to hers, kissing him deeply. Now was not the time for explanations. Besides, there was nothing to say, because she had never been anything but who she was with him. Determined, bold. Wanton. A woman who knew what she wanted. She arched against him, letting her body speak for her.

"Emily." He broke the kiss, and the ragged whisper of

her name was like a cry from his heart. He began to move within her. Deeply. Erotically. Expertly. Delighted, her fingers dug into his back, as she met his thrusts. He groaned as his rhythm increased, his breathing as ragged as hers as their passion climbed.

Her body moved with his into the rhythm of the sensual dance. His sure strokes and the pulsating heat of him as he moved deeply inside her created an intoxicating pressure that built within her. She cried out as his arousal touched her sweetest spot, and then she could think no more. Her heightened senses were alive with passion, yearning, and that delicious, almost torturous anticipation as her body began its slow, frenzied climb to climax. When she could stand it no more, she gasped, and his name burst from her. "Brett!"

Brett's mouth covered hers, swallowing her cry as he sought his own release. He thrust deep, his hands on her hips. She bent her leg up against his hip to better accommodate him, moved her hands over his buttocks, and relished the guttural sounds escaping him. His body was sweat slicked and hot against hers. She felt his muscles strain beneath her hands. A while later, his body shuddered against hers as he found his own release. And then his body collapsed, flush with hers.

Emily closed her eyes and clutched him against her heart, savoring the feel of Brett's arms around her, his body pressed to hers. She blinked back the moisture in her eyes.

Later, he summoned a last vestige of energy and twisted his body so that he lay on his side next to her. He drew her back into his arms and cradled her close. Her protector.

She was safe, cherished. And loved. For the moment, she let herself believe it. She drifted to sleep listening to his heartbeat against her cheek.

Chapter Twenty-five

✦

Emily glowered at the immovable, slumbering lummox beside her. "Get up! You need to go," she hissed as she shoved Brett's bare shoulder.

Dawn's light was not as beautiful as poets penned it to be, nor was day as jocund as Romeo described. It was dangerous, and like Romeo, Brett must *"Be gone and live or stay and die."* She slapped his cheeks, desperate to avoid a Shakespearean tragedy.

He groaned and opened his eyes, blinking up at her.

Mesmerized, she watched as his befuddled blue eyes cleared and then softened. Her heart did a ridiculous flip. He looked handsome, lazy, and sinfully satisfied. When he flashed his disarming smile, she forgot all about the time and the dangers it posed.

"Good morning," he murmured and cupped her cheek.

She expelled her breath. "You sleep like the dead."

"A naked nymph kept me awake all night, but I have no complaints." He eyed her robe, firmly belted, and he frowned. "Why are you dressed?" He shifted his gaze to the ribbons of light streaming over the Aubusson carpet, and then he shot to a sitting position. "It is morning."

So much for her heavy-lidded, lazy Casanova.

"Yes, it tends to arrive inconveniently early, but with consistent regularity."

He grunted, tossed the covers back, and snatched up his clothes. *Interesting.* He slept like the dead, but awoke prepared for battle. Well, perhaps with his weapon down.

She grinned as she admired the muscular thighs, firm buttocks, and broad shoulders. Pity that glorious view was all too soon covered. She frowned. "You are good at dressing quickly." With shirttails hanging loose, buttons misaligned, and his hair deliciously disheveled, the man still stole her breath. "No doubt you are well practiced at fleeing a woman's bedchamber."

He sat beside her to tug on his boots. "I promise you, this is a first. My involvement with you has always courted danger. But this is not how I plan to announce our betrothal to my future father-in-law. It could lead to bad residuals come the nuptials."

The grin curving her mouth froze. "What did you say?"

He glanced at her and seeing her expression, he paused, and then grimaced. "I did not mention that last night?"

Numbly, she shook her head. He ran a hand through his hair, and the chagrined flush staining his cheeks surprised her as much as his words.

"I told you I loved you. I said that much." When she simply stared, he planted his hands on her shoulders, his voice tender. "I am a cad, aren't I? I should have done this better. Flowers and candlelight. Romance. Poetry. Lady Emily Chandler, I love you. I adore every clever, delightful, beautiful inch of you. I cannot live without you. I would like to make our wonderful, strange alliance permanent. Will you marry me?"

She recoiled and tears pooled in her eyes. She shook her head and swallowed. "I . . . I cannot."

His hands fell from her shoulders. "Excuse me?"

Tears streaming down her cheeks, she jumped from the bed. She needed distance, and a moment to let her pounding heart settle. She swiped at her wet cheeks. "Please, I explained at the beginning that I would not marry—ever. I cannot."

Brett's features softened and he spoke gently, as if she were a skittish colt. "Emily, I understand you suffered when Jason died, that you are afraid to love and lose again, but Emily, you are no coward. You are a vibrant, passionate woman, who deserves to live life to the fullest. Who deserves a second chance. Life is full of risks, and you cannot hibernate—"

"Please. It is not about risking love or loss again. It is not! Because I . . . I do love you. I do." The words burst from her heart, momentarily stunning her. But they were the truth, and he deserved to hear them. To know that she was not cold or incapable of love. That what they had shared was special. She could, at the very least, give him this much.

"I do not want to love you because it hurts so very much, because I have to let you go. I cannot marry you." He stood and moved toward her, but she held up her hand. "Do not come any closer," she cried. "It is not about love and loss. It is about me!" She pressed her fist to her heart.

"I do not understand."

"No, you cannot. I will explain, and then you must go. When Jason died, I went to a very dark place. And it . . . it was bad."

"Emily, I know about that period," he said softly, his eyes warm. "Daniel told me about your escape to the Lake District. And I know about your withdrawal from society. You needed time to heal. And it is understandable because . . . after last night, I know that you are not a virgin. That you and Jason—"

"It is not about that!" she cried, exasperated. The man was clearly different if he had no qualms about her past sexual experience. But while it gave her pause, it did not change matters. "That is true, but it is not the reason why I avoided social engagements. I—"

"Emily, I understand."

"No! You do not. I did withdraw socially. I also discouraged any men's feelings for me. Unlike you, most English lords looking for a bride are not as forgiving of a ruined young woman, which is what I am."

"Emily—"

"Listen to me! That was my choice and I do not regret it, but it does not explain my withdrawal or my trip to the Lake District. Julia took me there, not because I was grieving or because I was ruined, but because I was fighting madness."

Brett stared at her and his expression softened, no signs of aversion to her confidence. "Grief can feel like madness. It can be dark, unrelenting, and all consuming."

She pressed her hand to her temple and forced herself to continue.

"Grief does not make you cut off all your hair, or slice at yourself with a knife, or—wade into a lake seeking to—to drown yourself. That is madness, in all its ugly, stark, bitter truth. And that is inside of me." She thumped her chest. "It was in my father, too. When my mother died, he rejected Jonathan for nearly a year and ran away. I am my father's daughter, and this darkness is in me, hovering beneath the surface and threatening to drown me again."

"Emily . . ."

His voice was so tender it nearly broke her. "You deserve someone whole. Someone strong. Someone who can give you children without the fear of those children carrying this stain of madness. You deserve that second chance, but I can only give it to you by . . . by letting you go," she cried, cursing the hitch in her voice. She blinked at the tears blinding her.

He was quiet for a long time and then shook his head. "I know you believe these things. And I know it must frighten you. But I see someone entirely different." His gaze was steady on hers, bright and warm. "I see someone brave and strong. I see a courageous woman who loves so deeply that she had to fight to go on living when she lost that love, but she found the strength to do so."

Stunned silent, her lips parted and she simply stared at him.

"I see someone who, despite fears and a darkness she fights

against, seeks to redress a wrong done to a man she loved—no matter what the cost or the danger is to herself. I see a woman who is a warrior, whether or not she is fighting to save herself, or someone else she loves. I see the woman whom I have fallen in love with, completely and irrevocably."

She blew out a breath and shook her head. "You are speaking like a love-struck fool."

He grinned. "I prefer besotted, because I was a fool once in love, but no more. You are the woman for me, and you said you love me. I will hold on to that for now. We can figure out the marriage part later—or not. Either way, I will not give you up."

Just when she regained her footing, the man kept tipping her world askew. "You . . . you will stay with me even if I refuse to marry you? What about children?"

"I hope to have them. And I hope they have your blue eyes and obduracy. Well, maybe a diluted version of that trait. But until I can convince you to marry me, they can wait. And so can I. I am not going anywhere." He walked toward her.

Too stunned to retreat, she could not tear her gaze from his, nor did she protest when he drew her into his arms and cradled her against his heart.

"Everyone deserves a second chance. You are not some mad Ophelia. Ophelia drowned. You did not. You are very much alive."

She sniffed. "I tried, but Agnes would not let me. She dragged me back to shore."

"Well then. I owe Agnes my most sincere apologies for every bad thought I ever had about her. She deserves an increase in her wages and will have a position in our household forever."

She snorted, and the sound of it in this bittersweet moment appalled her. If she was not mad already, the man was driving her to it.

He pressed his fingers under her chin, lifting her face to his. "Not to belabor the point, but I usually do achieve what I set out to accomplish. Once you become tired of my asking for your hand in marriage, I have faith that you will say yes. I suggest you decide if you want to reside in England or sail to America, and think about our wedding. After all, you are good at planning."

"You would live in England permanently?"

"I will live where you are. I am not bound to either country. Home is where you are."

Her heart leapt. She needed to free him, but he had her so muddleheaded that she could not think straight. *Weddings? Where to live?* The man was madder than she. "I will . . . I will think about it."

"I would expect you to do no less." He kissed her on the lips, and then drew away. "Now as much as I wish to stay, I best go so that your father is not arranging our nuptials before you agree to them." He winked and then left her alone with her baffled thoughts.

She frowned at the door. The man *was* a besotted fool. She may love him, but she could never marry a fool. Most men would be delighted with a lusty affair. But he had to talk of love and marriage and make her waver in her convictions.

She crossed to her bed and dropped onto it, staring blindly at the floor. The clock chimed and she shook her head, hoping to clear it of her jumbled emotions. A slip of paper on the carpet caught her eye, and in a daze she bent to retrieve it. Curious, she read the ink scrawl and all thoughts of love and romance fled. She shot to her feet, crumpled the note in her fist, and swore.

Drat and blast him!

The man was a fool all right, a duplicitous one at that! If Brett thought he was meeting Winfred without her, he could very well think again.

All the more reason she could not marry the man. They would kill each other before the year was out.

Chapter Twenty-six

❧❧

BRETT cursed the pending shipment that was keeping him tied up at the office. He needed to delegate more. It was time to trust in Jenkins's management, but relinquishing responsibility did not come easily to Brett. After his debacle with Janice Wentworth, building his company had saved him. For Emily, her escape to the Lake District had abetted her recovery.

They had both escaped their pain in different ways, but Emily was still running. Running from herself. From something she feared percolated deep inside of her, waiting to boil over.

He blew out a breath. He had suspected Emily hid something, but he could never have fathomed what it was. He recalled her nerves during those first few forays into society, and he had seen her crumble when she received Little's news about Jason. But these were but cracks in her fortitude. She had always shored them up, lifted her chin, and forged ahead. Daniel had recognized her strength, conceding that having a single-minded purpose had been good for her.

Why couldn't Emily see that?

And if she truly loved him, she should want to fight for him as she was fighting for Jason. Brett frowned, because there was the true sting in her rejection—that she was willing to give him up.

She believed he deserved better. Well, so did she. He rubbed his temple, a headache sneaking in as another pesky thought disturbed him. Emily had said she loved him, but maybe . . . maybe it was not enough. Could it be Janice all over again?

And once again, he was a fool.

His heart lurched in denial. Emily was not Janice. He just had to convince Emily to fight for them. *For me.*

He did not have time to brood over the matter, because his office door swung wide and Daniel entered.

He slammed the door closed behind him, a scowl contorting his features.

"Emily?" Brett blurted, shooting to his feet.

"Damn right, it is Emily. What the devil did you do to her?" Daniel thundered. "She is supposed to be ill, but then she is making plans for me and Julia to escort your sisters to some bloody masquerade ball in Kent while she recovers. A masquerade, mind you!" He paused, narrowed his eyes, and stabbed his finger at Brett. "Ill, my arse. She is plotting something, so she needs everyone out of the way. What is going on? Have you finally found the evidence implicating Drummond?"

Expelling a breath, Brett sank back into his chair. "No, not yet. But I would not mind getting Miranda and Melody out of town for a while. But I need you here. There might be trouble." He recounted Drummond's threats.

"Bastard. What do you plan to do?"

"Not run away as Emily would like," he grumbled. It still irked him that she thought he would abandon her—even if she wished to protect him as he sought to protect her. They made a pair. "I gave her my word and I am keeping it. Hopefully, we can collect the evidence from Winfred before Drummond unleashes whatever machination he is hatching. Then we can hang the whoreson and be done with matters."

"What if Winfred does not have anything useful?"

"I will keep looking and watch my back while I do so. I have no other choice," Brett said with a shrug. "I have men observing Drummond, so he cannot make a sneak attack. Did you meet with Roberts? Or uncover anything on Drummond's finances? We still need to determine motive."

Daniel sank into the chair across from Brett's desk. "Drummond did lodge the allegations against Marsh, but someone else corroborated them, so there was little Roberts could do but dismiss Marsh."

"It does not cost much to bribe another into committing slander," Brett said. "We learned that from Wentworth. What about Drummond's finances?"

Daniel leaned forward. "That was interesting. The man has no debts, does not gamble, nor does he keep a mistress. He has been spending generously to finance his sister's first Season. The income from his estate would not cover these expenses, so I thought that was something until I learned that the Earl of Dayton is financing everything. The man is a family—"

"—relation. So I have been told—repeatedly," Brett muttered. Daniel's information was not helping to alleviate the throbbing in his head.

"For someone who has embezzled a fortune, Drummond lives like a Spartan. Are you sure you are pursuing the right man? Did you know that he and Jason *were* friends prior to the viscount's posting in India? Lord Roberts said the two were at university together, and Julia told me that Drummond introduced Emily to Jason. Actually he reacquainted the two, as they both grew up in Bedfordshire."

Drummond was guilty. Brett knew it deep down in his bones. Had sensed it since first setting eyes on the blackguard. Something simmered below his polished veneer. Something sly and insidious. "He is guilty, but damned if I know why the man would embezzle money he does not need and is not spending. He has his reasons. He just has yet to reveal them. But make no mistake, the man is a snake."

"More important, if you are right, he is a murderer who

has now leveled serious threats against you. Have you considered withdrawing for a while? I can—"

"You sound like Emily," he said, scowling. "That is another mistake Drummond has made, believing me to be a coward who would flee. He wants to move all the pieces aside, so he can make his next move. The man has a plan, and we need to stay one step ahead of him. But in addition to the meeting with Winfred, there is another reason I cannot leave. I have an obstinate, thickheaded woman to woo and wed."

"Is that so?" Daniel grinned.

"It is. She said she loves me, so she cannot take it back. I will not let her."

Daniel jumped to his feet, grabbed Brett's hand, and pumped it vigorously. His other hand clasped his arm tight. "That's marvelous. I had hope, but you both were being so bloody slow-footed about the matter. I thought I would have to knock your thick heads together, and that could have gotten messy. Julia will be ecstatic."

His friend was babbling. Worse, he was right, not that Brett would concede that. "Ah . . . about Julia. You cannot mention it to her quite yet."

Daniel's smile faded, and he dropped his hand. "Why is that? You said that Emily told you that she loves you. Have you proposed?"

"Of course, I proposed," he snapped. *Just not very well.* He refused to concede that either. "Emily is being contrary about matters, but she will come around."

"You are supposed to have a way with women, have three sisters, and as you like to boast, you know women well. So pray tell, what the devil went wrong? Last I knew, Emily is a woman." He arched a brow.

"Emily is not like most women. She can be deuced opinionated about things, but she will come around. I am marrying her. I have made up my mind, and I can be as single-minded as she," he declared with more conviction than he felt.

"You are that," Daniel said straight-faced, but there was a betraying twitch to his lips. "I trust you to take care of matters, then. Perhaps it is premature to announce the nuptials until Drummond is rotting in Newgate, and you are safe from his threats. We need to determine a plan—"

The office door crashed open again, slamming against the wall. Brett really needed to start locking his door. He forgot his irritation when Jenkins stormed in, red-faced and fists clenched.

"The bloody custom officials are confiscating our goods," he roared as he slapped a sheet of paper into Brett's hand and began to pace, gesticulating wildly. "The cotton, the tobacco. Everything. Claimed the shipment is under investigation. Something about a question about the goods not being able to fetch enough money to pay the customs duty due to the inferior quality of the cotton fibers."

"Hell and damnation," Daniel swore. He leaned over to study the paper Brett held.

"Drummond," Brett snarled. He scoured the document, which claimed all the goods unloaded from the *Bostonian* to be impounded until further notice. He clenched his jaw, and then stiffened. "Wentworth! Emily said Drummond had mentioned Wentworth. Drummond must have colluded with the bastard, using Wentworth's clout to lodge the complaint. Wentworth has been seeking to undermine the business for years, and Drummond is aware of my history with him. Damned if he didn't use it to his advantage."

Devil take it, he'd thought he had time. He had been a fool, and the cost of it could be dear.

"Christ. This could cost a fortune," Daniel said, echoing Brett's fears. "I will speak to Lord Roberts and explain our history with Wentworth—if the bastard is indeed involved. Add to that our suspicions against Drummond, and it should give Roberts reason to intervene, or at the very least, forestall any bales going up in the Queen's Pipe before we can corroborate our allegations and discredit Drummond."

Brett nodded and collected his jacket. "I would accompany you, but I need to head to the London Dock House and speak to the Court of Directors who oversee the docks. Jenkins, gather up all the documents that pertain to every damn bale of cotton on the *Bostonian*, as well as a complete list of its inventory. The customs officials have their own paperwork, but in light of these allegations and our history with corrupt officials, I do not trust it not to be tampered with." He paused, and as an afterthought added, "And find Baines. He is familiar with many of the dockworkers. He might be able to dig up, sniff out, or bribe someone for information."

"Right, sir." Jenkins nodded, spun, and departed the room.

"I owe you, or rather, Emily, an apology," Daniel said. "Drummond looks like a fashionable coxcomb, so I did not take him seriously. I will not make that mistake again. Let us finish the bastard, so we can plan a wedding."

"Do not put the horse before the cart," he grunted as he shrugged into his jacket. "Emily has to accept me first."

"Do not forget to speak to Taunton," Daniel added cheerfully.

"One crisis at time." He sighed.

Leave it to Daniel to find another obstacle for him to clear. Earls did not like their daughters marrying untitled commoners. Hopefully, Taunton, like his daughter, was different, but it did not matter. He would smooth over the man's reservations, handle this company crisis, destroy Drummond, and convince Emily to say yes.

This was not in the order of his priorities, but necessity took precedence. After all, he could not very well marry Emily while he and his company were under attack. Therefore, he needed to move quickly.

Chapter Twenty-seven

❧❧

EXHAUSTED from haggling with the customs officials, it was early evening when Brett wound his way home to Keaton House. The matter was far from resolved, but he had been given the full six weeks' time that was allotted for unloading inventory to address the complaints lodged against his company.

"My pardon, sir," Burke said upon his arrival. "I was advised to inform you that when you arrived, you were to meet Taunton and Bedford in the earl's—"

"Curtis, in my office. Now," Taunton barked, peering into the foyer and leveling a steely-eyed look on Brett. He then turned on his heels and stormed off.

"As I was saying, the earl's office," Burke finished with a dip of his head, his features impassive.

At the sight of Taunton's thunderous expression, Brett slid his finger beneath his cravat. Christ. Could Taunton believe the allegations? Indignation burned hot on Brett's cheeks, but Taunton was a fair man, he would hear Brett out. *Wouldn't he?* With a heavy step, he made his way to

Taunton's office, wondering if the bloody day would ever end.

He paused at the sight of Emily. She was seated on the infamous settee, a handkerchief balled in her fist.

She rose to her feet when Brett entered. "I am sorry. So very sorry. It is all my fault. You warned me not to pursue my course, that it had repercussions, that it was dangerous," she said, her eyes brimming. "And now you are paying the price for it."

"I *told* you Curtis tried to talk her out of investigating matters," Daniel said to Taunton. Daniel stood at the hearth, one arm draped over the mantel, his stance casual. Clearly, he sought to dispel the air of tension that permeated the room.

"For *that* matter, and that matter alone, he still lives." Taunton sat behind his desk, his face implacable. "What the devil were you thinking, not bringing this matter to my attention immediately? Allowing Emily to—"

"Please!" Emily cried, whirling on her father. "I am three-and-twenty and responsible for my own actions. I have explained to you that I made Mr. Curtis give me his word not to speak to you. I forced him into an untenable position because he believed I would pursue my course regardless of whether or not he provided his assistance. Mr. Curtis's sole objective in helping me has been to protect—"

"—you from yourself. Splendid," Taunton grumbled. "I have been so busy trying to stop Jonathan from stabbing everyone with a wooden sword that I have been remiss in watching over you girls. I thought you two were more level-headed." He balefully eyed Emily, then Brett, and finally his gaze came to rest on Bedford, who dropped his arms and shifted.

"Now see here, my situation with Julia was entirely different. It did get rather heated, but—"

"I take full responsibility for all my actions, but even in light of recent events, I have no regrets," Brett stated. "It is an honorable goal that Lady Emily is pursuing, seeking justice for the man she loved."

Emily's eyes widened, and a tremulous smile curved her lips.

Taunton leaned back in his chair and studied Brett. "The pursuit of a just cause is indeed a worthy endeavor. However, it is the manner in which this has been—"

"*Please*, we have been through this," Emily said with strained patience. "I understand that I have needlessly upset you, and for that I am sincerely sorry. I know you only have a care for my welfare, but as you can see, no harm has befallen me. You should be thanking Mr. Curtis for his protection, and you can do so by helping to ensure that these fraudulent charges against his company are dropped. There are investors to consider, both here *and* in America. They will be harmed should any profits be lost. And . . . and we cannot sit back while perfectly good inventory is burned up in that odious Queen's Pipe or kiln or whatever it is!" Her voice rose, righteous indignation emanating from her.

Stunned, Brett's lips parted and he blinked at Emily, his heart thumping.

Emily had approached her father, not to aid *her* cause, but for *him*—to rescue him. She was the bravest of women, risking the lion's den.

At Taunton's baffled look, Daniel explained Emily's reference, amusement lacing his words.

Taunton harrumphed. "It appears my daughter has acquired a keen understanding of the shipping business and its investors. I take it I have you to thank for this unique education, Mr. Curtis?" He arched a brow at Brett.

Daniel had a sudden fit of coughing.

Brett shot the idiot a quelling look, while cursing the heat that climbed his cheeks. He opened his mouth to respond, but the moment had passed, because Taunton had turned his narrow-eyed scrutiny on Emily.

"It is a sad day when a man has not one daughter, but two, who court danger, and then take their father to task for reprimanding them for doing so. It is during situations like this that I most miss your mother. She was far better at disciplining you girls than I."

Emily grinned. "I miss her, too."

Taunton continued. "Now then, these charges. I have no doubt that they are trumped-up. I will have a word with Lord Wentworth, see if I can determine his understanding with Drummond. I will also speak to the custom officials and ensure that a thorough investigation of the matter is completed before any inventory is destroyed. With Bedford and myself pressing for answers, they will have to take heed. Emily is right in regard to the business repercussions. As she has sagely pointed out, there are investors to be considered, and they would not be pleased to see profits recklessly burned."

Brett swallowed. "Thank you, sir. I appreciate your confidence in the integrity of the company and me. You will not be proved wrong."

Emily circled her father's desk and leaned over to kiss his cheek. "I promise to be more forthcoming with my plans."

Taunton harrumphed again, somewhat mollified. "I suggest you start now. What do you plan to do about Drummond? As you say, justice needs to be served."

Emily explained about Winfred. "We are meeting with him next Tuesday."

Brett's eyes shot to hers. "Did he contact you?"

Emily's eyes widened, her expression one of guileless innocence. "Did I not mention that he wrote? It must have slipped my mind in the upheaval of recent events."

Slipped her mind? Brett gritted his teeth, tamping down the urge to snort. Nothing escaped her. He had wondered what had happened to that bloody note. He would not put it past her to have picked his pockets while he slept.

Taunton drummed his fingers on his desk. "And this meeting is to take place in a private and well-guarded location?"

Brett took some satisfaction in seeing Emily's smug expression falter. "No. It is not," he said. "Winfred plans to meet us in the Wapping district by the docks. It is not the safest of venues, and so I plan to take a few men with me when I go to meet him. *Alone*." His eyes bored into Emily's.

"And how, pray tell, will you identify him?" Emily challenged, undaunted. "Do you plan to approach every man you see? Or is he planning to wear a red flower in his buttonhole?"

"She has a point there," Daniel said, clearly enjoying Brett's predicament.

Brett nearly snarled at his friend. "You do not seriously think that she should accompany me to the dock area, where—?"

"The decision is not Daniel's or yours to make, but mine," Emily said coolly. "You agreed to assist me in order to keep me safe. Between your hired men and yourself, I trust in your ability to do so. You need me to identify Winfred. Besides, he is already skittish and likely to flee again if I am not there. I promise to be very careful. We can take my father's coach. No one would dare accost us in that."

Brett snapped his mouth closed, well aware that she was once again cleverly leading him in the direction she desired. Like leading a damn draft horse to water.

Taunton interceded. "She is right. I will give you my coach and more men. Bedford, you will accompany them. With a show of force, not much should transpire."

"He is the expendable one, not me," Daniel protested. "That is why Emily sought his assistance in the first place." When Emily whirled on him, Daniel winked.

She laughed. "I know you would have aided me heroically, but with the birth of the twins, Julia needed you more than I. I did not want to put you in the position of having to keep things from her. That would have been far more dangerous than this investigation."

"A wise woman. Very good of you to consider that," Daniel agreed affably.

"Now then, is there anything else I need to know?" Taunton said.

Brett made a bold decision—or a reckless one. "Yes, sir. There is one other matter. When everything is resolved, I plan to marry your daughter. That is, once she agrees to my proposal. But I am a persistent man. I shall prevail."

Emily's mouth gaped open. When she recovered, she glowered at Brett.

Unrepentant, he could not stop the beaming smile from curving his lips.

"Do not post the banns," she said, a hard edge in her tone. "This is still under discussion. Now then, gentlemen, we are quite finished." Without a backward glance, she sailed regally from the room in a swish of skirts.

"She is nothing if not decisive," Daniel said. "I understand why the two of you butt heads. You will have to work on your wooing. More flowers and poetry."

"Takes after her mother and sister," Taunton said, sighing. "I suggest a stronger arsenal than flowers and poetry, but you have my blessing. The two of you are well suited. Single-minded to the point of reckless."

Brett took no umbrage at Taunton's comment. After all, he had what he sought—his consent.

>=<

EMILY DID NOT have a light because she could identify Brett's room by counting the doors. She had wisely decided against carrying anything that could be construed as a weapon. The man had the audacity to declare himself to her father, like some heroic suitor of yore. The decision was hers alone to make. Daniel had to win Julia's hand and Brett would have to win hers.

She began to knock, but thought better of it. She turned the knob and slipped inside, closing his bedroom door quietly behind her—and locking it. She opened her mouth to berate him, but then shut it. After all, the fortress was secure. One could take a moment to admire the view.

Brett stood with his trousers on, nothing else. One arm was braced on the mantel, while the flickering firelight played over the planes of his body in an undulating dance. He was beautiful, smooth as marble, yet so vibrantly alive.

A riot of sensation spiraled through her. Desire. Excitement. Need. She ached to slip her arms around him, to feel him cradle her close and love her. She blinked, her throat tightening.

She had done the right thing in rejecting him. She was freeing him from a life of uncertainty. From wondering when the blackness would strike again, and if it did, would she have the strength to battle it back a second time?

But oh, to be loved by such a man.

He must have heard the catch in her breath, for he turned, and straightening, he gave her that slow, devastating smile. And when he opened his arms, she was lost.

She dashed across the room and flung herself into his embrace, his arms folding around her. She might not have him forever, but for tonight he was all hers.

"I had hoped you would come."

"It was a mistake. We have both made them today. You should not have spoken to my father."

"You spoke to him on my behalf. I could only do the same on yours. It is customary to ask a father for permission to marry their daughter. Since I have not had luck in the past, I thought it best to alert your father of my intentions, so I know if I face friend or foe. I can only handle one vengeful earl at a time."

"You know my father would like nothing more than to see me wed. And he thinks favorably of you since you assisted Daniel with winning Julia."

He kissed her temple, and she savored the warmth of the fire and their embrace. After a moment, she leaned back to see his face. "I am deeply sorry about the shipment. I warned you to flee while you had the chance. I wanted—"

"Shh. I am not a poor, powerless clerk like Marsh. I have powerful friends. The Duke of Bedford *and* the Earl of Taunton are demanding a full investigation into the charges. I do not always approve of the power your aristocracy wields, but when it is in the pursuit of righting a wrong, well, I appreciate their hoisting their banners on my behalf. The Court of Directors, who oversee the docks, will not dismiss two powerful peers of the realm. Now then, dare I hope you braved my room to lay down your arms and finally accept my proposal?"

How easy it would be to concede. He was an easy man

to love. "I am considering it." She did not wish to break this spell that had woven around them. Refused to let the harsh light of reality intrude.

"I see you need more convincing. Alas, I have no flowers. So I will have to do my best to romance you. To love you," he murmured softly, pressing his lips to her brow. "I do, you know. With all my heart."

He was good at romance. At loving her. She could feel her resistance melting.

She sighed when his arm slid under her legs, and he carried her to the bed. He lay her down gently and then with a predatory grace, he climbed onto the bed and knelt over her. Those dark, lucid blue eyes locked on hers as he leaned over, slowly untied the belt of her robe, and then spread it open. He sucked in a sharp breath. She wore another gown from her trousseau, one of silver satin that shimmered in the flickering firelight. The heat of his admiring perusal sent her pulse thrumming and warmth searing through her.

His words escaped on an exhale of breath. "You come with formidable armor."

"Yes, well, let's hope not for long," she whispered and lifted her arm to cup his neck and draw him down to her.

His husky laughter wrapped around her, vibrating through her body. He dipped his forehead to hers, and spoke with aching tenderness. "Love me, Emily. Be mine."

She cupped his cheeks and spoke the words from her heart. "I do. I am." Then she kissed him, and all was right with her world.

Chapter Twenty-eight

≫⋍

THE days leading up to their meeting with Winfred crawled, but Emily had no complaints about the evenings. During the day, Brett was at the docks, where he reviewed the *Bostonian*'s inventory with the customs officials. The goods in contention were safely secured in one of the dock's many cavernous warehouses.

The evenings belonged to Emily, to smooth out the frustrated lines furrowing Brett's brow. To curl up cradled in his arms and savor his wooing her with words of love and poetry. Brett was proving as single-minded as she in the quest of his goal, and in his arms, he made her believe in buried dreams.

She stifled the urge to giggle, because while the man might be well read, his verse was abysmal. She knew Brett was different—his poetry confirmed it. Not many men would pen a romantic poem featuring bawdy battles. If the man were not so besotted, he would see that he was making her half mad.

She would give him her answer soon—but not today. Today

they were due to meet Winfred. Over a year ago, she had reread Jason's letters and became convinced that there was foul play in regard to his death. Nearly two months had passed since she and Brett had entered into their strange alliance. It was hard to believe that after so much time had passed, that she was finally nearing her goal. Today, she hoped to collect the damaging evidence to convict Drummond. And then, only then, would she be free to consider her future.

She neatened the skirts of her dove gray carriage dress and hurried toward the foyer to meet Brett. The sight greeting her caused the smile curving her lips to freeze and her eyes to widen. She stopped short, too stunned to react. In the back recesses of her mind, she prayed Brett was running late. If he was on time, she sincerely feared for Melody's life.

A tall, dark-haired stranger held Melody tightly and swung her off her feet, twirling her in his arms. Melody's laughter rang out like chiming bells. The man's features were hidden, his head tilted toward Melody's upturned face, and his rich laughter melded with hers.

"He best be armed, because if he is not, he is going to die."

Emily whirled to find Brett had stolen silently upon them. She held up her hands, hoping to avoid bloodshed. "Wait! There must be some explanation. Let us stay calm and listen to it."

"Calm? Why should I be?" Brett protested, his brows snapping together. "The man disappears for nearly half a year, leaving his sisters alone to deal with their harridan of a mother, while still reeling from their own grief. While he neglects his title, his responsibilities, and disappears to who knows where, with nary a word to anyone and doing . . . ? What the devil *have* you been doing?"

The stranger stopped spinning Melody and set her on her feet. Laughter brimmed in his eyes as he straightened to his full height, which equaled Brett's. "It is good to see you, too, cousin. I am touched that you have given me a thought, because word has it that you are in far deeper trouble than I. So I have chivalrously returned to help dig you out. Please, no thanks are needed."

The enigmatic Duke of Prescott.

Emily caught her breath. With thick, raven black hair, rich cobalt blue eyes, and that infectious laugh, he was almost as striking as Brett. *Almost*, she loyally affirmed.

Brett snorted. "All slanderous lies. However, I am late for a meeting, so your overdue explanations and excuses will have to wait." He caught Emily's elbow and made for the door, but Melody blocked his exit.

"Andrew will assist you. If you do not want me penning that letter to Lady Janice Wentworth, you best allow him to do so," Melody said, a hard glint in her eyes.

"You would not dare." At his sister's jutting chin, Brett blew out a breath, and narrowed his eyes on Prescott. "Fine. I did promise Taunton I would bring extra men with me. For once, you might prove useful."

"I am at your service," Prescott said, dipping his head. "You have always been there when I needed your help, so I am here to return the favor. It is past due." He winked at Melody and followed Brett to the door. "Of course, I love to assist a damsel in distress. I take it this fair damsel is the Earl of Taunton's . . . ?"

"Daughter. Lady Emily Chandler," Brett bit out, pausing to begrudgingly make the introductions. "As you can see, she is not in distress and is quite capable of taking care of herself. Bedford is meeting us at the docks, but an extra duke along could not hurt. God knows, your infernal country does bow and scrape before them."

Emily covered her mouth to stifle her laughter at Brett's crotchety display of gratitude. She dipped into a curtsy. "Your Grace."

Prescott bowed, Brett's temper rolling off him like water from the prow of a ship. "The pleasure is mine, but please, let us not stand on formality. Call me Prescott. I have yet to use my title, so it will be good practice to flaunt my ducal power on your behalf, Curtis. Again, no thanks are needed."

"Slow down," Emily hissed at Brett's broad back, unable to respond as Brett practically dragged her down the front stoop of Keaton House. Her father's gleaming burgundy town coach awaited them at the bottom of the steps.

Once settled inside the cab, Brett gave directions to the driver and alerted the footmen to be on alert for anything suspicious, which aroused Prescott's interest.

"I had heard that customs confiscated one of your shipments. Is there something else I should be looking out for?" Prescott studied Brett more carefully.

"You ask a lot of questions for a man who has many unanswered of his own," Brett said, but with an air of resignation, he updated Prescott, curtly answering his array of probing questions.

Emily could discern nothing wrong with Prescott's mind, and again pondered the comments she had overheard in regard to his intelligence. Truth be told, it did not matter. She knew the most important thing about the man—he had returned when he had learned that Brett was in trouble. That was all that counted.

"You should know, your mother passed on your parting missive to me," Brett said, changing the subject back to Prescott. "It sent her into apoplexy, which I take it was your intent."

Prescott shrugged. "I only confirmed all she ever expected from me. She should have been pleased, because you know how Mother loves to be right."

"She does indeed. Well played," Brett said, smiling. "So you did not return for a painting? For A. W. Grant's *Adrift at Sea*?"

Prescott paused, a flicker of surprise lighting his eyes. "You know about that?"

"Brett bought the painting," Emily supplied, her mind on the enigmatic note Prescott had left his mother. She was disappointed when they did not elaborate. "But Brett believes it to be a forgery."

"So it is. A clever young woman replicated it," Prescott said.

Her eyes widened. "What . . . ? What will happen to her?"

"She will become my duchess of course." Prescott beamed, clearly delighted with his choice.

"But of course," Brett drawled. "Talent such as hers should be rewarded." Laughter danced in his eyes.

"Exactly. I surmise that Mother will disapprove of an art forger for a daughter-in-law. As my very existence gives her enough with which to find fault, perhaps we should keep my duchess's eccentric pastime between ourselves. Agreed?"

"Eccentric pastime?" Brett echoed and shook his head. "Has the lady accepted your proposal?" His eyes met Emily's. "I have learned that it is wise to get a woman's acceptance before announcing the nuptials."

Prescott shifted on his seat. "There are a few details to work out before I ask for her hand. We had a slight disagreement, but—"

Brett threw back his head and laughed. "Welcome home, Drew. I needed some amusement. My thanks to you for providing it. For my appreciation, *Adrift at Sea* is yours."

"No thanks needed, but I will take the painting." Prescott smiled.

Brett updated Prescott on family matters, and his cousin inquired after Bedford. As the two men bantered, it was clear that Prescott and Brett's friendship was a deep bond. Emily smiled because Brett might be forced to realize that not all English aristocrats were worthy of his disdain.

❧

"COULD YOU NOT have chosen a better meeting place?" Prescott grimaced.

They were meeting Winfred in a tavern in the Wapping district in East London, not far from Brett's offices. Dock laborers bustling to their jobs mixed with sailors and immigrants, and a chorus of foreign dialects rose above the din. Public houses lined the streets, despite the putrid smell of raw sewage from the nearby river. Emily pressed her handkerchief to her nose. The May day also threatened rain, which contributed to the bleak and depressing atmosphere.

Brett responded as they turned off Wapping Lane and onto

a side street. "Winfred chose the location. With no means of contacting him, we could not change the venue, or believe me, I would have." He addressed Emily. "Stay in the carriage until—"

"No! He wishes to meet with me, not you. Between the coachmen, your men, Bedford, you, and Prescott, I shall be quite safe."

Brett emitted a beleaguered sigh. "Fine, but first give me a minute to assess the area. That is not negotiable," he added when she opened her mouth to protest.

The carriage drew to a stop, and at Brett's nod, Prescott alighted first. Brett waited until she acquiesced to his demand before he turned to follow his cousin.

"I do not see a tavern. You said the *Jolly Tar*?" Prescott said.

At Prescott's query, she opened the door to peer outside.

Prescott ventured down the alley ahead of the coach, while Brett stood a few paces from the door, surveying the area.

She glanced back toward Prescott, who began to return to the coach. Suddenly, his eyes widened and he frantically waved his arms. "Behind you, Curtis! Get down!"

Emily gasped as Prescott broke into a mad dash in their direction. Before she could react, Brett lunged and slammed the carriage door shut, causing her to stumble backward, nearly tumbling to the floor.

"Go!" Brett bellowed. The sound of his fist pounding the coach's side, urging it to move, echoed in her ears.

When she regained her balance, she scrambled toward the door and grasped at the latch with unsteady hands.

The handle was ripped from her fingers in the wake of an explosive pistol shot. The noise caused the horses to startle with whining cries, and the abrupt jerk forward upended her to the floor.

The bellowing commands of the coachmen, who fought to calm the animals, drowned out her cry.

"Don't shoot! Hold your fire!"

She recognized Daniel's authoritative voice.

"I want them alive. Follow them! There were two!"

"Brett!" Emily cried. Shouts, pounding footsteps, and the jangle of the horses' harnesses and clacking hooves rent the air. *Brett.* When the coach rolled to a stop, she scrambled to her feet and tore at the latch, but it was yanked open from the outside.

Prescott stood outside, his eyes sharp as they roved over her. "Are you all right?"

"Yes, of course." She pressed a hand to her thundering heart. "Brett?"

Grim-faced, Prescott pursed his lips, but made no reply. He reached in and pulled the steps down, bounding into the cab. "Lift him up to me."

She stumbled onto a seat, her shaking legs unable to support her. Her hands rose to her mouth.

Prescott grasped Brett's unconscious form under his arms. Daniel and another man hefted up Brett's prostrate figure from the outside.

No! The protest sprang to her lips, a prayer from her heart.

Prescott laid Brett on the carriage seat, his long legs dangling off the side, his blood-soaked cravat tied around his head. *Not again.* She fought to draw breath, her chest tightening. *Please.* She could not do it again. The pain. The loss. The grief. Fear was like long talons sinking into her, biting deep, pressing her down.

Daniel leaned into the cab and fired off directives. "Get him to Taunton's. I will send for Taunton's physician. I want to remain here to see if we can catch the bastards. I also need to locate one of the men Brett hired and who has disappeared. Go."

Jaw clenched tight, Prescott nodded and knelt beside Brett to press another handkerchief to his temple.

The door shut, and the coach bounded forward, driving with increased urgency.

Prescott glanced her way and managed a reassuring look. "He is alive. The man's aim was off. Brett has a thick head, so I have faith in his resilience." Prescott shrugged out of his jacket. "Here. You are pale as a ghost. That is shock." He leaned over and folded the garment around her. "Stay with me. Brett needs you. Head wounds bleed a lot. He looks worse than he is."

She struggled to still her tremors. "How? We had so many men . . . How could—?"

"The bastard did not withdraw his pistol until he was nearly upon the coach." Prescott clenched his jaw, his eyes dark. His attention returned to Brett, and he brushed blood-streaked strands of hair free of the binding.

In a daze, she followed his movements. His tender gesture cut through her grief and severed her stunned immobility. Her heart thundered, and a protest sprang to her lips. She needed to do that.

She refused to let him go. She would not lose Brett. He was alive. The darkness could wait. Brett needed her.

With unsteady hands, she shrugged off Prescott's jacket, and knelt beside him in the tight confines of the cab's floor space. "Let me." She moved Prescott's hands aside, and gently brushed her fingers through Brett's hair. She gazed at his ashen features, the long lashes, and his body so ominously still. She pressed her mouth to his ear, whispering the words of her heart. "Hold on. Hold on for me. I love you."

Chapter Twenty-nine

❧❧

"GOOD lord, is he all right? What the devil happened?"
Her father's booming voice rolled off Emily, so
intent was her focus on directing Prescott to Brett's bedchamber. Sully supported Brett beneath his arms while
Prescott carried him by the legs, and she hovered beside the
two men—close to Brett.

She shoved open the door to his room and dashed ahead
to yank back the bedcovers. "Gently!" she cried, biting her
lip as they lowered Brett onto the bed. The site of his still
form, pale features, and the ominous blood-soaked cravat that
bandaged his head tore at her already frayed nerves.

She cursed her shaking hands as she leaned over to
remove Brett's boots, but her father's grip on her arm drew
her back. "I need—" she began.

"It is all right, Emily," Prescott interceded, giving her a
reassuring smile. "Let me tend to him for a minute. He is
my cousin, I love him, too."

She opened her mouth to protest, but her father's housekeeper Petie then rushed into the room and hurried to assist

the men. With reluctance, Emily allowed her father to draw her away from Brett's side, but kept her eyes locked on his figure.

"Emily, what happened?" her father said gently.

She moistened her lips to respond, but she stammered, finding it difficult to articulate the words. "He was . . . he was shot, but he will be all right. Daniel has sent for Doctor Malley. Prescott told him to duck, but he . . . he did not heed the warning because he was protecting me. He . . . he lunged at the cab to shut the door. I had opened it. Why did I open it? He told me not to, to wait inside, but I . . . it is my fault. I never should have . . . I . . ." She was babbling, could not seem to stop until her voice broke on a sob.

"Shh. None of that." Her father drew her into his arms and held her tight. "It is *not* your fault. That fault belongs to the man who pulled the trigger. It is his alone to carry. Brett Curtis vowed to protect you, and he did. He is an honorable man, and you would not love him so if he was anything less."

"He is reckless and foolish . . . and thickheaded," she cried, drawing deep, ragged breaths.

"And that is fortunate considering the location of his wound. He is strong; he will come through. After all, he has you to fight for." Her father pressed his handkerchief into her hand and drew back to smile at her.

"Well, I—"

Doctor Malley's arrival curtailed her response. She turned to follow him, but to her annoyance, her father once again intervened.

"Please, love, let the doctor see to him," he said gently but firmly. "Brett is all right for now, but you are not. You have been through a shock. Once the good doctor finishes, you can return. Prescott will get you should he wake or you are needed."

"Well, I . . ." Conflicted, she glanced over her shoulder, but seeing Doctor Malley lean over Brett, Prescott close beside him, she nodded. "Just for a minute." She let her father guide her into the hall, but then whirled and grasped his arm. "Melody and Miranda!" Good lord, she could not forget Brett's sisters.

"They are at the park with Julia, the twins, and Jonathan. They will—"

"Sully must collect them. Instruct him to do so immediately. They need to be here. They will want to be with Brett should . . ." She paused, unable to finish the thought. "They will want to be at his side during this time. He must not be alone." She pressed a hand to her head as she fought to collect her scattered thoughts. To push aside the shock and grief that warred within her.

"No, of course not. We will arrange a bedside vigil. Everyone can take a shift."

But she needed to do more. Surely there was something she could do or she would go mad.

She tamped down that thought as well and pressed an unsteady hand to her brow.

"Here, you need to sit. You cannot help him if you do not have a care for yourself." Her father guided her to a nearby chair and collected another to move it beside her. "Ah, here is Agnes. She will sit with you while I see how the doctor fares. I will return for you as soon as he is finished."

She nodded jerkily. She did not like to concede it, but Julia had always been better at nursing wounds than she. She cursed her squeamish stomach and unsteady hands.

"He will be all right, miss. He is fighting strong," Agnes said. "Besides, he needs to do right by you. Marry you properly."

Emily emitted a hysterical laugh. The man was so bullheaded that she could almost believe he would not deign to let a mere bullet to the head thwart him. Leave it to Agnes to know just what to say to her.

She drummed her fingers on her thigh, unable to sit still, strung so tight with nerves. She was better at planning—with Brett. She closed her eyes, but then immediately opened them.

Drat and damnation.

She should have thought of it immediately.

Brett was not safe so long as Drummond remained free.

She needed to find Winfred. She dug out the note from her skirt pocket, the one Winfred had ostensibly penned, and whirled on Agnes to thrust it impatiently at her. "I need you to return to Halford's and show this to the footman who rooms with Winfred. Ask him if this is Winfred's hand." Emily desperately wished to go with Agnes, but she refused to leave Brett.

Agnes frowned. "You think it is not?"

"I wonder if it was a trap. Those men were after Brett. They could have killed Prescott or Daniel, but the only shot fired was at Brett."

Agnes blew out a breath. "Of course, miss."

"You told me you are friendly with the footman who shares Winfred's room. I know you have spoken to him on this matter before, but it is now imperative that you press upon your friend our need to speak with Winfred very soon. Each day Winfred does not come forward further endangers himself and others."

"I will, miss. Ralf will assist me." She winked at Emily. "I think he fancies me."

"I have no doubt," Emily said, a half laugh escaping her. "And Agnes, if Winfred is there, you must convince him to come here. I must speak to him as soon as possible."

Agnes bobbed her head. "That I will, miss. I promise."

Emily bit her lip as Agnes scurried off. It might not be enough, but it was something. She glanced up as the door to Brett's room opened and her father reappeared, waving her inside.

She almost mowed him down as she dashed to reach Brett's bedside.

Later Miranda and Melody joined her vigil. And that was where Agnes found her when she returned from her errand.

Emily turned, her pulse racing at the beaming smile that split Agnes's face.

"Winfred has sent word! He is returning tomorrow and will come here directly."

Expelling a breath, Emily grasped Brett's hand and

squeezed. Perhaps, just perhaps, this nightmare was winding to an end.

≫≪

"Emily, sit. Burke said he would bring Winfred here as soon as he arrives, and your wearing a hole in the carpet will not expedite matters," Julia said.

Emily turned, her hands cupping her elbows. "I cannot. That is all I have been doing. All I could do until now."

After spending a night sitting vigil in the easy chair in Brett's room, her body had paid the price. She felt aches and pains in muscles she did not know she had. When others had shared her watch, she had been able to sleep on the nearby settee, but her rest was fretful and uneasy. Doctor Malley's assessment of Brett's recovery had haunted her.

The good doctor had launched into a lecture on the complexity of head wounds and the complicated workings of the mind. He ominously pronounced that only time would tell the true nature of Brett's injury. The wretched doctor then sought to alleviate their concerns with reassurances that on the other hand, Brett could wake up speaking impeccable Latin. She snorted. Brett's Latin was atrocious, so his prognosis looked bleak indeed.

"What was that?"

Daniel's question startled her, and she waved her hand airily, but froze when Burke appeared at the door to the drawing room.

"Mr. Reginald Winfred," he intoned. After Winfred entered the room, Burke discreetly departed, closing the drawing room doors behind him.

Heart hammering, Emily stared at the young man. He was slight of stature, with a shock of brown hair peeking out of his hat and wide brown eyes that surveyed their group. He clutched a satchel against his chest, and her breath caught at the sight of it.

It was a large leather portfolio.

She pressed her hand to her stomach. She recognized it, having purchased the case for Jason just before he had embarked for India. It was her parting gift, and she had even taken care to have his initials sewn into it.

Winfred removed his hat and dipped his head. "It is just Winfred. I rarely acknowledge the Reginald part, but your butler seemed insistent upon the matter."

"Welcome, Winfred, and thank you for coming," Julia said, keeping a straight face, but her lips twitched. "Please, have a seat. There is much to discuss."

"Thank you, Your Grace," Winfred said.

Emily took her seat on the settee beside Julia, while Daniel and Winfred settled in the chairs across the coffee table.

"Allow me to apologize, Lady Emily," Winfred began. "I would have returned the viscount's portfolio to you much sooner had I known you were looking for it." He leaned over to hand the satchel to her.

She caught her breath and laid it almost reverently on her lap, running an unsteady hand over the battered leather. Half of her wanted to tear it open and dig inside, but the other half of her had questions for Winfred. "Not that I am not grateful for your care of Jason's personal effects, but I am interested to know how you came to safeguard this particular item and for so long."

"Well, it is where the viscount kept his diary and his personal correspondence. Why, he saved every letter you wrote to him. As it was private, he directed me to safeguard it in the false bottom of his trunk. When the viscount died, I thought it was right that the trunk go to you, per his request. You should have your letters back, and I knew you would take good care of his diary."

"So if the portfolio was sent to Emily with Jason's trunk and then on to the Bransons, how did you next acquire it?" Daniel said, breaking the silence that had followed. At Winfred's hesitation, Daniel continued. "Please, you can speak freely here. You are among friends who appreciate your coming forward."

"I was residing at the Bransons after the viscount's funeral and was there when the viscount's trunk was delivered. When I heard his brother planned to turn the contents over to Mr. Drummond, I took the portfolio into my safe-keeping. It was personal, you understand. I did not want *that man* to have it, refused to let him touch the viscount's things," he said, sneering at the reference to Drummond.

He turned to Emily. "I planned to give it back to you. But when your father delivered the trunk, he explained that it was too difficult a reminder for you. I thought perhaps later when you were married and had someone else to care for, you might be ready then."

Emily blinked back her tears, and clutched the portfolio to her chest. "Thank you, Winfred. You were right and kind to think of that. I shall be forever grateful to you."

Winfred flushed, but gave a shy smile.

"You did not care for Mr. Drummond?" Daniel said, returning to Winfred's earlier comment, his tone neutral.

"No, Your Grace, I did not," Winfred said curtly, his smile fading.

"Is there a particular reason for your opinion?" Daniel pressed.

"There is," Winfred snarled. "I know a trickster when I see one. The man had a shifty manner about him, and he was always sniffing about the viscount's room." He drew a deep breath, and again spoke directly to Emily, his expression contrite. "I should have come forward sooner, but I had no evidence against the blackguard, just suspicion. I also had heard what happened to Mr. Marsh when he spoke up, so I did not think anyone would listen to me, a mere servant."

"I understand, Winfred. It is all right. I, too, wish I had acted earlier," she said.

"Well, I was right glad you wrote to me. After my room was ransacked, I asked for a week's leave. I took the time to visit Mr. Marsh, who you had warned me had been recently assaulted and that is why you had concerns for my safety. I had not seen Mr. Marsh since the viscount's funeral. He confided to me your plans to implicate Mr. Drummond in the viscount's death. He asked me if I could help, particularly in finding Drummond's valet." He straightened in his seat and lifted his chin. "I can, and that is why I am here."

Emily squeezed Julia's hand so tight she sucked in a sharp breath. "Winfred, do you . . . have you found evidence that could implicate Mr. Drummond in the viscount's death?"

"I have," he stated, staring her straight in the eye. "When Marsh told me about your investigation, I took the rest of my week's leave to find Mr. Drummond's former valet, who left his employ after the viscount's death. I found out why he left. He was afraid, because he overheard Mr. Drummond berating a sepoy for his inaccurate shot at the viscount. Mr. Drummond said he was to kill the viscount, not wound him, so the man did not deserve the full amount that Mr. Drummond owed to him."

"Good lord," Daniel breathed.

Emily gave a sharp cry and covered her mouth. Julia's arm curled around her shoulders.

"He said more, too. He said Mr. Drummond had opium stashed in his room, and it was gone after the viscount's death. I saw Mr. Drummond leave the viscount's room right after he died. It was Mr. Drummond who gave the opium to the viscount. I do not know how he did, but he must have done so, because that is what they say killed the viscount."

She sagged in her seat. She knew it! She had been right. Right all along. She wanted to cry in anguish and shout in triumph.

"Drummond will hang," Daniel declared. "Will Drummond's former valet testify to this? Is he willing to speak to a magistrate? More important, we need to ensure his safety until he does so."

"He is. He was scared to do so, but I convinced him to step forward. I told him the viscount's brother would no doubt give him a generous reward if Billy did so. If we both gave our testimonies. But I—" He paused to swallow. "I can do no less for the viscount. I just wish I could have done something sooner."

Recovering, Emily smiled at Winfred. "This is enough, Winfred. Jason would be proud of your stepping forward like this."

Winfred flushed, and ducked his head.

"We have Drummond on charges of attempted murder, but let us see if we can implicate him on embezzlement as well," Daniel said, and nodded toward the portfolio.

Still reeling from the turn of events, Emily blinked. "Yes, of course."

"Oh, my mistake, the key." With a sheepish look, Winfred leaned over to hand it to her.

Not daring to breathe, Emily unlocked the satchel, slid it open, and extracted a stack of envelopes. They were tied with a rose-colored ribbon that she recognized as one of her own. Through a blur of tears she ran her finger over Jason's name and address that was penned in her hand.

She recalled Winfred's words. *He had kept all your letters.* She swallowed the lump in her throat, and smiling wistfully, she hoped they had given Jason the same comfort that his had given her.

After a moment, she reached back into the satchel and withdrew Jason's diary. Not ready to review its contents, she placed it with the letters, exhaled, and then removed the hefty leatherbound ledger that barely fit into the confines of the portfolio. She held it in her hands for a moment, her pulse racing.

She opened the ledger to the middle, and then gave a choked laugh. "He has not made my journey easy." Reams of columns and rows with figures were scrawled across the page in Jason's meticulous hand.

Daunted, she flipped through the pages, and then caught her breath when a sheaf of paper slipped loose. Curious, she lifted it and her eyes widened. "My pardon, I spoke too soon. What was I thinking? Of course, Jason would neatly tie up all his accounts. He was so meticulous about his work, would never leave anything to chance. He used to try my patience when he gave detailed instructions in regard to a simple task or problem, but not this time. For once, being annoyingly, wonderfully, magnificently fastidious is his most admirable attribute." She lifted her face and smiled through the sheen of tears blurring her eyes.

"What is it?" Julia took the sheet, her eyes skimming

over it. "Good lord. It is all here in painstaking detail. It is Jason's testimony to the embezzlement of funds and then a full accounting of Drummond's culpability." She laughed and turned to Emily, her eyes shining. "Do you understand what this means?"

Daniel beamed at Emily. "Of course she does. You probably never doubted that you would succeed, because once you set your mind to something—"

"—there is no talking you out of it," Julia finished with a laugh. "I am so proud of you. So very proud, and so is Jason. I just know he is smiling down at you, never doubting that this moment would come. It must be why he sent the trunk to you."

Emily drew back and swiped at her eyes, her head spinning. She had gotten justice for Jason. She yearned to revel in her triumph, but victory was bittersweet. Something was missing.

Someone was missing, she corrected.

She needed Brett. She pressed her hand to her heart.

This triumph was not hers alone.

Brett had been there from the very beginning. He deserved to be here at the end. "Brett should be here. I need him to be with me."

"He will be," Julia murmured, and squeezed her hand.

"He will come through," Daniel said. "After all you two have been through, he deserves to see Drummond's face when you charge the man with embezzlement *and* murder. Rest assured, he will not miss that moment. You have both earned it."

Emily nodded, grasping onto their conviction like a lifeline. Brett would come through. She refused to contemplate anything less.

Chapter Thirty

※≈

AFTER Winfred had departed, Emily was once again settled in the easy chair beside Brett's bed. The shooting had occurred yesterday morning; surely he should wake soon. She clutched his hand in hers and curled her fingers around his wrist, the rhythmic beat of his pulse a comforting balm.

"I have news."

Emily jumped, unaware of her sister's approach.

Julia squeezed her shoulder. "That boy who works for Brett, Baines, is it? Well, Daniel engaged him to help with the search for the thugs who attacked your carriage. Daniel said that Baines can find a piece of copper wire buried in the stink and mud of the Thames, so it took some time, but he has scouted out the two thugs' hideout. Father has engaged Runners to apprehend them, so they should soon have answers as to who hired them. No doubt that will add one more charge on which to hang Drummond."

"And when Brett wakes up, he will be able to identify the men," she said with conviction. Sighing, she frowned at his still form. "Stubborn, headstrong man. I told him he needed to protect himself and stop worrying about me. I warned him."

Julia circled her chair and knelt before Emily. "And I understand he told you much the same. You know, when Brett wakes up, I doubt his first question will be about the men who shot him. It will be something closer to his heart, and which only you can answer."

"You have been talking to Father," Emily muttered.

"I cannot tell you how to respond, Emily. I know how much you loved Jason and the toll his death took on you, so I understand that it is frightening for you to risk loving another. But have you ever considered that the reason you took Jason's death so hard was because it came during a time when you had suffered so many losses? First, Mother died, and Father was lost to his own grief. I was struggling to care for Jonathan and keep the estate afloat. It was a bleak period, and Jason was like a bright beacon of light. When that was snuffed out, you must have felt as if you were plunged into darkness again."

Stunned, her lips parted, her mind reeling at the implication of Julia's words.

"He is a good man, Emily. You have fought so valiantly for Jason, perhaps it is time that you fight for yourself," Julia said softly. She closed her hands over Emily's and squeezed. "You deserve love. You deserve Brett. Not many men would risk their lives as he did." She stood, gave Emily's shoulder a gentle squeeze, and turned to leave.

Emily pressed a hand to her temple. Frowning, she recalled her gut-wrenching loneliness before Jason, her despair over her mother's death, her father's inability to cope, and Julia's absence. She had been so young and so very alone.

Could Julia be right?

Could it have been a confluence of tragic events that had so shattered her? She blew out a breath, because the reasons for her breakdown no longer mattered. It was not important. The last two days had taught her what was important—that if there was darkness in her, she was older and stronger now.

She may stumble and falter, but she would not fall, and if she did, by God, she would pick herself up and forge ahead. That was all she could ask of herself—or of anyone.

It was the only good news to come out of this horrid nightmare, because if this did not break her, nothing would.

She straightened in her chair, lifted her chin, and smiled at Brett. "Well then. Now you have to wake up in order to propose properly. I need to begin planning our wedding. Such things take time." She waited a moment, and then poked him in the chest when she received no response. "Are you listening? Please wake up. My nerves are frazzled, and I am not the only one suffering over you. Melody and Miranda are walking around half dazed and with red-rimmed eyes, and Daniel and Prescott are very sour-tempered."

She sighed.

"If you wish to hear what I have found, you have to wake up, you thickheaded lummox." She poked him again. Hard.

A groan escaped him, and she yanked her finger back, her pulse racing. "Brett?"

His eyes fluttered and eventually blinked open. He shifted his gaze around the room until his eyes locked on her. And then he simply stared.

She could see his pupils constrict as they came into focus with what she hoped was recognition. Her heart pounded, and the silence stretched taut. When she could stand it no longer, she bent over him. "Do you know who I am?" She took care to speak slowly and articulate each word.

He stared at her blankly.

She did not dare breathe. Nerves strained, she resisted the urge to give him another poke. When he finally responded, his words were a near whisper, so she leaned close.

"A sharp-taloned she-devil who has been poking and prodding me. And I am *not* a lummox."

She straightened. "You are, regrettably, the same. I will never forgive you for upsetting me, your sisters, Prescott, and Daniel, for worrying everyone senseless." She drew a shuddering breath and blinked furiously.

He moistened his lips. "Drew and Daniel do not have much sense to begin with, but I am sorry for upsetting you and the girls. I should have ducked as Drew advised. Fortunately, I have a hard head."

With a half laugh and half hiccup, she pressed her lips to his temple. "It is a brilliant head."

When she pulled back, his eyes softened and his gaze roved over her features as if memorizing each one. "I love you," he said with tender solemnity.

She smiled, her heart pounding. "I love you, too."

"Marry me, Emily."

Her breath hitched and her eyes blurred. "Of course, I will marry you. How can I not? You are as mad as I. You stop bullets to protect me, and compose verse comparing me to the fair Athena. More important, I am mad. Madly in love with you." She brushed his hair away from the bandage on his temple and pressed a gentle kiss on it.

When she sat back, his hand cupped her cheek. "You are not the only one with a fair hand with ink and pen," he said, his voice husky with emotion. "I told you I would wear you down." His hand slid to the nape of her neck and with a gentle urging, he drew her to him. Their lips met for a long, lingering kiss.

This was the real triumph of her quest. That this beautiful, brilliant man had fallen in love with her. He had stood by her, supported her, and believed in her. Her heart swelled with joy.

After a few moments, she drew back. Light-headed, she rested a hand gently on the blankets covering his chest. "Now then. You need to regain your strength. To get better so that we can meet with Lord Roberts and deliver the ledger and Jason's diary to him. We need to finish what we started so that I can begin planning our wedding. I—"

"You are good at planning," he said with a smile, and tried to pull her back to him. "You will have the wedding organized in a day. What I need is— *What? You have Jason's ledger and diary? How? You met with Winfred? Alone? Devil take you! After all—*" Brett struggled to rise on his elbows, ignoring her protests. "Blast it, my head is pounding!"

"That is what happens when a bullet grazes it. Lie down, you thick-headed fool!" Desperate, she pressed on his shoulders, but he struggled against her. "Please, are you trying to rip open your wound? For goodness' sake, I did not meet Winfred alone. He came here, and Daniel and Julia were with me. I will tell you everything once you lie down, you obtuse man! I cannot marry you if you kill yourself."

"I am getting up. Hang Winfred, but I am going with you to Lord Roberts. It is my company that charges were brought against and . . . and devil take it, I am as weak as a newborn babe, so let go." He slapped at her hands.

"Dash it, he is still the same. I had hoped the bullet might have softened his hard head."

Recognizing Daniel's amused drawl, Emily whirled to see him framed in the doorway, Prescott next to him, and Melody and Miranda crowding behind them. "Do not just stand there," she cried. "Get in here and get him to listen to reason."

The room flooded with people, Taunton and Julia joining the chaos. Brett was forced to lie back as Melody and Miranda fussed over him, grasping his hand and sniffling.

"You are all right? Do you recognize me?" Melody said, leaning close.

"Let me think," Brett murmured and scrunched up his features. "Thunder? Is that you? What happened to your harness?"

"He thinks I am his horse!" Melody squealed, her hand covering her mouth.

"Oh for goodness' sake!" Emily said, exasperated. "He is teasing. He is fine."

Melody dropped her hand and narrowed her eyes. "I cannot believe I shed one single tear over you. Drew is right. Your head is too thick to pierce." She bent over him and kissed his cheek. "You are a wretched older brother. Miranda, Mr. Jenkins is due to pay another call this afternoon, and I need your help in determining what I should wear. I might have to go shopping. *Again*."

"Jenkins? Another call? Shopping? Again?" Brett roared, but grimaced and pressed a hand to his head.

Miranda moved his arm aside to press a kiss to his bandaged head. "You need to rest, because your memory is not entirely returned. You forget, Melody gives back as good as she gets." She tucked his blankets around him. "Welcome back. You had everyone worried. Do not do it again."

"I never worried," Prescott said. "I warned you to duck, not my fault that you never listen to me—or Lady Emily for that matter. We heard your bellows in the other room."

Brett struggled to sit up, then seeing everyone crowd closer, he relented. "Fine. I will stay in this infernal bed under one condition. No one confronts Lord Roberts without me. Arrange for the meeting tomorrow. The throbbing in my head should be better by then, so you can all stop mollycoddling me. Except for Emily, who has agreed to marry me, and I am holding her to it."

"I think . . . ," Taunton began, but as Brett's words registered, the squeals of excitement drowned him out.

Julia rushed forward and gave Emily a fierce hug. She was then passed on to her father, Melody, and then Miranda.

Prescott and Daniel came over and pumped Brett's hand.

"I never doubted you would prevail," Daniel said. "No mere bullet can thwart you."

"I always wanted an older brother," Julia said, and leaned down to kiss Brett's temple. "Welcome to the family."

Emily smiled as Daniel and Prescott congratulated her.

"I have every faith that you will get him to listen better than he does to me," Prescott said and winked.

"So, son, you need to regain your strength," Taunton said, restoring order. "We have toasts to make, and you have a wedding to plan. As for meeting with Lord Roberts, we will do so the day *after* tomorrow." Her father's tone brooked no dissent. "And we are *all* going. A show of force is warranted."

Emily caught her father's hand and beamed. Then she glanced at Brett, who appeared to be weighing his options.

"Fair enough," he relented. "Two dukes *and* an earl is gilding the lily, but if you insist."

"We do." Daniel and Prescott spoke in unison.

"And stop maligning dukes," Prescott said, "or I still might petition the king to draft a patent of nobility, transferring the title to you."

Emily sputtered out a horrified laugh. *That* was why Brett was so determined to find Prescott. To stop him. She grasped his hand in hers and lifted it to her lips, a smile curving her lips. "Your Grace."

Brett scowled and turned on Prescott. "I appreciate your warning me about those thugs trying to shoot me, but now you can disappear again. This time, I promise not to look for you."

Prescott simply laughed.

"Pay him no mind," Daniel said. He leaned close to Prescott and added sotto voce, "He is always an ungrateful, ornery cuss when he is bedridden."

"And take Daniel with you," Brett said, narrowing his eyes.

"Gentlemen," her father interceded. "If Mr. Curtis is to recover, he needs his rest. Emily?"

"In a minute." Once they departed, she squeezed Brett's hand. "Two dukes, one earl, and my thickheaded protector." When he grinned back, her smile broadened. She brushed his hair from his temple. He was not different after all.

He was the same arrogant, clever man with whom she had fallen irrevocably in love. And she was absolutely mad—to marry him.

Chapter Thirty-one

❧❧

THEY were joining Lord Roberts in a meeting room in his offices located on Cheapside in a grand Elizabethan mansion. Its frontage boasted three bays that were four stories high, a cornice balustrade, and imposing Doric pilasters, making for a majestic and imposing welcome to any visitor.

Brett had never seen Taunton carry a cane before. Brett assumed the accessory to be another aristocratic affectation, but Taunton assured him that the feral lion's head gave opponents pause. Brett also had to concede that Daniel and Drew both carried a disdainful ducal scowl rather well. Emily's ivory gown threaded with blue ribbons broke up the austerity of their black and blue jackets. A spring flower amid dark storm clouds.

He wished he could ease the lines of worry furrowing her brow. A bandage covered his right front temple, but other than mild pain if he moved abruptly, he was quite recovered. Once they finished with Drummond, he looked forward to proving to Emily exactly how healthy he was.

A clerk met them in the foyer and ushered them into the spacious meeting room. "My lords, the Duke of Prescott, the Duke of Bedford, the Earl of Taunton, Lady Emily Chandler, and Mr. Curtis," he announced. After delivering the array of formidable introductions, the clerk departed with a bow.

Drummond was seated at a mahogany table polished to a gleaming sheen. A flicker of alarm crossed his features before he tamped it down. He rose slowly, nodding a curt greeting. When his gaze fastened on Brett, his eyes turned hard and assessing.

Brett stiffened at the sight of Wentworth, surprised to find him seated beside Drummond. He appeared to begrudgingly rise to his feet. Brett grunted. The man had always been a pompous arse.

Lord Roberts surveyed the group through gold-rimmed spectacles. The tall, sharp-featured man dipped his head. "For those of you who are not acquainted, allow me to introduce Mr. Lawrence Drummond and the Earl of Wentworth. Please, everyone be seated."

Brett drew back a chair for Emily and then sat to her left across the table from Drummond and Wentworth. Taunton flanked Emily's right side, with Daniel beside him and Drew one seat further down.

Roberts waited until everyone was seated before reclaiming his own chair at the head of the table. "I see you have brought a strong contingent in your defense, Mr. Curtis," he said, arching a brow at Brett.

Before Brett could respond, Wentworth sneered. "I do not know what this is all about. As I have explained to Lord Taunton, facts are facts, and opinions to the contrary cannot alter them."

"That is true when the facts have been unequivocally established," Taunton said mildly. "However, the customs officials have yet to find anything to justify these charges. Thus, the facts are still in question. Or am I mistaken?" Taunton cocked a brow.

Wentworth drew himself up. "There have been problems with imports from Curtis Shipping in the past, so it is not—"

"My pardon," Daniel interceded. "But I was a full partner in the firm during that particular charge to which you refer. Therefore, I can attest to the fact that those allegations, like these, proved groundless. I am surprised you are familiar with the incident, considering it was not public knowledge." He smiled thinly, eyes narrowed.

"I do not need to account for how I come by my information," Wentworth snarled. "But in regard to this complaint, Mr. Drummond brought to my attention—"

"You once warned me to choose my friends with care. I suggest you heed your own advice," Daniel said coldly.

Brett grinned at Wentworth's apoplectic expression. Pity the arse could not choke on his indignation. But they were not here for Wentworth. "My pardon, but I think it is time we turned our attention to the real purpose of this meeting. Lady Emily?"

"What?" Drummond blurted, red-faced. "Surely you cannot be serious."

Wentworth took equal umbrage. "What is the meaning of this? This is a business matter, not an open forum for ladies to profess their—"

"That is enough!" Lord Roberts's booming voice silenced the room. "Mr. Curtis is right. It is my responsibility to investigate nefarious dealings within the East India Trading Company, and that is what I am doing."

Wentworth furrowed his brow. "I do not understand. What the devil does this have to do with the charges against Curtis Shipping?"

"If you will be patient, all will be explained," Lord Roberts said, his tone brooking no further interruptions. "Many of us are apprised of the history of one of my investigations, but for those who are not, I will briefly summarize. Four years ago, Mr. Drummond brought to my attention that someone in the company was embezzling funds from the Calcutta factories. Per Drummond's recommendation, I appointed the late Viscount Weston to investigate. After the viscount's death, I had no evidence to substantiate the charges of embezzlement, so I believed the matter closed. However, his fiancée has uncovered new information that has recently come to light, thus reopening this investigation."

"*You* brought Jason's name to Lord Roberts's attention?" Emily said and stared at Drummond. "*You* lured Jason to India? Why? I do not understand."

"Because he desired to go!" Drummond bit out. "And I thought he could handle it. Alas, he could not." He addressed Roberts. "Due to Viscount Weston's abuse of opium, any information that has come to light in regard to his tenure with the company cannot be taken seriously. The man was not of sound mind."

"That is a slanderous lie, one of many of yours," Emily cried. "Jason never took the drug. We have sworn statements from his clerk and his valet affirming that. The two men who knew the viscount's habits as well as their own. It was you who spread slander about Jason and ruined Bertram Marsh. You then blackened Jason's legacy to undermine any accusations he made."

His Athena. Brett grinned, almost pitying the whoreson.

"You then sought to damage Mr. Curtis to stop him from assisting me, hence the false charges against his company. You knew I was searching for more information, and you could not allow me to find any because it would prove *you* embezzled the money. You were the man Jason had implicated, and you murdered him to silence him!"

"What? Good lord, you are as mad as the rumors attest!" Drummond shot to his feet. Ashen faced, he appealed to Roberts, his voice shaking with rage. "You cannot listen to a grieving madwoman and her egregious accusations. She has never recovered from Viscount Weston's death, therefore anything she says—"

"That is enough!" Brett leapt up and circled the table, his face but inches from Drummond's. "Not one more slanderous word, or I will rip your tongue out of your mouth and silence you once and for all. Lady Emily has only brought to light the late viscount's charges. *His* words, not hers, condemn you."

Drummond visibly swallowed, a sheen of perspiration

glistening on his brow. Every man had risen when Brett stood. After a taut impasse, Drummond clenched his jaw, his expression thunderous.

Wentworth, florid faced, did not retreat. "Lord Roberts, you cannot listen to this slanderous drivel. Good lord, Drummond is related to the Earl of Dayton, while this man is . . ." His gaze raked Brett with scathing contempt. "He is but a mere tradesman, a colonial, who—"

"Speaks the truth," Lord Roberts said coldly. "Viscount Weston's missing ledger along with his sworn testimony detailing Mr. Drummond's culpability were turned over to my care yesterday." He eyed Drummond, his tone cold. "Then there is the testimony of your former valet, a William Dean."

"What?" Drummond gasped.

"Your valet has testified that you hired a sepoy to assassinate the viscount," Lord Roberts continued. "When he failed to do so, you then provided the viscount with the opium that did succeed in killing him."

"You cannot be serious!" Drummond barked. "These are lies, hearsay, and slander."

"Yes, well, you would be more familiar with those than I," Lord Roberts said, his eyes hard. "I deal in facts and the truth. Those are irrefutable, as is the evidence against you. You will be charged with embezzlement, but will hang for murder."

A low moan escaped Drummond. He swayed on his feet and blindly reached out to clutch the edge of the table in a white-knuckle grip.

"As to the other matter, all charges against Curtis Shipping have been summarily dismissed. The customs officials have declared the imported cotton fiber to be of the finest quality, and the goods were accepted," Lord Roberts said. "Mr. Curtis has the right to charge you and Lord Wentworth with libel for filing a false statement against his company."

Looking dazed at the turn of events, Wentworth pressed his lips together, for once, wisely holding comment.

"No. I have no interest in Wentworth, and I plan to file

another charge against Drummond—that of attempted murder," Brett said, locking gazes with Drummond. "You penned the note from Winfred arranging to meet us at the *Jolly Tar*, and you hired two men to kill me. Both have been apprehended, and they, too, have implicated you. Pity you cannot hang twice."

"You bitch!" Drummond suddenly roared at Emily, his face contorted with rage. "It is all your fault! From the very first, it was your fault."

"What?" Emily gasped, recoiling.

Brett froze. After a stunned moment, he shook his head, marveling that he had been blind to so obvious an answer, one that had been staring him in the face all along. He advanced on Drummond, who stumbled away from the table. "You planned it all from the very beginning. It was never about the money or the viscount. It was about Lady Emily. You wanted her for yourself."

"*That* was his motive!" Daniel exclaimed, slapping his hand on the table.

Drummond glared at Brett and snarled, "You can have her! I was a fool. She picked Jason even though she was mine!" He thumped his fist to his heart. "I loved her first!"

Emily flinched and pressed her hand over her mouth.

"Good lord," Taunton breathed.

"I had planned and waited for years. I had finally disposed of Jason, luring him to India, for God's sake. I sought to console you in your grief, but you disappeared on some trip with your sister, forcing me to again bide my time. When you finally approached me, it renewed my hope. But you kept harping about Jason's letters. I thought I had destroyed all the evidence against me.

"I had been so careful. I exiled myself in that blistering-hot, heathen country, working for a company that was imploding with corruption. It was so easy to poison the viscount tea's, cover it up with the appearance of an opium overdose, and then bribe an official to corroborate the means of death."

Emily had moved to Brett's side. At this, she emitted a strangled cry. He reached over and gave her arm a squeeze, wishing he could do more. Wishing he could strangle Drummond for the pain he had inflicted upon her. Hanging was too good for the bastard.

"I had considered everything but Jason's bloody honor. I should have known the man would keep his own private ledger with detailed accounts of his investigation. He was so maddeningly meticulous about his records and accounting. It is not surprising he found a way for you to finish his work from beyond the grave," he snarled at Emily.

Wild-eyed, Drummond's gaze darted over each of them.

All the men had also circled the table, following Drummond and his macabre confession as he edged toward the door.

"Stop!" Drummond's hand shot up. "Do not come any closer. This is finished. None of it matters now. I am leaving. I have the funds to do so, don't I? Do not try to restrain me." His hand slipped into his jacket pocket, and he withdrew a pistol. He swung it over the group, his hand shaking, and sweat beading his brow.

The silver flash of the gun shattered Brett's stunned immobility. He shifted in front of Emily, cursing when she struggled to shove him aside.

"You big lummox, you will not get shot over me again!" she bellowed, pounding his back.

Thankfully, Daniel and Drew moved in to flank him.

"You do not want to do that, Drummond. It is over," Lord Roberts said evenly, holding his hands up as if to tame a wild animal.

Drummond's eyes fastened on Brett, and a perverse smile curved his lips. "If I cannot have her, no one can."

"You will have to go through me to get to her," Brett declared, ignoring Emily's shriek of protest.

"And me and Bedford," Drew added. "With only one shot, you will not get away."

Taunton stepped forward. "I may be old, but I can still stand up for my daughter, but I prefer to do it at the altar."

"No!" Emily cried, and another pounding rained on Brett's back.

He grunted, but held his ground.

"You are all mad. Do not move or I will shoot!" Drummond warned.

Brett's patience with the mewling bastard snapped. He was done with the man. When Drummond brandished the gun and his arm swung high, Brett seized the moment and lunged. He caught Drummond's arm in a viselike grip, thrusting it upward.

A vicious expletive tore from Drummond as he fought Brett's grasp.

Daniel and Drew rushed to aid him.

In the scuffle, the pistol fired, Emily screamed, and hearing her cry, Brett's heart stopped dead.

He abandoned Drummond to Daniel and Drew, and whirled.

The seconds between the gun blast and his locating Emily safe in her father's arms were the longest of his life. Heart hammering, he nearly collapsed with relief.

The bullet had cracked and splintered a strip of molding along the ceiling.

The two Runners, who had been posted outside to escort Drummond away, burst into the room. Drew and Daniel relinquished Drummond into their custody. The Runners then escorted Drummond's defeated figure from the room, Lord Roberts following.

And just like that, it was over.

Brett did not give a damn. He had eyes only for Emily. When her father released her, she flew into his arms, and he crushed her close. She was all that mattered. Safe, warm, and in his arms.

"What were you thinking? Stop trying to catch bullets with your hide or your head. I cannot bear it," she cried and buried her face against his chest, hugging him tight.

She was perfect. He pulled her away and gripped her shoulders. "Lady Emily Chandler, I adore you." Oblivious to their audience, he lifted her off her feet and swung her around, her laughter mingling with his. When he set her on her feet, he was unable to let her go, but curled his arm around her waist and beamed at her.

Drew stepped forward and bowed. "I trust you to keep him out of trouble, because now that my debt is paid, I have my own woman to woo. She thinks I am a lying, deceitful bastard, so it might take some time. But I have faith." He winked.

Daniel slapped Brett on the back. "Congratulations again."

A snort broke through the felicitations. "Taunton, surely you cannot sanction this. An earl's daughter with—"

"The man she loves, and who has proved his worth by saving her life, not once, but twice after today. No approval is necessary. She has made her choice, and it is a wise one."

Wentworth fumed, but eyeing the group that had closed ranks around Brett, he snapped his mouth shut and stormed out.

"My protector." Emily tossed her arms around Brett's neck. "Thank you for helping me win this battle."

Brett ignored the quiet exodus behind him as the group gave them a moment of privacy. He pressed his forehead to Emily's temple and smiled. "It is about time you surrendered to me."

"And you to me. Now we can savor the spoils of war."

"Another one of your brilliant plans, my love." He leaned down to kiss her lips.

Best damn alliance he ever made.

Chapter One

✦

LONDON, ENGLAND
MAY 1855

SOMETIMES a woman runs out of choices.

Alexandra Langdon glowered at the door, willing herself to turn its brass knob. She didn't belong inside the chamber. She risked discovery, expulsion, and scandal. Her stomach growled and reminded her why she was entering anyway. What did the pampered heirs inside their exclusive enclave know about hunger? The hollow, empty rumble of it. The slow, insidious gnaw of it. She had experienced it for so long, it was like a familiar adversary. One she vowed to conquer.

That is, if she could open the damn door and cross the forbidden threshold.

There was money to be had inside the gentleman's card room. The Duke of Hammond hosted the grandest balls of the season. The cream of society attended, and while wives and debutantes danced the night away, husbands and bachelors sought refuge behind these doors. Rich men with fortunes to win or lose at the turn of a card. Alex just needed to possess the winning hand—and she would.

Her father had given her a gift and she planned to use it. It was the only thing he had given her. For this, she loved and hated him.

She shook her head, wiped her clammy hands down her black dress trousers, resisted the urge to readjust her masculine wig, and once again, crossed into forbidden territory.

The familiar smells assaulted her first, a mixture of cigar smoke, whiskey, and men. The noise hit her next, the murmur of conversations, the rumbles of masculine laughter, and the crack of billiard balls striking together.

Burgundy carpet covered the floor, and dark wood-paneled walls were crowded with the familiar paintings of foxhunts. Red-coated riders leaned over straining horses, galloping after their prey. Alex's sympathies lay with the fox. She knew the desperation of seeking safety in hidden crevices, the terror of being hunted. Her lips pressed into a determined line. Like the fox, she needed to keep alert for fear of getting caught.

Alex stepped farther into the room, eyes locked on the card table in the far corner. A game had broken up and new players were claiming the vacated seats. One of those chairs was hers. If she reached it in time.

A group of men blocked her path. Her head barely topped their shoulders as she circled them, threads of their conversation drifting to her.

"Kendall is back."

The name echoed, ringing familiar to her. It had circulated throughout the house since her arrival downstairs, voiced in hushed tones that reverberated through the guests like a rippling tide.

"I thought he had returned last fall."

"Well, he's in town. And word's out that he's here tonight."

"Christ. Does Monroe know?"

"More important, does Monroe's *wife* know?" Laughter followed.

"*Only* Monroe's wife? What about all the other women?"

Alex had no interest in the antics of some Casanova. The room overflowed with them. Oiled hair neatly groomed, snow white cravats, and hands curled around crystal brandy glasses. It was no surprise that these men would be petticoat chasers. The sport didn't give blisters, mess their hair, or soil their jackets. Bitterness washed over Alex as she sought to bypass the group, but their next words brought her up short.

"Last time he sat at a table, he lifted a fortune off Lambert and Eldridge."

"Didn't Samson challenge him to a duel?"

"Rumors have circulated, but unlike you, Peters," a man drawled, "Kendall is mute on the gossip he generates, and Samson has disappeared."

"Remind me to avoid Kendall's table," someone muttered.

A gambler and a rake. Her dislike for the man grew.

Dismissing him, she continued forward, intent on her goal. Two seats on opposite sides of the circular card table remained vacant.

She set her sights on the closest empty chair. As she neared it, she studied the four men already seated. She recognized the two viscounts conversing with each other, Lords Linden and Chandler. Lord Richmond, an earl, had been introduced to her once before. Lord Filmore was a welcome sight. She had lifted fifty pounds from the rake in their last encounter.

But that was over six months ago, and the money hadn't gone far.

None of the gentlemen rose to greet her, nor did they draw back her chair. It always surprised her, but it shouldn't have. They nodded, murmuring her surname in that familiar greeting men exchanged, dropping titles and first names.

Before she breached society's rules and claimed her seat, she studied her surroundings. A mahogany bar lined the wall opposite her. Light from the chandelier danced off the crystal decanters and glasses littering the bar surface. A gilded frame mirror hung above the setup. Alex didn't immediately recognize the stranger staring back at her. When she realized it was her own image reflected in the glass, she drew in a sharp breath.

A young man with brown hair, startled blue eyes, and a crisp white cravat tied about his neck returned her stare. A red flush climbed her throat and stole over hollowed cheeks. She tore her eyes from the reminder of her gaunt appearance.

Her blue jacket had needed to be taken in further, only the padding filling her out now. It was little wonder she sweltered and yearned to yank off her cravat and draw a cooling breath.

The disguise was a necessary evil if she wanted to play for these stakes. Card rooms existed for women. She could try her hand at the genteel games of piquet or whist, but no fortunes would be laid on the tables, no hundred-pound bets. She needed to be here where serious money could be won.

She lifted her chin in determination and braced herself to wish the man in the mirror luck, but her view was blocked.

A new player had claimed the remaining chair opposite her.

Her eyes rose from his pristine black evening jacket, tailor-fitted over a tall, muscular frame to study his face. This time, she did retreat a step. Not because the man was handsome, though his classic aristocratic features were striking. He had chiseled cheekbones, sensual lips, and an enviable mane of thick, raven black hair. The room held a banquet of beautiful men, and while Alex was aware of them, her hunger was directed elsewhere. There was something more about this man, something beyond a handsome face and figure.

It was in his eyes. They were storm-cloud gray, cold as slate and hard as steel. Alex couldn't look away. They were hypnotic, riveting. He frowned, shattering the spell that had held her transfixed.

Weak-kneed, she circled her chair to drop into her seat. The hairs on the back of her neck prickled.

He knew.

It was the only possible reason for the black scowl directed at her, for she had never seen the man before in her life. Her eyes snapped back to his but he turned away, dismissing her. He collected a brandy from the tray of a passing waiter and folded his tall, lean body into his seat. He set the glass on the table but did not drink from it, instead shoving it out of reach and turning to respond to a comment from Richmond.

This man had no interest in her. Her tension eased and she exhaled. She needed to remain focused. *Focused players win.* She eyed his untouched glass of brandy. *Sober players win.* Her father's words echoed. Drawing a steady breath, she started to remove her gloves, but paused. Her hands would give her away but it couldn't be helped. The risk had to be taken. She slipped the pair off and lowered her hands to her sides.

Richmond addressed the group. "Kendall, you know everyone?"

Her eyes shot up.

Kendall.

The womanizer and gambler. But of course. It was inevitable that fate would seat this man at her table. Of late, fate had been less than kind to her.

"Actually, I don't." Those compelling eyes leveled on Alex.

"Right. Alex Daniels is new to you," Richmond said by way of introduction. "Daniels returned from abroad last year, grand tour and all." He addressed Filmore, a slow smile curving his lips. "Filmore, you remember Daniels, don't you?"

Daniels. She had chosen the name from a stallion who had triumphed at Ascot despite one-hundred-to-one odds against him. She hoped for similar luck.

Filmore grinned. "I do. You left with my money the last time we shared a table. You've been scarce these last few months. Good of you to make an appearance. I like to be given the chance to recoup my losses."

She opened her mouth to respond but noticed Kendall frowning at her again. She didn't like it, or the effect it had on her pulse. If she'd had a fan, she would have snapped it open and given him the cut direct. Without her fan, she turned away from him to respond to Filmore, lowering her voice to do so. "My apologies, Lord Filmore. I so enjoyed spending your money that I've returned for more." She couldn't bring herself to drop his title, cross over into the intimate address of men.

Chandler grinned. "The gauntlet has been tossed. Let's hope you brought your purse, Filmore." He lifted his glass in a mocking salute.

Filmore settled back in his chair and eyed his friend. "Did you bring yours, Chandler, or are you wagering another one of your father's prized stallions?"

Chandler laughed, unperturbed. "The earl managed to reclaim him. Admittedly, not at the bargain price at which he'd originally purchased him." His grin was unrepentant.

"He must not have been too upset over your bartering his prime bloodstock. After all, you still live," Linden commented dryly.

Chandler shifted in his seat. "There was a bit of a row, but there are benefits to being the earl's only heir—no spare."

The men laughed, with the exception of Kendall. Alex didn't know where Kendall had left his sense of humor, but she abhorred these fops' cavalier attitude to betting their estates, their father's stables, or treasured family heirlooms. If they didn't need their pampered luxuries, there were those less fortunate who did.

"Shall we deal the cards, gentlemen?" Richmond asked, lifting the deck and waiting for Filmore to cut before he dealt the first card to Kendall. "Opening bid is twenty-five pounds."

Beneath the table, Alex's hands clenched her thighs, her fingers digging deep. She had pawned her last piece of jewelry to enter this game, hoping to double its value. Glittering baubles were of little use, for there would be no more Seasons for her.

The round circled and returned to Kendall, who drew two cards and addressed the group. "Gentlemen, I'll raise you fifty."

"Aren't you missed in the ballroom?" Linden muttered as he tossed in his note, flicking off a piece of lint from his bright blue jacket. "Not by the men, but by the ladies?"

Kendall merely raised a brow, refraining from comment.

Alex ignored the banter. Good Lord, seventy-five pounds. Her necklace had garnered a mere hundred. She studied her cards. It was a good hand. *Langdon luck*. Her father's voice bolstered her flagging courage, and she added her note to the growing pile, stamping down her nerves.

"Recently returned to town, Kendall? I haven't seen you at White's or the last few balls," Linden said.

"Unlike you, Linden, I'm selective in the invitations I accept," Kendall returned, his eyes on Chandler, who scowled at his hand.

Filmore suppressed a laugh, but kept his attention focused on his cards.

"You have something in common with Daniels here." Richmond nodded to her.

"He's been scarce as well."

"Yes. Well, I've had other priorities." She waved a hand. Her eyes met Kendall's, and his narrowed as if he heard the lie in her words. She cursed him for appearing to read her so well, for looking so damn arrogant and handsome.

He was a distraction she didn't need.

"You both missed quite a spread at Warden's." Chandler added his note to the pile. "This season's debutantes are prime stock. I fully intend to sample a few of the fillies."

"Bloody hell, Robbie, haven't you had enough problems with horses?" Filmore snorted. "Gentlemen, shall we raise the bet another twenty-five?"

The cards circled to Linden and he folded his hand. "I'm out."

Alex did the math, calculating that after the round she would be left with . . . with nothing. Nothing didn't go very far. Past experience had taught her that stark, bitter lesson.

But she only needed one more card. *Just one more.* She wondered where her heady rush of Langdon luck was and feared it sat at another table.

She gnawed on her lower lip, then froze—no tells. She surveyed the table, but they appeared unaware of her frayed nerves.

The room was stifling. Why did men wear cravats? Like a noose around one's neck, they choked. She glanced up and noted Kendall appeared to have once again read her mind, for he removed his black evening jacket.

The man proceeded to brazenly roll up his sleeves and bare his forearms. She was riveted to every movement of his crisp white dress shirt sliding back to reveal his muscular, bronzed arms. She swallowed. Good Lord. It was indecent. He cocked a brow at her, and she stiffened. It was her move and all eyes rested on her.

She was suddenly grateful for the hateful cravat, as it hid the burning flush stealing up her neck. She met the bet and turned to await Richmond's play, avoiding Kendall. Why did his return to town have to coincide with hers? Like an ominous shadow, he darkened her mood and her hopes.

"Have you received news from the front?" Richmond addressed Kendall.

Alex turned, surprised by the question but glad for the sobering distraction. News of the Crimea should help her regain her focus, cool her burning cheeks.

Kendall's hand paused in placing his bet, but then he shrugged. "Nothing the papers haven't covered."

Linden leaned forward, his expression thunderous. "That bloody Russell should be fired for his libelous dribble. He's—"

"Accurate," Kendall cut the viscount off, his eyes hard. "Pity Lord Raglan's command wasn't as competent as Russell's pen. It might have saved a lot of bloodshed."

A taut silence stretched over the table.

Alex was stunned. Kendall hadn't served up the usual loyal drivel glorifying hard-fought campaigns or extolling a long life for the empire. Kendall voiced the dark and bitter truth.

She had heard murmurs of William Russell's reports in the *Times* publicizing the troops' suffering from shortages of food, clothing, and medicines, but she didn't need to read his accounts. She had heard from the soldiers themselves, and her heart had bled for them, for the carnage the Light Brigade had left after its disastrous charge at Balaclava last October.

She swallowed and glanced up to see Kendall's enigmatic eyes resting on her. She dropped her gaze and blinked furiously, cursing her momentary lapse and his words for touching her. But they had. Contrary to the opinions of some, she was not made of stone.

"Yes, well, to those who fought with courage." Richmond broke the silence, raising his glass in a toast, the others following suit. "Their glory will not fade." He echoed the poignant line of Lord Tennyson's tribute to the fallen men.

Kendall's hand tightened on his glass before he lifted it in response, but he set it down without drinking and turned to Chandler. "I believe it's your bet."

Frowning at Kendall's untouched brandy glass, Alex's head shot up. For a span of time, she had forgotten the game. That had never happened to her before. *A bad omen.*

She shook off the thought. She had a good hand, a solid hand. Her last card had completed her full house. The Langdon luck had come through.

Chandler sighed and tossed his cards onto the table. "My glory has faded. I fold."

"No more prized bloodstock to throw into the pot?" Filmore quipped.

"Not tonight. This evening my sights are set on the fillies downstairs, but I won't be riding them if I waste my time and money here with you gentlemen."

Inwardly, she cringed at the vulgarity.

"I'm out as well." Richmond folded his hand and leaned back in his chair. He withdrew a cigar from his jacket and waved a passing servant over for a light.

"Gentlemen, shall we call this hand?" Kendall asked.

Alex edged forward in her seat, heart pumping. She would win.

Fillmore tossed down his cards. "Pair of kings." At Linden's snort of laughter, he shrugged. "Worth a bluff. But I believe I'll join Chandler downstairs."

"Gentlemen, let's hope you have more luck with the ladies than at cards," Kendall said, spreading his hand on the table. A straight flush.

Linden whistled, shaking his head. "Christ, Kendall, tell me you're joining the others downstairs. Leave a man something to hope for in the next round."

"There's still hope. Daniels hasn't laid down his hand," Richmond said. "Alex, any chance you have a royal flush?"

Alex jumped as all eyes locked on her. She concentrated on drawing a steady breath as the room spiraled around her, a whirlpool sucking her down.

She had lost. *Lost everything*.

One hundred pounds; her meager fortune gone. She couldn't move. Couldn't think. She blinked at the cards. Heat flooded her body, and the smell from Richmond's cigar gagged her. In a flash, she knew what ran through the condemned's head before the noose tightened and their feet flailed beneath them in those final seconds of life. Nothing. Absolutely nothing.

It took all her strength to spread her cards over the table rather than grip the edge of it and hold on for dear life as the room spun. After she ceded victory to Kendall, Filmore slapped him on the back, but their words and laughter barely penetrated her dazed fog. She had never seen a straight flush. Hoped to never see another.

Chandler and Filmore shoved their seats back and rose.

It took her a moment to realize Filmore had addressed her. He had to repeat her name and his invitation to join him and Chandler downstairs.

She moistened her lips, not trusting herself to speak. Willing her legs to support her, she slid back her chair and stood.

Yes. Escape. Flee the scene of her ruin. Find a private place to think or curl into a ball and will the world away.

She cleared her throat and managed to voice an

appropriate parting to the table. Her feet followed Chandler and Filmore while she marveled at her body's ability to function when her mind could no longer.

Voices and masculine laughter floated through the room, a river of life flowing by without her. She jumped at the explosive clatter of billiard balls, the noise shattering her daze. In a flash of clarity, she sent her companions ahead under the auspices of getting a stiff drink to drown out the bitter taste of her loss.

She had faced ruin before. It had not beaten her, and it would not beat her now. *The Langdon well of luck might be bone-dry, but the Langdon spirit will revive.* She heard her father's words and closed her eyes.

She wished he would shut the hell up.

He had gotten her into this mess in the first place. She slid a finger underneath her cravat and tugged at the tie.

A waiter carrying a tray of drinks passed. Alex summoned him over when suddenly a steel grip curled around her upper arm and she was dragged to the side of the room. Speechless at the audacity, she stumbled, gasping when the hold tightened to steady her. Before she could recover, her captor reached across her and shoved open the adjacent window. A blast of cool air whipped in, fanning her flushed cheeks and shattering her shocked immobility.

"Still going to pass out?"

Her head jerked back at the words. Enraged, she yanked her arm free and whirled around to confront her assailant. Her words died in her throat and she staggered back a step. Steel gray eyes bored into hers.

Kendall.

Why had he followed her? What more did he want?

His eyes narrowed on her. "When's the last time you ate?"

"I beg your pardon?" Indignant, she met his gaze before her eyes strayed to the pulsing beat in the column of his throat, mesmerized by the strip of golden skin. He had discarded his cravat and opened the top buttons of his shirt. It was scandalous. She smelled Richmond's cigar on him. His linen shirt stretched over broad shoulders and clung to a rock-solid body standing intimately, dangerously close. Too close.

Towering over her, he was formidable. She stepped away until the wall braced her back and cut off further retreat.

"Christ." Kendall spun her around again to face the window, prodding her toward it. "Breathe."

She cursed the man but sucked in deep, calming breaths of the cool air. She damned him for being right and herself for being a fool. She couldn't afford to pass out or lose her wits. Thanks to him, she had lost enough this evening.

The urge to faint passed along with the fleeting hope that Kendall would disappear. Collecting the shattered remnants of her dignity, she planted a hand on the windowsill and braced herself to face the man, ignoring the staccato rhythm of her heart.

His brow furrowed, the now-familiar frown curving his lips. Minus the scowl, the man was striking. She noticed he was thin, not gaunt, but pure sinew, hard angles and whip-cord strength held in tight rein.

Confused at her train of thought, she pressed her hand to her temple. Suddenly aware the gesture made her appear as if she still planned to faint, she jerked it down.

She drew in a steadying breath before meeting those eyes. "Thank you." The words nearly choked her, but years of ingrained etiquette forced them out.

"Christ. You fools get younger every year. How old *are* you?"

She stiffened and thrust her chin up. "Old enough."

His lips pressed into a firm line, but he did not question her further. After an interminable silence, he spoke. "I've ruined enough men's lives, but I draw the line at boys. Here."

She stared at him blankly until she realized he was shoving something at her. She nearly gasped at what he held. Her notes. Blood rushed to her face. He was returning his winnings to her.

"Take it," Kendall demanded.

Her hand lifted, then snapped back to her side where she

curled it into a fist. No, she couldn't. If she accepted it, she could never show her face in a card room again. She bit her lip. She felt like the fox fleeing those hunters, wondering if the escape route before her led to safety or another trap.

She needed to think, but he never gave her the chance.

Swearing, he caught her hand and dumped the notes into it, curling her fingers around them. He wore no gloves, and she shuddered at the touch of his bare skin against hers. His hand was hard, his fingers calloused.

"Next time, don't bet what you can't afford to lose." He turned away.

"I'll pay you back." Finding her voice, her words bounced off his broad back.

"Don't bother." He didn't break stride as he answered. "I don't want it." He was clearly done with the matter. Done with her.

Stricken by his response, she stared at his retreating figure in silence. His gracious gesture burned to ash under his scorching dismissal. The transaction meant nothing to the man. To her it meant everything.

Everything.

To Kendall she was simply a prick at his conscience, a blister he felt compelled to lance. While surprised he possessed a conscience, she hated him for it. She recalled his comment about the men he had ruined. His words disturbed her, but envisioning his cold, slate gray gaze, she believed them. After all, he had nearly ruined her.

Realizing she stood blankly staring at Kendall's back, she searched her surroundings. She feared facing censure for not honoring her bet. But no one glanced her way. Only Kendall was privy to her loss of face.

All the more reason to detest the man.

She blinked away the moisture blurring her vision as she shoved her notes into her trouser pocket, hiding the incriminating evidence. She withdrew her gloves and shoved her hands into them. Damn him. He wouldn't make her cry. She never cried.

She needed to get out of here.

Ducking her head, she fled the room, suppressing the urge to run. Why bother? There was no escaping the man. Storm gray eyes were branded in her memory. No matter how fast she fled, they would follow.

A tale of love, deception, and redemption
in the face of mortal danger…

from
Victoria Morgan

For the Love of a Soldier

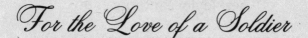

Captain Garrett Sinclair, the Earl of Kendall, has returned
to England a changed man. As a survivor of the legend-
ary Charge of the Light Brigade, he has spent months as a
remorseless rake and dissolute inebriate in order to forget
it. But Garrett has also made powerful enemies who want
him dead…

Desperate and down to her last pound, Lady Alexandra
Langdon has disguised herself as a man for a place at the
gaming tables. But when a hard-eyed, handsome man wins
the pot, he surprises her by refusing her money. Indebted,
she divulges an overheard plot against his life, and prom-
ises to help him find his foes—for a price…

Praise for *For the Love of a Soldier*

"This book is an absolute gem…a remarkable debut novel."
—PennyRomance.com

"Morgan deftly handles returning soldiers' trauma within
the context of a love story and adds spice with a bit
of mystery and unexpected secrets."
—*RT Reviews* (4 Stars)

victoriamorgan.com
penguin.com

M1346T0713

Discover Romance

berkleyjoveauthors.com

See what's coming up next from your
favorite romance authors and explore all
the latest Berkley, Jove, and Sensation
selections.

See what's new
~
Find author appearances
~
Win fantastic prizes
~
Get reading recommendations
~
Chat with authors and other fans
~
Read interviews with authors you love